JUST IN TIME
FOR A
HIGHLANDER

GWYN
CREADY

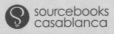
sourcebooks
casablanca

Published by Sourcebooks Casablanca, an imprint of Sourcebooks,
Inc.
P.O. Box 4410, Naperville, Illinois 60567-4410
(630) 961-3900
Fax: (630) 961-2168
www.sourcebooks.com

Printed and bound in Canada.
MBP 10 9 8 7 6 5 4 3 2 1

For Jeanne Lowther, who called me a good girl.

One

WITH A SHRIEK OF FRUSTRATED BLOODLUST, DUNCAN jerked to a stop as the crossing signal turned red. The musket-wielding French soldier he'd been chasing sprinted to the safety of the opposite sidewalk, nearly knocking down two young women carrying Macy's bags in the process.

Och, Duncan thought with irritation. *There's only one thing you can count on with Frenchmen: they run better than they fight.*

One of the women looked at Duncan and grinned. At six foot one with flaming red hair and a Scottish burr, he was used to being noticed. However, the kilt—his grand-da's from the Korean War—inevitably turned the looks into something more prurient. A gust of wind blew down Pittsburgh's Grant Street, and he palmed the wool against his thighs. Sometimes he wished he lived in a world where a man's bare legs weren't the object of such fascination.

"Reenactor?" the woman called.

He lifted his carved wooden sword and blank-filled pistol and gave her a lopsided grin. "Battle of Fort Duquesne."

A roiling gray now edged the blue sky. Duncan hoped the storm they were predicting would hold off until after he was in the air tonight. He hadn't been home to Scotland since Christmas, and by all rights he should have skipped the reenactment since he could only spare a week of holiday time. But there were so few battles in North America in which the Highlanders had fought, he'd hated to say no. His grand-da was his last immediate family member still around, and the old guy was in his eighties. Duncan knew a visit was in order, and he fought off a wave of guilt he knew he deserved for putting the reenactment first.

The walk light turned green just as a band of Seneca warriors, bows drawn, emerged on Fourth Street. In this particular battle, they were allied with the French and therefore his enemy. Not only that, but their leader, a blustery fellow named Dylan, had been a complete arse the night before in a debate over rugby versus gridiron. The Senecas spotted him and Duncan's adrenaline surged. *Time to teach the old boy a lesson.* With a nod to the women, he lifted his sword and flew directly into the hail of rubber-tipped arrows.

God, how he loved a battle.

Two

"NOTHING COULD HAPPEN TO MAKE THIS DAY LESS perfect." Smiling, Abby wiggled her toes in the cool grass, happy that, for once, her clansmen had lost themselves in the joys of a late summer afternoon rather than in the potential it held for a clash with the English.

Undine smiled and shook her head. "That is an invitation to trouble if ever I heard one. Besides, do you not see those clouds? There is a blow coming to be sure."

"Bah. I have no interest in your portents, my friend. This is 1706. We have abandoned the world of superstitions, potions, and charms, or have you not heard?"

"Perhaps *you've* abandoned them. But there are more than enough believers among your clansmen and on England's side of the border to keep my coffers full."

The bodhran's beat echoed, slow and steady, across the field, and the tin whistle's seductive notes hung in the air like summer cherries on a tree.

"You are right, of course," Abby said. "And I would never begrudge you an income, though I cannot help but wish it were different. I tire of fighting their superstitions." She sipped Undine's velvety smooth pear wine. Undine was a renowned fortune-teller and conjurer. Pear wine was the least potent of her elixirs. "This is wonderful," Abby said, "but different than the last. What did you put in it?"

The corner of Undine's mouth lifted. "No more than you can handle."

Abby watched with longing as the young couples made their harvest dance promenades across the freshly cut field, their eyes aglow and hands held fast. That sweet, besotted time held a faraway charm in Abby's mind, like a childhood pleasure one had outgrown. No more than half a dozen years separated her from the dancers, but at times it felt as if it might be a thousand.

"Don't they just look as if they might burst with the pleasure of it all?" she said with a sigh.

"What you need is a dance."

"What I need is a man."

Undine's brows rose. "At last, something I can help you with. I know a lover's spell that will—"

"Not that sort of a man."

"A husband then? Of the two, I can tell you which I'd recommend."

"Ha! If I needed a husband, we both know where I might find one."

As if he'd heard her, Rosston Kerr, Abby's cousin and leader of the family sept that had broken from Clan Kerr in Abby's youth, lifted his gaze from the circle of men at the far edge of the dancing area and met Abby's eyes.

Undine sat up, inserting herself neatly between

Rosston and Abby, though Abby was certain Undine could not have seen him from where she'd been lying.

Undine drew up her knees, wrapping her arms around them. "Help me understand, my friend. You do not want a husband, and you do not want a lover. For anything else, I recommend a dog."

"But I have a dog, don't I, Grendel?" Abby scratched her beloved wolfhound's ears, and he lifted his head briefly and made a wuffle. "What I need is an agent. A strong arm. A fist. A mind possessed of ideas."

"So few parts of a man are truly useful, and you have not mentioned a single one of them yet. There is, of course, Rosston."

Abby grimaced. "And a will that lacks a selfish motive."

"I am intrigued," a voice said, interrupting. "Were such a man to be found, he would be the object of every free-thinking woman between Edinburgh and the Irish Sea."

Abby turned. A woman her age or slightly older with bright red hair, deep blue eyes, and an open smile stood behind them.

"I'm Serafina Fallon. I am here to seek help." She gave them an anxious smile.

Miss Fallon's hair had been pulled into an efficient knot but a few loose tendrils framed her face, and the contrast of the copper against the pale skin was striking. Abby was reminded of a Norse goddess.

"I beg you to rest easy," Undine said, standing to offer her hand. "I'll be able to help you."

Miss Fallon hesitated. "How can you know? You do not even know what I seek."

"I know what you seek, just as I know what finding it will mean to you."

Abby was not surprised to see Miss Fallon's forehead crease. Despite Undine's gentle air and willingness to help, she had a way of making those who sought her counsel uneasy.

Undine, sensing too late the impact of her words, said, "But, here. Join us. The wine is cool, the cheese is sharp, and the grapes, plump and sweet. I am Undine, which you undoubtedly know, and this is my friend, Abby Kerr."

"So you're a part of Clan Kerr then?" Miss Fallon said. "Your musicians are wonderful. I was told I would be well entertained here. Please tell your chief he has exquisite taste."

"I'll be sure to pass along your compliments," Abby said, giving Undine a private smile.

Undine handed their visitor a mug of wine. "Here. Sit down. Relax a bit before we turn to the business that brought you here. We were talking about the sort of men we would choose if describing them were as easy as finding them. I was just about to tell Abby my own requirements."

Abby gave Miss Fallon a smile. "This should prove interesting. Never in life have I heard Undine express the need for a man."

Miss Fallon's gaze went immediately to her boots.

"Ah," Undine said with a wry chuckle. "I knew you had heard of me. One can hardly be the whore of Cumbria without generating some sort of reputation."

"Do not let Undine mislead you," Abby said. "She is no more a whore than I am the queen of France.

Such a reputation is the blind behind which she hides her true profession."

"Which is…spell casting?" Miss Fallon said, with a note of both hope and uncertainty.

"Spell casting, aye." Abby smiled. "And other things."

"Oh, I am glad," Miss Fallon said. "For I, too, am in need of a man."

Undine twirled a lock of her pale hair. "Three lovely women, each in need of a man. If the Kerr clansmen had the slightest inkling, we'd probably be bowled over by the fiercest charge Scotland has seen since the days of William Wallace."

Abby laughed. "Hang on to your mug, Miss Fallon."

"I shall. Oh, but please call me Serafina." She took a quick sip of wine. "I'm afraid my situation might be a bit different than yours. I want a husband, 'tis true, but only for a night."

Undine choked, and Serafina flushed.

"The situation you describe is hardly unique," Abby said, and Undine added, "If we could only find the man uniquely hard for it."

Serafina whooped, then immediately slipped a hand over her mouth when two nearby clansmen turned. "Bah," she said under her breath. "Hard I have had. I cannot recommend it. Give me biddable any day."

Abby snorted, and one of the clansmen lifted a disapproving brow.

"You are a widow, then?" Abby said. But the look of discomfort on Serafina's face made her wish she hadn't asked.

"My fiancé left me," Serafina said flatly. "And the blackguardly bastard left me with a pile of debt so steep I can hardly—" She stopped herself. "But this is not the time. You have been gracious enough to invite me to sit with you. The ride here was long, and the wine and music are wonderful. Please, continue. I should consider it a great kindness to listen to something for a quarter of an hour other than the sound of my own complaints."

Before Abby could respond, she spotted Murgo, one of her clansmen, striding toward her. The way his hand rested on his hilt made her certain the day's pleasantries were over.

"I beg your pardon, milady," he said. "We have received a report of a party of English soldiers on foot two miles south of the Greenlaw Bridge."

Abby groaned inwardly. Colonel Bridgewater of the England's northern armies would not rest until the clans were obliterated. He was a prig, more concerned for his own glory than the safety of England's citizens. Men like that were dangerous—sometimes more dangerous than the most bloodthirsty opponent. She weighed her options. "Tell the men to gather in the field beyond the river. I will give my orders there. Everything here should be ended and the families taken to the castle."

He gave her a pained look. "I dinna think we need to go to such an extreme over a handful of English soldiers."

"Is it a handful or a party?" she demanded, reaching for her boots. "There's a difference. And even a handful of English soldiers can be the harbinger of something more."

"The clansfolk are enjoying your family's hospitality. Why don't we wait until the dancing is over?"

"'Tis *my* hospitality they enjoy, not my family's, and they may continue to do so within the confines of the castle, where they will be safe from attack."

A hint of rebellion rose in Murgo's eyes, but he held his tongue. "As you wish, Chieftess. In the field beyond the river, as soon as possible." With a quick nod to the other women, he hurried off.

The insolence. Abby felt the blood rise in her cheeks. He wouldn't have argued if he'd been talking to her father.

Serafina regarded her with shock. "You are the head of the clan?"

Abby would never get used to the surprise this caused. She felt like the cadaver of the three-eyed pig the surgeon in Coldstream kept on his shelf in a jar. "Aye. For nearly two years now. I want you to follow Undine back to the castle. Undine, will you please tell Bobby to bring me my horse."

Serafina looked at the growing line of men heading in the opposite direction. "Surely you're not planning to join them in battle…"

Undine snapped her fingers. "Grendel, come."

The music had stopped, and the men were dousing the fires. Mothers with babes were hurrying their children toward the castle, which stood to the east, outlined against the darkening sky.

Abby brushed the dirt from her gown. She wished she'd been wearing a riding skirt. She also wished she'd thought to bring a weapon. The soldiers' appearance was likely to be nothing, but no one would take Clan Kerr by surprise. Not while she was in charge.

By the time she reached the river, the men were

standing in informal lines, arranged by family, those on horses in the back. Rosston and the men from his family stood closest.

"I did not expect your invitation to include a battle, Cousin," he said from his mount as she passed. Given his height and the preternatural size of his steed, it was like a bit like walking before Apollo.

"Let us hope it does not," she replied. "I shouldna like to be considered an unwelcoming host. I thank you and your men for standing with Clan Kerr." She gave a grave nod to the clansmen at his feet.

"Never let it be said that the Kerrs of Linton do not support their fellow Kerrs. We have not forgotten the old alliance." He bowed deeply, his blue eyes sparkling.

The faces of her own men were bright with emotion. In a few, especially the younger ones, she saw fear. In others she saw suspicion, though she did not know if it was a response to her or the threat of Englishmen a few miles from their village. In most, however, what she saw was desire for direction from the leader who would drive them into the fight. She would gladly serve them in this role. Unfortunately, it was Rosston upon whom their eyes were trained.

"We do not seek battle," she said, raising her voice to be heard by those at the farthest edges of the gathering.

A few groans rumbled through the crowd, and Rosston opened his mouth to silence the noise, but a pointed look from Abby stopped him. *Dammit, where is my horse?* She felt like a child, standing before the men on their mounts.

"We do not seek battle," she repeated, "but we will

not tolerate an act of aggression by the English. Not on the Kerr lands. Not ever."

The men cheered.

"We must hope for the best but prepare for the worst. That is the only way. Are you ready?"

The sound of hoofbeats made her turn. It was Undine on Abby's mare, Chastity.

"Bobby had her tied at the gate," Undine said, dismounting.

Abby ground her teeth. Even the groomsmen denied her the respect she deserved. She took a deep breath to arm herself with dispassion, letting it wrap around her chest and limbs like chain mail. From her saddle, only a bow and quiver hung—no pistol. But she'd cut out her tongue before she'd let the men know her groomsmen had failed to prepare her mount properly.

She lifted a boot into the stirrup.

"Wait." Undine reached in her pocket and brought out one of the distinctive twists of orange paper she used for her magic herbs.

"Not this," Abby said. "Not now."

"I know you do not believe in my herbs," Undine said a touch hotly, "just as I do not believe in your war. But I have no doubt my herbs have kept you safe." She loosened the paper and touched a finger to the powder then ran it across Abby's cheek. "In any case, your clansmen *do* believe, and they like to see their chief so anointed. Look at them. They watch *you* now—not Rosston—every last one of them."

Undine was right. Abby could feel their eyes upon her. Perhaps the power of the concoction was not in the spirits it evoked, but in the belief. "Thank you," she said meekly.

"On the other hand, they may simply be imagining you without your gown."

Undine clapped her hands twice, releasing a puff of powder over Abby's head. Then she placed the paper in Abby's hand. "The rest is to be used for your strong arm."

"My what?"

"The man you seek."

"Good Lord, Undine. This is hardly the time."

"Nor is it meant to be used now. Keep it with you. When you're ready, sprinkle a tiny pinch in front of you. Dissolve another pinch in wine, then drink— only a thimbleful."

Abby could feel the odd warmth of the contents. "What's in it?" She began to open the paper.

Undine clapped her hand over Abby's. "Not here! Great skies, not with so many people around. Use it in an enclosed space, when you are undisturbed, with the thought of the strong arm in your head."

A dirty floor and an upset stomach were the only things Abby could imagine being the results of such an exercise. Nonetheless, she dutifully refrained from rolling her eyes and slipped the paper into her pocket. She put her foot back in the stirrup and mounted Chastity, whose large brown eyes shone with anticipation.

Undine said, "Be safe, my friend."

Abby nodded, grateful, and clasped her friend's hand. She might not believe in the power of Undine's herbs, but she did believe in the power of friendship.

With a cluck of her tongue, she geed the horse to

a trot, and the men fell in line behind her. Together they made their way through the forest, toward the rise from where they could view the Greenlaw Bridge.

"Pass the word to spread out," she said in a low voice to the man beside her. "But stay out of sight behind the trees. And let silence reign. So long as the soldiers stay on the road, we will not act. But if they raise their guns or leave the road, we will consider that an act of aggression. No one is to move without an order from me."

She knew what to say—had listened in awe to her father's battle stories a hundred times over—but from her mouth, the words sounded hollow and untrustworthy. How could clansmen used to being led by a man put their faith in her? Aye, she had negotiated a much-needed peace in the borderlands. But her clansmen did not value peace as much as they should, and now she was asking them to follow her, a woman untested by battle, into whatever happened next.

The men spread out as they'd been told. From her perch on Chastity, she could see the bridge, though the road on the farside, the road on which the soldiers were approaching, disappeared quickly into a vale below, hiding them from view.

She could feel the uncertainty of the clansmen behind her as clearly as she could the day's damp heat. A few men shifted. She heard a belch, some whispering. Moisture gathered on her back.

"Quiet," she commanded.

She had three dozen or more clansmen here, if you counted the boys, which she did, and at least as many swords, but they had less than a dozen pistols and even fewer horses. If the English soldiers were out on a harmless but misguided exercise, she would not jeopardize the fragile peace to make an example of them.

Damn you, Bridgewater. Why did you have to choose this of all days?

The muffled sounds of boots hitting the hard-packed dirt grew closer, and the faint scent of gunpowder that always hung in the vicinity of the English army stung her nose. By the noise alone, there were more than a couple dozen men—well more. So much for the reports of her scouts.

Her hands shook. She could almost hear her father's voice. "When ye confront an armed man, take his measure by his hand, not his eyes. Every man with his finger on a trigger has fear in his eyes or he's a bloody fool. But the hand of a man actually willing to pull that trigger is as steady as death. 'Tis the hand that tells the tale."

The first soldiers marched into view, and a palpable, untamed energy rose from the men behind her. This was the most dangerous time. One man could start a war that a thousand could not undo. The nerves in her skin flashed like tiny pistol blasts.

The English soldiers marched carefully, their eyes on their sergeant. Had the men miscalculated their location? To be fair, the Kerr lands sat on the border and the soldiers were only two miles north of it, but it would take a pretty piss-poor soldier to overshoot by two miles. Or was this a trick?

Soldiers continued to crest the hill, their well-shined boots and buckles catching the setting sun. Ten. Twenty. Thirty, she counted.

Her fingers jangled in the reins, dampness turning to raw sweat where flesh met flesh.

Forty. Fifty. Sixty. *Sixty*. Sixty and a few more.

Sixty soldiers. An entire *company*. Each with a musket. Clan Kerr had the advantage of position and surprise, but position and surprise do not prevail in the face of sixty muskets. What was this well-armed company attempting? Should she let them continue? Her mind raced through a dozen possibilities.

A twig snapped.

The sergeant wheeled in a circle and raised his musket, followed instantly by his men.

"Stop!" Abby cried and charged from the shadows.

"I am Kerr of Clan Kerr," she shouted. She stopped halfway between the soldiers and her men. "You have wandered over the border into our lands."

Terror thundered in her veins. Sixty-odd barrels stared her down, the great majority guided by hands as restless as hers, but at least one pair, the sergeant's, was immovable as stone. Her mouth dried.

"You have found yourself in the middle of a day of festivities." She hoped she'd spoken aloud, as the sound seemed to rumble around her head like marbles in a bucket. "My men mean you no harm."

She made a forward gesture with her hand, and the front line of her clansmen emerged just far enough to be spied. It was a Clan Kerr feint of long-standing to suggest many more men stood behind them.

"Attack!" a clansman shouted.

"*No*." Abby turned to her men. "We do not need to fight." Many clansmen had reached for their weapons, and the hands of her men were steadier than those of the English soldiers. Fearing what the next unexpected noise would bring, she pulled the twist of paper from her pocket and held it in the air.

The Kerrs gasped as one. They knew from whom the orange paper had come, and everyone on both sides of the border had heard the stories of Undine and her magic. What power they ascribed to this particular mixture of herbs, Abby did not know, but she hoped it was the power to end this confrontation without the firing of weapons.

She waved the paper again and her men retreated a pace. With her arm still in the air, she turned to the soldiers, and more than a few of them stepped back as well. Undine had earned her reputation.

"I repeat," Abby said, "we mean you no harm."

She did not order the soldiers off her land. She had learned early in her tenure as chief that men did not take kindly to orders from a woman. Instead, she prayed the sergeant would come to this idea on his own, though she damned the world for forcing her to finesse rather than demand action. Even the most plank-headed man would have an easier time of it.

Suddenly, something stung her fingers and she heard a loud *pop*. Someone had shot the paper from her hand.

For an instant, Undine's powder sparkled in the air like a tiny shower of Chinese fireworks. Then the world became a maelstrom of pounding hooves and musket fire.

❧

Duncan cleared the bench and raced through the park. His heart thrummed like an engine and his feet moved like Mercury's. He'd narrowed the distance between him and the band of Senecas to little more than thirty feet. Step after furious step, like a man-machine, he closed the distance. The ancient hunger for devastation squeezed his balls. He could feel it like a magnet, lifting him from his shoes and delivering him to his triumph. And if the Senecas made the mistake of running under the pedestrian bridge, they were done for. A company of English soldiers had disappeared under the same bridge a few moments earlier. In this battle the Highlanders and English were allied against the French and Indians, and as much as it pained him as a Scot to be on the side of his countrymen's ancient enemy, he had to admit there was nothing in his life as a bond trader that equaled the thrill of herding his prey into a wall of waiting redcoats.

Three

DUNCAN'S WORLD EXPLODED INTO GUNFIRE, SMOKE, and charging horses—*horses?*—and the grass turned thicker and taller under his feet, tripping him.

For an instant, he thought he would fall, but he caught himself and kept running. The Senecas had disappeared, as had the bridge. Only the wall of musket-toting redcoats remained, but they weren't lying in wait to ambush the Senecas. They were ambushing him.

"No, no," he shouted. "I'm with—"

Something whistled by his head, and a pellet of dirt flew skyward. Blood pounding, he hit the ground and rolled. A terrified scream split his eardrums, and he realized with an embarrassed jolt the scream was his.

One of the bloody redcoats loaded his gun with a real charge!

But the balls kept coming and the dirt kept flying. Duncan rolled to a stop near a stump. He was under real fire from real muskets or, worse, someone with an automatic weapon. A shot split the stump, and he nearly shrieked again.

With heart ready to burst, he jumped to his feet and flew for the trees. He was dimly aware of the clash of swords, the grunts of men, and the stench of powder. This was like no reenactment he had ever seen. Men were screaming. A man was biting the arm of another soldier. Another was kicking a fallen Scot.

He was nearly to the trees when the sight of a beautiful young woman on a rearing horse brought him to a stop. It looked as if she had lost hold of the reins, and he wondered if he—anyone—should—

"Don't move."

A redcoat with bushy brows and a head like a jar advanced on him, bayonet ready.

The hell with that. Duncan ran to the left, hurtling over limbs and roots, and the soldier ran in parallel. He could hear the man's labored breathing behind him. He saw the clearing ahead and realized if he ran any farther, he'd be in plain sight of the men with real shot. Wheeling in a half circle, he withdrew his pistol and cocked it. The man froze.

Don't just stand there, you idiot! Turn and run!

The man's eyes flicked left and right. Duncan couldn't wait. He took three long strides and fired.

The soldier was so stunned he dropped his weapon. When the smoke cleared, he was slapping his chest, searching for a wound. Duncan took three more strides and brought his fist into the man's chin. The man spun in a circle and went down.

The only shot I'll need. Ha!

He grabbed the man's bayonet, which looked eerily new, with oiled joints and polished metal. But the rivets lacked the precise machining of those on the usual reenactor weapons. A shiver went down Duncan's back.

He took a deep breath and scanned the battlefield. It wasn't the triangle of green at the confluence of the Monongahela and Allegheny Rivers Pittsburghers called "the Point." The rivers were gone, the city skyline was gone, and the parkland into which he'd been herding the Senecas was gone. Nothing looked the same. It was as if he'd been lifted bodily from downtown Pittsburgh and placed in the untamed hills of…well, Scotland.

The skirmish seemed to have slowed a bit. Occasional shots rang out, and a handful of Scots in the distance were aiding what appeared to be a fallen comrade. Another Scot arrived, and the men made an opening for him. Duncan's stomach rose: the shaft of an arrow was sticking out of the thigh of the man on the ground.

Duncan considered himself a brave man, but he was losing control over a barely reined-in fear. Where the hell was he?

A howl of pain made him turn. Just beyond the trees, a soldier in a sweat-stained cap had his knee on the back of a boy and was twisting the boy's arm to the point of breaking.

"How's that, you filthy turd? Lot of good that bow arm will do you when I'm done."

Tears streaming down his face, the boy cried, "No, no! Stop! Oh, please!"

The boy's scream turned shrill and Duncan charged. He flew into the soldier's back, and both of them landed hard on the ground.

Duncan yelled, "Run," and the boy wrenched

himself free. The soldier scrabbled for his knife, and Duncan took the man by the arm. "You think it's fun to beat up someone half your size? Not so fun when it's me, is it?"

The knife flew free. Duncan kneed him in the stones and lurched for the blade. Duncan had grown up on the streets of Edinburgh and knew how to fight. But the redcoat had no scruples either and thrust his boot hard into Duncan's kidney. Duncan landed in the grass.

With stars in his eyes, Duncan climbed to his feet. The soldier grabbed the knife, triumphant. Duncan reached for his pistol. Hell, if it worked before…

"Get up," Duncan said.

The soldier eyed him dubiously.

"Get up and drop the knife. *Do it!*"

The soldier lumbered to his feet, still clearly weighing the possibility of using it. It was a good eight inches long, sharpened to a deadly point. If he decided to throw it, the blank in Duncan's pistol wasn't going to be much help.

Duncan raised the pistol and cocked it. "I'm about to put this ball through your heart."

"Put it down!"

A woman's voice came from behind him. He turned. It was the woman who'd been unseated from her mount. The horse was firmly under her control now, and she held a bow and arrow pointed expertly at the soldier behind him.

Gunpowder grime streaked her cheeks, and a mass of dark curls fluttered in the breeze.

"You heard the lady," Duncan said, giving her a quick nod of gratitude.

"I'm talking to you, sir."

Duncan blinked. The arrow wasn't pointed at the soldier. It was pointed at him.

The soldier snickered.

"But I—"

"Shut up," she said. "Drop the pistol."

"Let me finish."

The *twang* was like a whip crack. A searing pain ripped across his shoulder and the pistol flipped in the air like he'd been juggling it. "Jesus!"

The pistol landed with a thud and Duncan clapped his hand over his shoulder to staunch the stream of blood.

In a flash, she had another arrow nocked. This one was for the soldier.

"Private," she said, "I'd like you to tell your sergeant that the Kerrs wish you and your men no harm. We have been blessed today. No one has been killed in the skirmish. Your men stumbled into Kerr lands, and you must not do it again. Do you understand?"

The soldier spit and fingered his knife. "I don't take orders from women."

The arrow flew through the air with a whistle and carried the soldier's cap from his head to the oak behind him, where, with a ringing *thwap*, it burrowed itself in the wood.

Duncan heard the trickle of water and realized the man was pissing himself. He checked his own thighs. Dry, thank God.

A third arrow, already nocked, was aimed at the man's groin.

"Are you the soldier who can carry this message to your sergeant for me," she said, "or shall I find another?"

The man's eyes bulged. "I'll tell him."

"You are most kind. Thank you. You may go."

The soldier ran, stopping only to look back when he was safely out of arrow range.

Duncan's shoulder felt like it had been set on fire, but a reluctant look showed only a straight, clean flesh wound. The woman gazed at him with a mix of curiosity and something close to fear, though she did her best to hide it. He imagined that was pretty close to the look on his face as well.

She dismounted and walked around him as if she were circling a panther. The bow was at her side, but the arrow remained nocked. He took a step toward her and she jumped back.

"I mean you no harm," he said.

She snorted. "I imagine not—unless you are going to swat me to death with your wooden sword."

He flushed. "I had a pistol too, you know."

"Spent. I saw you fire it. How are you...feeling?"

The way she said it made it clear she knew he didn't belong here. He didn't know how she knew. Perhaps she'd seen him "appear," or more likely he looked out of place, but in either case he felt some small sense of relief that he wasn't facing this bewildering experience alone.

"A bit odd," he said with honesty. A twenty and the pen from his sporran had fallen on the ground, and he hurried to scoop them up. "I could have done without the arrow."

"I'll take that as a thank you."

"I'm not sure why."

"The man was going to kill you. He hit one of my

clansmen with the same knife at thirty paces before he cornered you."

His beautiful black Montblanc was ruined. The gold clip and nib were gone. "Well, my shoulder hurts like hell."

Her face softened. She came closer, and he lowered his shirt so she could look.

"Your arms don't look that strong," she said. "And the way you were carrying on doesn't give me a lot of hope that you're a man of ideas."

He jerked the linen back over his shoulder. "Thank you very much. Were you aware that that soldier was about to break a boy's arm?"

"I was. The soldiers did not come here to attack the Kerrs. My job was to bring the matter to an end as quickly as possible—something I thought I'd accomplished until I found you trying to start things up again with the private. You can't stay here."

"I don't want to stay here."

"Then go." She turned on her heel.

"Hang on! You can't just leave me here. I don't know how to get back."

"'Tis not my concern. I saved your life. Return the favor by leaving this place as quickly as possible."

He jumped to his feet and ran after her. "I don't even know where I am."

"For the love of St. Margaret." She gave him a despairing look. "You're in Langholm."

"*Scotland?!*"

"Is there another?"

"Yes. No. I don't know." She was heading to her horse, and the only thing clear to Duncan was that he needed to keep her here. "You can't go! I don't know how to leave. I have a flight tonight. I'm hungry. And my sword," he said, running out of reasons. "It's made of wood." He held it out lamely.

She pursed her lips.

Another woman bounded into view. Her hair was the color of pale honey and shone as if it were wet. Unlike the archer, who walked as if she were a queen, the second woman seemed to glide like a fish through water. She barely looked at him, moving directly toward her friend.

"Are you hurt? We saw everything from the castle."

"No, all is well, thank God. No one was killed, though William is hurt. Undine, do you see what your magic has wrought?" Abby stabbed a finger in Duncan's direction.

The woman gave him a full look and her eyes widened. "*Oh*. Oh, dear."

"What magic?" Duncan demanded.

Undine regarded him thoughtfully. "He's handsome, at least. And tall. That could be useful. But that hair…"

"If I wanted handsome, Rosston would certainly do. He at least wields a real sword." She took Undine by the elbow and turned her away from Duncan. "The poor man appears to have no skills beyond his fists," she said in a lowered voice. "And I think he's addled in his head—like Hal the sheep shearer."

"What were you thinking?" Undine demanded.

"What was *I* thinking?! 'Twas *your* herbs."

"I mean when you opened the paper."

"I *didn't* open the paper. It was shot out of my hand."

"*All of it?!*" Undine paled.

"Except for the part that flew in my mouth." Abby wiped the back of her hand across her tongue and made a sharp sound of disgust. "It tasted like burnt groats."

Duncan had had enough of being ignored. "What herbs? What magic? What are you talking about? Did you bring me here?"

Undine considered. "You could try to make do with him."

"*Make do?!*" Abby cried. "*You* make do with him! Can't you see this is the last thing I need with the clans right now?" She pulled herself onto the horse. "You need to get rid of him."

The "get rid of him" made Duncan's stomach tighten. "No. Wait—"

"Abby?" a voice called from beyond the trees. "Abby, are you there?"

"Oh, God help us, it's Rosston." Abby gave Duncan a warning look. "Don't say another word."

"No!" Duncan grabbed her pommel. "I want to go home! Send me home! I don't know what you two witches have done."

"Silence, you fool." She jerked the reins in an effort to keep the beast from lurching. The arrow fell from her bow.

A kilted clansman crested the rise.

"You, there!" Duncan called to the man. "Help me. These women have—"

Duncan felt a thwack on the head, and the world went dark.

Four

"BUT, UNDINE, FROM WHERE DID HE *COME*?"

Through the nauseating throb in his head, Duncan listened, eyes closed. He was lying on his side on cool stone. The mellifluous contralto belonged to the woman called Abby, and despite the pain, he smiled.

"'Tis not an easy question to answer," Undine replied thoughtfully. "The spell is a strong one. We could ask him, I suppose."

"I'm not sure the man could tell you the sum of ten plus two. And now I've had to tell Rosston he was a spy. What am I going to do when Sir Alan arrives?"

Rosston and Sir Alan. Duncan tried to pin those names into the memory banks in his tender head. Something wet and rough scratched his cheek.

"Grendel, leave him alone," Abby commanded. "He's our prisoner. We do not lick prisoners."

Grendel, whatever he was, made a soft noise of disappointment and thumped down. Duncan felt the tickle of fur against his leg.

Undine sighed. "I'd say drop him in the firth and be

done with him, but you've called him here, and now he is your responsibility."

"*I* didn't call him," Abby said.

"The herbs left your hand. I'm afraid it amounts to the same thing."

Herbs? Hand? Duncan strained to comprehend through the throbbing in his head.

"And, in any case," Undine went on, "are you certain you wish to be rid of him? There are one or two fine uses for calves as exceptional as those."

Duncan's eyes flew open.

"For heaven's sake, Undine. I am not going to enlist him as a concubine."

Undine made a regretful noise. "Pity."

"You do realize I'm holding the clan together by a thread right now, with little support from the men. We've been bleeding money for years, and we're on the verge of losing everything. If I can't convince Sir Alan to invest in the canal, I'll have to begin selling our land."

Duncan added this to his rapidly expanding data bank.

"You'll be able to convince Sir Alan," Undine said. "You are poised and intelligent and—"

"A woman. Do you know how many loans the bank made to women last year? One. The widow of the Earl of Straithmore, and that was only because her finances are controlled by her cousin. Sir Alan has no patience with the endless fighting of the clans. He is a man of commerce. He sees us as unruly brutes, who blunder about in a world of foolish superstition and meaningless feuds, and who would kill each other as soon as tip our caps."

"And how far from wrong is he?"

"This coming from a woman who says she is descended from the rape of a water nymph?"

Water nymph? The gears in Duncan's data bank seized. What the hell had happened to him? He rubbed his head gingerly and the urge to vomit receded. A few scraps of memory were coming back: The reenactment in Pittsburgh. The shocking battle here. The running. The boy. Abby and her bow—that bloody wench! She'd hit him with it, hadn't she?

Undine sniffed apologetically. "I didn't mean to suggest Sir Alan was entirely right—only that he was not entirely wrong."

"The clash today has marred our peace. Sir Alan wants his bank's investments to be free of unnecessary risk. I don't blame him. The last thing I need now is a man from God knows where calling us witches and telling Sir Alan he's been brought here by magic herbs. Sir Alan will run screaming from the castle before we even say hello. Clan Kerr must look worthy of his investment. And that means I need to hide the truth from him for at least the next twenty-four hours."

"I assume Rosston is still unaware of the shortfall?"

"Yes. And I should very much like to keep it that way."

"He willna hear it from me," Undine said. "Rosston does not care for me. He's kept his distance ever since I told him I put an impotence spell on the chief of Clan Armstrong."

"Did you?"

"Abby, the man's three score and eight. A sharp look will do it."

Abby laughed, and the lilting string of notes rose through Duncan's head like bubbles in champagne.

"The question remains," Abby said, "how do I send our unexpected visitor home?"

"The text is not quite clear on the point," Undine said after a pause. "It only says that one called to serve must actually serve before the spell can be broken."

"And 'broken' means he'll go back?"

"That is the part that is unclear."

Duncan opened his eyes. Grendel, it seemed, was a handsome wolfhound of gray and white with a long, slim nose and watchful eyes. Abby—at least what Duncan could see of her at this angle, which was one muddied boot tapping absently on an ancient rug about ten feet from him—seemed to be wrestling with a decision. Duncan wondered briefly why, if there was a rug available, he was lying on bare stone.

After a moment, Abby let out a resigned sigh. "Fine. He can stay. God help me. A clodhead with a wooden sword to keep fed and clothed. Well, if nothing else, I suppose he could help the swineherds."

Help the swineherds? A man who managed a platoon of bond traders, advised the CFOs of Fortune 500 companies, and lived in a doorman building in Manhattan's Financial District dragging pigs through the mud? Not. Bloody. Likely.

Abby added, "But I'll be depending on you to keep him out of sight."

Duncan opened his mouth, but his protest was drowned out by Abby's cry as she lowered herself into the gilded chair and jumped up again.

"What is it?" Undine said.

"Chastity threw me today on the field. I feel like someone has turned me over his knee and walloped me bare-assed. Can you look at it?"

Duncan froze. The top of a gilt-legged table blocked his view of Abby's unfortunate condition. He struggled to an elbow to see if that would correct the situation, and Grendel let out a low growl. Seeing his view had not improved, Duncan reached for the table leg. Grendel unleashed a string of barks so fierce Duncan felt like M-80s were going off behind his eyes.

"Grendel!" Abby shouted.

Grendel froze and so did Duncan, and it was only when Duncan returned his arm to his side that the dog stretched out again and relaxed.

"Thanks," Duncan mouthed to the dog. The dog made a whimper of regret and licked Duncan's nose. Duncan heard the rustle of fabric being raised.

"It's bad," Undine said. "One cheek is fine and pink, but the other will be as purple as bilberry jam by nightfall. I'll make you a poultice. That will help with the swelling. But for now, how about a goblet of wine?"

Abby sighed. "That would be lovely."

Duncan couldn't help but imagine that fine pink cheek, sitting like a perfect teardrop over a slim and willing thigh…

A knock brought Grendel to his feet again, this time barking happily.

"There's my good dog," said a third woman, leaning down to pat him.

She was slim and pretty, though not as pretty as Abby, with hair as bright red as Duncan's.

The woman said to Grendel, "We got to be great friends while we were waiting for your mama to return, didn't we?"

"Oh, dear," Abby said. "I'm so sorry, Miss—Oh, forgive me. Now I have forgotten your name. I know you told me outside."

"Miss Fallon. Serafina Fallon. Pray don't let it trouble you. We barely spoke before you were called off."

Abby's shoulders sagged. "Between the English and, well, other matters, today has not been the best of days. Did my servants take care of you while you were waiting?"

"Aye, they were quite attentive. I'm glad you are well. I understand the confrontation with the English was brief, thank God. If you'd like, I can return another time."

"No, no," Abby said, "we are most pleased to have you. And once things settle down, I am certain Undine shall be glad to help you in any way she can."

"I thank you," Miss Fallon said. "Oh! Who is this?"

The attention of the room turned to Duncan.

"Him?" Abby said disinterestedly. "He's my swinehe—"

"*Prisoner*," Duncan said, though the explosion of sound in his head when he spoke made him wince.

Abby marched over and crouched beside him, waiting until she saw his eyes focus on her. "You are not my prisoner," she said sharply. "If you were, I would hardly leave my door unbolted so that you could *go*." She stuck her finger pointedly in the direction of the room's looming entrance, violet-blue eyes ablaze.

Duncan looked beyond the doors, down the long gallery filled with centuries-old furniture and sconces filled with real candles. He shook his head. The floor might be cold, but the outside world—with shots flying, a sea of faces he didn't recognize, and no way to return to the world he knew—seemed even less inviting.

Abby made a grunt of satisfaction. "Then perhaps you'll want to tell Miss Fallon who you are."

Her eyes burned into him, the threat of expulsion clear, but he'd be damned if he'd say he was a swineherd. He pressed his mouth tight.

Abby growled and stood. "He's my swineher—"

"*Adviser*," Duncan said more loudly.

Miss Fallon looked at Abby. Abby looked at Undine, who shrugged.

"He's my swineherd adviser," Abby said with tight lips. "He advises me about swine."

"*Oh.*"

It was clear Miss Fallon had not heard of swineherd advisers.

Abby put a hand on her forehead and exhaled slowly. "Oh, for God's sake, it's too ridiculous for even me to believe. He's neither my swineherd nor adviser. But he has come quite recently into my charge, *much* to my regret, and I fear he will throw a turnscrew into my plans, something I cannot afford. We have a very important visitor coming."

Duncan pulled himself unsteadily to sitting. He felt like a sailor after three days of drunken shore leave. The three women—one dark, one fiery haired, and one blond—watched him as if they were watching the raising of a particularly ugly shipwreck. Grendel paced over and looked him in the eyes. He had a penetrating gaze for a dog.

Miss Fallon stepped closer and looked Duncan over carefully. Grendel wagged his tail. After a moment, the woman made a small sound of disappointment, and Grendel stopped.

"He's very handsome," Miss Fallon said, "but I'm afraid he won't answer my needs. The coloring is a problem, you see, as is his height. The man I seek must be shorter. Those additional inches will do me no good."

"Most women prefer tall men," he said, a little put out.

"Miss Fallon is looking for a husband," Undine explained, an amused smile on her face. "But only for a night. 'Tis rather a shame, when you think about it. As a turnscrew, it seems you would be perfectly suited."

Heat flew up Duncan's cheeks. He was hardly a prude, but, for God's sake, what sort of Amazonian love prison had he fallen into?

"Am I interrupting?"

A princely man with dark hair and arms the size of coffee cans stood in the entryway. It was the same man who had found Abby in the woods and witnessed her assault on Duncan. Duncan didn't like the way the women's heads turned, though he noted with some satisfaction that Grendel stayed with him.

"No," Abby said. "Do you have word of William?"

"The wound is clean and bound. The surgeon says he will be well again in time. I gave the man three shillings."

"Thank you," Abby said stiffly. "I would have paid him myself had I known."

"'Twas no hardship, milady. By the way, your servant mentioned something about Sir Alan Raeburn's imminent arrival. I was not aware he was coming."

"I do not clear my visitors with you or anyone, Rosston."

"No, of course not, milady." He took a step toward Abby in the silence that followed, but evidently changed his mind and stopped. "Is the man a spy?"

"Sir Alan? Don't be absurd."

"I don't mean Sir Alan," Rosston said with forced patience. "I am quite familiar with his position at the Bank of Scotland. I meant him." He ducked his head toward Duncan.

"What? No." Abby shook her head, distracted. "I was mistaken. The sum of what the man knows wouldn't get you a ha'penny in the deepest bowels of Whitehall."

Rosston waited. "Then he is…?"

"Him?" Abby said, apparently realizing an answer must be given. "That man there?" Panic rose in her eyes.

"Aye," Rosston said. "If he's not a spy, what was the idiot doing in the middle of Kerr land?"

Rosston had said "Kerr land" as if the "Kerr" involved had been him, and Duncan could see Abby had noticed it too. Duncan hadn't liked the man from the first, and his dislike was only growing. With a bit of unsteady maneuvering, he got his feet beneath him. Let the man call him "idiot" to his face.

"Abby?" Rosston said.

Abby jabbed her thumb toward Miss Fallon. "Why, he's her…her…"

"Her what?"

"Swineherd."

"Cousin."

"Husband."

"*Adviser*."

Rosston gazed narrowly at the four suddenly impenetrable faces. "I beg your pardon?"

Undine put down her wine. "He's her swineherd cousin's husband's adviser. Upon my word, Rosston. Pay attention. Miss Fallon brought him here to Langholm, and I think we would do ourselves and Miss Fallon a great service if we endeavored to keep that in mind."

Rosston scanned the room slowly, stopping for a long moment on Duncan's graceless ascent to his knees before returning to Abby. He made a courtly bow to Miss Fallon. "My apologies. I assume, then, Miss Fallon and her, er, associate will be joining us for supper?"

"I do not have time to trifle with a meal this evening," Abby said. "If you're hungry, please ask Mrs. Michaels to fix something for you. I'm sure there's more than enough left over from the festivities. I intend to review the paperwork for Sir Alan and go to bed."

"I pray you do not have much to review, milady. Sir Alan was spotted in town less than a quarter hour ago. He will be at Castle Kerr quite soon."

Duncan stood and the world began to spin. He grabbed the chair back, but it wasn't enough. He collapsed, crashing into the gilt-legged table as he fell.

Abby made a long, slow sigh. "We are ruined."

Five

ABBY WATCHED THE MAN WEAVE HIS WAY PAST THE top of the grand staircase and down the hall in front of her. In what part of Scotland did they wear such odd skirt-like plaids? The ones her men wore stretched from their shoulders to their knees. Had he come from another country? More important, what was she going to do with him? Or with Sir Alan for that matter? She hadn't even had a chance to wash her hands since she'd been thrown. Undine and her bloody herbs!

"Stop there," she commanded. "That will be your room."

The man turned, confused, spotted the open door, and grabbed the frame for support. He managed something bow-like to encourage her to enter first. She felt a faint crackle as she passed, like the air after a summer storm. He was taller than she remembered, taller even than Rosston, and the bedchamber seemed suddenly quite small.

"You can stay here until we figure out what to do with you."

He made his way to the cheval mirror, stripped off

his sark, and gazed over his shoulder at the reflection of his arm. The cut from her arrow must have reopened because a ribbon of red was visible in the tracks of the darker, clotted blood on his arm. His eyes were a rich sea blue, and she couldn't help but admire the wide, carved chest, dusted with bronze and gold, and the tautness of his belly. He lifted the red-blond locks at his nape and hissed when his fingers found the egg-sized knob.

"You're quite the bowwoman," he said, meeting her gaze in the mirror.

"My father wouldna teach me to use a sword. He said women have no use for them."

A ruddy brow rose. Had he heard something in her reply? Long ago, she'd learned to remove all emotion when she spoke of her father. She would have to take extra care around this man.

He crossed his arms. "Would you care to tell me why I'm here?"

She shifted. Anything she told him might be repeated to Sir Alan. He looked as if he'd managed to get himself under control, but who could judge such a thing? He didn't seem like the men she knew in the borderlands. He didn't seem like the men she knew anywhere.

"My life's been taken from me," he said. "I think I deserve an answer."

"You have been called here by magic, and I—"

"Whose? Yours?"

"No. I had nothing to do with it."

He eyed her skeptically.

"Undine is half naiad—water fairy," she added, seeing his confusion. "Or so she says. Without a doubt, though, she is a fortune-teller and potion-maker. 'Twas her magic that brought you here. Not mine." Abby thought of the long columns of household expenses and the dwindling gold in the Kerr accounts. "Were I possessed of magic, I would not have wasted it on you."

"And how will I—?"

"I cannot think about that now," she said. "I am about to receive a guest whose needs take precedence. For the present, you will have to wait here. Perhaps you can practice swinging your wee sword."

He gave her a cool look. "I know how to use a sword."

"A wooden one."

"I know how to use a steel one too."

"I am most glad to hear it. I'll have someone bring you something to eat."

"Rosston is expecting me at supper. Willna my absence appear strange?"

He was right, dammit. "I'll tell him you're unwell."

The man rocked on his heels for a moment, then threw his balled-up shirt on the bed. "No. I don't think so. I want to come."

She drew herself up to full height. "Perhaps you'd prefer to be locked into your room?"

"Perhaps you'd prefer to have me tell Rosston your clan is on the verge of losing everything."

He'd overheard what she'd said to Undine! What else had he heard? She considered calling for her guards. She also considered punching him in the nose. Neither, however, seemed calculated to reduce Sir Alan's anxiety about investing.

A dangerous incaution simmered in the man's eyes, and she could almost hear him shouting, "She's lying, Sir Alan! 'Tis the canal or the poorhouse for the Kerrs!" as her guards dragged him away. What choice did she have, short of having guards posted at his door? Even then she'd still have to worry about what he'd say to them.

"As you wish," she said. "But only under these conditions: You are to limit your conversation partners to me and Undine. Under no circumstances are you to speak to Rosston or Sir Alan. And you are not to mention the circumstances of your unfortunate arrival to anyone. We will see to your problems tomorrow, but for now I expect you to do as I say, when I say it. Do you understand?"

A drop of blood fell from his elbow to the rug.

She let out an aggrieved exhalation. "I'll have some towels and bandages brought to you. Until then, if you could manage to keep your blood off my rugs, I'd appreciate it. Do you understand?"

"Is Rosston your husband?"

The question startled her. "No."

"Does he want to be?"

"I don't know. Perhaps."

The man kept his unblinking gaze on her.

"Aye," she admitted, annoyed. "If you must know. Though it hardly matters."

"To you? Or to him?" He picked up his shirt. "Or to me?"

"To any of us," she said, refusing to consider what he might have meant by the last. "I have no time to tend to you like a bairn in clouts. There are clothes that should fit you in the wardrobe here. Can you get yourself clean, dressed, and to the dining hall by seven?"

"I am not here of my own free will. If you could spare me a modicum of hospitality, I'd appreciate it."

"Hospitality!" she cried. "Do ye not realize you're *alive*, under the protection of *my* clan, eating *my* food, and sleeping in *my* bed?" Her cheeks warmed as she realized how that last phrase sounded. "On top of that, you've just blackmailed me. What additional hospitality should I be offering?"

Those eyes turned gray, and she saw the tiniest flash of hurt. "Well, you could start by asking my name."

Oh.

She could hear her mother's voice. *Abigail Ailich Kerr, I raised you better than that.*

"I—I beg your pardon." Abby made an unsteady curtsy. "Today has been a mess"—she forbore naming the reasons why, since they prominently included him—"and dinner promises to offer more of the same. I am Abby Kerr of Clan Kerr."

"And I'm Duncan MacHarg." He offered his hand.

She hesitated. She had little desire to deepen their friendship. But a handshake was a greeting from a man to a man. She liked that. She took his hand. It was warm and firm—and large enough to make hers look like a small bird nesting in it.

"Abby Kerr," he said, the incaution in those eyes replaced by something kinder and a wee bit spellbinding. "I'll do nothing to harm your relationship with Sir Alan. I know what it is to have a lot riding on a meeting. I may be the last person you wanted to attend tonight, but I promise you may depend on me."

Nora, one of the younger kitchen maids, appeared in the doorway, and Abby pulled her hand free. The girl stared at Duncan with wide eyes.

"What is it?" Abby demanded, inexplicably flustered.

"Mrs. Michaels needs to know what dishes ye want to serve."

Abby exhaled. "Whatever can be salvaged from this afternoon. Tell her to use her best judgment."

Nora scampered away.

"I beg your pardon, MacHarg," Abby said. "I am needed elsewhere—everywhere, it seems."

He followed her to the hall, and they nearly bumped when she stopped to give him a second curtsy. This one was made even more self-conscious by the sight of Rosston peering at them from the doorway to his room.

"I'll see you at seven," Duncan said. "And I shall speak only to you."

"No, that's not what I—" She stopped. She could tell by the gleam in his eyes there was nothing to be gained by trying to correct him. She slipped her still-tingling hand in her pocket and hurried to the staircase.

Six

DUNCAN WATCHED THE SELF-ASSURED BOUNCE OF THE brown waves as she floated down the stairs. Being tall, Scottish, and reasonably good-looking, he was used to reducing women in America to tongue-tied teenagers. Abby, on the other hand, seemed entirely immune to his charms. He might as well be…well, a swineherd.

When he finally lifted his gaze, he saw they had not been alone. Rosston stood in the arch of a doorway, partially obscured by a statue. Duncan nodded coolly, a silent acknowledgment that Rosston's observation had not gone unnoticed, and Rosston turned and disappeared.

So that's how it's to be?

A servant dropped off a pitcher, ewer, and a roll of cotton wool as promised, and in a few moments Duncan had washed and bandaged himself. He imagined what it might have been like for Abby to do the tending instead.

He had to assume she was the de facto chief of Clan Kerr, but what sort of woman runs a clan? The last time there were working clan chiefs of any gender in Scotland, not to mention clashes between English soldiers and Scots clansmen, George II was king. The thought made Duncan dizzy.

How had Abby succeeded to the title? Had she no brothers? Duncan thought of the room full of aggressive, determined traders he managed, hardly more civilized than a regiment of bloody-minded clansmen. How did a lass of twenty-three or twenty-four command them? And how had the clan's coffers been mismanaged?

He looked around the room. A brocade-covered bed stood between carved tables. A tapestry of some ancient battle hung on the wall. A candle stood in a holder shaped to look like a lion rampant. He'd been in a dozen centuries-old castles like this on school trips or dragged by his mum on holidays to see "our history," but never had he stood in the middle of one, knowing that the furniture and decorations at which he looked were not part of Scotland's past but its present. A shiver went through him.

He didn't have to be a denizen of this century to know his torn and bloodstained sark was a no-go for dinner. He opened the wardrobe and looked at the array of linen and coats. Whoever owned them was tall and broad shouldered. He hoped it wasn't Rosston. He didn't want to spend a moment in that man's debt.

He found a sark embroidered with a tiny vine around the neck and down the front. Had Abby's hand done the work? He traced a finger along the twining leaves.

He heard a sound and turned. Grendel had appeared

and was turning in circles to make a place for himself on the empty hearth.

"Oh, I see. You're here to keep an eye on me, are you? As if I had anywhere to run. Perhaps you can tell me a bit about your mistress."

Grendel laid his head on his paws and looked at Duncan ruefully.

"Sworn to secrecy. I understand." Duncan bent to scratch the dog's ears. "There are no pets allowed in my building at home, I'm afraid. I have to get all my dog needs filled at the park."

Grendel rolled on his back and offered his belly.

A boy flew by the open door, firewood in his arms, and Grendel barked. Duncan recognized him as the boy who'd been attacked at the battle.

Duncan jogged to the door. "Hey." The boy spun around. He was twelve or thirteen, with a shock of brown hair that hung over his forehead. "Where are you going?"

"Firewood for Sir Alan's room."

"Come back here when you finish, will you?"

The boy shrugged, flipping the hair from his eyes.

By the time Duncan had tucked in his tails, the boy was back, wiping his nose on his sleeve. "What is it?"

"Do you remember me?"

The boy nodded, hesitant.

"My name's Duncan. Is your arm all right?"

"It is, sir. Thank you." The boy stooped by Grendel and patted the dog's head. His hands were filthy and the shirt he wore looked as if it was a size too small.

"Grendel is Abby's dog, is he?"

"Abby?"

"Er, Abby Kerr?"

"Oh, Lady Kerr. Aye, he is. He's verra good with sticks. I can throw them as far down the river as you can imagine, and he just jumps in and brings them back."

"Lady Kerr is, er, the chief of Clan Kerr? I'm not from around here."

"She is. My ma says Lady Kerr is too big for her saddle. I don't know as I agree, though. I've seen her in her saddle. She looks quite handsome."

Duncan coughed to hide a laugh. "What about you? Do you like her? Do you think she does a good job? Lady Kerr, I mean, not your mum. I'm sure your mum does a very fine job."

The boy shrugged. "I guess. She negotiated with an officer in the English army, and there haven't been any battles since last year at Hogmany—well, until today."

"Does Rosston help her? Rosston is the man with arms like small hams."

"I know Rosston. He was a hero at the Battle of Dunkeld. Everyone knows him."

"So, does he help her with the planning of attacks or anything else with the clan?"

"Lady Kerr does not plan attacks," the boy said. "I don't think she likes them at all. She certainly doesn't plan them with anybody."

"Perhaps they share a different relationship?"

The boy made a thoughtful frown. "They *are* related. Rosston's her cousin, though their families don't speak."

Feuding cousins. Very interesting. "She appears to be a little cool toward him."

"I dunno about that. He's the one who gave her Grendel."

Hearing his name, Grendel thumped his tail.

"*Hm.*" The giving of a dog was not generally the act of a mere acquaintance, though perhaps in this case it was a gift to mend the rift between the two sides of the family.

The boy had pulled a sausage from his pocket and the dog was running in circles, trying to earn a treat. The boy threw a piece, and the dog caught it in midair.

"What do you know about the canal?" Duncan asked.

"It's a big empty hole. The men started digging it three years ago. But they stopped."

"Why? Do you know?"

"My cousin Jack worked on it, and he says they ran out of money. But my ma says Lady Kerr pissed it away with trips to London and Paris to see her lovers."

Duncan's brows went up. "That's quite an accusation." Carnal appetites, fiscal irresponsibility, and consorting with, or at least spending time in the lands of, one's enemy—no wonder Abby was finding things hard going. "What do you think?"

Again, the boy shrugged. "I like her. She's always kind to me. And she's very good to Grendel."

Duncan smiled. Could a truer gauge of worthiness be found? "I take it you spend a lot of time here?"

"I help the cook when she asks," the boy said, "and I sometimes sleep in the barn. But I don't live here."

"What's your name?" Duncan said.

"Nab."

"Nab, I am in need of an assistant."

"A what?"

"A man to run my errands, do my bidding, carry my notes—"

"Answer your questions about Lady Kerr?"

Duncan searched the boy's face for the hint of a tease and had no trouble finding it. Duncan's ears warmed. "Er, aye."

"Am I to be a spy, then?"

Duncan blinked. "Let's see where assistant takes us first, shall we? How much does the cook pay you?"

"A shilling a week and breakfast."

Pursing his lips, Duncan considered what he should offer. He had a twenty in his sporran—useless here—and his wallet was in his hotel room in Pittsburgh. He had no idea where he'd get the money to pay the boy, but then again, Duncan had never had a problem making money, no matter where he was. "Let's make it two then."

"Three," the boy said stoutly. "Rosston offered me two to keep my eye on you."

Interesting. Duncan's investment in the boy was already paying off. "If I offer to pay you four, will you turn him down?"

Through the cascade of hair, Nab gave Duncan a careful look. "Do you *want* me to turn him down?"

Duncan wished every man in his employ possessed the same cold-blooded cunning. "Now that you mention it, no."

A pleased smile rose on Nab's face. "When do we start?"

"Well, the first thing I need is some valeting. I don't know your customs as well as I ought. It's very important to Lady Kerr that I look acceptable at dinner tonight. Can you take a look and tell me if anything looks odd?"

Nab grinned. "Your hair is a *very* bright shade of red."

"*Och*, a comedian. Those three shillings are starting to look like two again to me."

The boy laughed. "You'll need a different plaid. Those are too close to the Campbell colors. You can't wear that here."

"There we go. That's the sort of advice I need." Duncan waved at the wardrobe. "Choose carefully. I should very much like to outshine our friend Rosston tonight."

Nab's eyes came alive. "In that case, there's a really big sword and sheath in the Hunting Room. It's got a dragon on it, and jewels too. But it's too high for me to reach."

"A dragon? Well, we dinna want to miss that." Duncan stuck out his hand. "Nab, I think this is going to be the start of a beautiful friendship."

Seven

ABBY NODDED DISCREETLY TO HER SERVANT. SIR Alan's goblet was perilously low on wine, and she wanted him to be well lubricated before they moved into the Great Hall to start dinner. The library was sparkling, and she and the heads of the most important families stood admiring the pink-hued sunset through the western windows. Abby had no intention of mentioning the canal to Sir Alan tonight. Business is best done with breakfast in your belly, her father had always said. She wanted Sir Alan's first evening in the bosom of Clan Kerr to be one of pleasant and unexceptional repose.

The servant refilled the glass, and Sir Alan gave the young woman a lupine stare. Oh, dear. Always the risk of lubrication. Unfortunately, the woman filled Rosston's glass as well. Rosston's crimson cheeks betrayed a lack of moderation that appeared to have begun before his appearance in the library.

"I understand there was a run-in with the army this afternoon," said Sir Alan, taking another deep draft of wine. He eyed Abby closely.

"They haven't the sense to stay off our lands," Rosston said. "The point of our swords must be the reward for trespassing."

"The company had lost their way, I believe," Abby said. "When they realized their mistake, they left peaceably. It was hardly more than a moderately warm tête-à-tête."

"Like young lovers?" Sir Alan met Abby's gaze over the top of his goblet.

"Lady Kerr?"

Undine, in shimmering green silk, signaled from the doorway. Abby excused herself.

"I'm afraid I am the bearer of some unhappy news," Undine said. "William's leg is starting to swell. I fear a fever will o'ertake him by nightfall."

Abby's chest tightened with worry. "Will you—"

"Aye, I have. I've given him a marigold tisane. The other news is more troubling. Do you remember the company of soldiers this afternoon? I have it on good authority the sergeant is telling his officers the clan attacked first."

"What? No!" The tightening became a vise. If the sergeant managed to convince his officers the Kerrs were attacking the English, there was no telling what the army's response would be.

A servant carrying a platter of salmon cakes looked to Abby for instructions. Abby waved her in the general direction of Sir Alan. For God's sake, was she to be required to make *every* decision in this place? She could not outwit the English *and* know the right place to put the salmon cakes. There simply wasn't enough room in her head for all of it.

"Undine, I need you to go to the army headquarters in Bowness. See what you can find out. I know you have contacts there. Perhaps one of them has some influence with the colonel."

"I should prefer to stay to watch over William, but I suppose I can instruct a servant to care for him in my absence. May I have the use of your carriage?"

Abby agreed and gave quiet instructions to the footman, who hurried off. "And while you're there," she said, turning back to Undine, "I wonder if you could—"

She gasped. MacHarg had stepped into the hallway from the Hunting Room and was making his way toward the library. He'd shifted from his odd, skirted plaid to a longer Kerr one in a stunning crimson that set off the width of his shoulders. He looked a foot taller than he had earlier, and the setting sun was directly behind him, giving him the quite misleading appearance of wearing a halo.

Undine cleared her throat, and Abby's jaw instantly returned to its proper place.

"Oh, thank the gods," Undine said quietly. "I was afraid I had an apoplexy on my hands."

"He looks so…so…"

"Indeed he does. And the ripple of the linen is making me think your strong-arm plea has not gone unanswered. Is that not the sark you embroidered for Bran?"

MacHarg spotted Abby and smiled.

He made a low bow. His muscular knees, an hour ago caked with mud and blood, shone like pale marble. Abby was reminded of a statue of Mercury she had once seen in London.

"Good evening, Lady Kerr." He gave her a daunting

smile. She opened her mouth to reply; then her attention fell on the sword extending from his sheath.

"Where did you get that?" she asked, shocked.

"Do you not recognize it?" He pulled it free and brandished it with a laughably unskilled flourish. "It's yours, from the Great Hall. I don't believe I've ever seen one as handsome."

"You cannot—"

"Is something amiss?" Sir Alan had wandered over. "Your cousin says there's been some news about the army—something about a possible retaliation for today's tête-à-tête?"

Panicked, Abby searched for a convenient lie. "Er…"

"There has been," MacHarg said firmly. "Though not as you describe. The army has sent an apology via messenger. The sergeant who trespassed is new to the borderlands and misread his map. The transgression shall not be repeated." He gave Abby a conspiratorial look, and she bowed her head in gratitude.

Sir Alan narrowed his eyes. "And who are you?"

MacHarg gave Abby and Undine a stern, peremptory glare. "I am adviser to Miss…er…"

He'd forgotten the woman's name! "Fallon," Abby said quickly. "Of course, it's hard to remember since she just remarried."

"But you said 'Miss'?" Sir Alan looked confused.

"Did I? It's Missus. But," she added carefully to MacHarg, "she wishes you to continue to call her by her given name—*Serafina*."

Undine gave MacHarg a gentle elbow and said, "I think she may have a bit of a crush on you."

Abby trod hard on her friend's instep.

"*Mrs. Fallon*, of course," said Undine with a glare. "But how could she, since you are almost close enough to her to be her brother?"

The servant with the salmon cakes returned, evidently determined to engage Abby in their disposition.

Sir Alan regarded MacHarg with interest. "And where is this Mrs. Fallon with whom you share such a familial-like relationship?"

"I am here." Serafina sped down the hall, a vision in fawn velvet, and came to a dead stop in front of MacHarg, no doubt trying to recall the exact connection she and he were supposed to share.

"There you are, my dear." Abby gave her a gentle kiss. "You know Duncan MacHarg, of course. And here is the guest I was telling you about, Sir Alan Raeburn. Sir Alan is in today from Edinburgh."

Serafina made a small "*Ooh!*" followed by a deep curtsy, indicating she remembered who *he* was, at least.

Sir Alan bowed, letting his gaze travel over Serafina's ample bosom like a fox eyeing a pair of goose eggs. Despite his age, Sir Alan had lost no interest in the hunt.

"A pleasure," he said to her. "And how, again, are you related to Mr. MacHarg?"

"I believe he is something in the way of an adviser," said Rosston, who had edged his way into the circle, "through a swineherd connection. Good evening, Miss Fallon."

"'Missus,' I think you mean," Sir Alan said, and Rosston frowned.

Abby prayed everyone would remember how they were related to one another for at least the next hour or two, or it was going to be quite a long evening.

Sir Alan said, "I give you great joy of your recent marriage, Mrs. Fallon."

Serafina looked as if she'd swallowed a porcupine. "Er…what?"

MacHarg made a deep-throated *proceed with caution* noise, and Serafina, catching on, grasped his arm tighter and gazed at him with love. "I'd say it took us both by surprise—"

Abby coughed and shook her head.

"—and I can't wait to introduce you to him, Duncan. I know you will like him."

The long moment of silence that followed was broken by Undine's snort. "Well, I would certainly love to stay for the rest of *this* dinner, but I'm afraid I have business that takes me away tonight. With any luck, I shall see you on the morrow."

Undine exited, and Sir Alan said to MacHarg, "I am told you are an adviser. Pray, sir, on what do you advise?"

Clearly happy to have become the center of attention, Duncan held up a theatrical hand. "Actually, that's a rather interesting story. Like you, I suppose, I had aspirations in banking, but after my first year of university, things took a wee turn. You see, I fancy myself a bit of a—"

If Abby could have reached MacHarg's instep, she would have forgone her heel and plunged his sword through it instead. In place of that, she fired off a look that would have flattened a lesser man. Just because Sir Alan was talking to him didn't mean her proscription against talking to Sir Alan had expired.

"A bit of a what, sir?" Sir Alan said.

MacHarg, paling, considered. He snagged a salmon cake from the platter. "Fisherman. That is to say, I advise on fish *and* I fish. I am all fish, truth be told."

"Oh, well, I am a man of fishing myself. A very fine stream runs through my property in Fife. You must try it sometime."

Another servant appeared and met the eyes of the footman, who immediately straightened and announced dinner was ready. The group moved into the Great Hall. Abby had purposefully put MacHarg in the middle of the long table, between Serafina and Undine, so that he would be as far as possible from both Sir Alan, who would be seated next to Abby at one end, and Rosston, who would be seated next to his men at the other.

However, her plans were not to be. Serafina, who had stopped to rearrange her skirts, was swept up by Rosston on the way to the hall, and MacHarg was repeating a particularly drawn-out story to Sir Alan about the enormous size of a salmon he had once caught. It seemed to Abby, who had almost no interest in fish except those Mrs. Michael baked into her pies, as if gentlemen these days were almost as invested in the size of their catches as they were in the size of their—

"Battering rams, milady?" Sir Alan had paused to observe the pair of intricately carved columns of wood that hung in an X over the dining room's massive hearth. "Rather an unsubtle touch." He smiled.

"My grandfather used to say the larger the weapons, the fewer the wars."

"Is that a sentiment you and your father also share, Lady Kerr?"

And just who was being unsubtle now?

"Perhaps," she said with a forced chuckle. "Though I suspect it was for different reasons. My father liked his swords sweeping. I prefer my peace that way."

MacHarg said, "I understand the people of the borderlands have been quite pleased with the peace Lady Kerr was able to negotiate. More than a year now, is it not? That has to be a record."

He raised his goblet and Abby's cheeks warmed. That was the second time he'd helped her navigate a difficult situation. She found herself flustered by his support. The last few years had been so turbulent and her ascension to the chieftainship so fraught with controversy, she had grown used to expecting every decision to be a fight and every fight to be fought alone.

While she was most grateful for his help, she was very interested to know the source of his information. His "reinterpretation" of the army's message—patently false—was predicated on knowing that a messenger had come to Kerr Castle. And now for him to know she'd brokered a peace with the English army a year and a half ago? Was he a borderlander? But no. Everything about him was a degree divorced from the expected, from the cut of his clothes to the odd length of his hair to his sometimes surprising choice of words or phrases, suggesting that the odds of him being from the borders were small. On the other hand, there was no mistaking that lovely, deep rumble for anything other than a Lowland burr. She looked at him and he gave her a lopsided grin. But even that, she had to admit, carried a note of something in it marking him as an outlander.

She lifted her glass in thanks. He gave her a generous smile.

"Sir Alan, surely you didn't come to Kerr Castle for fishing?" Rosston popped a gobbet of lamb in his mouth.

"I did not. Though I could surely be tempted." He gave MacHarg a gentle poke. "No, I am here to talk to Lady Kerr about her canal."

Abby pushed a small mound of peas around her plate. She had hoped to keep the nature of his visit between Sir Alan and herself.

"The canal?" Rosston leaned forward. "I thought the project had been abandoned?"

Sir Alan had not gotten to be on the board of the Bank of Scotland by being lured into indiscretion, and he could judge enough in Rosston's tone to know that the answer, if any were to be given, must come from Abby herself.

"I am looking to reopen it," she said.

"And from where are the funds to come?" Rosston demanded a second before the answer came to him.

Sir Alan buried his attention in his oysters.

"You are bringing a *bank* into this?" Rosston shoved his chair from the table. "This is a family matter. Your father would not agree. *I* do not agree."

A clansman whispered, "Nor do I," and a few others nodded.

Abby felt the focused gazes of her men. "Rosston, this is hardly the place—"

"No," he said, voice rising. "You dinna bring outsiders into something like this. We settle these things on our own. You dinna open our—"

MacHarg adjusted his chair. It moved no more than

an inch, but the scrape carried such menace Rosston stopped in the middle of his sentence.

Abby sat with dread, waiting for MacHarg to say something that would irretrievably transform this discussion from a point of order between a chieftess and her cousin to a bollocks-driven brawl in the middle of her dining hall. But MacHarg only picked up his wine and waited politely for Rosston to finish.

Abby relaxed a degree. "Thank you, Rosston. That will be all."

He flung down his napkin and stalked away.

With the throb of blood in her ears, she said, "I am so sorry, Sir Alan."

"I see my presence here is upsetting to some of your men," he said. "I wonder if I should go?"

"No," she begged. "Stay. Please. Enjoy your dinner. I'll talk to Rosston."

Sir Alan tapped the edge of his plate. "Milady, I think it might be best for all concerned if you were to invite me back when there is some consensus among your men. As I understand it, each has a vote, does he not?"

"Aye, but not to the degree you think." Abby felt like weeping. She bit the inside of her cheek.

"Perhaps, if you were able to convince Rosston, he might be able to help you convince the rest. I understand his side of Kerrs carries quite a bit of influence and, dare I say, with their investment, you may not need me and my bank at all."

"Thank you," she said, though she felt no gratitude at all. "I appreciate your advice."

He nodded. "'Tis the least I could do for a young lassie like yourself."

Abby reached for her goblet and drank.

Eight

DUNCAN AMBLED DOWN THE SEEMINGLY ENDLESS COR-
ridor of doors, candle in hand, searching for his room.
The dinner had proceeded, though after Rosston left,
no one seemed to enjoy it. Abby managed to convince
Sir Alan to delay his departure until morning but not
to reopen a discussion of the canal until she had what
he termed "the unshakable support of the Kerr men."

Abby had carried on stoically, even keeping the
evening's conversation afloat with something akin to
cheer, but Duncan had seen the distress in those eyes.
He'd wanted to tell her everything would be all right,
but such a thing would have been both condescending
and disrespectful, not to mention unlikely to be true,
and he suspected she'd had enough condescension and
disrespect to last a lifetime. Nonetheless, it had taken
more than a little willpower to keep his mouth shut,
just as it had taken more than a little willpower to keep
from running after Rosston and introducing his bulk
to one of the tapestry-covered walls. As well-intended
as the acts might have been, neither would have served
his hostess well.

Night had fallen during dinner, and rain had come, pounding the walls of the castle before moving on to the west just as the first guests rose from the table. And now, the strange, sometimes off-putting, Scottish mists were rising like walls of ghostly fire over the river. The sight sent a wave of homesickness through Duncan. His grandfather's house, situated not far from Langholm, had often been enveloped in odd and fascinating weather, and his visits there as a child, far from the city streets of Edinburgh, had formed in him a deep and unchanging love for the majesty of the Lowland hills.

Homesick when you're in the middle of Scotland? A fine fool you are. And yet home—and his grand-da— seemed more remote to him now than when he was in New York, half a world away.

Outside a wolf howled, and Grendel appeared in one of the doorways, ears raised.

"Do you hear your pack?"

Grendel made an agitated noise, and Duncan scratched the dog's ears. Duncan didn't know how he had come to be here, more than three hundred years in his past, and wondered for an instant if he, like Grendel, had been responding to some ancient and unknowable call. But while finding out how he got here would be interesting, Duncan knew he needed to concentrate on discovering something more useful— namely, how to return.

Grendel made another noise, in sympathy with his wild brethren, and leaned reluctantly against Duncan.

"Poor fellow. I'm afraid we must both be resigned to stay awhile."

His heart cramped. *What day was it? Still Sunday?* He had been intentionally vague with grandfather about his arrival, protecting his options in case an emergency arose at work, but at some point his grand-da would begin to worry.

The muffled sound of a man's voice—deep, gruff, filled with anger—rose behind a door at the end of the hall. With Grendel at his heels, Duncan padded to the door at the cross section of two halls. Duncan looked left, right, and behind him. No one in sight. He leaned closer. A woman was speaking now, her voice as agitated as the man's but quieter and appeasing. Duncan couldn't make out the words, though the disagreement was heated.

He jerked away when he heard footsteps approaching on the other side, and thank goodness he did. The door banged open, barely missing him, and slowed to a stop far enough forward to block him from view. Abby, stiff with upset and clutching her skirts, ran down the hall, pulling Grendel into her wake. She disappeared into a room and slammed the door behind her, stranding the dog, who flopped down sadly.

Duncan moved around the open door and gazed in. It was not a room but a tight, round stone stairway rising higher into the castle. He stepped inside cautiously.

The walls were bare save for narrow slits cut through the rock at eye level every four steps or so. A chill went through him despite the evening's warmth. The slits were for arrows. He was standing in a battle-ready turret.

With whom had Abby quarreled, though? Whose room was at the top of these stairs? He felt certain he could guess.

He heard a noise and slipped back into the hall, closing the door with a *click*. He was halfway to the door into which Abby had disappeared when Nab ambushed him from the other direction.

"There you are."

"Where is everyone?" Duncan asked.

"*Och*, there's a fiddler playing in the upper bailey and a quite decent game of dice. A lot of men are watching. I think Murgo's going to lose his goat, though. I passed Sir Alan outside the Great Hall. He was looking for you."

"Was he?" Duncan said, still looking abstractedly at the turret door. "Say, I might take a walk, possibly until quite late. If I wanted to swing by after that to chat with Rosston, where exactly in the castle do you think might I find him?"

Nab considered this for a moment. "Well, he's usually up with the owls. I think no matter how long you walk, you'll find him with his men, so probably in the bailey."

"Right," Duncan said, disappointed. "But let's say my walk were to take me as far as, say—"

"I cannot recommend walking much beyond the castle walls," said a man holding an armload of papers who was cresting the stairs. "Not tonight. Between the wolves and the soldiers, 'tis not a night for a lone stroller." The man, of middle years, had thinning hair, bright eyes, and the face of a kindly, curious bird. He held out his hand. "I'm Jock Kerr, Lady Kerr's steward.

Though if you're ever looking for a companion, I do enjoy watching the stars."

"I'm Duncan MacHarg. I'm, er, Mrs. Fallon's adviser. A pleasure to meet you, Mr. Kerr."

"I saw you at dinner," he said, taking Duncan's outstretched hand. "Call me Jock."

"Oh, aye. I can see it's not going to be too hard memorizing last names around here."

Jock laughed, his eyes wrinkling with pleasure. "No. Though it does make knowing who to trust a wee bit trickier. Even the bad ones are called 'Kerr.'"

Duncan smiled. "Are you involved in her ladyship's canal?"

Jock looked down at the paper in his hands, spotted the two-inch-tall "Kerr Canal Plan" calligraphed on one of the top sheets, and grinned. "*Och*. Just a bit. Lady Kerr is still hoping for a discussion with Sir Alan tomorrow. I'm trying to get the key issues laid out on paper for him."

"The idea of a canal is not universally embraced, I take it?"

"You noticed that, did you? Well, it *is* a financial risk. Then there are those in the clan who feel the canal will attract an unwelcome element."

"The English?"

Jock's snort was all the answer he needed.

Duncan knew enough about business to know that building a canal could make you fantastically wealthy. But if you built one in the wrong place, or at the wrong time, or without the right support, you could also be wiped out, as easy as snapping your fingers. Scotland's Darien scheme, a forerunner to the scheme that built the Panama Canal almost two hundred years later, had brought Scotland to its knees financially at the end of the 1600s, and would, in many ways, be the driving force behind the country's submission to England's demand that they join them in a union called Great Britain.

He also knew that no canal of any magnitude existed today, even in disuse, near Langholm. If Abby's canal had been built—which he doubted—it had failed.

Jock gathered his papers to carry on, but Duncan had one more question. It was essentially the same question he'd asked Nab earlier, but he knew Jock would have a more informed point of view. "Lady Kerr's rise to the chieftainship has not been an easy one, has it?"

Jock's gaze traveled to the hall's far window, as if remembering a time long ago. "Her father, Lachlan Kerr, was a devil of a man. Caesar couldna hold a candle to him. He ruled the clan with an iron hand, and they loved him—those who didn't feel the sting of his lash, that is. When his health started to fail, and Abby was his only surviving heir, the clan had the choice of supporting her, a wee lass who'd never lifted a sword, or Rosston, her cousin from the estranged side of the family. Many were surprised the clan wanted Abby. Being a direct descendant of Lachlan was more important to them than experience leading men. In truth, I think there were those who thought they'd be able to control her. But I knew she would never stand for it—she was a wicked bowwoman with a mind of her own even then. Once she was chosen, I knew she would lead even if it meant fighting them one at a time to prove she could."

"Her father must have been proud. They wanted his daughter, his blood."

Jock scratched his chin. "Her father refused to approve the line of succession. 'No girl will run my clan,' he said. 'Not as long as I draw breath.' He threw his support behind Rosston. Banished Abby from the castle until the matter was settled. She lived for a year with a friend in Cumbria. Lachlan wouldn't even let her into Scotland."

"Her mother allowed this?"

"Dead when Abby was just a girl. Not that it would have mattered. Lachlan didn't temper his opinions to please his wife."

"What happened? She's obviously the chieftess."

"The clan overruled him. Halfway through the year away, Abby survived an attack. There were some among the clan who thought Lachlan had sent the man to kill his own daughter. I suppose the truth will never be known. But that was enough to turn the tide in her favor. Lachlan saw his last great effort thwarted by his own men. He was furious. He used his last shreds of power to negotiate a compromise between Rosston's sept and his men. Abby has their support, but the alliance has not been an easy one."

Duncan could imagine. With Rosston looking over her shoulder, ready to take over at a moment's notice? He wouldn't want to be in her boots.

"One more thing," Duncan said. "You mentioned Lady Kerr was Lachlan's only surviving heir. I take it she had brothers?"

"Oh, aye. Two. One younger. He survived only a day or two after birth. And her older brother, Bran. Bran was six years older and the apple of his father's eye. Handsome, brave, a true warrior. He was killed in battle when Abby was fifteen. You're wearing his sword."

Duncan winced. No wonder Abby had been so upset.

"I must excuse myself," Jock said. "Lady Kerr and I are meeting before dawn on this. She never gives up, I'll give her that."

Each man bowed, and when Jock was out of ear-shot, Duncan said to Nab, "What a tough position to be in."

Grendel, who still lay curled at Abby's door, let out a long, canine sigh.

"You know what?" Duncan said. "Let's take the dog for a run, shall we? We can do that much for her."

Nab whistled for Grendel and headed for the stairs. Duncan left his candle on a table to light his way on his return, but what he heard when he passed Abby's door brought him to a dead stop.

Nab was halfway down the stairs when he noticed Duncan wasn't behind him. "What is it?"

Duncan pointed to the door and whispered, "She's crying."

Nab rolled his eyes. "What about the walk?"

Duncan shrugged, helpless. "I'm sorry."

"C'mon, Grendel," Nab said. "We don't need anybody else to have fun."

"Stay within sight of the castle now," Duncan called.

Nab, who was already running through the entry hall, laughed. "Jock might be afraid of the wolves, but I'm not."

Duncan hesitated before knocking. The sobs were quiet but steady.

"Lady Kerr?"

"Not now." It was a plea, not an order.

"Lady Kerr, please."

She didn't respond, but he heard steps and, after a long moment, the door opened. Her eyes were as red as cherries, but it was clear in the moment before answering, she'd wiped her face dry and was determined to keep further tears at bay. She gave him no greeting and shut the door quickly once he'd entered.

The space was much more than a bedroom. It was an apartment of sorts, three times the size of the room she'd put him in. The main space, covered in thick wool rugs, held shelves of books, a settee and chairs in front of a hearth, and a large desk scattered with ledgers and papers. To the side, in a wing off the room, was a four-poster bed draped in plum satin, and a large wardrobe. On either side of the bed were doors, which led, Duncan assumed, to a bathing area.

"You cannot stay long," she said, wiping her nose with a handkerchief. "I have a reputation to uphold, and my clerk is not here."

"I won't. No one saw me enter, in any case."

She nodded. "Thank you."

She looked so unhappy. "I am sorry, Lady Kerr."

"For what? You had nothing to do with these tears."

"But I am sorry for them, nonetheless. More important, though, I am sorry for this." He pulled the sword from his sheath and laid it on her desk.

She closed her eyes. "Who told you?"

"Your steward. I'm sorry for your loss, and I'm

deeply sorry for taking the sword without your permission and reminding you of it."

A fresh tear striped her cheek, but she gave him a wan smile. "If you were hoping to keep me from crying, I'm afraid you have said entirely the wrong thing."

"You'll find I have a knack for that. It seems to be my trademark."

Her shoulders hitched. "I miss Bran. I miss having someone to talk to, someone who would understand. Sometimes it's just so…"

She covered her face.

"I came here to apologize," Duncan said, feeling his own throat tighten, "and I've upset you. I'll go."

"No…no. Please. Stay. I feel as if I could just talk to someone for a bit—about anything other than the clan—it would help."

Duncan stepped closer. He was not an inexperienced seducer, and many late nights in bars, empty offices, and hotel rooms had taught him that in this moment, he could take her in his arms and kiss her and that she would likely kiss back. But he dared not attempt such a thing. He knew one false word, one false move, would instantly destroy the tiny bit of trust he'd built here with her.

"I would be happy to stay, Lady Kerr. I will do whatever you wish."

She took a step and reached for him. To his surprise, she kissed him hungrily.

With the little part of his mind not focused on the melon taste of her mouth and the dizzying scent of lilacs in her hair, he battled to control his hands. What *she* chose to embark on was one thing. He would not take the role of aggressor. In fact, he was so afraid of overstepping his bounds that when she broke away, he found himself cupping the back of his head with both hands.

"*Och*," he said, "that was wonderful."

But the look on her face was embarrassment. "Well, that explains why no one wants to talk to me. That was unthinkably rude. I do apologize, MacHarg."

Duncan twisted and turned, fingers still laced, trying to find a way—*any* way—to rescue the moment. "I—I—"

A noise in the hall made her straighten. "I'm sorry, but you must leave. I must also ask you not to mention our meeting. 'Twould make things uncomfortable for me."

"No, of course not." He was stumbling backward toward the hall, propelled by the sheer force of her will. At the door, he made himself stop and gather his thoughts. He did not want to leave, and he certainly didn't want to leave her regretting what had just happened.

"Lady Kerr, if you want me to stay the night, I would consider it an honor. And you can be absolutely assured that whatever happened in that bed would stay strictly between you and me."

He heard a giggle and turned.

While he'd been making his impassioned plea, the young maid who'd interrupted them in his room earlier in the evening had appeared in one of the doorways beside the bed, holding a large tin jug. She eyed Duncan with amused interest. The noise Abby had heard hadn't been in the hall; it had been in the bathing area.

"Your bath is drawn, milady."

Abby cleared her throat. "Thank you, Mr. MacHarg," she said quite formally, "for the honor of the offer, but I think you understand why I cannot accept it."

Duncan, you imbecile.

He reached for the knob. "I wasn't lying when I said it was my trademark. You can count on it to pop up at the most inopportune times."

Nora snickered, and Duncan's heart dropped sixteen stories. "No, no, no! That's not what I meant. I meant my—"

"I know what you meant," Abby said, smiling. "I wish you a good night."

Nine

DUNCAN RETREATED, HIS CHEEKS BURNING LIKE FIRE.
But no matter how embarrassed he was, the glow from
those seconds in her arms would outshine everything
for many, many hours to come. He could endure a
lifetime of Nora's snickers for a reward like that.

Happily whistling "Walking on Sunshine," he
picked up the candle he'd put down earlier and
walked all the way to the end of the hall before he
realized he didn't remember which room was his.
He turned and spotted something he hadn't on the
first pass. His wooden sword was leaning against one
of the doors—the door, he had to assume, that was
his. He gazed at the carefully burnished wood and
shook his head. Neither potent nor artful. A perfect
metaphor for him in the eighteenth century. On the
other hand, who had just been kissed by the most
enchanting woman between John O'Groats and
Lands End? Duncan MacHarg, that's who. Perhaps
if Duncan were very lucky, he could extend those
few seconds of happiness to an hour or even a particularly glorious eight in the time he had left here,

assuming, of course, there would be an end to his time here.

He opened his door and set the candle on his bedside table, where he discovered a decanter of what turned out to be very fine whiskey. With a freshly poured glass, he returned to the doorway. He could see the faint light emanating from the space under Abby's door and smiled. Was it candles or just her enchanting glow? He would have said angelic glow, but there was definitely a streak of something other than the temperament of angels to her. And that made him smile even more.

Abby's door opened and Nora emerged, jug in hand. Then Abby herself appeared, in a diaphanous slip, half-hidden by the door, to relay some instructions. Nora listened, curtsied, and headed for the stairs. Before closing the door, Abby looked down the hall. Her eyes, unsteady, met Duncan's, and his heart quickened. A footman making his rounds crested the stairs and looked surprised to see Duncan in the doorway. In explanation, Duncan pointed to the mists off the loch visible through the window at the end of the hall. "Quite a sky."

The footman nodded politely, turning in the opposite direction, and when Duncan looked for Abby again, the door was closed.

Duncan stared at that door for a good five minutes, debating. At last, he came to a decision. With a deep, uncertain breath, he swallowed the rest of the whiskey and placed the glass on the table just inside the room.

When he looked up, Rosston was tapping lightly on Abby's door. Duncan ducked back inside and watched, unseen. Abby's door opened and Rosston slipped inside.

For many moments, Duncan stared at the door, walloped to his core. Only when Grendel bounded up the stairs, wagging his tail madly, with Nab half a staircase behind, did he break his gaze.

Nab looked at his benefactor with curiosity.

"Is Lady Kerr in love with Rosston?" Duncan asked without preamble.

"I should hope so," Nab said. "They are betrothed. The wedding will be at Michaelmas."

Ten

ABBY CUT THROUGH THE GURGLING WATER LIKE A BIRD extending her wings, and the cool of the liquid balanced the warmth of the sun on her naked back. The loamy smell of the river filled her head, and she could feel the grit and disappointment of the day before slowly being washed away.

"I am in love with the sea," Serafina said, coming up for air, "but I must admit swimming in such placid waters, with the larks singing overhead and the early morning sun sparkling among the reeds, is quite lovely."

"It's called Candle Pool. It is one of the most magical places in the borderlands—or so Undine says." Abby turned on her back to float, putting her hands behind her head. Their clothes were heaped under the boxwood overhanging the bank, and a bountiful breakfast of boiled eggs, sausage, and buttered bannocks sat wrapped in a basket awaiting them after their swim.

"Do you believe in Undine's magic?" Serafina asked.

"Indeed I do," Abby said, snorting. *I shall be dealing with the effects of it for many days to come.* "If you are worried about her ability to help you, you mustn't.

She is very good at seeing the truth, sometimes even better than one wishes. She'll be able to guide you."

"'Tis not the truth I need," Serafina said sadly. "Far from it. I need someone to pretend to be my former fiancé so that I may collect cargo that, when sold, will repay the money he stole from me. I was hoping Undine might give me a spell that would help conceal the identity of whomever I hire."

Abby smiled and ran her arm over the surface of the water, sending ripples in all directions. "I have no doubt that will pique her interest. She is at least as fond of concealing secrets as she is of exposing the truth. Her magic, it seems, can be quite potent."

Serafina's face softened. "Did her magic have something to do with Mr. MacHarg?"

Abby started. "Why do you ask?"

"Well, my powers are nothing compared to hers, but it took nothing like magic to see there was something going on between the two of you at dinner."

Abby dove under the water to hide her reddening face. The memory of MacHarg's lips on hers had stirred her half the night. Even Rosston's quarrel-filled late-night visit had not erased the memory. She'd been sorely tempted to accept MacHarg's awkward but well-meaning invitation. She smiled to think of the intriguing sparkle in his sapphire eyes and those arresting calves. If only Nora hadn't been there....

But dallying with an outsider was a risk she couldn't afford. Rosston was pressing her to announce their agreement to marry. He'd already told the men closest to him the ceremony would be at Michaelmas, which had only made her feel even more coerced.

She dreaded the thought of marrying him, but a clan chief, especially a woman without the full support of her men, does not always get to marry whom she chooses. If she had to marry Rosston, she would, but if she could get the canal financed before the money was gone, she wouldn't have to depend on an alliance with him to save her clan.

She surfaced, flipping soaking strands of dark hair over her shoulder.

"I am inclined to take your silence as an affirmation of my suspicions," Serafina said, smiling.

"You are as much a fortune-teller as I, then," said a voice behind them.

Abby turned. Undine stood on the high bank, having apparently emerged from the rosebush-lined path the rise hid from view. Her face glistened with the perspiration that always comes with a summer carriage ride.

"You've returned!" Abby cried. "I trust things went well?"

"Well enough, I think." Undine threw down her bag and began unbuttoning her gown. "I spoke to my contact, who was eager to discuss his own troubles as well. He promised to do what he could to settle the army's agitation and send a private message."

"Oh, thank God."

"And I stopped at the castle before coming here. William is doing better."

"Thank you, Undine."

"But for now, I think I must examine your face. Something has changed." Undine's dress dropped at her feet and she skimmed off her chemise. With a trim dive, she entered the water, her limbs as lithe and powerful as a mermaid's tail.

In an instant, her head cleared the water directly in front of Abby. She examined Abby's face with blade-like sharpness. Abby knew protestation was futile.

"You kissed him!" Undine declared. "Great skies! You *kissed* him!"

"Keep your voice down." Abby fought the smile that appeared, uninvited, on her face.

Undine turned to Serafina. "What happened at dinner? What did I miss?"

"There was a palpable cloud of attraction hanging over the table," Serafina said, grinning. "'Twas hard to see the food, the air was so thick with it."

Abby sputtered. "That's…that's outrageous. 'A cloud of attraction'? Don't be ridiculous."

Serafina laughed. "I cannot account for the hours after dinner, however."

"The hours after dinner were spent bemoaning Sir Alan's refusal to negotiate a loan," Abby protested.

"Sir Alan will change his mind," Undine said with her usual certainty. "And that is all the 'bemoaning' you will admit to?"

Abby squawked. "For heaven's sake! I barely know the man."

"And yet…" Undine tilted Abby's chin with a finger. "And yet 'tis quite clear you kissed him."

"I…well…a *kiss*." Abby shrugged, the thump of blood in her ear.

Serafina squealed. "He is very handsome. And *big*!"

Undine chuckled. "If only we knew. I suspect he casts a noble shadow."

"Undine!"

Serafina clapped her hands. "Perhaps that's what changed Abby's mind," she said. "I believe until she escorted him to his bedchamber, she was quite against him joining us at dinner."

Undine smiled. "'Tis astonishing what the sight of a deftly prepared joint does for one's appetite."

"Ha. Ha." Abby sent a spray of water in their direction. "You two should be on the stage. Surely, some Covent Garden theatre is looking for entertainers. I shall have my fastest carriage prepared."

Undine added with a flash of sympathy, "'Tis a shame Abby is betrothed to another."

"Betrothed?!" Serafina said. "No! To whom? Can't your magic help her, Undine?"

"I've tried. I'm afraid my magic is powerless against Abby's brand of determination."

Abby sighed. "I do not wish to marry, believe me. But if I cannot fund the canal, the only way to hold the clan together will be through an alliance with the leader of another, wealthier clan."

Serafina gasped. "Rosston."

"Aye," Abby said. "But you do not need to gasp. He is a good enough man—though a wee bit bull-headed at times."

"A wee bit?" Undine did a backflip and disappeared under the water.

Serafina's face grew serious. "Oh, Abby, forgive me for offering unasked-for advice, but you mustna marry a man you don't love. I should have never said 'aye' to my fiancé. I had my reasons, 'tis true. But it turned out to be the biggest mistake of my life. I was very independent. I had an inheritance from my father. It wasn't large, but it was enough for me to live on and run his small shipping business. Then I met Edward and, well, I think I was overcome by his kindness to me and the breathtaking blue of his eyes. 'Twas like standing atop Ben Cleuch and staring down into the loch below."

Abby thought of Duncan's shining eyes. "Oh?"

"And then each day, he did a little more and a little more. 'Twas just to take some of the burden of running the business off my shoulders, he said. But soon enough he made me feel as if I was unnecessary, and soon enough after that, I *was* unnecessary. 'Twould never happen with a man who truly loved you, of course, but with anything short of that…" Serafina paused, then added with a note of concern, looking at the spot where Undine had disappeared, "How long can she stay under?"

"A long time." Abby smiled, but Serafina's story had left her vaguely unsettled. "They say her mother was a naiad."

Serafina's eyes widened. "You're joking?"

"No family is without its dark secrets, I suppose."

Undine surfaced with hardly an intake of air. Her wet, blond curls clung to her back like scales on a fish.

"The bottom is especially clear today," Undine said. "And there's a spectacular school of shad down there, all blue and shimmery."

"Ooh!" Abby swam toward the steep outcropping on the opposite bank. "I'm going to dive."

Undine swam in a slow circle around Serafina. "When we finish here, the two of us must adjourn someplace quiet for a talk about your cargo."

"Thank you. I don't know when the ship is expected. It could be anytime between now and the end of the month. I just hope to be prepared."

Then, in a louder voice for Abby's benefit, Undine said, "But tell me, Serafina, do we think this nobility of Mr. MacHarg's is ever going to be tested?"

Abby, who had been too busy weighing the bone-tingling excitement of MacHarg's kiss against the risks of succumbing to that excitement to be bothered by a bit of teasing, sniffed. "I have no doubt I'd find it unwavering," she said and dove into the water.

Eleven

DUNCAN MADE HIS WAY ALONG THE SUN-SWEPT path—if the lightly trod grasses could be called a path at all. The morning sky was a vibrant blue, but neither it nor the sun's rays had been able to penetrate the gray unhappiness that hung over him since finding Rosston outside of Abby's door. Nab had told him Undine would be returning that morning, and Duncan intended to flag down her carriage the instant she arrived, so that he might press her for the spell needed to reverse the magic that had brought him here. Nab had also told him that Rosston was "as rich as a sultan," which got Duncan wondering if Abby saw the marriage as a way to save her clan. She certainly didn't display a lover's affection for her fiancé in public.

Duncan made his way down the path Nab had recommended to reach the main road, rather than waiting inside. The day was fine, and in any case, Duncan was determined to put as much distance between him and the castle as possible. The last thing he wanted was to run into Rosston radiating self-satisfaction and bonhomie in the afterglow of a night in Abby's bed.

Duncan's first errand that morning had been to see Sir Alan, who, with the lure of a bit of salmon fishing, had been convinced to take a tour of the canal site and see the work done to date. Nab had said it was impressive, and Nab had been right. Sir Alan had left for Edinburgh far more open to the idea of a loan than he had been before the tour. In fact, he'd said he'd collect his overseer in Cumbria and return in a few days for another look. If Duncan could talk to Sir Alan uninterrupted, money man to money man, he was sure he could wrap up the deal. Abby would be thrilled, and Duncan couldn't wait to see her face when he broke the news. Rosston may have won her hand, but what might Abby think when she realized the only man who could give her what she really wanted—a way to save her clan without marrying—was Duncan?

The lush, green fields turned to rolling hills blanketed with heather, shrubs, and trees. As beautiful as it was, he was glad he'd convinced Nab to find him a pistol with real balls to shoot. One couldn't be too careful in the borderlands, he knew. The path took a winding turn up and around a steep rise. At the top, he froze.

He was perched on the bank of a river. On the opposite bank, in full view of heaven and earth, stood a very naked Abby, toes gripped around a jutting ledge and arms curved over her head. Her breasts, lush and full, shone pale against the golden brown of her shoulders, and the damp triangle of raven curls below her belly glistened in the dappled light. She executed a precise arc, her perfect bottom the apex of the oval, and slid into the water with hardly a splash.

Undine and Serafina treaded in the blue pool with her, each as naked as Abby herself.

Duncan jumped out of sight, blood buzzing.

The breathtaking image was not only seared into his brain, it was galloping at a feverish clip through some less genteel parts of his body as well. In all his years, he had never witnessed anything as ball-gripping as Abby Kerr's dive.

He hurried on, ducking to keep from being seen, then slowed and stopped, the sound of Abby's laughter too enchanting to leave behind.

Nothing, of course, would induce him to return to the rise. That would be ungentlemanly. But as far as he knew, there was nothing untoward about *listening* to a naked woman. Well, perhaps there was, given the thoughts tumbling through his imagination. But what was in a man's head was between a man and his conscience, no one else.

He walked a little farther, found a shady spot under a tree, and sat. Her nipples, small and rosy, had been stiff with the chill of the water. He wondered what it might be like to run his palm lightly over the tips or to take one between his teeth. Would she cry out or squirm—or arch like a satisfied cat?

The women were talking now—the lower notes of Abby's voice mixed with Serafina's higher soprano and Undine's clipped cadence. He couldn't hear what they were saying, but it didn't matter. They were talking like friends, in quick streams of banter and laughter.

Three naked women. Six creamy legs. Three glossy mounds.

He closed his eyes, imagining them in his bed as he watched, a tangle of warm limbs—Serafina, reticent but curious; Undine, aloof and practical; and Abby, lost in the pleasure. They would suckle and kiss and probe, their skin pink with their exertions, the scent of their joining like the lush, perfumed air of a tropical forest.

And he would come to the bed, weaving himself among them—

His eyes opened. *No, no, no. Interesting but not quite right.* He thought some more.

He would come to the bed, pulling Abby from the tangle, her cheeks flushed, and she would roll on top of him, tan and eager, as the other women faded into nothingness.

Aye, that was it. His eyes closed.

He would feel her perfect, round bottom straining against him, and he would cup it as she lowered herself over him, her flowery scent stirring a maelstrom of desire.

He was fully hard now, as hard as he'd ever been, the plaid folds tented comically over his cock. He reached under the fabric and grabbed it, his hand a poor but serviceable substitute for the heavenly tightness of Abby's quim.

She would move slowly, eyes shut, working to find her own pleasure at first. And then she would have it, and those violet eyes would flutter, and his heart would catch, afraid the world-ending pleasure of their joining would be over if he made the slightest noise.

Hungering for a taste of her, he would roll her bud

slowly, until his thumb was slick with her desire. Then he would suck the salty-sweet honey from it.

Oh God! His hand was moving so steadily, he was going to finish before he reached the part where he pleasured her. With effort, he slowed his movement and returned to his daydream.

She would ride him now, her arms extended over her head, as graceful as a dancer's. Her breasts would be so smooth, so warm.

His hand quickened. His balls burned with single-minded need.

Mewling thickly, she would writhe over him, scorching his already-burning loins, and he would stare in awe of this stunning, smart, wicked-tongued woman who had stolen his heart, knowing he was completely in her power—

A twig snapped and his eyes flew open.

He stared into the blue eyes of a living, breathing Fury, her chemise clinging to her damp breasts, her arrow pointed directly at his balls.

"You goddamned Peeping Tom," Abby said. "Take your hand off your cock, and stand up and take your punishment."

Twelve

DUNCAN JUMPED TO HIS FEET AND RAISED HIS HANDS. If the arrow didn't kill him, the shame of being caught ministering to what would undoubtedly be the last willing erection of his life would. On the whole, he thought he might prefer the arrow.

Abby scowled. "Tell me why I shouldn't put this through your heart."

Heart. Much better. "I'm so sorry. I don't know what I was thinking—"

"*Och*, no? Then you're a bigger fool than I thought. What exactly did ye see?"

"I...I..."

"Come, MacHarg. Don't add lying to your list of sins." She pulled the string tighter, and the bow made a terrifying groan.

"I saw you on the rock about to dive," he admitted.

"And?"

His erection, which had faltered in the crosshairs of the bow and arrow, was finding its second wind. The wet chemise was more than even the fear of death could vanquish. He shook his head. "I can't say."

"*Now* you've found your modesty? *Speak*, MacHarg. My fingers are starting to ache."

"You were naked," he said quickly, hoping to stave off the coup de grâce.

"*And?*"

He wished he could jam his bloody cock between his legs. But he didn't dare move. He closed his eyes. The shock of cold metal made him jerk back instantly, and he banged his head on the tree trunk. She had pressed the flat head of the arrow against the bottom of his chin.

"Closing your eyes is not a good idea in this kind of engagement," she said.

"Nor is getting too close," he said, summoning bravado. "I might make a grab for your arrow."

She snorted. "I canna recommend it. Your shaft-grabbing skills are estimable, I know, but the arrow-head would split your windpipe like an ax through an apple before your grip even tightened."

His throat felt very soft and exposed.

"What else did you see?"

He shook his head. She pressed the steel hard enough to pinch.

"Your nipples!" he cried. "The tan on your collar-bone! A scar on your back! Jesus, what do you want to hear?"

She glared. "What about Undine and Serafina?"

"*Who?* Oh, right." The fire in his cheeks rose. "Sorry. I barely noticed them."

Abby's squinted eye opened for an instant and just as quickly reverted to its former state.

She stared down the length of the arrow. With a

disdainful *hm*, she lowered the bow. He dropped his arms and exhaled. Then she took his pistol and slipped it under her quiver strap. "Where is your home, MacHarg?"

He could feel the accusation in her words—only a spy or a fool hides himself within earshot of the clan leader—but no one would question Duncan's loyalty to Scotland, not while he drew breath. "Edinburgh," he said, squaring his shoulders.

"You're a liar. You're a Scot. That I can hear in your voice. But you're something else too."

Subtle changes happen every year in a dialect—word choices, rhythm. A Scots accent three or four hundred years ago was different than a Scots accent of the twenty-first century. Duncan could hear the difference himself. But he also knew eighteen months in New York City would alter a man's accent more than five hundred years of natural changes. The last time his grand-da heard Duncan ask for a cup of "caw-fee," he'd been horrified.

"My mother's Dutch," Duncan said and immediately regretted it. Was Holland Scotland's ally or enemy now? He wished he knew his history a wee bit better. Three hundred years ago, alliances had changed practically every month.

"You dinna sound Dutch."

"Because I'm an Edinburger, I told you. We're on the same side."

She made a dubious noise. "There are plenty in Edinburgh who would line their pockets by selling Scotland to the crown."

This was history Duncan knew as well as he knew as his own name. Maybe better. Scotland was "sold" to England via the Act of Union in 1707, an agreement between the countries that deprived Scotland of independence and formed the country known as Great Britain. The year lived in infamy in the minds of Scotsmen. And the polarizing debate over whether or not the agreement should be entered into had begun in Scottish parliament in 1705. Duncan now knew in what time he'd landed, give or take a year.

"Aye, well, I'm not one of those damned traitors," he growled.

"Dinna let me find ye eavesdropping on me again, MacHarg."

"Send me back and you'll not have to worry. Or have you forgotten that it was you and that witch's magic that brought me here?"

Undine swept into the small clearing, appraising the scene with cool detachment. Unlike Abby, she'd taken the time to dry off and dress. "Did I hear my name?"

Duncan blanched. He knew little of witches but he doubted they enjoyed being referred to in the tone he'd just used.

"I only want to go home," he said as explanation.

"And I should like to send him there," Abby added angrily. "Undine, 'tis time to clean up your mess. I've had enough."

"*My* mess?" Undine's eyes flashed. She walked in a circle, regarding him and Abby as a teacher might regard misbehaving pupils. "Mr. MacHarg, did ye, in the moments preceding your unfortunate transfer, express some sort of deeply felt sentiment—perhaps involving your sword?"

Abby snorted a second time, and Duncan tugged

at the wooden hilt angrily. "I most certainly did not."
Then it hit him. Undine saw the change on his face
and eyed him sharply.

"I might have said something about loving a
battle," he admitted.

Undine silenced Abby's guffaw with a look and said
to Duncan, "I had the pleasure of standing beside Lady
Kerr in the moments preceding your transfer, so my
understanding in this instance is more precise. Abby,
ye professed a keen interest in acquiring something
you considered very important. Do ye happen to recall
what that was?"

She gazed at her friend, tight-lipped. "Peace in
the borderlands."

"Oh, come now," Undine said. "Your objective
was a bit more personal than that. Ye wanted a man."

Duncan raised his brows, and Abby said fiercely,
"What I wanted was a strong arm. And may I add,
I'm still waiting."

Undine crossed her arms. "So last night's kiss was
something neither of ye desired?"

Abby cut her gaze to Duncan, her eyes filled with
fiery accusation.

"Don't look at me," he said. "I certainly didn't say
anything. Blame the witch. She knows things."

"Mr. MacHarg, if ye call me that again, I shall
slip a tonic in your wine that will cause your stones
to shrivel to the size of field peas. While this would
undoubtedly curb certain impolite habits, I dinna
think it is something ye would much desire." She
straightened her skirts and carried on. "I am not
denying my role in this. I merely point out that ye two

share in the responsibility. But let us not wallow in regret and blame. There is but one way for MacHarg to free himself of Abby and Abby of MacHarg."

"How?" they demanded in unison.

"'Tis a simple matter—in theory at least. The objective of the spell must be fulfilled. In short, MacHarg must serve Abby as a strong arm. And Abby must truly be served."

"But he is hardly more than a simpleton!" Abby cried.

"I have been friends with you a long time, Abby. Ye have never given yourself to a man who could be described as a simpleton, even by the most ungenerous observer."

Abby nearly choked. "I did not *give myself* to him!"

Undine cut her gaze to Duncan, and his grin died instantly. "And ye, my friend, need to make yourself useful. Ye are a pathetic reprobate who has apparently spent his life getting by on bluster and what one might loosely describe as charm. Learn to serve the chieftess properly. She will teach ye what ye need to know."

"I will *not*," Abby said hotly.

"Ye will if ye wish to be rid of him. Once he has fulfilled your objective, the spell will be broken. Do ye understand?"

Duncan gave the tree root a sullen kick. "Aye."

Undine turned to Abby.

Abby's look could have burned holes in steel. Duncan was grateful that, for once, he wasn't on the receiving end of it.

Undine pulled a twist of orange paper from her pocket.

"Not another of those," Abby said.

"This one is for his return." She handed it to

Duncan. "When you have fulfilled your purpose, the herbs will warm. That is how you'll know when you can return. Abby, you must do everything you can to help him."

Abby said, "Tell me again why I shouldna just abandon him to the buzzards on the slopes of Craignaw?"

"Well, my dear, I am hardly an expert on your religion, but I should say your priests might view this with an unfavorable eye. More to the point, however, Craignaw is a two-day ride, and ye canna afford the time."

Duncan, who had grown tired of the swipes at his character, slipped the paper in his sporran. "Or you might consider the cost to your fortunes of having Sir Alan arrive only to find his stalwart fishing guide left for dead in the Grampian Mountains."

"Sir Alan is as unlikely to return to Castle Kerr as I am to cross the Alps on an elephant."

"Wrong, Lady Kerr. He will be here Thursday."

Abby swung around. "What?!"

"That was the reason I came to find you, ye ken? I ran into him this morning on his morning walk. Naturally, our talk turned to fishing—"

"Naturally."

"—and while he couldn't stay longer now—he has business in Cumbria—I did convince him to join me for a fishing party at my hunting lodge on the River Esk upon his return."

"You have a hunting lodge on the Esk?" Abby said, incredulous.

"Well, no. But I assumed you did."

Abby made an aggrieved huff, but Duncan knew

he'd nailed his first assignment. Hell, it hadn't even been an assignment. He was like the applicant who'd arrived for his interview at Duncan's firm with fifteen pizzas and revised business strategies for the firm's three biggest clients. Everyone rolled their eyes, but a year later the guy was Duncan's second in command.

He waited for Abby to acknowledge his triumph. She chewed the inside of her mouth as if considering the digestibility of a particularly tough piece of mutton. "Well done," she said at last.

Undine let out a laugh, then caught herself.

"What?" he demanded.

"That's what she says to Grendel."

Thirteen

"YOU'LL NEED TO WALK FASTER IF YOU INTEND TO keep up."

Abby strode through the thick yellow gorse as if it were fog. Duncan's bare knees seemed to be scraped by thorns at every turn. "I am doing the best I can. I'm not as familiar with the path as you are."

She turned sharply enough to rattle the arrows in her quiver. "Your best may be good enough in Edinburgh, where buckled slippers and fancy assembly-room swords stand in for experience, but it willna be good enough here, ye ken? Here, ye need rough boots and rougher arms—or you may find yourself dead."

Duncan had watched Abby slip her shapely calves into a pair of well-worn knee boots after Undine had left the clearing. The rowels were tarnished, the shafts were dusty, and when she pulled them on, clods of dried mud tumbled from the soles to the ground. Nonetheless, the dead self-assurance with which she tugged on the thick leather, on top of the unanswered erection, had just about driven him mad with desire.

"Dead from thorns?" he inquired. "I believe even I might survive that. Ow! Dammit!"

She shook her head and resumed walking. "I suppose I shall have to provide you with a pair of boots too."

"I'm sorry I no longer have access to my own wardrobe." In which, he declined to add, she would find no boots.

"Ye seemed to have no trouble availing yourself of the wardrobe in your room last night. You may as well have taken Bran's boots too."

She turned away abruptly, and Duncan could tell she regretted mentioning her brother.

"I considered it," he said softly, "but I could tell I'd upset you last night. It's enough to mourn a dead brother. You shouldna have to watch an interloper stumble about in his boots."

She said nothing, just continued walking.

"I didna have a brother, nor a sister," he went on. "It was just me, my mum, and my grand-da. I canna imagine what it would have been like to lose a sibling."

She veered right to avoid a fallen tree. He gave up trying to have a conversation and concentrated on just keeping his footing. The path, such as it was, had grown steeper and the rocks strewn across it larger.

"What about your da?"

Duncan looked up. It was the first thing she'd said in many minutes.

"I didn't have one."

She gave him a sidelong glance and climbed onto a wide boulder.

"Well, I mean, I did. But he left when I was a bairn.

He skipped out on a list of debts as long as my arm too. He was not a popular man in our neighborhood. I don't think there were many who missed him."

She hesitated before hopping to the ground. "You?"

Duncan shrugged. "Maybe. A bit. But it was more the idea than the man."

She pointed to a break in the ridge ahead of them. Duncan returned his attention to his feet.

"Bran was the most popular man in the clan," she said.

Duncan cringed. The death of a popular heir must have made her transition to chief even harder. "We never know how the losses we've survived will end up guiding us. My da's debts were the reason I went into finance. I used to think—" He stopped. How much did he want her to know of his life in the twenty-first century?

"What?"

He shook his head. "Not important. But he's the reason."

Her eyes, which had momentarily brightened, returned to their guarded blue-purple. Duncan felt as if a bank of clouds had passed between him and the sun.

As they reached the top of the hill and began down the other side, he considered the situation from her perspective. Though he'd told her he was from Edinburgh, she had to know he wasn't from the Edinburgh of 1705 or 1706. If he were, he'd have simply said "Later, lass" after the end of the skirmish and hopped the first coach back to the city. And yet, she didn't seem fazed by him either. Annoyed, yes. Deeply annoyed. But she didn't display either the repulsion or fascination he'd expect from a person who'd just met someone from another century. His best guess was that she thought Undine's magic had transported him either from a place in the present time that was hard to get back to, say the East Indies, or from the borderlands in a year near but not identical to her own. It was probably better for both of them if she continued to believe that.

The slope began to angle downward again, and they followed the curve of the hill.

"Here we are," she said. "Langholm Abbey. Well, all that remains."

Before them, at the foot of the hill, perched on the near side of a dramatic bend in the river, stood an ancient stone-built chapel, whose narrow, vaulted window slits pointed unashamedly at its roofless top. No doors hung in the wide doorway, and the blankets of pink flowers that grew in heaps along the hillside. He tried to think if he remembered such a site near his grand-da's home, but neither the river bend nor the ruins seemed familiar.

"A bit down on her luck, is she not?"

"I dinna ken why people assume things like abbeys and ships and carriages are shes."

"Because they possess a certain transcendent beauty?" he offered.

"Because they can be commanded by men, more like." She trotted toward the structure.

"I canna argue with you on ships," he said, following quickly. "But abbeys? They are not exactly commandable."

"Perhaps you should make an inquiry of Edward VIII, who commanded this one be turned to rubble."

"Why are we here?" he said when they'd reached the front.

"This is your hunting lodge, my friend. Certainly, the only thing on a river I can muster for you. The fortune of the Kerrs is tied entirely to Castle Kerr. We do not maintain a host of lodges throughout the borderlands."

"I think Sir Alan may notice the lack of ceiling in his room. Perhaps, though, if we arrived after dark? And provided him a canopied bedstand?"

She gave him a dry look. "My men will be able to manage a new floor and reed roof by the end of the week. 'Twill be up to you, however, to convince our guest of the charms of rusticity."

As if eighteenth-century Scotland weren't rustic enough. "And what do you want me to tell him of the canal?"

"MacHarg, I appreciate the opportunity you have arranged with Sir Alan. Truly I do. However, I dinna plan to rely on the persuasive abilities of a man I hardly know, who stumbled into the borderlands with neither wits nor weapon at hand, and who may be as happy to see my clan fail as succeed. I will sit down with him myself, after you have delighted him with the pleasures of fishing the Esk."

He was the opening act, not the headliner. An irrational disappointment overcame him. He was good at negotiation—very good. Bridges, roads, canals—they all needed financing. He could do so much more for her if she would just let him.

The sound of thumping hooves rose beyond the ridge. Abby stiffened. "Hide yourself."

"I'm your strong arm, remember?"

"A strong arm obeys. Hide."

The edge in her voice told him more than the words. He opened his mouth to argue—

"*MacHarg*."

With a sigh, he relented. He topped the chapel steps in two strides and tucked himself behind the largest intact wall.

"Abby, if it's dangerous, shouldn't you—"

"I didn't say it was dangerous. *Be quiet*."

He could see her but not the path. If the person on the horse threatened her, Duncan didn't care what his "orders" were. His sword might be wooden, but it still packed a wallop. And his fists worked just fine.

The hoofbeats grew louder and louder till they stopped just outside the chapel. Abby maintained her hold on the bow but didn't raise it. Duncan tightened his grip on his hilt.

"'Tis an odd place to find the head of Clan Kerr," a male voice said.

"I find a long walk clears the head."

"I'll never understand the risks ye take," said the voice, considerably softer and, as such, at once familiar. "I should hate for something to happen to ye."

Duncan gritted his teeth. He'd been exiled to the ruins not to keep from unnerving a potential threat. He'd been exiled to the ruins to keep from unnerving Rosston. Bloody hell.

"Nothing will happen to me in these hills, Rossie. I've been walking them since I was a lass. Besides, I have my bow."

"And a pistol, I see. Good for you. Would you like a companion for the rest of your journey?"

Oh, great.

"I would," she said. "But I can tell from your packs you're on your way somewhere. I have no wish to detain you. I know you have business you need to address."

"I wish it were otherwise. My men are here, at your command. I shall return tonight or tomorrow morn at the latest. Perhaps then we can sit down as we have talked about and decide what is best for us… and for the clans."

Duncan waited for the ax to fall. *She* would decide, not him. *Tell him, Abby, tell him.*

"Aye," she said, weariness in her voice. "Perhaps it is time at that. By tomorrow, I shall know my mind."

Duncan nearly lost his footing. Abby gave him a tiny sideways glare.

"Tomorrow, then," Rosston said.

"Wait," she said and moved out of Duncan's sight. Closer to Rosston. *Next to him, no doubt.* Duncan tortured himself for an instant, imagining the scene.

"Will ye give me a proper good-bye?" Rosston asked.

His voice had grown husky. Duncan wished to be any other place on earth.

A muffled "*mm*" from Rosston that would be branded in Duncan's memory forever, then, from Abby: "Godspeed."

"Go back to the castle," Rosston said. "For me." A plea, not a command. Perhaps he was trainable, after all.

The horse trotted off. Abby appeared again in Duncan's view, offering him a nodded "all clear."

He bounded out, stung by the double lashes of incompetence and jealousy.

"I don't want to hide again," he said, not caring if he sounded like a sullen child. "I want my pistol back."

Abby readjusted the strap of her quiver, tactfully choosing not to point out the situation that just passed was not one that had required a weapon. "Is that really what ye want?"

"*Yes*. I don't want to be hearing hooves and wondering whether I'll be massacred in the next minute. I need to be able to protect myself." *And you* hung in the air, though he knew her amusement would kill him if he said it.

To her credit, Abby didn't even smile. "I know what it is to long for the power to protect oneself, MacHarg. And I will give ye your pistol. But if you are to be my strong arm, you will need more than that." She handed him her bow, and reached for the buckle on her belt.

"I don't think I would make much of an archer," he said uncomfortably.

"Good. Since I don't have a year to teach you the skills." She tossed the belt and quiver on the ground and retrieved the bow. "Did I not hear ye say ye knew how to wield a sword?"

"Yes." Duncan had aced two years of fencing classes and considered himself if not quite an expert then certainly the most skilled of his reenactor friends. He had a beautiful lunge.

"Show me."

He squirmed a bit. It was one thing to back his instructor into a corner in the heat of an encounter. Doing his moves with a wooden sword while Abby appraised him felt very different. With some trepidation, he withdrew his blade and angled himself into the *en garde* position.

"This would be better if I had someone to fight," he said.

"Perhaps we can arrange that. But for now, please, just begin."

Soles flat and body carefully balanced between his feet, Duncan advanced and retreated. The wooden sword was, of course, weighted differently from the fencing saber he used in class, but the principles were the same: Loose but controlled grip, point angled slightly downward. Non-sword hand in the air for increased agility. Eyes focused in the middle distance but alert to tiny movements at the edge of one's vision that betray an opponent's next move.

He advanced, retreated, and jump lunged, followed quickly by an advance, retreat, and flèche. With each movement, the familiar sense of mastery increased. He thought of her father refusing to teach her to use a sword and wondered if he might be the man to open this world to her.

He extended his attack over a wider area, thrusting his sword left and right with a graceful ease. With a beautiful crossover, he turned his line of attack ninety degrees and prepared for a beautiful—

Thump!

The sword flew from his hand and hit the chapel steps.

Like an eighteenth-century Babe Ruth, Abby recovered from her swing and ran a finger along the length of her bow, searching for damage. "I think," she said flatly, "you may need a bit of polishing."

"You wouldna have done that had my blade been steel."

"No. You're right. In that case, I would have put

an arrow through your heart when you turned your back. You need to learn to fight. 'Tis nothing to be ashamed of, MacHarg. No man is born with the knowledge of it. How do you think the lads learn?"

He had a sudden vision of himself standing a head above a class of preteen boys. After coming into possession of a small upright piano courtesy of a moving neighbor, Duncan's mother had forced him to take lessons at age fifteen. He remembered the abject shame of performing in a recital alongside schoolkids who had learned much faster and played much better than he did. He had no wish to repeat the experience.

He shook his head. "No."

"I know just the teacher."

The nightmare re-formed in his head, and instead of being outgunned by a bunch of kids, Duncan stood before Rosston as he explained the proper grip in the sort of tone one reserves for half-wits and five-year-olds.

"*No*. I have all the skills I need."

She stared, eyes blazing. "Then our effort is at an end, MacHarg. I need a *strong* arm, not a dead one. My steward will provide you with your wages, and I will tell Sir Alan a family matter in the north required your attention."

The prospect of being cast off in the borderlands brought him back to the reality of his situation abruptly. He couldn't survive, and, worse, he would lose his one chance to show Abby how much he could help her.

She was already climbing the rise, and Duncan had to jog to catch up. "Wait. I've changed my mind."

"I canna teach a man who dinna wish to learn."

"I want to learn! I swear I want to learn!"

She turned. "You will do as I say when I say it, aye? And you will learn to do it *before* I say it?"

"Yes."

"Then get down on your knees, and make your oath to me. I am your chieftess and master."

He fell to his knees, bowed as much by her words as by the force of her will. "What do I say?"

"The words must come from you."

Duncan had never made an oath. He'd grown up in the Presbyterian Church, which seemed to require nothing more than regular attendance and some careful listening. He'd never been a scout or a fraternity brother, or even a husband. He'd never promised anyone anything. How had he gotten to be thirty years old without making a promise to something beyond himself?

He looked at her, so purposeful, so sure. What had she given up to take on this role? He thought of his own self-interested life, working hard, playing hard, pursuing any and every amusement he found interesting.

"I—I dinna have the words, Lady Kerr. I'm no speechmaker."

"For this, I am Kerr," she said gently but in a manner that brooked no deviation. "I stand for every Kerr who lived and breathed and every one who will live and breathe. The sentiment must be yours."

He closed his eyes and searched, but found no feelings to put into words. Then he thought of Abby, alone and determined, and something stirred in his chest.

"I swear to your purpose, Kerr, whatever it may be.

I swear to protect you in the best way I know and to get to know better ways—the best ways. I swear to put your needs before mine in all things. I swear myself to you for as long as I am with you."

"Longer," she said quietly. "Forever."

"Forever."

"If you're a spy, MacHarg, I shall cut out your tongue and stuff it down your throat."

"I'm not."

He opened his eyes, and a smile had come to rest on her mouth.

"Well done—er, I mean to say you did well."

"Do I get knighted?"

She chuckled, a beautiful contralto trill that reminded him of something out of one of the Bach concertos his grand-da used to play. "I do not knight people, MacHarg. I am nae a queen."

"No, a queen does not require quite so much sacrifice."

The chuckle turned into a full-throated laugh.

"Surely I get *something* for such a pledge." He knew what he'd have chosen had the world been a different place.

She pulled an arrow from her quiver and laid the tip on his shoulder as if it were a scepter. "You are a clansman of the Kerrs. You are of us and with us, as if you'd been born to a Kerr mother. Your blood is ours and your body is ours, just as our body is yours."

She made no acknowledgment of the other meaning one might derive from the last of her words, though he knew she had realized it because her voice had changed just the tiniest bit when she said it.

"Are ye ready, MacHarg?"

"Yes."

"Then stand. 'Tis time for your first lesson." She started down the rise again, toward the chapel.

He climbed to his feet and brushed off his plaid, looking around. "What can I learn here?"

"*Och*, there's always something to be learned from a church, don't ye think?"

"I...guess."

She walked to the back of the chapel and stopped. After a look around, she removed a ring of keys from her pocket.

"I thought you said the chapel was abandoned?"

"I said it was in ruins, MacHarg, not abandoned. Scots do not abandon things that are useful. Dinna make me doubt you're a Scot."

She stripped off her quiver strap and laid it and her bow against the chapel wall before dropping to her knees. Closing her eyes, she stretched her arm behind some brambles that hugged the corner of the structure. He heard the scrape of metal and against metal. Then she withdrew her hand, returned the key ring to her pocket, and reached back. She withdrew one sword and then another from the place she'd unlocked.

"Hidden storage. Impressive."

She tucked a loose strand of hair behind her ear. "One never knows when a few weapons will be needed."

He picked up the sturdier of the two swords. It was considerably plainer than Bran's sword. Nonetheless, it was serviceable and striking, with a well-honed edge to the blade. He didn't dare swing it. Not after what had happened the last time. "Are they both for me?"

She chuckled. "Neither is for you. Unless you earn one, of course."

"And how might I do that?"

She picked up the remaining sword and swung it hard enough to have sliced his belly wide open had he not leaped for his life.

"What the *fuck*?"

"That's a verra impolite word, MacHarg. Have you forgotten there's a woman present?" She swung the blade again, backing him so far across the uneven surface, he lost his footing.

He fell with a *thump* but managed to hold on to his weapon, and rolled instantly to his feet. He blocked her next swing, barely, and the clang exploded next to his ear. Jesus, was she going to kill him?

He retreated two steps and met another powerful swing. The metal rang in his hand. Adrenaline pumping, he shoved her back and jumped to the right, where her moves were unlikely to be as strong.

For a woman of five two, maybe five three, she had incredible reach.

"I have the longer sword," she said, answering his thoughts. "Typical man, you chose the heavier one. Now you are paying the price."

Her sword met his, once, twice. His heart pounded like it never had in class. Of course, in class the blades hadn't been sharpened.

Sweat poured from him as he fought. Her feet barely moved, yet she always seemed to be a quarter turn from him. "You told me you didn't know sword fighting."

"No, I told you my father wouldn't teach me. Eyes

up. I'm not going to kick you. I'm going to slice off an appendage."

The fog of shock had lifted at least, and his reflexes were there. He caught her blade high and then low.

"Your left side is exposed," she said. "You might as well drape a target on it."

He pulled his shoulder back. Her shoulders, straight and true, formed a perfect perpendicular line with her spine and, he noted somewhere in his head, pressed her breasts firmly against the neckline of her gown.

"*Pay attention*," she said. "I'm backing you over the same rock that tripped you earlier."

He held his ground and beat her back a step. His arm felt about as responsive as a bag of sand at this point, despite the electricity charging through it. He took the hilt in both hands for added strength.

"Oh, good," she said. "You've shortened your reach even more."

She was a deft fighter, replacing height and strength with surprise and finesse. He had held off her challenge with brute force, but he could see the exceptional art in her movement, the deliberate beat of her tanned arms, the stretch and return of her swanlike neck—

His foot turned underneath him and he faltered.

She threw down her sword, exasperated.

"What?" he said, grateful to catch his breath.

"You pay no attention! How many different ways are you going to give me to kill you?"

"Don't quit. Please."

Her eyes flashed. "Take off your clothes."

"What?"

"If you want to learn, get undressed. My father

said the only way to get a man to pay attention is to put his balls between him and a sword. 'Tis the way every boy in our clan was taught." She picked up the sword and stuck the point in the ground, waiting for Duncan's decision.

Duncan was of several minds about taking his clothes off. However, he was of one very singular mind about putting his balls in harm's way.

"I dinna think so."

"MacHarg, have you forgotten the oath ye just took? Take off your clothes."

Duncan considered his options. He wanted to learn enough of sword fighting to avoid more embarrassment. That was primary. His also knew his only hope of escaping this wretched place was to fulfill his mission as a strong arm, at least according to the witch, and everyone here seemed to bow to her wisdom. There was the oath, of course, though he had a vague sense that being required to satisfy a thirst for voyeurism was beyond the limits of even a clan chief's powers. But most of all, he had a primitive and surprisingly titillating urge to find out what would happen if he let Abby have her way.

He met her eyes. "I have no problem taking my clothes off if that's what you want."

"Then stop talking and do it."

Despite his bravado, he found himself fumbling with the brooch as he unpinned his plaid. "Tell me," he said as the fabric's heavy corners dropped to his waist, "might the opponent sharpen her skills by shedding clothes as well?"

Abby rolled her eyes.

"I'll take that as a no." Grabbing the belt's hasp in one hand, he slipped the supple leather from the silver. The wool fell to his feet. The sark, gleaming white in the morning sun, flapped around his knees.

A light burned in her eyes, but prurient curiosity was only part of it, he thought. Another part was a teacher's assessment of raw materials. Still another was the self-satisfaction the powerful take in looking at their possessions. Taken as a whole, Duncan found himself reluctant to take the last and final step. He shifted.

"Are ye under the impression I havena seen a man's balls before?" she said. "I grew up with a brother, father, sixteen male cousins, and two hundred and thirty fellow clansmen. Be assured your balls will not merit the slightest notice."

He steeled himself, slipped the linen over his head, and dropped it on the ground.

Between weights, running, and fencing, he had a rock hard stomach and shoulders that were naturally broad and intentionally sculptured. The reaction of various bed partners had taught him he cut a handsome figure. Yet, as he felt Abby's eyes slowly measure the worth of what she saw, inch by inch, it took all the self-control he had not to jerk his hands into impromptu fig leaves.

"Your arms are workable," she said without any particular enthusiasm, then, more to herself: "The hocks are strong. Perhaps the balance can be improved." She chewed her lip, lost in observation. "'Tis not as bad as I imagined," she announced, bringing her sword to the ready position. "You have the frame of a fighter. Let us try to match that with the trained instincts of one."

Duncan barely had time to grab his sword before the first swing seared his side. "You cut me!" He glanced long enough to see blood, and she cut him again, this time his shoulder.

"That's two points for me. Three, and our game is over."

He could tell from her tone it was not an outcome he should hope for.

Both wounds stung, though he dared not look, concentrating his attention instead on fighting off her parries.

Her swings were harder now, and infinitely more precise. The hair on his neck stood on end with the proximity of mortal danger. He wondered for an instant if she actually intended to kill him, and the thought roused a fierce survival instinct in his belly. As he fought, the world became a blur around the circle that held her face, her hands, and her sword.

In the small space of his forebrain not dedicated to keeping himself alive, he began to muster a tiny offense. For seven or eight entire seconds, he pushed her back from her impenetrable foothold, till an unexpected lunge, whose windy wake tickled the hairs on his scrotum, destroyed any sense of advantage he'd felt.

But he had seen the surprise on her face. And his swings grew more assertive because of it.

That's right, Lady Kerr. I am not who you think. And you do not own me.

He saw the bored certainty of victory on her face, and it inflamed him. He became an arm and a head, and she, a beating neck, a vulnerable heart, an unprotected flank. They might have been fighting an hour or a minute. The notion of time had no place in the battle being waged.

The mortal danger of the fight was doing something to his thinking. He felt alive, centered, brutish. He'd never wanted to vanquish someone, a longing far different than merely winning, but he wanted to vanquish Abby. He wanted to see her on her knees, abject, at the mercy of his wishes. It was a revolting desire, entangled with a primal longing that flushed his cheeks and tightened his testicles, but no amount of modern scrupulousness could flush it from his head. He was half-hard and didn't care if she saw it.

Recognizing the fiery determination on his face, her blade work sharpened.

Her eyes flashed, defiant, as she beat him back.

You willna reign over me. You will know my tyranny.

His breath came ragged now, but his arm was steel. At the third massive blow, the sword flew from her hand.

He thrust himself between her and the weapon and watched the full knowledge of her defeat come over her. It was glorious.

He could kill her now. A tiny animal part of him wanted to, he recognized in horror. She saw the part too, and pulled a knife from her belt.

"I willna kill you," he said, voice ragged.

The *but* hung in the air between them, as heavy and sharp as an ax.

"Nor will I take you against your will," he said. "But I will have ye. Fair and square."

He threw down his sword.

In her eyes a dark, rapturous fire blazed.

"Say ye'll have me."

"I am warrior, MacHarg, not a blushing milkmaid. I know what I risked."

In two strides he was against her, crushing her body to his and tasting her mouth. It was savory and hard, like an exotic, muscular fish. He pulled up her skirts and ran his hands across her bare thighs. Her buttocks were high and round. He squeezed them, savoring the heavy silken weight.

She hissed. "I'm bruised there."

"And you'll be more."

He extracted himself from her biting kisses and pressed her onto her knees. He could see her silent curses for him in her half-lidded eyes. His legs shook and he nearly came, so hungry was he to see her take in the thick, symbolic bit of her defeat.

But claiming the spoils of war required a deeper trespass.

He dropped to his knees as well and pushed her firmly onto the grass. Then he climbed on her, his cock as hard as his blade and just as intent on penetration.

"I have a knife," she said, reminding him of the steel in her hand. "And I will use it, I warn you."

"'Twill be the only way to stop me."

With a low growl, he plunged into her, driven by a need so ancient it seemed to come from outside him.

In the far reaches of his consciousness, he took remote note she was not a virgin, a fact which only fueled his need. In a much more immediate part of his mind, he was aware of her blade, pointed at his carotid, its length sparking in the sunlight. If she were to kill him now, in this moment, it would be deserved. However, he would die unrepentant.

She was slick, ready, responding roughly to his movement.

He licked the salt of her skin and brought the taste back to her mouth. Focused only on his need, he hammered her, deep as he could go, charging toward a brutal release. His balls, hot and tight, readied their contents.

The chill of a steel point against his rib brought him to a sudden stop.

"Too soon," she commanded. "And too fast."

He dared not move. The thrust he longed for would put the blade into his heart.

She shifted her hips and clasped her long legs around his back, tucking her heels under his thighs. With the blade still burning into his flesh, she drew her quim along the length of his cock until the head caught the entrance of the moist hollow between her legs. She mewled, digging her nails into his back, and repeated the movement, again and again, until he thought he'd die.

"If you're going to kill me, do it now. I cannot even breathe."

The corner of her mouth rose. She withdrew the blade and brought the arm around his back.

He dropped into her, relieved. The release, once so close, had receded, and he pressed himself furiously into the work of recalling it.

Flush with color, her lips parted like a thirsty bud, and he kissed her, grasping her silky chestnut hair. She had nearly bested him in the fight, and now her throaty sounds and immodest hips threatened to get the better of him here as well.

A fly bit his buttock and he jerked. But it wasn't a

fly. She had positioned the tip of her blade a scant inch or two above his flesh.

He swore but slowed. It was the only way to keep the point from piercing him. Without a word, she had driven him into a rhythm of her own liking. Sweat beaded on his skin as he strained to minimize the force of his thrusts. He was a draft animal, bridled to plow, the prick of her blade like the farmer's whip.

At last she arched. The knife slipped from her flailing fingers. He drove himself hard into the beautiful, sharp-witted, imperious woman who had mastered him.

With a cry, she arched again, and, obeying an unspoken command that she was not to be encumbered with a child, he wrenched himself free of her body and released his seed with a roar.

But seed or no, she was his, just as he was hers, and he would serve her like this whenever she commanded.

Inebriated with lust and joy, he collapsed beside her. The lilac scent of her hair and satin smoothness of her skin and the deeply satisfying sigh of pleasure she made thrilled him. He shoved Rosston firmly out of his head. With a strong arm, Abby need not marry Rosston. Hell, she needn't marry anyone. With Duncan beside her—well, perhaps a step or two behind—Abby could handle anything.

❧

As the wild flush of pleasure receded from her body, the cold lens of reality returned. She closed her eyes and buried her face in Duncan's dangerous, warm chest to try to fend it off, but each moment that passed made the fending off harder.

He wrapped his hand around her hair and kissed her. "Tell me, chieftess, what is lesson two?"

Oh, ye foolish, foolish girl. What have ye done?

Fourteen

HAVING REACHED THE POINT WHERE THE SUN'S WARMTH crosses the line between pleasing and discomfort, Duncan, stirred from his muzzy, relaxed sleep, lifted his arm from where it curled around Abby and rolled to his back to cool off, eyes still closed.

The light dimmed, and Duncan said a grateful thanks to whatever cloud had chosen this moment to sail by.

"Mr. MacHarg?"

Duncan bolted upright and found himself under both the shadow and somewhat nervous observation of Jock Kerr, the steward, on his horse. "We don't usually find our guests quite so far from the protection of the castle," he added with a sigh of relief. "I was afraid perhaps you'd been attacked and left for dead."

Duncan reached for his sword, only to discover it, along with Abby, had disappeared. He glanced around.

"Did you lose something?"

"No. Yes, I suppose." Duncan found his sark, which he pulled over his head. "Though I was no' robbed." Except perhaps of a bit of self-esteem. How had Abby gotten away without him noticing?

"But you're bleeding."

Duncan had almost forgotten the wounds, numbed as he'd been by anesthesia of pleasure. "Oh, that. I…fell in the middle of the stream. Cut myself on the rocks."

"Indeed?" Jock eyed Duncan with something short of credulity. "The cook can dress them for you. The shoulder one, especially, looks quite deep. What brought you to the river here?"

"Er…bathing."

"Nearly two miles from the castle? Good Saint Margaret, you *are* a modest man."

His plaid, sporran, and wooden sword were where Duncan had dropped them, but the steel sword was nowhere to be seen. Duncan hopped to his feet and reached for the pile of wool. "I was actually here for the fish—that is, I was looking for a good place to find them," he said, catching Jock's quick scan for poles or lines. "The bathing and nap came after." He doubted there were many in Abby's time save the feebleminded who spent the shank of the day sleeping, and the man's mildly piteous look didn't surprise him.

"And?" Jock said.

"And what? Oh, the fish. Yes. Quite good. Sir Alan will be pleased."

Jock's brows rose. "Sir Alan is returning?"

Had he said too much? "Aye. I believe I heard Thursday."

"That *is* good news. Odd that Lady Kerr didn't mention it."

"Oh," Duncan said, at once attentive. "Did you see her?" He busied himself in the rearrangement of his plaid.

"Aye. We were supposed to be reviewing the old accounts for the canal, ye ken, though she arrived near an hour late, which is not like her. She had a good reason, though."

"Did she?"

"Said she fell in a pile of horse shite."

Duncan winced. He opened his sporran and gazed at the twist of orange paper. The herbs smelled like flowers, which made him think of Abby's hair. Oh God, how wonderful it had been to possess her.

Jock took a long look at the chapel's crumbling walls. "Lady Kerr said we are to rebuild the roof here— which is how I happened to be out this way. Do you suppose the roof is connected to Sir Alan's visit?"

This time Duncan knew better than to reply.

"I hate to see her take on any new expense," Jock added, "though I guess even we can afford a bit of reed and wire," he said, dismounting.

"Is it that bad?"

The steward shrugged, the same sort of noncommittal and eminently Scottish gesture Duncan's grand-da used to make when Duncan asked when his father might be expected to visit. *Grand-da!* The thought hit him like a stomach punch. Would he worry when Duncan didn't arrive? Or would he remember the other times Duncan had canceled a flight home when a critical project at work forced him to rearrange his priorities? Duncan's cheeks burned with shame at the thoughtlessness.

Jock wandered behind the chapel and squinted at the leaning steeple. "Of course, if it comes to that, I suppose I can pay for the damned roof myself."

"Is it cash flow or other troubles?" Duncan asked,

wrapping the belt around the voluminous fabric. He wished he had access to an ATM. He had enough money in his checking account alone to rebuild the chapel several times over.

"Are you a bookkeeper?" Jock pulled out a small notebook and began entering figures.

"Of a sort. I used to help men with money to invest." Several thousand of them, actually.

"The canal was Lady Kerr's father's dream. It was supposed to ensure the dominance of the Kerrs in the Lowlands. I thought—and still think—the idea is a good one. If you control an improved means to move goods from the west side of Scotland to the east and back again..." He paused. "Well, that's how it was supposed to be, though it dinna come to pass. Lord Kerr was in tight with Rosston's father, Colm Kerr, at that point—one of Lord Kerr's cousins was Colm's wife—but that was before the families split. They were investing in the canal as a partnership then. But the investments Colm recommended were not exactly sterling choices—at least that is my reading of the account books."

"Your reading? Did ye not manage the books then?"

"For most things, I did. For the canal, Colm's steward was the manager."

Duncan heard the note of hurt in the man's voice. "And look where it got them."

Jock sighed. "I know. Yet 'tis no salve to know another man ruined them. Will ye be staying through the visit of Sir Alan?"

"I will be here for a while, it seems. Lady Kerr has asked me to stay. To help where I can." Not exactly the truth, but as long as they were resorting to salves for one's self-esteem, he decided he would let Jock believe it.

"Has she?" Jock clearly saw little role for a shirker with few skills, but added with true gladness and only a hint of wonder, "I am glad to hear it."

"I am to be her strong arm," Duncan said, "an adviser in all matters of enforcement and conflict."

"Her strong arm?" The change in Jock's eyes from pity to respect gave Duncan a rush of satisfaction.

"Oh, aye." That, at least, wasn't a lie. Duncan intended to serve Abby in every way she desired and perhaps a few more. Rosston could take his attempt to pressure her into sharing control of the clan and peddle it somewhere else—at least while Duncan was here.

Jock opened his mouth to say something, then seemed to change his mind. "If ye are Lady Kerr's strong arm, I daresay ye get yourself back to the castle. She has just called a council of war."

Fifteen

ABBY CAST HER GAZE DOWN THE LENGTH OF THE LONG table slowly filling with the senior clansman of each of the seventeen families that made up Clan Kerr as well as the eleven that made up Rosston's sept. Twenty-eight identical chairs, twenty-eight caped footmen prepared to serve at an instant's notice. Abby met each set of eyes carefully, just as she'd watched her father do. The tapestries that lined the walls, fading with time, reminded the men of the glory of Clan Kerr, and the swords, glinting in lethal circles on the walls and ceiling, reminded them how that glory had been won.

There was one set of eyes Abby was careful to avoid, though the owner of those eyes was sitting not at the table, but just inside the door at the far end of the room. Undine's divining was the last thing Abby needed on this disastrous day. She knew well enough she'd been a fool to give in to the heady rush of a sword fight. She'd grown up around warriors. She was as familiar as anyone with the aphrodisiacal powers of battle. She didn't need Undine's prying gaze searching for the truth, like some uninvited surgeon digging through her head and heart.

But aphrodisiacs are curious things. Just like the infernal powder that had summoned MacHarg, they couldn't always be counted on to behave in the way one desired.

What she'd wanted this morning was to strut off from the fight, heady with victory, having forced MacHarg to his knees. What she got instead was his knees between her legs.

Flashes of heat exploded on her cheek and another in her belly.

She'd had men before—a lad who'd called her his wild Scottish rose, a prince in Paris, even a sympathetic English officer once—more out of curiosity than desire. She'd had her curiosity satisfied and even occasionally her body. But nothing had felt like those heated iron arms on her today or smelled like the scent of sea air that seemed to permeate MacHarg's skin. And nothing, nothing had ever been like the driving hunger with which they seized those moments.

He was a risk in every sense of the word—too smart to be the addle-brained interloper she'd first thought he was and not quite smart enough to be an enemy spy, he begot more questions than he answered.

Of course, look where your instincts got you this morning.

She had almost welcomed the unhappy news delivered by Nab, who had pelted across the hilly path to intercept her on her way back to the castle. It had focused her mind where it belonged—on her clan, not on the distractions of sword fights and summer swains.

The last clansman bowed and took his seat.

She rubbed a thumb against the inside of her palm, wishing for the reassuring, worn beech of her bow. With her weapon, she was the equal of the men in the room. Without it, she was forced into the position of their superior, a role in which she was far less comfortable.

She spread her hands and placed them on the table.

"A report has reached me," she said, "of English soldiers amassing at the border."

The men quieted instantly. Many looked surprised.

Cathal Kerr asked, "Was this the report ye received last night?"

"No."

Murgo Kerr leaned forward. "Do ye intend to act?"

The eternal conflict between men of war and a woman of a more tempered mind. The question was more than a question. It was the first volley in a familiar blood sport where the clansmen were one team and she another. But this time, she would prevail.

"No, Murgo. I dinna. I intend to do absolutely nothing."

❧

Duncan shoved himself past the guards outside the Great Hall door, hardly troubling himself to wrestle his arms from their grasp, though even he had to admit the trouble would have been quick in coming had not a clansman at Abby's table jumped to his feet at the same instant and shouted, "Have you lost your mind, woman?"

Stunned into stillness, the guards stared, mouths agape, and Duncan, instantly ready to launch the offending clansman into a different zip code, made it over the threshold before a cool touch on his knee brought him to a full stop.

"This is her battle," whispered Undine, who was sitting by the door.

He didn't know how she'd stopped him. He'd felt only the lightest touch.

"I'm her strong arm," he said.

"Not yet, MacHarg. Not yet."

Abby's shoulders trembled as she regarded the offending clansman, and the hard, blue ice in her eyes made it clear the tremble's origin was fury not embarrassment.

"Sit *down*, Murgo," she commanded.

Take care, Abby, Duncan thought, his heart pained to see her tested like this. *Anger can be as debilitating to a leader as timidity.*

Her fiery stare didn't waver, and Duncan swore she grew half a foot.

One by one, the other clansmen, whether out of disagreement with Murgo's tactic or pure discomfort, dropped their gazes. Not Murgo, though. Duncan would have jumped out of his skin had Abby pointed such a glare at him. After what seemed like an hour, Murgo wilted and dropped into his chair.

Duncan tried to catch Abby's attention, to signal his readiness to assist, but her eyes flicked past him as if he were a hat rack. *Dammit.* He might not be the world's finest swordsman, but he'd managed to best her at least, and, in any case, he could take on any man in this room with his fists.

He took a step closer, and the warning in her eyes stopped him.

"I dinna intend to act," she said, addressing the clans-men, "because I am in possession of information that ye are not. Robby, open the side doors." She nodded to one of the footmen, who did as she commanded.

In streamed several dozen boys, none more than ten, clearly awed at being invited to enter the esteemed gathering.

The looks on the older clansmen's faces, however, ranged from confusion to shock.

One of the smallest boys, who looked about four, ran to a nearby man and clutched his legs. "Da!"

Abby said, "I have gathered your youngest sons and grandsons here to witness our council—twenty-eight in all, one boy from each family."

Some boys climbed onto the laps of their relatives, others stood alongside.

"Welcome, lads," Abby said warmly. "Let this serve as your first introduction to the workings of the clan."

Abby, however, was the only adult remotely close to smiling. Duncan felt the back of his neck tingle.

"We were talking about the English army," she said in the same tone a much-loved teacher would use. "The clan has received a report—well, I did, to be clear—that the army is doing a little sword rattling over the border to scare us. However, I have a source who is very close to the English army and, like I, values peace in the borderlands. He knows some things that no one else knows."

"A spy!" whispered one obviously thrilled boy, who was immediately shushed by his father.

"That's correct, Charlie, a spy. This spy has put

his life on the line many times to help our clan. His information is sterling. He is paid nothing for his risk. You must never pay a spy. A spy who works for gold can be bought by the highest bidder."

Charlie nodded, wide-eyed.

"This spy assured me the sword rattling is a mute-show meant to prod our clan into an attack. The army is under strict orders from old Queen Anne not to stir up trouble during the negotiations to unite our countries. I believe the spy, so Clan Kerr will not be mounting an attack—nor will any other clan whose chief I can convince. And yet, someone in this room, someone who is not a clan chief, took it upon himself to decide what this clan should do. Men?"

The men at the table looked at each other, uncertain what response she was asking for. It turned out, however, the men in Abby's directive were not the men at the table, but the footmen at the perimeter of the room, who each drew a short sword from a sheath on the wall and pointed it directly at the back of the man seated before him.

The men leaped to their feet, tossing boys to the ground, but none had arms to respond.

Abby said, "I should like every man here who is sworn to my leadership to raise his hand now. Lads, you too. No one is too young to make this vow."

The boys, deciding perhaps this was part of the ceremony, lifted their hands at once. The men's hands rose more hesitantly, but each did rise. Undine flicked Duncan's leg with a fingernail, and he lifted his hand, belatedly remembering he, too, was a part of this now.

"One of you, unfortunately, is a liar," Abby said.

"One of you, upon hearing the news of the English army's sword rattling, decided to take matters into your own hands this morning. You gathered your sons. You went to the border intending to stir up trouble. And you turned back when realized you weren't prepared for what you saw. I do not blame your sons. What, after all, is a loving child to do when his father commands him? But you…you are spineless and false. Do ye have the courage to admit your treachery?"

The men stared blankly, but the boys were enthralled, save one—a lad of six or seven, who looked up, terrified, into the shifting eyes of his bearded father.

The man squeezed his son's shoulders, and the boy steeled himself. Duncan didn't know what was going to happen next, but he knew he wanted Abby to look to him for help. He made his way to where she stood. The fire in her eyes nearly set him ablaze, but he took his place beside her.

"Repeat your oath before God." Her voice filled the hall. "All of you—if you dare."

The men repeated words in Gaelic Duncan didn't recognize. His grand-da had tried to teach him the language, but Duncan had had no interest and knew only the everyday phrases he'd heard his mother and grand-da say. He recognized only two words in the oath: *blood* and *death*.

The bearded man did not move or speak. But at a pause in the oath, when the other men pressed their hands to their hearts, the man closed his eyes for a long instant. Then he opened them and launched himself through the open door, leaving his son behind.

The footmen, stock-still, waited for Abby's command. Duncan grabbed her arm. "Choose me," he said.

She shook her arm free. "Sit down."

"No." He hardened himself against her gaze.

"Damn you," she said, and Duncan knew she'd given in. "Go! Make him repent."

Sixteen

DUNCAN FLEW OUT OF THE CASTLE'S MAIN DOOR WITH the sword he'd torn from the wall into the blinding sun of the castle bailey. The steel felt awkward in his hand, improperly weighted and already slippery with sweat. The man was bloody fast and had the advantage of knowing the twists and turns of the grounds far better than Duncan.

Make him repent.

The man pulled a long dagger from his plaid and ducked through a door in the bailey wall, slamming it behind him. As Duncan expected, the door was locked when he reached it, and no amount of pulling would open it. Duncan spotted an open archway fifty feet farther on, began to run toward it then paused. If the locked doorway and archway led to another bailey, the man would run not toward the archway, where he'd expect Duncan to emerge, but away from it. Duncan did an about-face and retraced his steps at a run. As he'd hoped, there was a second door, this one unlocked, thirty feet in the opposite direction. He ran through the darkened room to the door at the other side and emerged within fifty feet of his bearded prey, who was heading directly toward the open castle gate.

They flew by the castle guards, who were uncertain which man to stop, and sprinted for a quarter mile, but Duncan slowly and inexorably closed the distance. Angling into a scattering of outbuildings, the man turned too quickly and fell. Duncan caught the man's plaid before he could climb to his feet. A single swing of Duncan's sword flung the knife from the man's hands. The man scrabbled to escape, but Duncan put his full weight on the man's leg.

"God, ye'll break it," the man cried. "Ye'll break it!"

But Duncan sensed the fine line between pain and destruction, and held his pressure. The man was boxed up against a low stone wall with nowhere to move. For being the height of the day on a working estate, the world around them seemed eerily quiet. The only movement Duncan registered was a hawk sunning himself in a gentle glide across the southern sky.

Make him repent.

"What's your name?" Duncan demanded.

"Harry," the man said through gritted teeth.

"Why did you betray her?" Duncan's anger was growing—irrationally, he thought, given Harry's de facto surrender.

The man spat, and Duncan pressed his weight harder, no longer shrinking from what would be a nauseating crack.

"No lass…can run a clan," Harry said in gasps, sweat running from his forehead, "especially one whelped as she. She's a wild thing, she is…a whore, plain and simple—and without the sting of her father's strong hand, she'll bring doom upon the Kerrs."

"Are ye under the impression a clan chief should be well loved?"

"Fouck ye. She wouldn't make a pimple on the arse of her brother."

Duncan brought the sword point to Harry's heart.

The man called in Gaelic for Jesus.

Duncan's blade glinted in the sun. He knew what was expected. The pulse in Harry's neck beat furiously. One swift thrust and Harry would bleed out in seconds. Duncan had done this in reenactments dozens of times, but confronted with a real foe and a blade polished to lethal perfection, he was unable to move.

His impotence bathed him in a white-hot fury, and he tried to redirect his anger at the man on the ground, but it was as if he were trying to punch his way out of a fog.

The man closed his eyes and braced himself. "Tell my son I love him."

"Get out!" Duncan roared. "Get out! Run till your feet are bloody. Run till you collapse! Run till you reach Inverness, then board a ship and run some more. If you ever, ever show your face in Scotland again, I will kill you, and your son, and everyone related to you."

He pushed himself from Harry's leg, sick with self-loathing. Harry's shocked eyes followed him, waiting for the trick, but when Duncan thrust his sword into the soft ground, Harry grabbed his knife, scrabbled to his feet, and ran for his life.

Duncan dropped to his knees. He'd failed her. He'd

failed the clan. He'd let a traitor run free. And he'd forever parted a father from his son. He jerked the sword free from the ground and threw it as far as his failed strength would allow. Then he put his hands on the sun-warmed earth and vomited.

Seventeen

THE SUN HAD FALLEN IN THE WESTERN SKY, SPILLING ITS blood-red light over the hills. Duncan had spent the rest of the day walking numbly. He eyed the low, wide castle at the top of the rise with reluctance, but the fact remained, he had nowhere else to go. He was lost in this time, with only one person who had the remotest interest in him, and her interest went only as far as teaching him what he needed to know so she could be rid of him.

Unlike Harry, Duncan knew he owed Abby the truth of his failure, and he intended to give her just that and accept the fate that would come with it. With a sigh, he began up the hill that led from the town's small square to the castle gate.

"Mr. MacHarg, is everything all right?"

Duncan jumped. Serafina stood in the shadows beside a tall stone cross, the sign of the market town. He realized how he must look, with bloody shirt, hands and knees covered in filth, and plaid streaked with vomit.

"I slipped. It's nothing."

She peered at him thoughtfully but held her tongue. Then she whistled, and Grendel, who had been sniffing the perimeter of a distant shop, came bounding toward her, carrying a huge stick. Spotting Duncan, he turned abruptly and ran directly at him, thick tail thumping.

She smiled. "I wanted a walk, and he looked like he wanted to play."

"*Och*, I'd say so."

Duncan bent to bury his hands in the dog's warm fur and was rewarded with several licks to the neck and ear. Feeling unworthy of the dog's enthusiastic affection, Duncan took the stick and tossed it across the square. Grendel raced away.

"Has Undine been able to help ye?" he asked.

"We've conferred, but she's reluctant to lend a hand at present. I am to wait a bit, she says, until the sands of the universe have shifted and her magic returns to its former potency. She says her spells of late have disappointed."

Duncan felt another stab of self-pity. The sky's crimson stain was resolving into a thin rose band across the horizon. In a quarter hour, a million pinpricks of light would labor to take the sun's place and fail miserably—just like Duncan.

"Is there a chance I could help?" He took the stick from Grendel and threw it again. "I don't know what help you need, and it's nae my business, but I am able-bodied, at least, though I seem to lack most of the skills that make a man valuable here."

Serafina's mouth rose in a gentle smile. "Is that what Lady Kerr told you? Ye mustn't pay her too much mind—at least not today. She's carrying the weight of Ben Nevis on her shoulders."

Serafina had turned her gaze toward the eastern tower of the castle, the structure's only round tower, whose crenellated roof bit the sky and whose narrow windows rose, each higher than the last, till they reached what appeared to be the tower's only inhabited floor, a horizontal line of flickering lights. Duncan recognized it as the tower with the winding staircase he'd explored the day before.

"I suppose you're right," he said.

"I am right. And I thank you, Mr. MacHarg, for your offer. I dinna think ye can help, but the story is no secret, at least between us, so listen and tell me what ye think." She gathered her wrap more tightly around her shoulders. "The story begins two years ago. I met a man and fell in love—"

"The start of many a good story," Duncan said. Grendel had returned again, but Duncan held up his hand to tell him the game was over for now.

Serafina gave him a rueful smile. "Less good than foolish, I assure ye. He was an Englishman. Perhaps I should have known better. I behaved incautiously, thinking the promises he'd made gave me leave to be." Duncan dropped his gaze, and Serafina said, "Still interesting, no? Just not very happy."

"I'm sorry."

Grendel dropped to the ground with a sorrowful sigh and looked at his pack mates with disappointment.

"Poor thing," Serafina said, and Duncan sensed a change was coming in the story. "My da died not long after—my ma had died when I was young—and

I came into possession of a small inheritance. I should have left Edward then and there, but he was so comforting, and I was so sad…"

"I, too, lost my da. I can understand your sorrow."

"Edward said he knew how to take a little gold and make it into a lot of gold. We would marry in style, he said, and live on the Royal Mile. Under those circumstances, I agreed." She knelt to rub Grendel's ears. "My father had owned a merchant ship, Mr. MacHarg. I knew it was possible for poor men to become rich overnight. But Edward was not a good investor. He tried importing silk from Shanghai, then sugar from the West Indies. Nothing worked out for him. My little heap of gold became a long list of debts. But I loved him, foolish girl that I am, and we'd created a life together. Then I found him in our bed with another woman. That was the end for me, finally. I spent the last month we were together imagining the ways I might kill him—poison, a ball to the forehead, a knife to the belly."

"I am most certainly not the man ye need then."

She laughed. "No, Mr. MacHarg, I am not looking for a murdering brigand. Foolish I may be, but wicked I am not. I want only what is mine."

"And that is?"

"One shipload of cargo remains. It is to arrive in Edinburgh in a few weeks, a bit earlier than Edward expects it. If I can claim the cargo, I know men who will pay top dollar. I will be able to erase the debts and clear my name. But I need someone to pretend to be Edward."

"I should think any man—or a big enough bribe—could help you with that."

"Ye would be right except in this case. The supernumerary on the ship is Edward's cousin. They were the dearest of friends as children, though they haven't seen each other in nearly thirty years. The transaction was conducted by post, and I'm certain Edward's cousin would do nothing to hurt Edward's interest."

"You could claim Edward was ill and sent you in his place. You are his wife, after all."

"That would work very well if I *were* his wife, Mr. MacHarg, but the wedding he promised never took place. The investments were in Edward's name, and the debts are in mine."

Duncan thought there ought to be a special place in hell for men who bankrupted others. "I would be most happy to serve as your husband."

She gave him an uneven grin. "A more tempting offer I am unlikely to receive. But I must decline. You see Edward's father was verra short, and his mother even shorter. I need a man who is no more than nine or ten inches above five feet, with golden hair; a wide, square jaw; eyes the color of honey—and as full of his own importance as the King of France. I daresay ye would not do, even if ye were as blond as Cupid and just about as tall."

Duncan chuckled. "No, I suppose I miss on all counts. Could ye not advertise for such a man? Must ye wait for Undine?"

"There is verra little chance this effort will succeed, MacHarg. Not without a great deal of luck and all the magic I can muster. I have heard Undine can help those she chooses."

"Except of late. You see, I was summoned by her magic."

Serafina's jaw dropped. "For Lady Kerr?"

"Ye see? Even ye can't help but wonder why."

"You misinterpret my surprise, Mr. MacHarg. 'Tis not for your unsuitability. 'Tis because I applaud Lady Kerr's unashamed pursuit of her desires."

A wave of heat crashed over his cheeks, and he found himself at a loss for words. "I—I—You must understand Lady Kerr sought a strong arm, nothing more."

"Aye, but perhaps Undine's magic was responding to something more, something Lady Kerr didn't even realize she needed."

He thought of waking up abandoned outside the chapel and of his humiliation with Harry. "Aye, well, she still doesn't know she needs it—and for very good reason."

"'Tis only my opinion, but what I think Lady Kerr needs is a pair of sympathetic ears not an arm or a fist. She's in a very hard position with the clan, and I imagine getting those would please her more than anything."

Duncan gazed at the tower, thinking of his own experience leading men. His "clan" worked in a cushy office in Manhattan, but leading them was challenging enough—the competitiveness, the politics, the backstabbing. Abby had to deal with all that, as a woman barely more than twenty, in a world where the stabbing was done with a real sword.

He looked down at his hands, the ropy knuckles, skin caked with dirt. No doubt he'd serve Abby better with his ears than his fists. But he'd never get the chance, not now, not after failing her so miserably.

He was awakened from his reverie by a short growl. Grendel had evidently decided the time for sympathetic listening was over. He had laid his stick at Duncan's feet and prompted him with a comically fierce curled lip and a wriggle of his hind quarters.

Serafina laid her hand on Duncan's arm. "I am a very poor judge of men, but this much I ken: ye may lack the skills to be Lady Kerr's strong arm, but any man who's loved by a dog as much as ye are has all he needs to be her friend."

With a resigned sigh, Duncan bent to pick up the stick. "Come, dog. I think it's time we return you to your mistress."

Eighteen

NAB CAUGHT UP WITH DUNCAN AS HE AND GRENDEL climbed the castle's long, curved stairway.

"Did ye kill him?" the boy said, running to keep up.

"I owe our chieftess the honor of the first report," Duncan said grimly.

"Was it hard?"

"Harder than anything I've ever done." He stopped, and Nab nearly ran into him. "Listen, I must give you some money for your help. Tell Jock I have authorized you to collect my pay. It's only a day's worth, but I hope it will cover what I owe."

Nab eyes clouded. "Are you leaving?"

"I...I am unsure in what circumstances I will find myself after I talk to our chieftess." He began to climb again.

"What about Rosston? And Lady Kerr?"

Yes, what about them?

"Lady Kerr kens what is best for the clan," Duncan said. "Whatever she does, ye can be sure it's the right thing."

"Then you dinna want my report on Rosston?"

Duncan paused. Two clansmen from Rosston's sept walked through the hall below, talking. Duncan caught Nab's eye and the boy quieted. One of the clansmen looked at Duncan and nodded. Duncan signaled to Nab to follow him upstairs.

"I suppose if I've already paid for the report, I might as well have it." Duncan looked both ways, then slouched against the wall.

"The whole thing or just the interesting bits?"

"The whole thing."

"Rosston was at Langholm Abbey today."

Duncan froze. *Please, God, let Nab not have seen what happened after the sword lesson.* But the boy's face showed nothing more than an earnest desire to please. Duncan cleared his throat. "And?"

"And he practically begged Lady Kerr for a kiss." Nab made a face like he was sucking lemons.

"Did she give it? No, I dinna want to know. And you shouldna be telling me, either."

"When I am a clansman," Nab said, "I shan't bow and scrape like that. Perhaps it's different since Lady Kerr is chief here, but when I find the girl I'm going to marry, I will expect her to do my bidding."

"Is that so? Well, then I daresay you should prepare yourself to be a very lonely man."

Nab looked at him, thunderstruck. "Do you do what a girl tells you? Other than Lady Kerr, of course?"

Duncan thought dreamily of the knife poised over his back and her throaty, "Too fast…too soon." "I might," he said. "If the reward was right." He lifted his shoulders in an unregretful shrug. "I think ye'll find with a woman you love that the reward is often right."

Grendel's ears went up, and he bounded down the hall.

Abby turned the corner, faltering when she saw Duncan. Grendel circled her, tail wagging.

Duncan stood straighter as she made her way toward him. Nab bowed. Abby met Duncan's eyes, and for a foolish instant his heart rose, imagining she intended to invite him in. Then he realized she awaited his bow as well.

With a flush of embarrassment, he bent his head.

"I've been expecting you, MacHarg."

"There's more," Nab said to Duncan.

"Later," Duncan replied. "I am here to give you my report," he added to Abby.

"Please come in then. And leave the door ajar."

Nineteen

DUNCAN FOLLOWED ABBY TO HER DESK. SHE SUNK into the chair and Grendel settled immediately at her feet. The skin under her eyes was stretched thin, and she rubbed her temple with her palm. She made no indication Duncan should sit.

He was at once aware a third person shared the room with them.

"Mr. MacHarg, your absence this afternoon was the cause of some concern."

The witch. He turned to find her leaning against Abby's bookcase, her pale, feline eyes considering him. If Abby had been concerned about his well-being, she was certainly doing a thorough job hiding it.

"I—I—found myself diverted by another matter."

"Indeed. Well, we are glad to see you returned to us."

Abby reached for a ledger and opened it. "I hope you dinna mind if I review my accounts while you talk. Jock will be arriving soon, and I need to give him proper instructions."

"Do you ever allow yourself a distraction from your work, milady?"

Their eyes met, and Duncan flushed. He hadn't intended to make reference to their morning's activity, and she struggled to hide the whirlwind of emotion on her face.

Duncan had given up thinking any moment he'd shared with Abby would be unknown to the witch, who appeared to have the ability to peel back his skull and read his most private thoughts. Nonetheless, as he wished to tell Abby that their time together had meant a lot to him, he stepped closer to the desk to at least make what he said harder to overhear.

"There can be no sin in the occasional pursuit of joy, milady, especially when your pursuit also brings joy to others."

The brilliant blue in Abby's eyes turned transparent, and for an instant Duncan thought he could read every emotion they held. Then she returned her gaze to the account book, and he was once again on unsteady ground.

"May I have your report?" She reached for the ink pot and uncorked it.

Duncan's mouth dried. The quill was duly swabbed and began to scratch across the page. If he *had* killed Harry, would she have heard the details of the final bloody thrust while totaling her expenditures?

"I didna kill him," Duncan said.

The scratching slowed but didn't stop.

"He's still alive."

"I heard what you said, MacHarg."

Duncan wished he could see her face, read his fate in those striking eyes, but she didn't look up. "He ran for his life. He willna trouble you again, I think.

But I—I—I couldna do it." The muscles in Duncan's throat felt as tight as violin strings, and he'd wanted to add that he'd had every intention of obeying her command, had willed himself to do it, but nothing in his twenty-first-century life had prepared him for taking the life of a man who was not, at that instant, intent on taking his.

Abby laid down the quill and stretched her slender fingers, giving her hands the look of tiny pink starfish. Yet, these were hands that could kill a man, that had certainly wounded him—and pleasured him too. The relationship she had with life and death here was so different from his relationship with it in his own time.

"Harry was the man who told me my mother died," she said, gazing beyond the narrow window. "I'd been catching frogs at Candle Pool—the same place ye came upon today. I was but seven. My mother had been thrown from her horse. Killed instantly. Later my father said English soldiers had been chasing her. But 'tis just as likely that was a story he made up. My father threw himself over her body. Wouldn't let anyone near. Wailing, crying, people running around—a fine stramash. But that was my father, ye ken. Harry found me at the pool. He told me God had called my mother to his side, which sounded frightening and beautiful to me. He said I wouldna see her again except in my dreams, and that that would be enough. He sat with me, catching frogs the rest of the day. When it was too dark to see, he took me to his house for a chicken pie and a mug of beer. He wouldna bring me back to that madhouse, ye see." She closed the account book and looked at him. "But no man can challenge my authority and live, MacHarg. Not here. Not now."

"I'm sorry. I—I—couldna do it." Duncan hung his head.

"Do not expect me to thank ye for it. Your failure diminishes my authority. Every failure to obey an order diminishes my authority. You bear that."

Blood thumped in Duncan's ears. Grendel made a sympathetic whine but stayed at Abby's side.

"Go," she said to Duncan. "I'm done with ye."

Twenty

WHEN THE DOOR LATCH CAUGHT, ABBY LAID HER HEAD in her hands, fighting back the sting of tears. *Harry, my dear Harry*.

Undine *tsked*. "That was shameful, Abby."

The rebuke was too much. "Shameful, was it?" she cried. "I lead a clan! I dinna have the luxury to forgive."

"Have you forgotten what it is to be a novice? To have the commitment without the ability? Did your brother cast you off when you failed in your reconnaissance and were taken by that English soldier?"

"I was twelve!"

"You grew up with the clans, Abby. He did not. This is a life he didna choose."

Abby walked to the fire to warm her shaking hands. Why did everything about Duncan MacHarg affect her in twice the proportion it should?

"Where did he come from, Undine?" It was a question she should have asked the moment she saw him, but she'd been afraid to hear the truth. "Why is he so different?"

"I canna tell you."

"Why?" she said, her irritation with Undine unexpectedly full-blooded. "Because ye deem me unworthy of your insight?"

"No," Undine said curtly. "Because I dinna know. My magic is not the sort of thing I can control with certainty. If it were, you and I would be walking the gardens of our new home, Versailles, and stuffing ourselves with brandy and cakes. As of late, it has failed me in ways in which it has worked perfectly before. I wonder, perhaps, if the more I use it to agitate in matters of the world, like this bloody war, the more tenuous my hold over it becomes..." She shook her shoulders as if shaking off the grasp of an unpleasant suitor. "However, if you're that curious about where he is from, 'tis no hard matter to find out. Ask him."

Undine was right. It *was* easy enough, and yet she hadn't done it. Why?

"Perhaps it isn't where he is from that concerns you," Undine said, hearing Abby's thoughts as always, "but rather that he will be returning there."

Abby blushed to the roots of her hair. "Don't be ridiculous."

Though English by birth and disposition, Undine produced a flawless Scottish "*Och.*"

"I am concerned about both," Abby said pointedly. "I am responsible for the canal and the farms and the safety of people. I cannot afford to have the consequences of a miscast spell ready to wreak havoc here like an unexploded mortar."

"You have convinced me, but I don't think I'm the one who needs convincing."

Abby ignored the jibe. "You canna know how matters of life and death change one's responsibilities."

"Can't I?" Undine's eyes flashed.

Undine had no more love for the clans than she did for the English army. Her wisdom was doled out equally to both sides, which was why she was allowed to walk freely between the two. In her words, her auguries were "neither facts nor lies." They were illustrations of what might be—carefully fashioned reflections of the seeker's pride or weakness or, more rarely, strength and, as such, carried tremendous power to affect the hearer. Men paid dearly for Undine's counsel. And she never broke their trust. No English officer would hear of a clan chief's craven fears, and no clan chief would hear of an English officer's vainglorious ambition—which made Undine's recent entrance into the dark business of working to undermine Colonel Bridgewater fraught with risk.

"The secrets men tell me stay secret," Undine had once told Abby. "But the secrets they withhold are fair game—and the ones they withhold are far worse."

It wasn't that Undine loved the Scots. Abby had not fooled herself into believing that. Undine had made her dislike of the clansmen's hunger for vengeance clear. It was that Undine had decided after a harrowing spate of attacks by both sides in the last few years that she would join the rebels who worked to foil those who sought war, no matter what flag they carried.

Abby, too, harbored a deep desire for peace, and, therefore, supported Undine in her endeavors and occasionally benefited from her intelligence work. It was Undine who had brought the news of the troops amassing at the border and of Harry's betrayal. But if the English army—and Colonel Bridgewater in particular—were to discover their favorite fortune-teller was working against them, her head, and the heads of her rebel friends, would decorate the tallest spikes the army could find along the border.

Because of this, Undine's "Can't I?" was a fair question, and Abby regretted having strayed into a battle she would not win and had had no right to start.

"I apologize, Undine. 'Twas a thoughtless thing for me to say."

"Especially as you seem to be quite content to benefit from my risk taking."

"I said I was sorry."

"As did MacHarg. Am I more deserving of your apology than he? The only quality that costs a king is compassion. And a king who spends not a shilling on it is nae more than an empty crown."

Overwhelmed, Abby shook her head. "I am nae a king, Undine."

"You are a queen. More is expected." Undine put her hand on Abby's shoulder. "We cannot be perfect. But we can always be better."

Abby laid her hand on top of Undine's and, though she'd never had a sister, was reminded for an instant of what it had been to have the love of a mother. "How did you get to be so wise?"

Undine laughed. "If ye believe as I do we only learn from mistakes, then the wiser the woman, the more foolish choices you will find in her past."

"If that's true, I am certainly on the road to being the wisest woman in creation."

Undine must have heard more in Abby's answer than Abby intended, for she said, "If you are thinking of taking him to your bed, I beg you to move cautiously."

"What an idea!" Abby examined the toe of her boot. "What would possess you to even say such a thing?"

"I have been around enough young lovers to know where a kiss leads, and you have too."

Abby had almost forgotten about that kiss, so lost was she in the memory of this morning's joining. The gentle warmth of his lips—aye, he was capable of great gentleness too—the scent that had filled her head from the moment he'd walked into the bedchamber, the rumble of his baritone as he offered his companionship for the night. Rosston had tried that tack once too. But with MacHarg the words had felt like a sweet and unplanned outpouring, not a maneuver on a long, fiercely fought campaign. She smiled. The words had to have been unplanned. They'd been too awkwardly offered to be anything else.

Undine said, "The look on your face would inspire a dozen Leonardos. Have you told MacHarg ye are betrothed? And dinna say ye are not because the discussions have been started even if the conclusion is far from clear."

Abby shifted. "Our exchanges have not been the kind that lend themselves to that sort of conversation." She touched her mouth, remembering the day's more brutal kisses. "And in any case, that is not the sort of information that affects men much, I find."

"Dear friend, do not lie to yourself. That man has a heart—and a growing hope to be the man you'd like him to be. I can see it as clearly as I can see my hand."

"Oh, Undine," Abby cried, "dinna steal into his thoughts too. He has not learned to harden himself to your wicked tools."

"I didna steal in," Undine said haughtily. "The only tools I need are two eyes and a willingness to see. You might try it once."

An anguished howl split the quiet of the night. Grendel jumped to his feet.

"God help me," Abby said. "Not again."

A second howl followed, more piercing than the first.

"Where is she? Where is the nurse?" Abby leaped from her chair. "Fetch Robby, would you? Hurry!"

Undine and Abby parted in the hall, and Abby flew to the tower door and up the stairs, with Grendel on her heels.

The man was tangled in his covers, his head on the floor and a foot kicking the footboard like an angry mule. The ropes meant to hold him hung useless from the bedposts. Bloodied spittle seeped from his mouth—he'd cut his lip—and he dug at the collar of his nightshirt, tearing the fabric and leaving bloody gouges in his flesh. Grendel barked furiously.

"Stop it, stop it!" She grabbed his hands and pulled them from his neck. "You're going to kill yourself."

He was swinging his fists wildly now, and one caught her temple. The world blurred for an instant.

"Stop it, you fool!" Where was the nurse? Where was Undine?

She bent over his bulk, sheltering herself as best she could amid the swinging arms, and looked for a way to loosen the bedclothes. Another blow caught her head, and she lost her balance.

With arms across her face, she held back the worst of the blows. "Stop! *Stop!*"

"Bitch! Bloody, foucking *bitch*!"

A pair of hefty arms scooped her from the barrage.

With a well-placed shove of his foot, MacHarg disabled her attacker. He deposited Abby in a nearby chair and dropped on her attacker like a berserker, pinning the man's arms to the floor as easily as if they were stalks of sparrowgrass.

"Call her a bloody, foucking bitch again," MacHarg snarled, "and I'll break yer bloody, foucking arm. Who the bloody fouck are ye anyway?"

Abby rubbed her aching temple. "May I present my father, Lachlan Kerr."

Twenty-one

ASHAMED, SHE WATCHED AS MACHARG BLINKED, OWL-like, and lifted his gaze from her father's face, now contorted in pain, to hers.

"Your father?"

"Aye." The familiar heat crawled up her neck and cheeks. It happened every time she had to bring someone new into the particular sort of madhouse that existed within these walls. The new nurse had been the last, and she found herself wondering if Duncan thought less of her for having such a man as a father.

Lachlan's groans slowed and he opened his eyes. She hoped Duncan was holding his arms tightly. "He gets like this sometimes. I dinna ken why."

She watched Duncan take in the ropes on the bed-posts and the relative obscurity of the location. "Does no one know he's here, then?" he asked cautiously.

Her father took a deep breath and let out a howl that filled the room and nearly split her head in two.

Duncan jammed a hand over the struggling man's mouth. "I withdraw the question."

MacHarg had had to gather her father's wrists in a

single hand in order to stopper the man's mouth with the other, and she watched as he shifted his weight to keep his quarry contained. There was something about the way his orange-blond hair caught the firelight as he moved that made Abby think of a ginger cat with a mouse.

"Then he's not a…prisoner?" Duncan readjusted a slipping foot.

A prisoner? *Ha.* If she could release him, she would have done it gladly. "Of his mind and body. Nothing more."

Lachlan relaxed and Duncan freed his mouth.

"Does he…speak to you that way often?" Duncan asked.

"Moira, Moira, forgive me," Lachlan wailed. Grendel, who had taken an uneasy post in the corner, whined with him.

"Da, it's nothing," she said softly. "You have to stop struggling. He doesn't mean it," she said to Duncan, "not all of it, at least. Moira is my mother. After the apoplexy, he couldn't speak at all for the longest time. When his tongue came back, his memory was gone. Then the nonsense began—just a little at first—he'd left his pony at his gran's, we needed to secure the portcullis, the dead king was coming to visit—and then it got so ye were just as likely to get nonsense as anything else. Betimes he's violent. Others, he's like a block of wood, unhearing and unseeing." She gestured to the bed. "We need to get him tied up again, though. At least until he settles."

With Duncan doing the lifting and restraining, Abby was able to resecure the ropes with no more than two kicks and a mild scratch to thank her for her effort.

Her father quieted, emitting only an occasional mournful sigh. The lax, unmoving side of his face drooped like a candle that had been held too close to the fire, while the other half twitched as if it were being struck by tiny bolts of lightning. The best thing now would be to get some food in him and get him to sleep. His untouched dinner sat on the table next to the bed.

"I can take care of him now," she said. "The nurse should be here shortly. I thank ye for your help."

"*Ye goddamned besom!*" Lachlan jerked the ropes so hard the bedposts shook.

Duncan frowned. "I think I will stay awhile, if ye dinna mind."

Or even if she did, Abby thought, for the readiness of his stance said he would be planted in place until he deemed it safe to leave her unattended.

"I—I—What I mean to say is it is not necessary for you—"

Molly, the new nurse, bounded up the stairs, breathless. "My deepest apologies, milady. His lordship had been crying half the morning for his mother to make him a bit of spun sugar for his birthday." She cast her eyes to the floor. "I know I shouldn't leave him, but I thought how nice it would be if Cook could make him something to ease his mind. Please dinna dismiss me. I willna do it again."

"Dinna trouble yourself," Abby said. "'Twas just a matter of getting him back into bed. I'm sure my father appreciates your efforts on his behalf. I know

I do." Abby had had enough trouble finding a girl patient and skilled enough to stay with her father. She was hardly going to dismiss her over a bit of spun sugar.

Undine and Robby, her burliest footman, clattered up the steps. Abby held up her hands to signal the time for panic had passed.

"Thank you, everyone. My father is settling down. Molly, you're tired. Have a rest. Get the cook to give you a nice bowl of soup. We'll be fine here." She found herself looking to MacHarg for confirmation, which he gave with a small nod.

Undine, Molly, and the footman descended the stairs, leaving Abby to negotiate the odd but not entirely unpleasant sense that MacHarg was her partner in this.

Her eyes went to Lachlan's dinner. MacHarg wouldn't be a partner in *this*, she thought. No one should have to be. She found a cloth near the ewer and wet it to wipe down her father's bloody lip. When he was clean, she sat down and took the plate on her lap. The soup would stay where it was. She couldn't bear for MacHarg to witness that debacle, and it was likely cold now anyway. Spearing a morsel of chicken, she adjusted the stool so that MacHarg would be directly behind her, blocked from view.

"My da had Alzheimer's," he said quietly.

Abby stroked the corner of her father's mouth, encouraging him to open it. "What is Alzheimer's?"

"Oh, sorry." MacHarg coughed, flustered. "Well, 'tis something like what your da has. He lost his memory and then his manners—not that he had many to begin with."

"How long did it take him to recover?"

MacHarg hesitated, and she felt her heart fall. "I didna expect you to say he had. I just...hoped, I guess. For both our sakes." She put the morsel in her father's mouth and gently pressed his lifeless lips together to form a seal as he chewed. "You told me you grew up without your da."

"I did. But I knew where he was."

"And you attended him when he fell ill?"

"I wouldna call it attending. I am not as kind-hearted as you."

"I am hardly kindhearted." She gave her father another piece. "I treated you quite cruelly down there."

"I failed you."

"Aye, ye did. But it didna follow that I must add to your burden. No man comes to killing an expert. I was wrong to have expected that of you."

Lachlan's vacant eyes turned suddenly dark, and Abby, as always, started at the change.

"Who failed me?" he asked coldly, though the "me" came out as "eel" through his half-functioning lips.

"He failed *me*, Da. Not you. Quiet yourself."

Lachlan wrenched himself upright to see the man who'd done the failing. "Is this your husband? Your husband has hair like a raven."

"I dinna have a husband with raven hair or other-wise. Lay back."

"Who is he?"

"His name is Duncan. He's a MacHarg."

MacHarg stepped into the fire's light and made a hesitant bow.

"A MacHarg, is it? Decent enough farmers, though

they drink too much and have a verra dangerous streak of stubbornness in them."

Abby snorted. "Scotsmen who are stubborn and drink? I canna imagine it."

"Are you one of Ainsley MacHarg's men?"

Abby watched MacHarg's face, curious herself.

"Er, no," he said.

"Who is your chief then?"

MacHarg licked the corner of his mouth. "My grand-da. Gordon MacHarg."

There was no chief named Gordon MacHarg in the Lowlands, nor, did she suspect, in the Highlands, the Arrans, the Grampians, or the Western Isles, either.

"I dinna know him." Lachlan narrowed his eyes. "Who is your father?"

MacHarg stiffened. "He's dead."

"Drunkard?" Lachlan asked.

"Da!"

"Aye," MacHarg said. "And a thief."

Lachlan settled back on a pillow. "Well, we never mind a wee bit of reiving. Untie me, lass. And get your mother."

Abby's heart clenched. "Ma is gone. Visiting Auntie Ialach in Tayside. Will you promise to be still?" She untied the closest rope.

"Did she take the new gelding? Braw beast, that one is. Worth every shilling. But there's something I don't like about him." He squeezed his eyes shut, struggling to remember.

"He bolts," she said and felt MacHarg, who had ventured to the farside of the bed to untie the ropes there, pause.

"Aye, that's it! We can fix that, nae bother. Donnie's a gem with horses. Take him to Donnie, lass."

"I will, Da. In the morning."

Lachlan ran a hand through his thick, white hair and gave his visitor a long look. "MacHarg, I know you have come to the Kerr for a reason. What is it? I dinna lend money, but I can put you to work."

"He's been put to work," Abby said. "He is my strong arm."

"A strong arm who canna kill?" Her father turned his sharp gaze to her. "What other changes have ye made? Who were ye intending to kill?"

"Harry," she said, steeling herself. "He took his sons to carry out a raid against the soldiers in Cumbria against my orders."

"Your orders! Ye dinna order men! You're a lass!"

"I am the Kerr now," she said carefully, "as you are unfit for it. And Harry defied me."

"Where is Rosston? What does he say?"

"Rosston is not the chief. I am."

"Harry is *my* strong arm. A real strong arm."

"And ye poisoned him against me." She was intensely embarrassed that MacHarg had to witness this and struggled to hold on to her temper. "When the deal was struck, he took his oath, but he never accepted me. Ye told me yourself, no man can defy an order and live."

"Apparently one can when you're leading the clan. MacHarg, I see you drape yourself in the Kerr plaid. Have you abandoned your own clan, or are your father's thieving ways in your blood too?"

"Enough." She put the plate down hard and stood.

Her father was one step from lunacy. How did he still possess the power to reduce her to a shrieking child?

MacHarg unfolded himself to full height, and Abby felt rather than saw the tension vibrating in him. "I have taken an oath to the Kerr," he said. "My Kerr. The Kerr of Clan Kerr. I failed to kill Harry, but I will not fail again. I will kill any man who tries to harm your daughter, and if you are the father I think you are, you will thank me for it."

Lachlan ran a tongue over the gaps in his lower teeth and laughed. "My daughter can tack a man's balls to his horse at thirty yards. She dinna need protection, MacHarg. She needs a man men will follow."

"Both of you are wrong," Abby said hotly. "I need no man at all."

Twenty-two

THE CLACK CLACK OF ABBY'S BOOT HEELS ECHOED down the stairs. Grendel gave Duncan an accusatory look and followed his mistress.

Duncan knew the brunt of Abby's anger was directed toward her father, but he felt complicit too. He'd never irritated a woman in quite so many ways before. His experience of women, apparently more limited than he'd imagined, was that they *adored* him. They loved his hair, his accent, his stories, his height, the way he smiled. Their clothes melted off them; they invested their money in his firm; they waved him onto the bus without exact change. Yet there appeared to be no part of his personality that didn't drive Abby crazy.

Indeed, he'd bedded her—if you can call that three-megaton explosion by the chapel bedding—but he'd hardly breached the gates of the fortress known as Abby Kerr. He didn't know what she liked to eat. He didn't know if she'd ever been to Rome. And while Nab had told him she was to be married, the word "betrothed" had never passed her lips. Nor had "I'm in love," "There's someone else," or even, "I think we should proceed with caution." No, no caution for that girl.

Duncan sighed. He would eventually find the pitch on which she wanted to play, but until then, he was getting a very hard lesson in the rules of the game.

Lachlan, oblivious to the fury he had excited, was struggling to cut another piece of meat. Duncan thought of Abby emerging from the tower door last night in tears. Daughter, successor, caretaker—the very act of juggling those balls would be challenging enough, but with a man like Lachlan Kerr? *Och*.

Lachlan let out a frustrated growl as the chicken slid from under his knife.

"Perhaps," Duncan said with a disgusted shake of his head, "you shouldn't have driven your wee daughter from the room."

The man dug in harder, sawing wildly. The plate was creeping toward the edge of the bedside table.

"Oh, for the love of—*Stop!*" Duncan grabbed the plate just before it fell. "Has anyone ever told you for a man who depends on the kindness of others, you don't exactly engender goodwill?"

"Fouck ye."

"Oh, verra nice." Duncan seated himself on the stool with a sigh. "Despite your evident displeasure with my company, I intend to see that you have your dinner. We can spare your daughter that much, can we not?"

The heat in Lachlan's short Gaelic response gave Duncan a pretty clear idea of the man's thoughts even if the words were beyond his understanding.

"Is that an 'aye' then?"

Before the man could summon another stream of invective, Duncan nimbly swiped the knife from his hand, grabbed the fork, and cut the meat into a half a dozen pieces. He held out the plate, swept his arm around his back, and said in his best French accent, "The dining room proudly presents…your dinner."

Lachlan, evidently not a fan of *Beauty and the Beast*, was unmoved. This did not deter Duncan, who had earned money his last year of secondary school babysitting his six-year-old neighbor and watched *Beauty and the Beast* so many times he could sing every part, including Belle's and that of Gaston's chorus of buxom admirers. He forked a piece of chicken, twirled it in the air as if it were Lumiere's flaming candle, and brought it before the man's mouth.

"Be our guest."

Lachlan narrowed his eyes. But the chicken, moist and dark, was too tempting to pass up. He took it and chewed.

Duncan reached for the man's lips, to close them as he'd seen Abby do. Lachlan jerked away and brought his better, opposite fist to hold it closed.

"Fair enough," Duncan said.

"Where's Molly?" Lachlan demanded, as sullen as a child.

"Molly?" Duncan frowned, trying to place the name. "The wee dimpled nurse? Oh, aye, I can see where you'd prefer her to me. Unfortunately, Molly needs a rest from ye as well."

"Molly," Lachlan said firmly.

"Duncan," he replied. He held out another piece of chicken and quietly sung Lumiere's song. Duncan was no singer, but the tune was as enticing as the chicken, and Lachlan eventually opened his mouth.

They continued on in this way until the chicken was gone. Duncan returned the plate to the table and leaned forward to straighten the man's covers.

"There. That wasn't so bad, was it?"

Lachlan grabbed the front of Duncan's sark and jerked his face close to his.

"Get out of my home," he said, each word drenched in venom. "I can smell a man after my daughter's money and quim as far away as Edinburgh. Ye stink of it."

Duncan peeled the man's fingers off his sark, stifling an urge to break them as he did it. "I have more than enough money of my own, old man. I have no need of your daughter's."

"Then I guess I know what you *are* here for."

Lachlan swung his fist and Duncan caught his wrist.

"Listen, you filthy old reprobate. You're wrong about your daughter and you're wrong about me. She would have made you proud today. She stood before those men a leader. They respect her—not because she's stronger than they are, but because she's smarter."

Lachlan's eyes burned blue fire, and Duncan saw where Abby got her spirit.

"And as far as your daughter's money and quim are concerned," he said through clenched teeth, "she can do with them what she pleases. Should she choose to give both to every man between here and the gates of York, it'd be no more your business than it is mine. And if you ever, ever make her cry again, I'll come in here while you're sleeping and hold that wee pillow over your head until you bother her nae more. Do you understand me?"

Lachlan's scowl tightened. Then all of a sudden he barked a great, whooping laugh. "Only a fool would say such a thing—or a verra canny man. Let us hope you know which you are. Now get me my Molly. I need to piss."

Duncan let go of Lachlan's wrist. He was a force to be reckoned with—even in his dementia. Duncan wondered how poor Molly managed it. But as he had no desire to be handling the man's cock, he rose from the stool, knowing he would bend to Lachlan's will, just as he had to Abby's. Six hundred years of power brought something to the Kerr chiefs the titans of Wall Street could only dream about.

It dawned on Duncan as he gathered the dishes he had no idea where the kitchen was or how to find Molly or the cook, and he was just about to ask Lachlan when he spotted Abby in the archway at the top of the stairs. He wondered how long she'd been standing there.

"Leave them," she said, indicating the dishes. "Molly will get them."

"He may have found his niche at the castle," Lachlan said. "Dinna rob him of it."

"Da."

"He wants Molly," Duncan said, replacing the tray.

"She's coming. And she'll have your spun sugar," Abby added to her father. "But if ye make a bit of trouble before she comes, I'll tell her to dump it right out that window, do ye hear?"

Duncan met Lachlan's eyes. He fluffed a pillow

meaningfully and placed it behind the man's head before nodding his good night.

"Come, MacHarg," Abby said. "I should like to have a word with you before you retire."

Twenty-three

THEY EMERGED FROM THE STAIRWELL INTO THE INKY blackness of the hall, and she stopped. He had hoped the conversation would be conducted in her room and couldn't help stealing a longing look at her door.

"I thank you for your help up there," she said. "I had nae patience for it tonight. And you were…" She bowed her head, searching for words. Gratitude did not come easy to a clan chief.

"It was nothing, Abby. I've spent my life around"—he almost said "arseholes" but thought better of it—"men who are challenging. At least your father has an excuse for it."

"'Challenging,' is it?"

He could hear the smile in her words, though the soft planes of her face were no more than patches of gray in the darkness. The window that had lit the hall the night before showed only a vast expanse of twinkling black now. The moon would not rise for another hour, at least.

"I dinna ken how you do it," he said. "How do you lead with him second-guessing you? How do you keep the men attending to you, not him? And how in God's name did ye become the chief? I mean I know your brother died and Lachlan fell ill, but even then?"

She sighed. He could feel the urge to share the story with him welling up like a rising stream against a dam. But he could also feel her fighting it.

Break, he thought. *Break. Pour yourself into my dry bed. I will hold you safely.*

"'Tis such a complicated story," she said.

"I have all night."

Her longing was palpable, and his was too. They were like two magnets, held apart by nothing more than the friction of the rug and the fear of letting go. If she made the slightest move, the slightest sound to show him what she wanted...

"Duncan—"

The squeak of a door made them jump. Nab's slim back, lit by a single candle, appeared in the doorway to Duncan's room. He held the candle high, as if checking his work in the room, and backed out. He smiled when he spotted Duncan and trotted down the hall.

"I was wondering where ye had gotten yourself off to," Nab said, giving Grendel a vigorous rub. "I dropped off some supper and hot water. Undine said you might need some. Have ye finished making your report?"

Duncan wondered what the penalty was for infanticide in 1706. "Aye."

"Then let me lead you back. I was to return the candle to Undine if I didn't find you, but here ye are."

"Aye. Here I am."

"May I take Grendel for a bit?" Nab asked Abby.

"I'm certain he would enjoy it," she said. "Good night, MacHarg. Good night, Nab. No, Grendel," she said, making her way toward her room, "you stay with them."

Duncan swore he felt the brush of her hand when she'd passed.

The door of her bedchamber closed behind her. "Oh God."

"Tired, are ye?" Nab asked.

"And in mind of murder, aye."

"Oh?" Nab stopped scratching Grendel's ears. "Is it the sort of thing that when ye do it once, ye want to do it agin and agin?"

"It is," Duncan said. "Though I dinna mean actual murder, ye wee wicked louse."

They trooped to his room, and Duncan shut the door, collapsing against it. "Ye have the worst timing of any man, woman, or beast I have ever kent. You are too young to know better, but Lady Kerr and I were about to…well, that is to say, it was possible that she might have—might have, ye hear—a gentleman never assumes, and in any case—"

"Oh, I ken what you were about. That's why I stopped ye. Rosston put a sentry on Lady Kerr. The man's been crouching behind a door down the hall since dusk, peering through a crack, watching her comings and goings."

Duncan straightened. "You're serious?"

"Aye. And once I leave here, I intend to point Grendel directly at him. Knock the bastard on his fat arse."

The dog wagged his tail eagerly.

"And you're sure Rosston's behind it?" Duncan

skimmed off his soiled sark and wondered if perhaps his hiding place in the chapel had not been as hidden as he'd thought.

"Well, the man is one of his. Brutish fool too. Solomon is his name—surely a sign of someone's love of a jest. No man could be more thickheaded."

Duncan's ego plumped a bit at the fact Rosston was worried about him. "Perhaps it will do the man good to know he has a rival?"

"Rosston, do ye mean? Or you? I feel certain 'twill be no blessing for Lady Kerr."

Duncan's sense of triumph disappeared. "You are quite correct." He slipped his hands in the warm water Nab had delivered and doused his face and arms. "Today has not been the best of days. Leave the man, though. I should like Rosston to think his ruse has been undetected." Duncan reached for a towel and gave himself a vigorous rub. He could feel Nab studying him.

"I heard about Harry," the boy said.

Duncan had almost forgotten today's failure. "How? I only just told Lady Kerr."

"He stole a horse in Thrum's Ferry. The men were talking about it outside."

Abby was right to say he'd complicated things for her. "I am not much of a strong arm, it seems." He grabbed another clean sark from Bran's closet, conscious once again of his utter dependence on the generosity of Abby Kerr to survive in this world. "He isn't heading back here, I hope."

Nab shrugged. "I doubt it. I've never seen an exiled man return. Well, except for Lady Kerr, of course. And she had to be brought back almost in chains."

Duncan slipped the linen over his head. He had forgotten her father had sent her away.

Nab said, "But Rosston's man is not the only thing I must tell you about—"

A knock sounded and Grendel flew to the door.

"Come," Duncan said.

A gap-toothed maid with steely eyes opened the door. "The chieftess requires your assistance."

"Oh?" He brought the plaid up over his shoulder again.

"The smith is in need of ten feet of the thickest chain the castle has—as wide as your wrist, if ye please."

"Jesus. Is he penning an elephant?"

"I didna ask, though it seems unlikely. There are nae eilifints in Scotland, sir."

"Can it wait till morning?" Even in full light, carrying ten feet of four-inch-thick iron chain was going to be a hell of a job.

"Are ye ill? I can spare a girl if ye need help, though it's Katie, and even in the best o' times—"

"No, no, no. I can do it myself. I just—Never mind. Where's the chain?"

"There's a storage room at the base of the west tower stairs. I expect you'll find what we have there."

"And the smith?"

"East bailey, behind the old brewery."

Duncan groaned. Stairs, full darkness, three hundred pounds of chain, and an entire castle's width to cross.

The woman eyed him dubiously, as one might a one-legged man who's been handed a ladder, but seemed to decide in the end whatever happened wouldn't be her problem. He suspected he was never going to be asked to tote the best china though.

"You may let her ladyship know I'll take care of it."

"Lady Kerr *presumes* her requests will be fulfilled, Mr. MacHarg. 'Twould only be worth notice if you refused. And in that case I should call the castle guard." With a sniff, she turned on her heel and disappeared into the hall.

"*Well*." Duncan could think of no more to say that should be said in front of an impressionable young man. "Ten feet of four-inch chain. What in God's name is it for, do ye think?" he wondered, adding with a grin, "Maybe her ladyship's planning to lock Rosston out of the castle on his return, aye?"

"That's what I need to tell ye. Rosston's back. He's here—in the castle. I don't know what he'd been planning to do, mind, but after he left the chapel, he stopped at a crofter's cottage just north of here and came out with a small chest, which he brought back here and has been hovering over ever since. *That* is what the chain is for. To lock it up."

"Why would he need a three-hundred-pound chain for a chest?" The words had barely left his mouth when it hit him. "Gold."

Nab nodded. "He's let it be known this is his wedding portion to Lady Kerr. The date has been set. And the date has been moved. They are to be married in three days' time."

Twenty-four

DUNCAN SIMMERED AS HE DESCENDED THE DARKENED stairway to the main hall. Hospital orderly, unpaid muscle, and now pack mule for her husband-to-be. There seemed to be no end to the roles he could perform for her. His cheeks warmed thinking of the role she'd enjoyed most of all.

The castle was quiet, not surprising at this late hour, though he could hear the convivial noise the clansmen gathered outside in the bailey were making. After a few wrong turns and locked doors, he found the stairway to the base of the west tower. This was the tower he'd glimpsed to the left of Lachlan's tower when he'd stood in the town's market square. The only light came from a narrow window through which the northern sky's glittering sea of stars flickered and flashed. He thought of his grand-da, who loved the night sky. Was he too looking at the Northern Lights? He closed his eyes and said a prayer.

Hang on, Grand-da. I'll get there.

But if he wanted to go, he'd best fulfill the

requirements of the spell. He hadn't realized "strong arm" would be taken so literally.

By now, his eyes had grown used to the dark, and he could make out the different doors well enough. The first room held rugs, rolled and standing on their sides; the second casks, the peaty smell of whiskey in the air. He found the chains in the third, as well as pulleys, ropes, and stacks of scrap metal.

The chain sat in a rusty heap.

So you're to be wrapped like a miser's arms around Rosston's fortunes, are you?

He decided with some satisfaction that any man who needed a chest of gold to get into a woman's bed probably had a very small cock.

He lifted the first length of chain over his shoulders, and it was immediately clear he wouldn't be able to carry the weight of it all, which had to be close to three hundred pounds. He could bench-press two fifty, but this weight wasn't neatly attached to each end of a bar, and he'd be climbing stairs with it.

He needed wheels.

With a booming crash, he dropped the chain and headed back to the casks. Casks needed wheelbarrows. This room was deeper than the others, and darker. He was working mostly by hand and gut, feeling the ancient wood staves and rough iron bands, hearing the echo of his breath. The shelves ended a few feet before the adjoining wall, leaving an empty space. He stretched his hands forward, wondering if he'd found another hallway, but found only wall. The echo from his breathing changed tone, and he paused instinctively to consider the reason.

He reached for the wall again, and nearly fell when it swung away from him.

A bright light blinded him and resolved into a vision of Abby standing before a narrow stairway, one hand holding the now-open door and the other a flickering lantern.

"I was wondering how long it might take you to find this."

Twenty-five

THE LOOK OF SHOCK ON DUNCAN MACHARG'S FACE nearly made her laugh, but the way he looked at her when the shock dissipated took her breath away. She realized with a start she was on the verge of becoming foolish about him, and not just foolish like this morning. Foolish in a far more dangerous way.

She turned away, flustered. "I hope you don't mind, but I thought this was the best way."

"Why would I mind?" He brushed the cobwebs off his shoulders and peered up the stairs. "It's only time away from dragging a quarter ton's worth of chain through the castle like Marley's ghost."

"Marley?" She closed the door behind them and threw the latch.

"An acquaintance of mine. Dead." He looked around the small space. "More Kerr secrets, is it?"

"I don't know about more. It is certainly secret—at least until now."

"And what does a chieftess like you have to hide?"

There was an air of danger about him that made her senses come alive.

"Whiskey, weapons, and wealth," she said, "the three *W*'s every clan chief hoards."

He looked into the ascending darkness. "Given the steepness of these stairs and lack of shelves or storage, my guess would be that it is a different *W* the Kerr chiefs have wanted to hide, something a little, shall we say, more warm-blooded."

"Women. Aye, I suppose that's true as well."

"Barring yourself, of course, milady, whose desires would never run in the direction of such carnality."

She swallowed. This was a different Duncan MacHarg than the one she had known for the last day and a half. She found herself uncertain and a little scared.

"Indeed, my predecessors were known to bring the occasional woman here. Barring, of course, Cailean Kerr, the fourth chief, a buggerer of some renown whose only son was sired by the town's rather dim-witted but strong-as-an-ox stonemason, breathing new life into the Kerr blood and happily infusing generations to come with an irrepressible need to extend the castle's perimeter."

"Buggery is probably the least of the sins that have taken place here. I assume I should follow you."

"I…well, yes." His presence overwhelmed the small space. It was more than the size of him, though that seemed to have doubled since she saw him last. It was his tang of sweat and labor, the way his whiskey burr reverberated within these walls, and the inexplicable sense of him as a devil-in-a-box, ready to leap at her at any instant.

She hurried up the steps, already regretting her carefully plotted plan. A small fire, a comfortable seat, and a

chance to share the story of elevation to the Kerr chiefship with him was all she'd wanted. Their easy rapport
had stirred something in her she thought she'd locked
away forever, and the chance to unburden herself away
from the gossiping tongues of the castle had seemed an
elixir more powerful than wine. Now, as she hurried to
keep herself beyond the reach of the storm-like current
that seemed to pop from him, she wished she'd drunk
the claret she'd set out before sending the maid to him.

At the third turn, the small square door stood open,
revealing the silk, linen, and velvet that hung in the
wardrobe that shielded the stairs from sight.

He disappeared into it before she had a chance to
give a single word of explanation. She blew out the
lantern's flame and crawled in behind him.

Her head had no more than emerged through the
fabric when he caught her by the waist, lifted her to
her feet, and enveloped her in his arms.

"Your bed," he whispered.

She didn't know if this was a question or statement
about the room in which they now stood. In an instant
it didn't matter. His bruising kiss seared her mouth,
and his arms expertly maneuvered her against the
wardrobe through which they'd climbed.

"What am I here for, chieftess?"

Abby's legs tingled and she struggled to catch her
breath. Another kiss cut off any response but a hungry
return of his attentions.

He lifted her like a sack of beets and turned. A crash
of metal filled the room.

"Bloody goddamned quiver." He kicked the arrows
aside and laid her on the bed. "If ye want me," he said,

pulling off his sark, "ye will have to tell me exactly what you want me to do."

His chest, dusted generously with auburn curls, gleamed in the candlelight.

"Do ye understand?" he said. "Every step. Ye command me, aye? So give me your command."

He stretched himself over her and looked into her eyes, the iron of his arms as striking as the forged steel between his legs.

"I only wanted to talk."

He laughed. "Did you?"

His kisses trailed down her neck to the valley between her breasts. His hair tickled her sensitive flesh, and blood rushed to her nipples.

"Then talk," he said.

"Not here."

"Oh, not here." He swung her from the bed as he stood. "Where then? Here?" With an easy movement, he brought her thighs to each side of his hips and backed her into the tapestry-covered wall. He was ready. Through the silk of her gown she could feel it, and her own desire burned as he moved her slowly up and down.

"No," she whispered.

"Over here perhaps, then?"

His footsteps echoed on the worn wood, and he swung them both into the deep sill of her window. His hands slid up her gown and, finding her hips, arranged her over the peaked wool of his plaid.

Wildly unsteady, she anchored herself in the only way she could, with palms against the glass panes. He took the nipple that jutted before his mouth and tugged.

The hunger in her moan surprised her.

"Do ye want me to undress you?" he asked.

She closed her eyes and nodded.

"Say it, chieftess."

"Undress me."

He freed his hands from her skirts and unbuttoned the bodice. Then he lifted the silk over her head and tossed it to the floor.

In an instant, the straps of her chemise were around her elbows, and her breasts, freed from their bindings, swayed gently with her heart, which now beat even harder.

His eyes widened, not, as she had wanted, in desire, but in shock.

"Tell me what you see," she said.

"Milady…"

"You said I am to command you. I command you. Describe it."

He brought a hand to her shoulder and gently traced the scar's ragged outline. "A wound," he said, the hardness gone from his eyes, replaced with penetrating sorrow. "Healed, aye, but terrible nonetheless. I saw the other side of it, I guess, when I saw you diving. But that mark was no more than a line. What happened?"

"I was shot. 'Tis part of the story of my ascension to the chiefship—and an important part of my life—but I dinna wish to talk about it now. Not *right* now," she added, bringing a hand to the rough, tawny stubble of his cheeks. "I find I dinna want to talk at all, at least not with words. I want…what we have started."

His eyes, full blue, gazed at her through long, black lashes, and he pulled her into an embrace so gentle, she smiled.

"I willna break," she said. "I promise ye."

"No, it's not you."

Her face was buried in the lustrous waves of his hair, and her breasts pressed against the warm expanse of his chest. Yet even through the tenderness she could feel the hesitation.

"I dinna think…" He stood, taking her with him, then placed her on the floor and turned away. "I dinna think I can do what you want."

Abby flushed. She suddenly felt very exposed—and very foolish. "Why?"

"The truth?"

"Aye. Always." She returned her chemise straps to her shoulders though it hardly mattered. He gazed into the fire.

With evident effort, he relaxed his hands, which had balled into fists, and turned back to her. "I've never been so addled by a woman before. On the one hand, I should like to throw you in the bed, grab that bonny bottom, and bend ye to my pleasure. There's nae place on ye I shouldna like to bury my tongue, roll under my palm, or feel pressed against the head of my cock. If we dinna finish what we've started here, only an eager hand and the most wicked imagining will free me from the thought of you tonight—and for many nights to come, I should think."

The fire deep in Abby's belly flared. "But?"

"But ye use me. And ye lie—or withhold the truth. I dinna want to be the man who comes to ye when you've sent your husband from your bed—or your husband-to-be."

"It's not what you think."

He held up a hand. "The worst part is, I dinna want to be that man, but I know I will. That's the part I hate." His breath was ragged now. "But ye make it even worse for me."

"How?" Her throat was so tight, the word caught.

"Because I want you. You face such challenges. And you do it with such fierceness and determination. I want to be the man that you take to your bed—even if I'm not the only one."

Someone knocked, and Abby groaned. MacHarg was already reaching for his sark.

"The door's locked," she said under her breath.

"Abby?"

The voice belonged to Rosston. MacHarg met her eyes.

She said, "I should talk to him."

"Of course." He slipped the sark over his head stiffly.

She grabbed a blanket from the bed, threw it around her shoulders, and scurried to the door. MacHarg had retreated from sight.

Cursing Rosston from the depths of her soul, she unlocked the door and opened it a crack. She could feel MacHarg's exasperation at her back. "Aye?"

"I hoped we could talk." Rosston held out a bottle of old brandy.

"It's late. I'm tired."

"Jock said you missed your meeting with him. I was worried."

The meeting in which he'll tell me I have no choice but

to marry you, she thought. "Aye, my father was causing a wee stir."

Rosston sighed. "I'm sorry, Abby. I know ye struggle."

"It's done now."

"I have something that might set your mind at ease. I have brought to Castle Kerr—"

"I know what you brought," she said. "I had to order new chain for it from the blacksmith. What sort of mad man parades a king's ransom through the borderlands like that? Ye of all people should know better."

"I did it for you, Abby. I dinna want you to worry anymore."

His chestnut eyes reflected the fire's flickering gold. She knew he cared for her. But that just made it worse.

She gave him a heartfelt hug. "I know. And I thank ye for it."

"I burn for ye, Abby. Invite me in. Let my money save you."

She stepped back into the relative safety of her bedchamber. "Watch your words, Rosston. A less agreeable woman might think ye intended to buy your way between her legs."

"And a less prideful one might recognize such an offer as a generous and fair one." He swept her into a kiss that was urgent and brief. "I willna wait forever."

She had no interest in being forced into anything, including a kiss, and she gave him a firm push. He shook his head, disappointed, and disappeared into the darkness of the hall, bottle at his side.

She steeled herself for MacHarg's reaction.

He stood slouched against the wall, arms crossed,

staring moodily at the floor. "Ye seem to have an abundance of suitors this evening."

She held her breath, terrified he'd walk out.

"I'm not going to leave," he said, "because I want to hear the truth about the two of you. Even if it kills me, I think."

She tugged his arm, and he followed her reluctantly, but when he saw she was leading him toward the bed he stopped.

"I cannot."

"Lay with me. Or sit at least. When I was a girl, my friend Eleanor used to say 'tis impossible to tell a lie when you hold hands with another." She wove her fingers into his. "See? No lies."

"No lies?"

She shook her head.

"Are ye free to fall in love as ye choose?" he said.

She inhaled sharply. "Have I not taught ye to engage an opponent more craftily? Ye dinna start with the coup de grâce."

She pulled him onto the bed and lay beside him, so that they both looked up into the plum velvet folds of her canopy, clasped hands between them.

"I've been promised the truth," he said, "and yet ye dinna answer."

She took a deep breath. "Who is ever free to love as they choose?"

He wrenched himself out of her grasp, but she caught him again before he stood. "MacHarg, please. Who *is* free? Have you chosen the girls you've come to love? It's not as if we stroll through the stalls in Covent Garden and point to ripe peach and say, 'This is it. This is the one.' We may be offered a gleaming peach, yet for a reason we canna explain we willna be talked out of a bruised pear."

The muscle in his jaw flexed. She had gained a foothold.

"Sit," she said. "Please."

He laced his fingers back into hers and lay back on the bed.

She let go of his hand only for an instant as she stood, transferring the constancy of touch to their knees. He watched her, uncertain. With a deep breath for courage, she slipped off her chemise. Those sea blue eyes widened and grew more guarded. She crawled beside him again, taking his hand.

His silence lasted so long she nearly reached for the chemise again. His eyes remained fixed on the canopy ceiling.

"Ye have put me in an awkward position," he said at last.

"More awkward than mine?"

He chuckled, and she felt him relax a bit.

"Eleanor said ye canna lie holding hands. But I want to show you I can tell you the truth in the most natural position in the world to lie—in bed with a man, lying naked. Why, the words themselves prove it! 'Lying naked'!"

He made a small laugh but did not turn his head.

"I will tell ye the truth," she said, "and if I dinna, ye may do as ye wish with me."

"If ye dinna, I will leave."

"I know. And what bigger blow could a woman suffer than have the man she courts leave her naked on a bed after she has thrown herself at him? I have given you the weapon with which to eviscerate me."

"I hope not to use it." He stroked her palm with his thumb. "Is he in love with you?"

Love? An irrelevance for a clan chief. Yet the idea, once so elusive, seemed to glimmer in her mind's eye as a possibility for the first time in her life. "If he does," she said, "it is the love of a child for a toy he does not wish to share."

"Will ye wed him?"

"I believe I will, MacHarg. Not out of some wind-swept emotion. Out of necessity. I wish it were not true, but it is, and there we are." His hand did not loosen, and she let out a quiet sigh of relief.

"How much money stands between you and the altar?"

"Five thousand pounds. Though it might as well be fifty."

"And if you dinna get it?"

"I willna be able to pay my bills. My clansmen will go hungry. Children will die. Eventually the families will be forced to go begging to Rosston anyway. At least if I marry him, I will be able to maintain a nominal place as head of the clan."

"What if I can help you?"

"Are you a wealthy man, MacHarg?"

"In another time and place I am."

"That other time and place—"

"It's my time to ask questions, aye? Rosston says ye are to be married on Thursday—at least that's what Nab told me. Is it true?"

"Rosston said that? Scoundrel. No, 'tis not true. He

may wish it. But he needs to learn that wishing does not make it so. Not with me. I havena even accepted his proposal."

"But you will marry soon?"

If only MacHarg could understand she had no choice. "Aye."

He sat up abruptly and her heart skipped a beat, but he did not release her hand. Turning on the bed, he brought the full weight of his gaze on her. "The next question will be harder for you to answer," he said, "and if I should have to leave…well, I should like to have the memory of you like this safely tucked into my heart."

"You are a cheat, MacHarg."

The corner of his mouth rose, and his eyes traveled over her slowly. She knew her breasts were too small and her skin too ruddy to be a real beauty. But her hips were round and welcoming, and her legs, though brown, were firm and lithe.

His gaze was investigative, referencing a sizable volume of past experience. She knew him to be well practiced. She recognized him now as connoisseur as well. With a less consequential man, she might have felt violated by such scrutiny. Instead, MacHarg raised her to a pedestal beside the most expertly sculpted Diana. She wished, however, her body did not quite respond so plainly to his appreciation.

"In my land," he said, voice low, "women shave their mons."

"Have they lice?" she said with horror.

He laughed. "I dinna think so. Personally, I think they're mad. I hope they seek to please themselves, because they dinna please me—not that they should, of course. But I find your hair enchanting."

Abby had never thought of her hair as enchanting. She had never thought of her hair there at all. But she knew how much she was looking forward to drawing her palms across MacHarg's stubbled cheeks and braiding her fingers in the silk of his auburn waves, and wondered, in a Samson-like rumination, why anyone would give up even a scant inch of hair if they could help it.

"Touch it," she said, hoping to distract him from the question he intended to ask, which she was certain she already knew and had no wish to answer.

"Ye are a siren."

He lifted his hand, still holding hers, and drew his knuckles slowly across her mons.

"God help me," he whispered. "My grand-da had a beaver hat when I was a kid. It couldna touch this for softness."

Any other man would climb instantly between her legs. But MacHarg would not rest until he had learned what he needed to know. He laid his hand—and hers—on her belly.

"If ye marry him," he said flatly, "will ye still take me to your bed?"

The question was hard, not because she didn't know the answer, but because she knew the answer would hurt him.

"I am not a great clan chief, ye ken, nor daughter, nor friend, nor even child of God. However, it isn't because I dinna try. If I marry Rosston, I should like to be a good wife. I should rather try and do it miserably than take my oath with the intent of breaking it."

MacHarg stared, unseeing, at the place their hands met. He looked so handsome in her brother's plaid, the dark crimson a striking contrast to the copper of his hair and gold of his cheeks. Her words had hurt him, and she was sorry to have brought him pain.

He said, "It's for the best. I dinna think I could bear to have you in one way and be shut out of the others."

She squeezed his hand. "I could convince you, I think, even if ye were not inclined. But ye would hate me for it."

And that was that, she thought. The truth of the situation. She couldn't be with him, nor he with her. She wondered if male clan chiefs had to sacrifice even half as much.

He let go of her and stood. She reached for the discarded wrap, her nakedness now odd and uncomfortable, and lay motionless with it in her hand. She had no interest in watching him go.

When she lifted her head and turned, he had taken off his clothes.

"Then ye shall have to put off this wedding as long as ye are able." He lay beside her. "I willna be done with ye for a while."

He kissed her gently as he entered her. His rocking was so slow and her body so wracked with anticipation, she thought she might die for lack of air. The heat oozed through her body—belly, knees, the breasts he stroked—till it reached her toes, which stretched into the cool night air like a dancer's. This was a different MacHarg. Not the morning's warrior claiming his prize, but a man in the desert, savoring his last sip of water.

She memorized each part of him—his muscled shoulders and long crevasse on each side of his collarbone; the musky, salty scent of his neck; the wiry brush of chest hair; and of course the gold and russet curls around his thick, ivory cock.

Would she be able to hold on to the memories after she bedded a new husband? She closed her eyes and gave entrée to Rosston's shade, feeling his thumping thrusts, tasting his ale-soaked lips, yielding to that insistent gaze.

"*A leannan?*"

Her eyes flew open, though the word had been barely audible. MacHarg stared down worriedly.

"Have I done something?"

"No. Aye. Something wonderful." She smiled. He had called her "darling." She shooed away the ghost with no regret.

"Oh, good. I was afraid there was something else I should be doing—moving faster or slower, perhaps, or applying some wee spanks."

Her eyes popped wide. "Spanks?!"

"*Och*, I keep forgetting!" He flushed a deep red. "Ignore me, please. I am ungovernable—or so my grand-da says."

She held up her hand. "Are ye saying the women in your land—the wee lousy ones—like to be spanked?"

"I dinna…It isn't that I…I mean, they *do* ask for it sometimes, ye ken."

She blinked. "'Tis part of bringing a woman to climax?"

"Ye make it sound so vulgar."

"Make it sound less so."

He chewed his lip. "A spanking can, well, heighten the arousal. Some women like it—some men too."

She sat up so quickly they slipped apart. "Ye have spanked a *man*!"

He waved his hands wildly. "No, no, no. I havena spanked a man. And, please, no more questions. I should like this discussion to be over. I should like all discussion to be over."

Not being a fool, she laid down immediately, and he entered her again.

"But…"

He paused.

"Oh, dinna stop," she said, feeling somewhat foolish. "It's just…I dinna understand how a woman might enjoy such a thing."

He climbed to his knees, still lodged within her, and lifted her ankles over his shoulders. Cupping a buttock, he said, "Imagine I told you to count up all the wicked things you've done with your lovers— tempting them when they couldna possess you—"

"I have never—"

"—taking them in a kirkyard, under God's own midday sun—"

She clamped her mouth shut.

"—or pleasuring them like a wanton, with those fine, full lips."

Fire spread across her cheeks, and with an amused groan, he brought her hips more tightly against him.

"Then," he said, "after ye'd finished your counting, imagine I told ye that you would endure one hard crack for each transgression?"

Her belly contracted so hard around him, she felt light-headed. "*Oh.*"

"Oh, indeed."

If he brushes my bud now, even the barest touch, I will ignite.

He read her thoughts and didn't move.

After a moment, the danger passed, but the warm, hard hand on her arse still twitched in anticipation.

"I dinna think I'm quite ready for such a thing," her voice choked.

"That's fine." He brought his hand instead to the thick, dark curls below her waist, weaving in his fingers till they were as tight as a comb. Tucking his thumb against her bud, he lowered her to the bed and bent to his work.

She arched, the exquisite intersection of pressure and pleasure sending waves of warmth over her. His thrusts slowed or quickened as necessary to hold her in the searing flame tips of heat, and she writhed wantonly. He seemed to savor the pleasure of her groans as much as if she were a succubus and he the one being ravished.

She clasped his shoulders as the wave began to crash, and kissed him hungrily. He held her tight, as if she might disappear, and rode the wave with her though he was nowhere near his own peak.

"Oh," she cried. "Oh!"

When her breathing slowed and she opened her eyes, he was gazing at her, smiling.

"God, you're beautiful, Abby. I canna believe I'm holding you in my arms. Did I please ye?"

"Aye, ye did. I believe I might never enjoy a man again as much—even if I tried every one between here and the gates of York."

He clapped his forehead and she laughed.

"Ye heard?"

"Oh, aye. And I had to wonder how long you'd been imagining that particular scene."

"Well, just the one day."

She licked the salty-sweet skin of his shoulder and sighed. "Ye taste of goodness and badness both—honor and avarice, loyalty and lust. Does everything on you taste as good?"

His cock swelled inside her. "What are ye offering, lass?"

"Exactly what you think. I want to try every inch of you."

"Every inch is flattered. Deeply flattered," he said, adjusting his hips. "Though from my point of view, he is exceedingly well placed where he is."

"Ah, but ye cannot finish there, MacHarg."

"Oh?" Eyes glinting, he said, "Why is that?"

"Ye know perfectly well. No man of chivalry would even ask."

"I tend to be more chivalrous when I am not firmly planted between the legs of the most captivating woman for a thousand miles."

She giggled, thoroughly surprising herself. She swore she hadn't giggled since she was besotted with her first beau at thirteen.

He bestowed a series of kisses on her neck and cheek. "Tell me then where I might finish," he said. "And paint a pretty picture, for I am quite at home here."

"Well," she offered, stifling a smile, "you seemed to be most happily served by your hand earlier today."

He coaxed a nipple into a tiny ruby. "Alas, my hand seems to have found a place more to its liking."

"I have never known a man's hand to find a place

more to its liking than around his cock. Nonetheless, I will take you at your word."

He bowed. "Perhaps you have another idea?"

"Well, I am reminded of the story of Lady MacTavish."

"Is it a long one?" He thrust himself once again into her depths. "I find I am growing less interested in fending off the inevitable."

She pushed him out of her and onto his back. "Gather your fortitude, sir. You will need it for this story. Lady MacTavish was the most famous of the clan chieftesses—or perhaps I should say the most infamous. She was one of Robert the Bruce's most powerful supporters. Many men vied to lead her clansmen on her behalf. This was back when a woman could not be expected to lead her own clan. Not like now."

She rolled her eyes, and MacHarg gave her a charming smile.

"It is said she brought each candidate to her bed-chamber to personally measure his worthiness."

"And was this worth measured with a ruler or an hourglass?"

"Probably both. But the important part of the story is Lady MacTavish was not one to take any unnec-essary risks. Legend has it she had her two prettiest lady's maids put the men through a number of, well, I suppose you might call them exercises, before she did her own judging. The exercises were conducted in a way that brought no risk to the maids' carefully preserved maidenheads but still managed to force the candidate to thoroughly exhaust his reserves. This was done as quickly as possible, in the full view of Lady

MacTavish, apparently to satisfy her that it had been done properly."

"Are you joking?"

"*Och*, you have nae heard the half of it. The exercises ended with a blue ribbon being tied rather tightly around, well, the man's assets. The procedure ensured that the third exercise, involving her ladyship, whose own maidenhead, I believe, was but a faint memory, offered almost no risk of an unwanted child. More important, however, the ribbon, once tightened, guaranteed a certain unflagging constancy in the clansman, a quality most valued by her ladyship."

MacHarg shook his head. "I am in awe of her practicality."

"MacTavish clansmen wear blue ribbons into battle even today, though the sight of it never fails to make me laugh."

"Tell me," he said, crossing his arms behind his head, "in the story about to unfold here, in this bed, are you one of the maidenly attendants or the chieftess herself?"

She drew her gaze over his daunting length. "I am nothing if not maidenly."

"In that case, you have convinced me to abandon my original plan." He climbed to his knees, adding considerably to his daunting-ness. "But before you begin, allow me to give some brief instruction in how it should be done."

He inserted his shoulder between her thighs and brought his mouth to her bud.

She dug her fingers into his hair, gasping. His tongue warmed her already swollen flesh. Every flick, every caress stoked the fire. This release was coming faster and far more powerfully than the last. She arched hard, and he held her there, on the back-breaking edge of absolute pleasure.

"No, no, *no!*" she cried.

The next shameless caress undid her. He held her until the tremors subsided.

"You're a fiend," she said, dizzy with the reverberations. "Onto your back. Ye shall be paid with the same hellfire."

Twenty-six

THAT HAD THE OPPOSITE EFFECT OF WHAT I WAS EXPECTING.
Duncan unraveled Abby's dark, lustrous locks from his clenched fingers and glanced at the flushed cheeks of the woman whose head had just come to rest on his belly.

Well, not that. *That had* exactly *the effect I was expecting.*
From the waist down he was numb, as boneless and unmovable as a spatchcocked chicken. But his heart paced like a caged animal.

He'd severed himself from women before. With the ones who had exerted no claim on his heart, it had been easy—a dinner, a gift, an apology—his fault always. Breaking it off with the ones who'd worked their way into his blood had been harder. Even then, though, he'd scrupulously drawn the line when things had gotten complicated. But with the women who'd turned the tables and ended it with him…

Even when he'd accepted the facts intellectually, his body demanded closure. And the only way to get it had been to swive them within an inch of their lives. Dirty, mindless, nails-down-the-back fornication that left both of them gasping for air. Only then had he been able to shake off the blow.

But the last hour had not cured him of Abby. It had only deepened his addiction. What had he done to himself?

"Did you like it?"

"Yes," he said, almost afraid to speak.

"No need of lady's maids?"

"I could no more serve another than I could fly to the moon." Ever. He would never take another woman to his bed. He knew it as clearly as he knew anything.

"Don't be so sure." She smiled. "You haven't seen my ladies."

"Abby? I may call you Abby, may I not?"

She smiled. "As you have called me a name or two rather more shocking, I think Abby will be fine."

He had to ensure she didn't marry Rosston, and there was only one way to do it. "Abby, I have to go. Right away. As soon as we can manage it."

She sat up, the playfulness on her face gone. "Why?"

"It's for you. For us. I told you I have the money. I must get to it."

"MacHarg, I dinna mean to insult you, but I doubt a man in your situation has the money to—"

"I have the money. Believe me."

She took his hand. "I'll delay the wedding as long as I can. You dinna need to persuade me with promises you canna keep—"

"Abby, I have the money. It's in my home, not here. I'll collect it and return as soon as I can." The idea of finally doing something useful with his money thrilled him. He needed to find Undine, and he needed to think about how he'd make the money liquid in eighteenth-century terms. "With my money in your pocket, you need never worry again."

She gazed at him strangely. "You'll bring the money and then what will happen? Would we marry?"

"Yes, Abby, yes! Don't you see? Rosston will have no power over you."

"No," she said quietly. "Ye would."

"No, no," he protested. "You misunderstand. I don't want to marry you for your power. I want to marry you because"—the words seemed foolish now and calculated to ensnare her—"I care about you."

Something awful flared in her eyes. She climbed out of the bed and pulled the cover off it. "You are not the first man to try that tack," she said, flinging the satin around her. "But you may be the most scurrilous. Was all of this a ruse to try to position yourself at the head of my clan? For all his maneuvering, Rosston, at least, has had the grace not to insist on indulging in his wedding night before his wedding day."

He stood. "Abby, you're wrong."

She picked up his sark and threw it at him. "For God's sake, is there a situation in which you are not at ease with a cock-stand?"

With an aggrieved sigh, he jerked the linen over his head. "Abby, let me—Oh, Christ."

He didn't know how she'd gotten the bow into her hands, but for the second time that day, he was staring down the shaft of an arrow. "I might ask if there's any situation in which you are not at ease threatening mortal danger."

"Put on your plaid and go."

"I'm not leaving until we settle this—"

He heard the *twang* and resultant *thump*, but his head did not fully register the event until he looked down and saw the arrow's fletching still vibrating just below his balls.

"Remove your cock from my view," said Abby, nocking another arrow, "or I shall remove it from your body."

He huffed loudly, stepped carefully over the arrow now firmly lodged in her floor, and pulled the shirttail down as far as it would go.

"I did not bed you with the intent of stealing your place at the head of the clan. You sent me for the chain, ye ken, not the other way around. And I intend to give you my help despite your resistance to it."

She sniffed. "I am not resistant to help. I am resistant to the sort of help that comes shackled to obligation."

God, she was infuriating. Duncan scooped up his plaid and wrapped it several times around his waist. "Believe me when I say you have stripped me of any desire to obligate you further. The money will be a gift. Do with it what you will."

"I don't want your gift, MacHarg."

He strapped the belt around the plaid, thinking for an instant it would be far better applied somewhere else. "Perhaps you'd prefer to earn it?" He gave her a brief and meaningful look.

"Aye," she said calmly. "I would."

He nearly dropped the belt and the plaid. "You're not serious."

"Why wouldn't I be? I dinna want to be obligated to you or any other man for that matter."

"You would sell yourself instead?"

"Why not?" she said, gesturing to her body. "'Tis mine to sell, fair and square."

She meant it. "You're letting your pride get in the way of common sense."

The only response he received was a steely lift of her chin.

He almost pointed out that he was already sleeping with her for free, but apparently she had anticipated this thought, for the look in her eyes made it clear that that accommodation had ended. At once, the specifics of the negotiation took on a very concrete relevance for Duncan.

"All right. You said it was five thousand pounds to save the clan, aye?" He imagined the glorious weeks and months—and acts—it would take for her to work off a debt that size. "How shall we calculate this then?" he said, his eagerness increasing by the second. "Not that I would expect an upstanding lass like yourself to be versed in the commerce of the street, but do you happen to have any knowledge of the going rate for such a transaction?"

She snorted. "'Tis not the going rate with which you need to concern yourself, MacHarg. 'Tis the going rate for *me*. There's a difference, ye ken?"

He swallowed. The memory of that silken hair and those exquisite breasts was still clear in his head. "I do."

She lowered the bow. "The rate is five hundred."

"Per *night*?"

"Per ejaculation."

Today's two ejaculations would have already cost

him a fifth of the entirety of what he would lend her. On the other hand, there was something deeply arousing about the sangfroid with which she was negotiating this. If he had the money in his sporran right now, he would bend her over the bedstead, lift up his plaid, and—

"MacHarg," she said sharply, "your attention is wandering again. Do we have a deal?"

"Well, I…" The likelihood of effectively negotiating a lower rate cost of fornication while sporting a full-on erection did not seem high. Abby shifted, inadvertently exposing a long length of tan thigh. A dark and titillating desire took root in his head.

"What?" She'd seen the change on his face.

"I…I mean, if I am to pay such a price, I-I want certain stipulations." For a man who'd negotiated a dozen million-dollar deals, he sounded about as confident as a teenager trying to negotiate the price of lawn mowing. *Up your game, Duncan.*

"Oh? And what might those be?"

"Well, it's just one thing, really." God, did she have to look at him as if she was measuring his moral worth and finding it lacking? She was the one who had turned a perfectly normal commitment to copulate into a transaction. "I want to finish inside you."

She lowered the bow just enough to see over the arrow. "Why?"

There were many reasons, and he considered each. He wanted to feel when he came what he had tasted and touched. He wanted to feel her release the instant before he found his own. But these paled in comparison to the most important reason.

"I want to know if you're willing to risk getting with child."

He felt as if he had just bet far more than he could afford to lose and was waiting for her to turn over her cards.

He watched the careful calculus in her eyes.

"It's a considerable risk," she said objectively.

"Aye, it is."

"My reputation as a whore would be set."

"Nae. Ye could marry."

"You?"

It was as much a challenge as a question.

"Aye. If you wished it. I wouldna attempt to command your clan, Abby, or you, no matter what you may think. But in bed, when ye chose it, aye, I would. And you could be sure I would never, ever come anywhere but inside ye again."

"*Och*, a poet in our midst. I feel certain Edmund Spenser wishes he was as canny a hand with a sonnet as you."

"Now you're the one dragging your feet," he said. "I want to know ye risk as much as I."

"And what is it you risk, Duncan?"

It was the first time she'd said his name. The rich, throaty reverberation would live forever in his heart. "I take to your bed with no promise of a future with you."

Her grip on the bow relaxed. "I canna think of many men for whom that would be a concern."

"Well, it is for me. So what do you say?"

"I say I will take your offer of a gift, Duncan. Any man who could tell me that deserves to be taken at his word."

It took a moment to orientate himself to the sudden change in momentum. "You're saying you'll take the money—as a gift?"

"Aye."

"And ye willna have to marry Rosston?"

"With five thousand pounds in my pocket?" She made a distinctly Scottish noise. "I'm nae a fool."

Duncan felt light enough to fly. They had all the time in the world. Visions of the coming days danced in his head—days at her side, nights in her—He paused.

"And we can still...I mean when we're together— and alone, of course... Which is to say our, well, 'arrangement' is probably the best word—"

"Tell me, MacHarg," she said, cutting him off from what would have proved to be a very clumsy and possibly insulting finish, "does your position in this other land require you to conduct negotiations?"

He gave her a sheepish look. "Aye."

"And you've managed to make five thousand pounds at it?"

He laughed.

"Let me set your mind at ease. We will revert to the previous terms of our alliance, which is to say you will be free to try to earn your way into my bed any way you wish, and I will be free to judge whether you've achieved what you've set out to accomplish."

He shook his head as if clearing it. "Those were the previous terms? Clearly, I need to pay closer attention."

She smiled. "I'm been telling you that since I met you." She dropped the bow on the bed and put her arms around him. "As for the other...well, that, too, can be earned."

"I don't suppose you're going to tell me how."

"*Och*, I should think not. Suffice to say that, as in all things, attention and a good deal o' devoted practice will put you in the way of success."

He pulled her close, taking in the light scents of fire smoke and lilacs in her hair. He knew he needed to tell her the truth of his origins. And if Abby could accept Undine had the power to pluck him from another land, she could probably accept Undine had the power to pluck him from another century as well. But that could wait until later. The candles were starting to gutter, and her bed looked warm and inviting.

"This has been a day of so many reversals," he said, kissing her, "I dinna want to tempt Fate further. Will ye take me to your bed one last time to sleep?"

"My maid knocks at dawn."

"And I shall be gone a half hour before that."

She dropped the wrap and slipped back under the covers, eyeing him with a giddy smile.

He reached for his buckle. "I canna believe this is the same day that included me failing you so badly with Harry. I am very sorry, Chieftess, for the trouble I've caused you."

She waved away his concern. "Ye didna cause me trouble. Truth is, I didna really want Harry dead. I am not quite chieftess enough to kill a man I hold so dear."

Duncan gave a weak chuckle. "Well, I guess it's a good thing you sent me then—" The realization hit him like a truck. It was all he could do to find breath enough to speak. "Did you send me because you knew I'd fail?"

"Duncan, it's nae a crime to be unready to—"

"Answer me, Abby. Did you send me—pick me among all your men—because ye knew in your heart I couldna kill him?"

"'Tis not as simple as that. A chieftess does not always have the luxury to—"

"To what? Not use people? Not leverage their failings?"

"I dinna consider it a failing that your heart is a compassionate one, Duncan."

"But your men do. That is not a strength in this place, is it? I will never be a man like them in your eyes, will I?"

He saw the pity on her face and thought he might be sick. "Answer me, Abby."

Her lip quivered but there were no tears in her eyes. Just resignation. "No."

"And ye sent me after Harry not caring that my failure would nearly destroy me?"

"Aye."

The only clear thought in the furious storm in his head was that he needed to get away from her.

"Well, you have your wish, Abby." He opened the wardrobe and jerked the frocks out of his way. "You see I *am* learning to pay attention. I just don't like what I see." With a hop, he landed in the darkened stairway and didn't look back until he reemerged in the dark, whiskey-laden air of the cask room.

Twenty-seven

ALTERNATING BETWEEN SHAME AND FURY, DUNCAN stumbled blindly up the stairs to the castle's main floor.

A compassionate heart, was it? Well, he felt none too compassionate now. He needed to find Undine. Where did the white witch sleep in this place, if in fact she slept at all? Surely there was another way to get him home, and he would make sure she found it. He'd had about all he could stand of Clan Kerr.

He could hear the laughter and shouts from the men—the real clansmen—in the bailey. *Does anyone sleep in this godforsaken place?* He headed up the grand staircase to begin his search of the warren of bedrooms.

"MacHarg."

Rosston sounded drunk, though when Duncan turned, the man looked as steady as an ox, watching him from the bottom of the stairs.

"Where were ye just now? I've been looking for ye."

Did he look like bent on murder? Duncan couldn't tell.

"Walking," Duncan said placidly, continuing his ascent. "Couldna sleep."

"*Och*, I suppose Harry's death would weigh heavily on any man."

Duncan froze.

"I mean had he died. And if you were a man."

Duncan charged. Rosston might be a better man with a sword, but he had made the mistake of not unsheathing his sword before he spoke, and Duncan's first punch landed home an instant before Rosston's weapon could clear the metal.

One punch should have been enough. Rosston wove, eyes rolling, like a baby taking his first steps. But Duncan's ego was not so easily appeased. He lowered his center of gravity and unleashed a fist into Rosston's gut. The man doubled over, hands on his knees, vomiting his dinner onto the floor.

Only Nab's appearance kept Duncan from adding, "I just finished bedding your girlfriend, by the way. At her invitation. Who's the man now?" But he might as well have, for when Rosston finally lifted his head, he had murder in his eyes.

Duncan needed no further invitation. With an iron shoulder, he knocked the man to the floor and crouched beside him, showering him with punches.

"Stop it!" The horrified cry barely broke through the din of his fury.

He had a distant sensation of someone tugging his collar, then a clear apprehension of it. Abby jerked him off his feet. Several clansmen had appeared since he'd last taken notice. Nab held Grendel by the scruff of his neck.

"*Fool*," she said to Duncan.

"Take him to the barn," she said to the footmen,

"and bring Rosston to my room with hot water, towels, and a needle and thread."

Twenty-eight

THE CLANSMEN, WHO HAD NO SPECIAL LOVE FOR THE stranger in their midst, dumped Duncan unceremoniously onto the barn's dirt floor, which immediately enveloped him in a stinking cloud of dust.

"Fuck you," Duncan called matter-of-factly to the retreating figures. He lifted himself to his elbows and picked detritus from his mouth.

"*Och*," one clansman said. "Did you hear that? I think the poor fellow said he's in need of a pillow."

A shovelful of warm cow dung landed next to Duncan.

The men laughed.

Duncan let out several long oaths, the last consigning Abby to a particularly warm place in Hell for leaders who abuse their power. She'd been the commander of men so long the line between leadership and manipulation had begun to blur. From the moment he'd landed in this godforsaken time, his vanity had taken a bruising. But to find out his most useful characteristic as a strong arm was the dependability of his ineffectiveness had been devastating.

He dragged himself to a sitting position, and a rag

plopped beside him. He turned to find Jock standing behind him.

"'Twas a novice's error, laddie," the man said, gesturing toward the main castle hall.

"Ha!" Duncan wiped his face. "I'm hardly a novice. Rosston's lucky he can still walk."

"I didn't mean your fighting, ye clod-heid."

An image of a barely dressed Abby tenderly daubing Rosston's wounds sprung to life in his head. "Oh. Right." Duncan sighed. "I suppose that willna go down in history as the smartest move I've ever made."

Jock slipped a slim glass bottle from his coat. He uncorked it and handed it to Duncan. Duncan drank freely. Now there was a taste he could live with. He wiped his mouth and returned the bottle. "Thank you."

"You've taken a fancy to the chieftess?" Jock took a long draft himself.

Duncan schooled his features. He had no wish to expose the tenuous connection he and Abby shared. Scrutiny would certainly destroy it, and, worse, it would put Abby in a deeply embarrassing position. But a bullheaded crush on her would be understandable in any man between fifteen and fifty, and it would certainly explain his scrum with Rosston.

"Mm," Duncan said obscurely.

"You wouldna be the first man to have fallen in love with her," Jock said, "though you may be the first to press his suit with such, er…"

"Stupidity?"

"Unqualified abandon. Though there is *some* advantage to defying expectations, ye ken."

Duncan climbed to his feet and dusted himself off.

"From the sound of it, I'm guessing you'd recommend I give up?"

Jock gave him a sad, avuncular smile. "I am an accountant, after all. Our hearts might wish one thing, but I am unable to ignore the balance sheet. And to be fair, if the lady marries, it will have to be for money. She runs a rather large concern, as you have undoubtedly noticed. My own thoughts…" He stopped, eyeing Duncan carefully. "Well, 'tis not for me to say."

"No, please. Say it."

Jock lowered his voice. "Between you and me, I have encouraged her not to accept Rosston."

Duncan brightened. "You *are* a romantic."

The man laughed. "I wish it were so, lad, but, nae, I have seen what uneasy marital partnerships can do to an organization. The increase in assets may not be worth the loss of goodwill among the stockholders."

"You're saying the clansmen don't like Rosston?"

"Most do. But there are enough who don't to make the decision a risky one."

"Her father likes him. And, by the way, I was *shocked* to find out he's still alive."

"If you call that living," Jock said. "Aye, the chieftess has her challenges."

"She is quite good at managing them, though, isn't she? I mean for such a young woman. She is quite determined to be everything a male chief would be. She even handles a sword like one." He closed his eyes and remembered the lesson. He'd liked that almost as much as what had followed. A lesson where one learned better without one's clothes? That's the sort of studying he liked to do. Then it struck him and his eyes flew open. "Jock, who taught her to use a sword? Her mother?"

Jock laughed. "Hardly. I believe it was Rosston. They were thick as thieves when they were young."

Duncan gritted his teeth. That was exactly the sort of thing he could imagine Rosston doing.

Jock must have seen his face, for he shook his head. "Laddie, you're not much of a match for a wealthy clan chief. I advise ye to give it up." He extended his hand and Duncan took it.

Jock was probably right, and while Duncan had no intention of following the advice, there was no harm in letting the steward think he had.

"Well, I suppose there are other women in this place, aye?" Duncan said with a sheepish grin. "There's that maid of Abby's, and the new nurse, Molly—do you know her? Those eyes are quite fetching."

Jock hesitated. "The maid is Nora, but I'd stay away from the nurse. She is a favorite of Lachlan's."

There was something in the turn of the word that made Duncan look up. "You canna be suggesting…?"

Jock made an embarrassed shrug.

"The man's half out of his senses," Duncan said, appalled.

"But half in—and used to living like a lord."

"Good God! Do you think he can…? I mean, he is quite old."

"The vanity of youth." Jock chuckled. "I had a great uncle who spent every birthday with one of the beauties at the whorehouse in Langholm. On his sixtieth birthday, he treated himself to all six at once."

Duncan lifted the bottle, trying hard to unsee *that*

picture. "All right, but what is *her* motivation?" He hoped it was money—a *lot* of it.

"I think I know—and if I'm right, I fear 'tis none too good for our chieftess."

Other than accidentally walking in on such a scene, Duncan couldn't imagine how a dalliance conducted by Abby's father could affect Abby.

"Molly's motivation is power—at least by association. Lachlan wants a son to lead his clan."

Duncan's jaw didn't just drop. It nearly unhinged itself and took a turn about the barn. "But Abby's already assumed the chiefship. She is chief."

"At the birth of a younger brother, she would revert instantly to second in line."

Duncan turned over the scenario in his head. "But she'd at least be regent to her wee brother, would she not? Until he could serve on his own?"

"I doubt it. Lachlan would convince them to appoint a man."

Rosston. "But Lachlan wasn't able to sway the clansmen when he wanted Abby removed from consideration the first time. The clansmen like her, I think. It's grudging, perhaps, but it's there."

"That was different," Jock said. "Their only other choice was someone outside the family. A son fathered by Lachlan would be a different matter—very different."

The tenure of a clan chief seemed more fraught with peril than that of a Wall Street CEO. "Of course, if the clan has no assets and, therefore, no future, all that strategic copulation would be for naught."

Jock laughed. "I guess we'll have to hope for both

their sakes that copulation is its own reward." He tucked the bottle back in his coat. "There are some blankets in the eaves if ye get cold tonight."

Duncan said, "I don't suppose I'll be let back in the castle."

"Not tonight. Perhaps with a night to sleep on it, Lady Kerr will soften."

Despite his predicament, Duncan hoped nothing transpired in Lady Kerr's bedroom that would leave her seeing the world in a different way come morning. He glanced at the towering eaves and decided his plaid would be blanket enough.

The steward made his way toward the barn door.

"Hang on," Duncan said. "Have you seen Undine? I was hoping to talk to her."

"Gone till the morrow," Jock said, brows knitting. "'Tis no swipe at you, lad, when I say you may need to aim for a woman a bit less challenging—a tavern wench, a milkmaid. Nora is a good start. You never know, she may have been looking all her life for a devil-brindled lad with a head as hard as rock."

Twenty-nine

BATHED IN EARLY MORNING SUNSHINE, DUNCAN CUT through the pool's cool current like scissors through paper. There was nothing, he thought, like a hundred laps in bracing water to clear his head. Stroke, touch, turn. Abby be damned. Stroke, touch, turn. Rosston too.

On the last turn, he rolled onto his back and stared into the sky, letting his dying momentum carry him into the center of the water. His clothes, heaped on the far shore, might be a filthy mess, but at least the body put in them would be clean. He tried to clear his head of Abby, but every time he did, the ledge on which she'd stood, damp and golden limbed, would drift into view, making any sort of clearheadedness impossible.

Abby had a mess on her hands. Perhaps he was responsible for some of it. But she would survive. Even at her young age, she knew how to get what she wanted. Look at him. He'd been reduced to a bumbling knave in her carefully plotted drama, publicly rebuked and thrown off for a wealthier suitor, and yet, here he was, still determined to get her the money she needed. But that at least would give him the closure he needed to be done with this place and with her.

Damn you, Undine, ye great pale wraith. Get your cauldron-stirring arse back to Castle Kerr so I can—

"You're looking for me?"

Duncan plunged his nakedness below the water so fast his feet tangled in the weeds and he snorted a sinus full of water trying to right himself.

Undine sat on a rocky outcropping, inclined on her elbows to enjoy the sun. Duncan had looked at that outcropping no more than thirty seconds earlier, at which time it had been completely devoid of human habitation, as had every inch of rock and ground in a fifty-yard radius.

"Are ye in need of a swimming lesson too?" she asked as he coughed. "Abby's probably still abed, but there's a lad in the stables who—"

"I dinna need a lesson. I've had all the damn lessons I want. I'm ready to go back."

"Oh." She sat up straighter and wrapped her arms around her knees. "You've put Lady Kerr in the way of what she needs?"

He wasn't sure quite how to answer. As Undine seemed to know everything that transpired, he couldn't tell if her words were a sly reference to his liaison with Abby, a crueler reference to delivering Rosston into Abby's arms after the fight, or a perfectly straightforward question about whether he'd earned the right to be called Abby's strong arm.

Gah! Why didn't borderland women come with instruction books?

He treaded in place, hoping the combination of

sunshine and moving current made the water less than entirely transparent. "I, well, I have certainly made some progress," he said, hoping the answer would suffice no matter what the question had been.

"I see."

"But I need to go back to my own time. As soon as I can. Today, if possible."

"Unfortunately, Mr. MacHarg, that's not how the spell works."

"Look," he said, growing irritated, "I'll come back here. You have my word. Can't you just free me from it for a day—like a parole or something?"

"The spell is not some sort of whim. It was duly cast, and it stands—until it is fulfilled."

"But I need to help *Abby*, dammit."

He wished he hadn't raised his voice. He wished he hadn't used Abby's Christian name. Undine's eyes penetrated him like tiny tunnel borers, and he suddenly felt as if he couldn't lie even if he tried. "I am giving her ladyship the money she needs to avoid marrying Rosston. I *have* money," he added pointedly. "In my own time."

"Has Abby—and I see we can speak of her in familiar terms now, aye?—has she asked you for money?"

He shook his head. "Nae."

"So this is a gift?"

"Yes."

"And what makes you think she'd accept such a thing from you?"

Undine didn't know? Perhaps there was a limit to her capabilities. To test that theory, he pushed every thought of his sojourn in Abby's bed out of his head, concentrating instead on a red grouse that was hopping through the underbrush at the water's edge. If Undine would read his mind, let her discover his great love of birds, nothing more.

"Mr. MacHarg, has she given you the slightest reason to believe she would take money from you?"

Red grouse. Nest: found on the ground. Eggs: yellow and mottled.

"Mr. MacHarg," she repeated, with more than a hint of temper.

Mating habits: live in pairs. Food: heather sprouts. Fate: will be shot by the thousands in the future at the hands of Abby Kerr's noble ilk.

"MacHarg!"

It worked! Ha! Triumphant, he did a full somersault in the water. When he emerged, he found himself under Undine's fiery gaze, which severely tempered his glee. *Don't piss off the Wizard of Oz, lad. She's the one who'll be getting you home.*

"Does it matter if she asked for it?" he said. "If she turns me down, she'll turn me down. I want at least to give her a choice. I would think you'd want that for her too."

Undine fell silent. He had finally hit on something that resonated with the woman. She began to pace.

"You dinna come from 1706?"

It was a question, not a statement, which surprised him. He'd assumed she knew exactly when and where his home was. "No."

"I have to believe you come from the future. You're too quick-witted for a man from the past. Am I correct?"

Quick-witted? Duncan had spent the last two days

feeling about as quick-witted as a bucket of muck. And while he appreciated the compliment—one of the few he'd been paid since he'd arrived—he found himself hesitating to reveal anything specific about his origins. Age of Enlightenment or no, an end to the burning of witches didn't come to the British Isles until the 1730s, and he remembered the alarm on Undine's face when he called her one.

"You needn't fear me, Mr. MacHarg. In fact, I'm about the only person here you need not fear."

Duncan considered his options. He needed Undine's help. He had better be willing to let her know he trusted her. "Aye, I'm from the future."

This stunning, unfathomable admission she accepted as fact, her face barely changing. How many other men had said the same to her? he wondered. How many spells had she wrought like his?

"Across how many years have you traveled?"

Here he drew the line. Truthful he would be. Specific, no. "Many."

The implications of that statement washed over her, and her face fell.

"Well, then," she said, "I'm very sorry to have to tell you your money willna work here."

That he'd already considered. "I wouldna bring money. I'd bring gold."

But instead of admiring his foresight, she shook her head sadly.

"Gold works everywhere," he insisted. "It has since before Moses."

"Ye canna bring gold through time. The spell won't allow it."

"That's ridiculous. I—" He remembered his pen. He *hadn't* dropped it. The gold appointments had been stripped as he passed through the centuries. He felt a growing pit in his stomach. "Silver, then."

"No silver, no gold, no gems, no pearls. Nothing with concentrated value." Her face softened in something as close to kindness as he'd seen since he met her. "I'm sorry, Duncan. I'll do what I can to help you help Abby, but we canna do it with your money or gold."

Duncan's sense of purpose drained away like blood from a harpooned selkie. Money was the one thing he possessed that could truly help Abby. Aside from that, he was just a distraction—a harmful distraction, in truth. For the last few hours, the determination to be of value had given him his old assured self back. Without it, he felt himself drifting down and down—

An unexpected splash made him turn. Undine surfaced a dozen feet in front of him, naked. The mild fear he felt toward her soundly trumped any attraction, but his cock, as always, operated according to its own set of principles, and it shifted instantly to life. She was, despite everything, a beautiful woman. The contrasting tugs of attraction and repellence lent an odd, otherworldly sense to the moment.

No more than her eyes showed as she moved effortlessly through the water, reminding him of the crocodile in *Peter Pan*, though the sensuous curves of her hips and breasts were clearly visible below the surface.

"Do you not feel the power of this pool?" she said.

He hadn't until she'd asked. But now he saw that the waters around him churned and shifted according to more than her movement, and the pool's buoyancy increased, as if it was being infused with helium. If there was magic to be had here, he wondered if in fact it came from her, not the water.

Her hair had loosened from its tightly pinned knot. Transfixed, he watched the long strands swim in wriggling lines behind her, like a school of golden eels. He found himself wondering what it might be like to draw his fingers through it.

"The power of the water does not come from its potential for impropriety," she said, interrupting his daydream, "though that can be an effect. It comes from the power to concentrate your mind. What do you want, MacHarg? Think."

He closed his eyes and tried to sort through the conflicting desires in his head. "To go home. To free Abby. To prove my worth."

"That is three things. You defeat yourself before you even begin. Concentrate."

He did. He saw a red-haired man in a Highlander Regimental kilt—him, it must be, though the man was older—middle-aged, even—sinking on top of a young woman in a meadow. As they kissed, drumming rose in the distance, an insistent, forbidding drumming. The lovers vanished, replaced by the thunder of cannons and an acrid cloud of smoke that galloped toward him like a sandstorm, gaining speed and height as it rolled over top of the never-ending lines of redcoats descending the hills until it filled the sky with black.

Heart pounding, his eyes flew open. All of it, somehow, represented a danger to Abby.

"You saw it, didn't you?" Undine said, "The change that's coming?"

"Aye." The sense of devastation was as clear in his head as if he'd been part of the battle, and he struggled to slow his heart.

"Scotland will be destroyed. This is more important than Abby or Rosston or the canal or your vanity, MacHarg. What can *you* do to change what happens? Why were *you* sent?"

He didn't know. He could fight with passion but no skill. He thought of the English and what they would do in time to the Scots, though he knew it didn't happen—not in its ugly, disgusting entirety—until the 1740s.

Undine dove under the water and made a wide, easy circle around him. She moved like a great ray, banking with the barest effort and staying submerged for so long, Duncan's own lungs cried for air.

"There's a colonel in the English army," she said, surfacing without a gasp, "a cruel, vainglorious man, but a man smart enough to know the value the Kerr canal might represent to England. His name is John Bridgewater and he's pushing the English army to claim this piece of Scotland. It is my most heartfelt wish to remove him from power."

Duncan knew well the story of the Debatable Lands, the tiny sliver of Scotland that changed hands between England and Scotland again and again during the warring years. But he didn't have specific knowledge about a confrontation in 1706.

"How do you know this?"

"I have acquaintances on both sides of the border,"

she said with a mysterious smile. "Sometimes information makes its way from the English army to my friends here."

Duncan remembered Abby's reference at the clan meeting to the spy who brought her information about the army. He wondered if he was looking at the secret envoy right now. If so, Undine was involved in a very risky game.

"But you're an Englishwoman," he said, shocked. As such, passing secrets to the Scots made her a traitor.

"I am a believer in peace, MacHarg. Helping those transgressed against is a way to keep power balanced and guns quiet. There are a number of us who feel that way—a growing number."

Was Abby part of this mission too? The look in Undine's eyes made him refrain from asking. "I want to help Abby but I don't know how."

"Maybe it's enough that you want to," Undine said. "Maybe you simply need to keep that in your heart and the answer will come to you."

"*Och*." He hated not having a plan, not having a goal to shoot for. He was not one to stand on the sidelines. But if Abby was going to need help, that was going to be his only choice. "Waiting is the worst job."

Undine smiled. "We canna choose how we will be needed. But we can choose to accept our assignment with grace. I think you had better get dressed, though. Serafina has started from the castle to find you, and I should hate for her introduction to the future of Scottish soldiering to be illustrated in quite such vivid detail."

Thirty

DUNCAN HAD MANAGED TO DRESS HIMSELF WITH-
out feeling too much under Undine's observant
eye, and now they walked the path that would
return them to the castle. "What does Serafina want
of me?"

Undine looked at him, surprised. "I have no idea,"
she said, as if his assumption of her knowledge of
Serafina's state of mind had been akin to an assumption
she could fly. "I haven't seen her since yesterday."

"Then how did you—" He stopped. There was no
point in asking how Undine knew anything. He just
needed to accept it. Just as he needed to accept that
serving Abby meant stripping himself of preconceived
ideas of being her savior or protector.

"How has your strong-arm training been?"

"Well, I had my first go at swords yesterday—
stripped to the skin, of course."

Undine coughed. "Stripped to the skin?"

"Aye. I got the traditional first lesson. And I'm
surprised to say I think it really helped."

"I'm curious, sir. Who gave you your lesson?"

"Actually, it was—" He stopped. "There is no tradition of stripping, is there?"

Undine shook her head.

Idiot. "Fell for it, did I?"

"I'm afraid so. That must have been quite the spectacle. I'm afraid your teacher was having a bit of fun with you."

"Aye. So it seems." He supposed it was the price he had to pay for observing her diving session. Given what the naked lesson led to, it wasn't too much of a comeuppance.

Serafina came into view at the next rise. She was racing Grendel downhill, and Duncan was reminded how young she really was.

She saw them and waved. Duncan waved back. A thought had been niggling at him since they'd started back. "Maybe I do know why I was sent here, Undine."

She regarded him thoughtfully. "Oh?"

"Because I know what will happen."

Undine chuckled. "Dinna be so certain. First, no man knows everything. While you stand outside the castle wall waiting for the tyrant to fall as has been written, you dinna see the wagon that runs ye down. Second, the past is more mutable than ye know. A delayed attack here, a missed appointment there. Suddenly, the warp and weft has changed, even if the fabric remains whole. And third, even if ye do know, ye must take care. That kind of knowledge is a danger to possess. Do not let any but those you trust absolutely know about it."

"Are you saying I shouldn't tell Abby about the future?" *Or you,* he almost added, for she had asked him no questions about it since his admission at the pool.

"I'm saying use your knowledge with care, and dinna be too certain of it."

Serafina arrived beside them, cutting short the possibility of asking anything more.

Her energetic curtsy was punctuated by Grendel's barks. "I've been looking for you, Mr. MacHarg. I hope you have recovered from your run-in with Lord Kerr. Lady Kerr was up half the night stitching his chin. I dinna think the poor man has been having much luck convincing her he's the man she wants. I do wonder if the nursing session might have helped turn the tide for him."

"Duncan has fallen in love with Lady Kerr," Undine said abruptly.

"*Oh*. I'm so sorry. I shouldn't have said—"

"I have not fallen in love with Lady Kerr," Duncan said, rising from a round of Grendel ear scratching. "And she has *decidedly* not fallen in love with me."

"Then the fight was not about Lady Kerr?"

"Hardly," Duncan said. "Rosston made a comment regarding a member of Clan MacHarg that required a response. That is all."

Undine said, "I see you're rewriting history already, MacHarg."

"If it's any comfort," Serafina said, "Lord Kerr has not made an appearance since it happened. Of course, neither has Lady Kerr, and I—" Her face clouded. "Oh, dear. That's probably not a good thing, is it?"

Duncan groaned. If Serafina was right, he'd certainly been a fool.

Undine said to him, "Sometimes one forgets to weigh the cost of a lifetime of regret against the satisfaction of a few moments."

"I get it," Duncan said sharply. "I screwed up."

She touched his arm. "I meant Abby, my friend."

Clearly distressed by her misstep, Serafina said, "Sir, I'm sorry to have added to your burden. But if you're in love with Abby, you cannot let this lie."

"And that is my cue," Undine said. "There are some things over which even a fortune-teller has no power. Best of luck in untangling this." She hurried off.

Duncan, who was in no mood to be upbraided over his failures with Abby, said, "But this is not the reason you came looking for me," he said. "What can I do for you, milady?"

"I am full serious," said Serafina, who would not be diverted. "If you love her, you must act. And if you do not love her, say so now. I know ye wouldna lie."

"Well, I...I mean, Lord Kerr seems to have..." He wilted under her probing gaze. "Aye," he said, "I do love her if ye must know."

"I *knew* that was why the spell brought ye here! But have you told her?"

"What if I have? It didn't do me any good. She spent half the night tending to Rosston's cheek and the other half to his—"

"Mr. Mac*Harg*!"

"I was going to say *vanity*. In any case, Lady Kerr is rather angry at me right now."

"May I ask why?"

Duncan shifted. "It would probably be better if you didn't."

"I see. May I give you some advice?"

Her tone indicated what followed would be less like advice than a direct order. "Well—"

"First, get yourself a clean set of clothes. That plaid is filthy. Would ye wear a butcher's apron to a ball? Second, never make reference to any other suitor. 'Tis impolite, it betrays a lack of confidence, and it paints you as a churl. Third," she said, holding up a hand to stop his response, "apologize. Instantly. Effusively. And quite possibly from your knees."

Duncan crossed his arms. Regret was one thing. An apology was another. "*Mmphf.*"

"And fourth, kiss her. Thoroughly."

He shifted. "She might not let me."

"She might not *let* you? Mr. MacHarg, if that is your primary concern, we have a much bigger problem on our hands."

"What I mean is, she may not want an apology—or like me kissing her."

She gave him a fiery look. "You will bear up somehow. I'm sure of it."

"Your hair color suits you. Has anyone ever told you that?"

"Many. My father, especially."

"Was it his color too?" Duncan's had come straight from his grand-da through his ma to him.

"My da? No, black as coal, but he was my stepfather. My real father died before I was born. And my mother's hair was golden. I suppose it came through her people. I never met them. They came from up north."

Duncan brushed off his plaid self-consciously and offered her his arm. "Have you finished your instructions? If so, and if I promise to abide by them, will you do me the honor of telling me why you were looking for me?"

"There was a note from Lady Kerr. She has called a meeting of clansmen—"

"Not again!" He calculated the time it would take him to reach the castle.

"Dinna worry. The meeting is not till the strike of ten. But I was to fetch you and to tell you the meeting is to be kept secret."

"Oh. Well then." The bells at the castle had only just struck nine. What secret did Abby Kerr have to share with him?

"Mr. MacHarg, may I observe you are looking a bit smug for a man who needs to be guided by humility—especially as you are not the only clansman invited to this meeting."

Thirty-one

DUNCAN TUGGED THE BELT TIGHT OVER A CLEAN PLAID and sark, pinned the wool at his shoulder, and flew down the hall with Grendel at his side. He intended to be on time, at her side, and adding value from the start. He might not be the only man there, but he would be the handsomest, tallest, and smartest.

However, the Great Hall was empty. And after the footmen there claimed to know nothing of the meeting, Duncan began to wonder if perhaps Abby had played another trick on him.

"Any thoughts, old boy?"

Grendel looked in the direction of Abby's room and whined.

"*Och.* Are you sure?" Duncan could face her in a room full of men. Finding her lounging in bed, eating bacon and eggs with Rosston would do very little for his morning.

Fortunately, Abby did not answer his knock. On the chance he might catch her with her father, he headed up the stairs.

He rounded the top and found Molly standing by

the bed, bundling a blanket around her shoulders. Her cheeks were flushed. So were Lachlan's.

Duncan scooped her cap from the floor and handed it to her. "Do you know where her ladyship is?" *And does her ladyship know you are bedding her father?*

Molly gave him a piercing look. He hadn't seen her hair before. It was blond, which surprised him, given her dark brows and eyes.

"I havena seen her since yesterday."

He ducked his head toward Lachlan, who seemed to be staring out a window that didn't exist. "Is he in his head?"

"Bugger yourself," Lachlan said.

Duncan sighed. "I'd like a word alone with his lordship."

Molly gave him a look, and she left.

"Pretty girl," Duncan said evenly.

"I thought ye were foucking my daughter. Or has she o'erthrown ye?"

"I feel certain the only foucking your daughter will be doing will be with her new husband. I'm told a wedding has been set for this week. She's marrying Rosston."

Lachlan's eyes narrowed. He wanted to believe Duncan, that much was clear, but he was canny enough to know that if a wedding date had been set, somewhere in the reaches of the sandstorm he called memory, he'd be able to remember someone telling him about it.

"The thing is," Duncan went on, "I have nae doubt the happy bride and groom will set about producing an heir *tout suite*. Winning over the clansmen is a tricky road, as you ken. Abby alone…" Duncan shook his head with regret. "The odds there are mixed at best. Abby with groom…better. Definitely better. But Abby with groom and son…" He ran a hand through his hair, pleased. "'Tis a combination I would not bet against. In fact," he said, stroking his chin, "I suppose any man could father the child, really, no matter who the groom was, so long as Abby could say she's produced an heir."

Lachlan purpled instantly, his tongue churning thickly.

"But that is not what I have come for," Duncan said. "You see, Lord Kerr, I am here on a very short visit. I have been tasked with helping your daughter overcome her financial difficulties. When I have done that, I will leave here. Forever. I should think that might be a very attractive proposition to you."

Lachlan leaned forward far enough to spit out, "Bastard," before collapsing back onto his pillows.

"The quickest way, it seems to me, is by breaking the back of this canal," Duncan said. "Or rather unbreaking it."

"Taxes," Lachlan croaked.

"Pardon?"

"Taxes. We paid too much."

Duncan had never met a Scot who didn't think he paid too much tax, so he didn't put too much weight on Lachlan's assessment. Nonetheless, the complaint sounded like a bone the man had been chewing for a long time.

"Taxes for what?" Duncan asked. "The canal?"

"I told Moira, look at the taxes. But, no, Lachlan, dear, that is for you. I must ride. Ride, ride, ride. She rides all day, but she doesn't look. She doesn't *see*!" He clutched his covers, terrified. "Where's Molly? I want Molly. Molly!"

The girl appeared so quickly, Duncan wondered if she'd been standing outside the door. He rather hoped she had. The message he'd delivered was meant as much for her as Lachlan.

He heard the first strike of ten.

"Dammit," he said and caught Molly's arm. "Where might a group meet if they're not meeting in the Great Hall?"

"Do ye mean the group Lady Kerr has called together? I hear they're in the Lady chapel."

The sad cry of "*Moira!*" resounded as Duncan hurried down and down.

Thirty-two

THE TINY CHAPEL SAT LIKE A TREE HOUSE ON AN ancient gray battlement wall that divided two baileys. A man Duncan did not recognize stood inside one of the chapel windows. He shook his head when he saw Duncan pelting across the bailey's worn cobbles.

Duncan strained for the sounds of talking and heard an upraised voice—not Abby's—though he could not make out the words.

God, he hated to be late for meetings. At his firm, the last person to arrive at meetings not only had to take notes, but refill coffee, stand, and pay a hundred-dollar fine. He doubted there'd be much coffee or note-taking here.

He hurdled over a largish trough, clearing it easily but failing to anticipate the orange tabby cleaning itself on the other side.

The cat screeched. Duncan's ankle turned, and he hit the ground palms first. He was scrabbling to his feet when he heard the *whoosh* and *smack*.

The arrow had missed him, only just, and spun to a stop after hitting the cobbles. Standing, he scanned the sight lines. No one on the wall. No one now in the chapel window. No one in any of the castle windows, though the curtain in one window fluttered suggestively. It dawned on him that the angled shadow behind him was cast by the tower in which Lachlan was situated. But there was no one in any of those windows either, at least no one he could see.

He waited a moment for another arrow—he'd just as soon have a chance to see his death hurtling toward him—then, concluding his attacker had meant to catch Duncan's attention not put him in an early grave, he crouched down and picked up the arrow.

There was nothing distinctive about the design. It was very plain, with feather fletches, and looked more or less like the same ones Abby had used—Duncan froze. Squinting, he gazed up at Lachlan's tower, did a quick spatial calculation, and followed the castle roof-line till he found what must be the window by Abby's desk. It was impossible to tell from where specifically the arrow had been launched, but Abby's window could not be ruled out. His heart sank.

The arrow's shaft was unmarked, though a small piece of paper, no wider than his thumb, had been quilled around it. He unrolled the paper. "Leave now and never return" had been written in a tight script. He tried to remember the look of the writing in the expense book on Abby's desk, but nothing concrete came to him.

He shoved the note in his sporran and took the stairs to the battlement wall two at a time.

This chapel was in considerably better shape than the one on the banks of the Esk. Red, blue, and emerald glass sparkled in the intricate scenes rendered in the window over the door, and numerous grotesques lined the chapel's roofline. The heavy door was propped open, and Duncan was surprised to see no more than a half dozen men. They stood in a close circle near the altar, most of them members of Rosston's sept. Unfortunately, Rosston was among them. Duncan stepped inside.

The men fell silent when they saw him. Duncan wondered if there was a bow stashed nearby.

"I saw ye trip," said one wearing a dun-colored cap. "Take care on those cobbles." As the warning seemed less concerned than amused, Duncan refrained from offering his thanks.

Rosston stood with his hands on his hips. With his dark coloring, sullen expression, and Abby's neat black stitches anchoring a fiery length of crimson across his chin, he looked like a cross between Oscar De La Hoya and a five-year-old child.

Duncan sighed. He walked up to Rosston, purposefully moved the arrow from under his right arm to under his left, and extended a hand.

"My apologies, Lord Kerr."

In truth, Rosston owed him as much of an apology as Duncan owed him, and possibly even a thank-you given what followed the smackdown, but Duncan knew the melee had upset Abby and he held himself responsible. He also knew that, unlike Duncan himself, Rosston looked liked he'd been dragged through a hedgerow by a four-inch chain.

Rosston did not take the proffered hand.

"Lady Kerr," one of the men said, and Duncan let his hand fall to his side.

Abby stood at the door, bow over her shoulder, beside Jock. The subtle greens and browns she wore made her look like a forest goddess in some Edward Burne-Jones painting. The look on her face made it clear she had witnessed Duncan's exchange with Rosston.

"Gentlemen," she said flatly, managing in three syllables to greet the group, imply the seriousness of what was to come, and suggesting at least one among them did not measure up to the characteristics inherent in the word. In this case, Rosston was her target, and the look she cast in his direction carried such stinging disapproval, Duncan nearly felt sorry for the man.

Rosston made an unregretful noise.

Duncan withdrew the arrow from under his arm and placed it with a firm snap on the priest's table. Abby's eyes narrowed, but he saw nothing in them that might betray a previous knowledge.

He was taking a seat on the front pew when a warning noise from Abby brought him up again.

"We will hardly be making our council here, Mr. MacHarg."

"No, of course not."

Rosston but not Abby caught the hint of mock obsequiousness in his voice and surprised him by smiling.

"Come, gentlemen," Abby said.

They trouped through a side door and down a dark stairwell—*Was the entire bloody place lined with hidden stairs?*—into a windowless, though Duncan thought probably not staircase-less, room. With only the scant light coming down the stairwell to guide them, the men took seats at benches on either side of a long table. Duncan wondered if the space had once been a classroom. Abby, perhaps responding to the sense of the place, clasped her hands behind her, teacher-like, until, one by one, the men fell silent.

"We have a problem with the English," she said.

One of the younger men snickered, but Rosston sat straighter and Duncan heard the strain in her voice.

"I've called you here today," she said, "because I know I can trust you. I received word today from someone on the English side who is sympathetic to our cause."

Undine again? Or is there another informant?

"Bridgewater is making immediate plans to attack, despite the fact the English army has strict orders from the queen not to stir things up during this delicate time."

The "delicate time" Abby referred to being the negotiations for the Act of Union, the treaty that would strip Scotland of its independence in exchange for ensuring the financial health of a few influential Scots. Duncan, swallowing his disgust, thought of the lines from Robert Burns:

> *We're bought and sold for English gold,*
> *Such a parcel of rogues in a nation!*

"The time is delicate for Clan Kerr as well," she added. "'Tis no surprise to anyone that we are in desperate financial straits. We can make a go of it with the canal if I can get a loan from the bank."

Rosston held his tongue this time. Duncan realized with a shock that Abby and Rosston must have reached an agreement on the subject. There was a palpable sense of negotiated truce in the air, and he wondered what other subjects they'd come to terms on. Oh God, how he regretted that fight with Rosston.

When he wrestled his attention back to the matter at hand, the men were discussing how to rally the clans to the border.

"No," Duncan said, interrupting. "We mustn't let the English army choose the mode of battle or the battlefield. We won't concede the terms of the fight to them."

"What choice do we have?" Jock demanded. "They're attacking."

"Perhaps ye think we can just send a footman over with an invitation," one of the young men said, then laughed.

"Well…" Duncan hadn't totally thought things out before he spoke—a very unwise move. But he'd watched enough war movies to know there was always a way for the good guys to outsmart their enemy. Then it came to him. "Say you're a man in charge of a large army who's not supposed to attack but wants to anyhow. What's the one thing that would make you wait?"

Rosston held up a hand to stop the snickering. "What?"

"If you heard the other side was going to attack you."

Abby looked at Rosston and nodded. "He's right."

"So we're going to attack the English army instead, just to choose our own time and battlefield?"

"Well, it's always better to do the choosing yourself," Duncan said, thinking of the choices Abby may have made in the last twelve hours. "It's called having the weather gage in sailing, and it gives you a distinct advantage. But I'm not suggesting we attack. I'm suggesting we let them *think* we're attacking."

"Shall we send them a letter?" the capped man said with sarcasm.

"No," Duncan said carefully.

"They'd ken it was a trick. And it would be," Abby said, getting into the spirit. "We have to make them think they found out about the planned attack on their own, right?"

Duncan grinned. "That's right."

"How?"

"I've got it! *The Man Who Never Was*!" Duncan remembered the movie clearly. It had been a fairly pulpy melodrama about England fighting the Germans during World War II. He had watched it with his father on one of the last days before the bastard did a runner, and his father had downed half a dozen cans of beer and ranted about the plot being "too bloody convoluted."

"The man who never was?"

"It's a"—he stopped himself before he said *movie*—"way of confusing your enemy. You plant a dead body with misinformation on it in a place where the other side will find it. For example, if you're going to attack Sicily, the papers on the body say you're going to attack Sardinia," he said, repeating the subject of the planted misinformation in the story. "The trick is making the other side believe the dead person is a person with insider knowledge of your plans."

"So we kill Jock?" the man with the cap said with a guffaw.

"No." Duncan smiled. "Not required. The dead

person just has to seem like a person who would be trusted with Kerr secrets. For example, he'd need to be wearing a plaid, and maybe carrying a flask with Kerr whiskey in it. He'd probably have a letter or two in his sporran in addition to the letter stating the plans for the attack—No, I take it back. The letter about the attack would have to be hidden on him somewhere…"

"The hollow heel in his boot?"

"A false back in his sporran?"

"Written on silk and stuffed into a wooden tooth?"

Duncan eyed his companions. "You people scare me. Aye, any of those things would do—so long as we could count on the English army finding the letter."

The man who'd suggested the wooden tooth grinned, revealing an entire set of them.

"Seems to me," Abby said, "the only problem is finding a dead man."

One of the younger men sized up Duncan.

"I'm sure Lady Kerr wasna suggesting we kill someone," Rosston said, though his tone suggested that wasn't an unreasonable idea.

"Then how do we find a body?"

Christ, the Middle Ages ended like eighteen years ago. Aren't people dying by the hour? "Well…" Duncan quickly paged through the random snippets of science fiction, horror movies, and episodes of *CSI* stowed away in the dusty rafters of his brain.

"We could rob a grave," Abby suggested.

"Unfortunately, we can't have the man be too dead. Alas, poor Yorick and all that. But you're definitely onto something. Does anyone happen to know the local gravedigger?"

Thirty-three

THE PLAN WAS SET. WITH THE HELP OF A BRIBE, Rosston's men would procure the area's most recently deceased body, dress it in Kerr-appropriate attire, and stow it under a blanket on a horse. Duncan felt a little guilty for the desecration of the deceased, but on the whole he thought God and the dead man would approve of an act meant to save others from dying. The man's family might have a different point of view, however.

Abby would draft the communiqué that would make the army think the Kerrs were planning an attack. Duncan and Jock were to equip the man with the other sorts of personal items—money, weapons, notes—that would heighten the verisimilitude when he was found. Where to plant him proved to be the biggest obstacle. Since England planned to attack soon, a quick discovery was critical. And they wanted the body to be found by a soldier, not a civilian, to ensure the information got to Bridgewater as fast as possible.

They finally decided on a tiny sliver of land just along the border known to be patrolled by the English army but little used by others. It was a risk because both countries claimed the land, which was why England patrolled it so heavily. So, the army would not greet trespassers with kindness, especially trespassers from the clan the army was planning to attack.

Duncan, Jock, and Abby climbed the great stairs of Kerr Castle in silence. They were to execute their tasks and meet again in two hours at a prearranged spot in the forest.

"Shall we sit down in my office?" Jock said to Duncan.

"Aye." He cast a sidelong glance at Abby. He wanted desperately to speak to her alone. "Let me gather some things in my room. I'll be there straightaway."

Jock nodded and made his way down the hall.

"We are under watch," Abby said under her breath. "Talk quietly and keep a respectful distance."

Talking quietly and keeping a respectful distance was the last thing Duncan wanted to do. But he obeyed.

"You know about Rosston's sentry, then?"

"Aye," she said. "Trust is not his greatest strength. But I understand his motivation even if I don't care for it."

She looked so beautiful, standing in the streaming sun like some angelic visitation. Her hair was pinned, but a few chestnut wisps had escaped, framing her face. He had promised to buy her freedom for her, but he had no way to do it. And now he had to tell her, even if it meant he was pushing her into Rosston's arms— that is, if she hadn't cast her fate with Rosston already.

"I need to speak to you about last night," he said.

Her eyes flashed, half-cautious, half-amused. "Which part?"

"The part I need to apologize for."

"Ye ken that still gives you a pretty wide field of choice."

"It does. I was thinking in particular of my engagement with Rosston."

She raised a wicked brow. "Now you're engaged to him too?"

Duncan's heart dropped to the bottom of his chest. "Did ye accept him, lass? I dinna blame ye, ye ken. If I were ye—"

"You are not me. And I am not a fool."

His heart stood poised on the precipice between relief and despair. "Then you are not engaged? I thought after last night—"

"That I should accept him? Indeed, you would be right. If I was in my right mind, I would. But I'm afraid I am almost as much out of my senses as my da. I am willing to believe a stranger from God only knows where, who holds my heart in his hands, will save me and my clan."

She smiled, such a sweet, trusting smile, it hurt him to see it. "Regarding that…" He cleared his throat.

"Aye?"

"I have found out from Undine that…" The words caught in his throat, and he swallowed them whole, knowing they'd destroy the perfect happiness he'd found. "…that the spell is stronger than she knew. It may be a while before I can return."

Even the tiny clouds of concern that rose in her eyes were too much for him to bear.

"You needn't worry, though," he said quickly. "We have Sir Alan returning from Carlisle on

Thursday. I promise we will convince him to invest in your canal."

"Then we best ensure the army doesn't make a move until then, I guess." She clutched her skirts, gave him a worried smile, and swept away.

Thirty-four

DUNCAN HAD BEEN TOLD THAT THE BRIGHT CRIMSON plaid he wore would not be a welcome addition to the group of travelers, who needed to progress as covertly through the woods as possible. As such, he had switched to a more muted green one and was just trying to decide what if anything to do about a loose button on his cuff when Nab opened the door.

"Have ye heard of knocking, ye wee whelp?" Duncan said.

"I kent ye were alone."

"What is it? Spill it before I box your ears."

"Her ladyship held a secret meeting today."

Duncan hid his smile. "Did she?"

"Aye. With her top advisers."

He was a top adviser now. "What was the meeting about?"

Nab shook his head. "I couldn't find out."

"Half pay for you. Tell me, do ye recognize this hand?" He slipped the note that had been wrapped around the arrow out of his sporran and handed it to the boy.

Nab frowned. "I don't. Was it for you?"

"Who else? It came wrapped around an arrow."

"Bloody hell."

"Does your mum know you talk like that? Who here can shoot a bow and arrow?"

"Most everyone, I'd say."

"I mean straight and true. As if it were one of Zeus's thunderbolts."

Nab thought. "Her ladyship, of course. She's the best—though she canna shoot as far as Rosston. He can reach the larch by the river from the battlement wall."

Interesting. "Anyone else?"

"No one else worth remarking on. Do ye think Rosston wants you to leave?" he added eagerly.

"I'm certain of it. But I just don't see him resorting to arrows and secret notes, do you?"

"His fists didn't do much good."

"*Och*, it takes more than a few punches to get through to a MacHarg." Duncan folded the note and put it back in his sporran. "We're far too stubborn."

"What's in the parcel?"

"What parcel?"

Nab pointed to the bedside table. Curiosity piqued, Duncan took a seat on the bed and examined the paper-wrapped object. There was no note on the outside or any indication the item was for him. He untied the string around it. Given the wide variety of feelings the inhabitants of Castle Kerr had for him, it could be anything from a bag of sheep shite to a—

"It's a sporran!" Nab cried. "A bonny one."

It *was* a bonny one. His grand-da's had gleaming white horsehair and three black tassels tumbling down the front. This one was not as dressy, but a skilled artisan had made it and the attention to detail was obvious. The leather had been tooled with Celtic knots and tiny silver beads then burnished to a rich golden brown, and the flap was covered with the thickest, darkest fur he had ever run his fingers through—

Beaver.

A fiery heat raced up his neck to the tips of his ears.

Nab gave him a narrow look, and Duncan tried desperately to think of anything but his night with Abby.

"It's from her, isn't it?"

"Never you mind, eh?"

Nab rolled his eyes.

With a happy tug, Duncan removed his grand-da's sporran and put the new one in its place. Then he emptied the contents of the first—his broken pen, a pencil he'd picked up somewhere, a slip of paper, Undine's twist of paper—and placed them inside the second.

"I'm going to be gone till nightfall," Duncan said, "perhaps a wee bit longer."

"Uh-huh."

"It's not what you think—not that you should be thinking anything, ye evil-minded mumper. I want ye to earn the other half of your pay today. Nose around. Without revealing why you're asking, see if can find out who in Castle Kerr keeps a bow in easy reach."

"If you're going where I think you're going, an arrow will be the least of your worries. Rosston will be aiming a mortar in your direction."

"*Hm.*"

"*Hm*, yourself."

Duncan tugged the sporran in place and headed for the door. "Take care, laddie. I'm on my way to see Jock about a few things."

"He was up working most of the night last night."

"Well, ye ken the man never stops working."

"Oh, he stops. I saw him with a whore a couple of days ago behind the tavern in town. He was hopping around like a man with a hot coal in his boot."

"Perhaps she was giving him a dancing lesson."

"If so, that's the third lesson she's given him this month. My cousin works in the stables there."

"Some men are verra slow learners. Now, shoo."

❧

Duncan looked at the small assemblage of belongings on Jock's desk and clucked his tongue.

"Coins, a small knife, a pencil, a bannock, a hunk of cheese, and, when Lady Kerr is done, the battle plans," Duncan said. "Is that enough?"

"I think the man must have a love letter from his sweetheart too, don't you?"

Duncan eyed Jock with curiosity. He didn't appear to be a man with much interest in love. On the other hand, he didn't appear to be a man with much interest in dancing either.

"I think a wee note would be appropriate, aye. Er, shall we have Abby draft it?"

"Oh, no, we can do it fine. Anyway, her hand will be on the attack plans. It canna be on the love note too. We can't have Colonel Bridgewater thinking the chief of Clan Kerr is in love with her courier."

God forbid. Or a man of even less substance.

"All right," Duncan said uncertainly. He was no expert at love letters—or of thinking like a woman, an activity he'd found to require considerably more intuition, diplomacy, and quick wit than he'd ever possessed.

Jock drew a sheet of paper from his drawer and slid it toward Duncan.

"Me?"

"My hand is pretty well-known here."

Duncan swallowed and reached for the quill. Dipping it in the inkwell, he said, "What exactly do you think Archie's lass would say to him?"

Archie was the name they had bestowed on their yet-to-be-gotten body. Duncan had already begun to think of him as a man of great determination and bravery, willing to sacrifice for the good of his countrymen.

"We need the lassie's name first, aye?"

"Why?" Duncan asked. "Oh, aye, for the signature at the end. How about Catriona?" His girlfriend's name at university.

Jock shook his head. "Sounds a bit wild."

Duncan couldn't disagree.

"Jean," Jock suggested.

Duncan's mother's name. "Too old-fashioned, aye?" He would definitely not be able to craft a love letter with his dead mother's face lodged in his brain.

Jock shrugged. "Jenny?"

"That'll do." Duncan began to write:

Dear Archie,

Now what? He gazed at the paper, utterly devoid of ideas.

"Come, lad," Jock said. "You're young. All this flowery language should still be in your head."

Duncan rolled his head from shoulder to shoulder and put the pen to paper.

I am writing to you today, my darling,

He paused. "Do ye think she kens Archie well enough to call him *darling*?"

Jock pursed his lips. "Are they engaged to be married?"

Duncan pictured Archie volunteering to deliver the battle plans to the nearest allied clan chief, and Jenny pacing the river near her home, worrying for her absent love. "No, but I think she knows they're going to be. He's saving to get her a pair of earbobs before he asks—those red ones lassies seem to like."

"Rubies?"

Duncan shook his head. "Too expensive. The other kind." He snapped his fingers twice, trying to force his brain to unlock the word.

"Garnets?" Jock offered.

"That's it!" Duncan had had great success with a pair of garnet earrings for one girl and a dainty garnet bracelet for another. There was something, he thought, about the warm crimson of the stone...

With a thoughtful noise, Jock settled back in his chair. "She should call him *darling* then."

I am writing to you today, my darling, because I was thinking of you

"'—and the last time we were together,'" Jock offered. Duncan nodded.

and the last time we were together. I smiled enough then to provide me with smiles for the rest of the summer. I'm counting the days till your return.

"That's when he's going to ask, ye ken," Duncan said.

And dearest Archie, please know I do not regret a thing.

Duncan smiled a little at that. He could almost see the empty field in which the two had done their joining, feel the sun on his face. He hoped Abby had no regrets about him. It seemed the best possible assurance a woman could give a man.

Jock leaned forward. "Do ye think they have…?"

Duncan nodded. "I do."

Jock laced his fingers together and tapped his thumbs against his lips. "Aye. I think ye may be right."

Hurry back to me. I cannot bear to think of you walking the hills alone.

All my love,
J.

Duncan tapped the corner of the paper, unwilling

to meet Jock's eyes. He hoped poor Archie had enjoyed a love as sweet as Jenny's before he died.

"Those bloody soldiers better not pass this around," Jock said, with an avuncular scowl.

"They won't. They'll be too busy hightailing the battle plans to Bridgewater." Duncan sprinkled sand on the paper and shook it off. Then, folding the paper and running the edges back and forth over an account book to simulate wear, he looked at the collection on the desk. "What else would a man have in his sporran?"

Jock said, "'Tis more than I have in my own."

"It needs a touch of the inexplicable. It's almost too perfect. The English were—" He stopped himself. He could hardly be telling Jock the English were expert at sniffing out German spies during World War II because the Germans insisted the IDs and paperwork their spies carried be perfect. "The English will be quick to spot anything that looks too good. It's the mistake or spot of inexplicableness that will make the deception believable." He looked around and spotted the loose button on his cuff. With a quick tug, he jerked it free and tossed it with Archie's other possessions.

"See," Duncan said. "Inexplicable."

Jock laughed. He brushed the items into a small rough cloth sack and looked at his clock. "It's too early to head to the woods. Do you have a pistol? The soldiers are unlikely to engage us with fists, ye ken."

"Aye, I have a pistol—and a sword."

"Good. We may need both. Bridgewater has quietly spread the word that a band of marauding Scots may be just what is needed to convince the queen to lift her ban on an attack. He'd be happy to slaughter us all and say his troops were under siege. Our best bet is to avoid the soldiers altogether, which is going to be a hell of a lot harder in daylight. They want Scotland, and nothing will stand in their way. Lady Kerr's canal will just be the fruit on the tart."

"Since you've mentioned the canal," Duncan said, stretching his long fingers to quiet the low-level fear tingling through his body, "what can ye tell me of the estate and its taxes?"

Jock's brows went up. "We pay what we owe, though it kills me to see it done."

"So you havena been hit with a big wallop recently?"

"*Och*, no. Just the same slow bleed. I dinna know how they expect us to feed our people and grow when they take as much as they do." Then, sensing that he had not put Duncan's curiosity to rest, he added, "Would you like to look yourself? 'Tis no more than you'd find in the royal tax rolls."

"Could I?"

"Ye may." He pulled a large blue leather book from his shelves and put it in front of Duncan. "This is every year since 1511. Before that, the Gordons owned the estate."

"And what happened to the Gordons?"

"Ye dinna want to know."

For close to an hour Duncan followed the Kerr accounts, from the Scottish defeat at Flodden (debts unpaid and a near bankruptcy for the estate), through a visit by Mary, Queen of Scots ("bedstead, ebony inlaid with silver and pearl, worthy of Her Majesty, £2,3") through the fourth Lord Kerr's elevation from baron to earl (investiture ball, commissioning of a set of solid gold plates with the revised coat of arms), to the present day (the failure of the canal, divestiture of land in Arran and Argyll, and the sale, piece by piece, of the gold plates.)

No outrageous outlay for taxes (though taxes, as Duncan knew, had been quite high) and nothing obviously amiss. Just a slow descent into near bankruptcy that began around the beginning of Abby's time as chieftess.

He closed the book and sighed. If Lachlan's hint about taxes had been more than the words of a man out of his senses, Duncan found no evidence to support his assertion, or of any sort of monetary mismanagement, in the accounts.

"An amazing overview of the family's history," Duncan said, handing the book back to Jock, who had spent the time going through correspondence.

"You canna tell the story of the lowlands without telling the story of the Kerrs."

Duncan looked at the clock. The witching hour. "Shall we head out to see how the next act unfolds?"

"Let us hope Shakespeare is'na involved. I shouldna care to find myself dead on a field like Hotspur."

Thirty-five

"I'D LIKE TO TALK TO MY FATHER ALONE," ABBY SAID.

Molly, who had been smoothing his quilt, made a quick curtsy of acknowledgment. Abby's opinion of the girl's talents had not eroded since her hiring a few months ago, but her sense of the girl's trustworthiness had. Though Abby could point to no missing flatware, no beau skulking in the woods beyond the castle walls, no sniggered impertinence, the sense was undeniable, and she had to force herself to return the girl's smile.

Lachlan had had a particularly bad morning, howling about Moira and thrashing in his bedclothes until one would have thought the castle was being burned to the ground and his bed used as tinder. Her burliest footmen had tied him into place, and he had finally exhausted himself into the sweaty, vibrating quiet she found him in now.

"I want your blessing, Da."

His eye, the one good one, searched her face. Did he see her? Did he understand what she was saying?

"I know you don't think I listen to you enough," she said. "But you always said a good chief must make decisions, and if the decisions are right, so much the better. Well, I have a made a couple of decisions. The first involves the clan. We canna go on the way we have been. The money is…well, it started going bad with the canal and hasn't gotten any better since. And now the English want to have their way with us. We've concocted a plan that will put them off for long enough to secure a loan for the canal if it works. But the plan is risky. If we're caught, the army will unleash itself upon us and the rest of the borderland clans. We will be held up to every clansman as an example of what happens to those who defy their English keepers. I will lose the support of my fellow chiefs, and the era of Kerr influence will be at an end."

She tucked the thin brown cloak more tightly around her. "The plan is a good one, though. You've met the man who thought of it. MacHarg is his name. He is…" She gazed at the base of the nearest bedpost. "Well, he is not the man I first thought him to be. He may not be skilled in the way we think of it, but he is loyal and true—and sometimes foolish, that is certain—but he fights with the heart of a true Kerr."

Her father jerked at his bindings hard enough to thump the bed forward.

"I'm no fool, Da. I had you for a father and Moira for a mother, after all. And I am beginning to trust the decisions I make. They may not be the decisions you'd make, but they work in the world in which I exist now. I've built a strong ally in Rosston. He is not the man I thought him to be either. We know the plan we are attempting is risky, and we have agreed that if one of us doesn't make it, the other will take the leadership of both families. We have left letters stating as much, and, for my own part, I am prepared to do what it takes to make his men obey me if it comes to that."

The tension in Lachlan's shoulders seemed to relax but nothing emerged from his questing lips.

"As for the other decision, Da, it seems I am to be married. Soon, I think, though I dinna know to which groom. A wee bit strange, isn't it, for a bride to stand so close to the altar she can smell the candles burning and still not know the name of her husband?"

She allowed herself to think of that long walk up the aisle, and how different she would feel in one case versus the other.

"I know my heart," she continued, "and I know my responsibility. In this instance, they are not the same. Oh, I know if ye could, ye would tell me nothing is more important than my responsibility." Her throat caught, and she pushed away the stinging in her eyes. "But I tell ye this," she said, voice rising. "Ye loved my ma more than I've ever seen a man love a woman. So dinna tell me I have to give that up. 'Tis not fair."

His face betrayed nothing. She didn't know if he even heard her. *Och!* Why did she even bother? Every discussion with him made her feel like she was arguing with herself.

"I will make this decision when I have to, and for once it will be without reference to anyone's desires but my own. If you can keep your own counsel, so can I."

Then suddenly, it was the old Lachlan, dark eyes burning like peat fire, and he growled, "Then why are ye here?"

The tower had two windows. One looked fifty miles east along the border, across the lands of the Armstrongs, Elliotts, and Nixons, the clans who had joined with the Kerrs in repelling the English for nearly half a millennium. The other looked south, to England and the army whose breath she felt on her neck every moment of every day. She turned from one to the other, wondering where her fate lay.

"I'm prepared to make these decisions alone," she said. "'Tis the first time I've been able to say that and mean it. But I love ye, Da. I have never known a better chief. Will ye not tell me that I have earned the right to lead this clan?"

He made a noise—disgust? agreement? imminent belch?—and closed his eyes. She waited. When he did not speak, she gave up and was nearly to the door when he said, "Come back."

Abby found a place on the bedside stool. "What is it?"

He extended his bony hand, the hand that had once seemed so strong and large to her, and clasped her arm.

"Ye have my support," he said, voice thick. "Ye always have. Whatever ye do, I'll be standing at your side and so will the ghosts of every Kerr chief before ye."

She had longed for the words since the day she took her oath, and air filled her lungs as if a crushing weight had been lifted from her chest. "Oh, Da."

He leaned forward, and she met him halfway, her cheek against his forehead. She basked in his reassuring warmth.

"Now promise me whatever happens ye'll take care of your ma and your sister," he said. "You're a braw lad, Bran. You'll make a bonny chief."

Thirty-six

DUNCAN BARELY RECOGNIZED THE SLIM FIGURE IN THE hooded cloak and white bonnet, standing alone among the trees. The Abby of his experience commanded attention in every situation—on horseback in battle, marching purposefully with her bow, certainly naked at Candle Pool. It wasn't her beauty or captivating eyes or the way her breasts sat round and high that drew the eye, though all of those had left indelible marks in Duncan's mind. But when she wore the mantle of her office, it was as if her gender melted away, leaving only the power, the determination, and the spirit.

But this Abby was foreign to him. It was as if someone had drained the sunshine out of one of Van Gogh's fields, or the pink out of Cézanne's peaches. Her natural luminescence had dimmed almost to the point of darkness. He hurried to her side.

"Abby, is everything all right?"

"Lady Kerr, if you please. Or Chieftess. You're late. Where is Jock?"

"He wanted to finalize something before we set out. He said he'd be only a moment or two behind me."

"A moment or two we don't have. Do ye have the items for the man's pockets?"

"Aye."

"I have the orders. We are to travel two miles to the south, to where lightning felled two of the tallest oaks, then another mile to the southwest. That's where Rosston and our body will be. That puts us in the heart of the Debatable Lands, and no more than a mile or two from the border." She looked at the pistol tucked in his belt. "Ye ken ye cannot take that. You and I are on a leisurely hunt for deer," she said, tapping her bow. "One does not shoot deer with a pistol."

In the Scotland of Duncan's day, one did not have the right to shoot deer on someone else's property whether they used a bow or not. "Are we on Kerr land?" he asked cautiously.

"No. It seems we are not very well versed in the rules of hunting."

Duncan knew what Scotsmen did to the men who stole their livestock. He did not care to discover if English soldiers on the Debatable Lands felt the same sense of proprietariness. "Oh."

"All the more reason to stay as minimally armed as possible. If we are found, 'twould be nice to have the hunting story hold a ring of truth."

"But, wait. They are hardly likely to believe the chief of Clan Kerr is unfamiliar with the local laws regarding hunting."

She laughed, and while he never liked being laughed at, he was glad to see the lines around her eyes relax.

"While most of the soldiers in the regiment have glimpsed Lady Kerr once or twice—and have no doubt described her in vivid detail to their drinking companions, you overestimate an English soldier's ability to overcome his lack of interest in a sickly, plump married woman." She opened her cape and turned.

Duncan blinked. She had the baby bump of a last trimester mother-to-be. All in all, he thought he'd rather have the soldiers believe they were stealing deer. Between being engulfed by a large and fairly ridiculous sense of protectiveness and feeling that a pregnant woman offered an English soldier twice the potential for mischief, Duncan's anxiety tripled.

"I...don't...think..."

But his thoughts remained half-spoken when a musket shot blasted through the quiet of the afternoon.

"Run," she said.

They headed deeper into the trees, hurtling over bushes and deadfall.

"Put down the pistol," she cried. "Hunters dinna use them."

"And pregnant women dinna long jump over fallen trees."

The shot had been far enough to their rear that Duncan couldn't be sure if the person firing had been aiming at them or shooting a turkey, a deer, or some other animal.

But if they were already in someone's sights, he had no desire to see he and Abby separated from a key source of protection.

After a hazard-filled four-hundred-meter sprint, Abby signaled for them to stop.

Bent over, gasping for air, Duncan said, "I dinna hear anything."

"No. If the shot was meant for me, I wonder how someone would know we were heading out now."

"The shot may have been meant for me," he said, bracing himself for the chortle.

But she didn't laugh. He glanced up. Did she know something she wasn't saying? "Someone shot an arrow at me this morning," he said. "In the bailey. It wasn't by any chance you, was it?"

"If I wanted to kill you, Duncan, I should hardly do it in public."

He looked at the thick woods surrounding them and the hairs on his arm stood on end.

This time, she laughed. "Is that why you're clinging to that pistol like a drowning man with a line?"

"Aye…well…maybe you're not the only thing I need to protect myself from."

"Apparently not. Well, it's not clear either of us were targeted. What we heard could have just been a stray shot."

She cocked her head, and he knew she, like he, was trying to sort through the rustle of leaves for the sound of footfall.

"Let's go," she said.

"Without Jock?"

"At this point, aye. We need to get to Rosston."

Duncan nodded. If Abby wasn't the person who'd shot at him, it moved another suspect to the top of his list: Abby's would-be fiancé.

Thirty-seven

AN HOUR LATER, THEY WERE REACHING A PLACE WHERE the pines began to give way to scrub. Abby had been unnaturally silent, failing to laugh after she drew a small wedge of cheese from her pocket and he reminded her she was eating for two. He swore she walked differently with the cushion under her chemise, and it had taken all his willpower not to leap to her aid every time they climbed a ledge or forded a stream.

She stopped behind the last small copse of trees. "This is it," she said, "where we are to meet Rosston."

"Then this is the Debatable Lands?" Duncan found it hard to imagine this nondescript barren slope represented anything of value.

"Not here. Do ye see the raised wall there, past that outcropping?"

The "wall" was no more than a small hillock of earth a few feet high and barely discernible, covered like everything else here with patches of rock and grass. "Aye."

"That's where it begins. The moment we step into

the open, we will be on disputed land. I must insist you lay down your pistol."

With a distinct sense of regret, Duncan put the pistol at the base of one of the trees and covered it with needles. "I do wish," he said as he stood, "we did not have to be quite so—" He froze. The rocky ledge above them to their west was intimately familiar to him. It was visible from his grand-da's kitchen window, accessible via the park that was adjacent to his land. Duncan's mouth moved wordlessly. He had played on this ledge hundreds of times in his childhood. They were standing more or less in the center of what would be, in three hundred years' time, his grand-da's garden. He felt slightly dizzy, as if the world had shifted under his feet, and the immediacy yet immense distance of the world he'd left behind took his breath away.

"Duncan, what is it?"

"This is my grand-da's land. We're standing on my grand-da's land."

"Your grand-da is Angus Eliot?"

He slumped against the tree trunk and sat, head in hands. "No."

"But—" She stopped, and realization washed over her face. "Oh."

She crouched down beside him, a trick with her rugby ball–sized belly, and touched his arm. "Duncan, we've never talked about this, mostly, I think because I've been afraid to ask, but—"

"I come from the twenty-first century. More than three hundred years from now."

The crouch devolved to a hard plop on the ground.

She made a quiet whistle. "I thought, well, I thought a few years, perhaps a decade. I had no idea... I dinna think you should tell anyone."

"Undine knows."

"What has she done? What have *I* done?"

"I suspect we all have a hand in it, somehow. In any case, I should never wish for it not to have happened. Not now."

But rather than the smile he'd hoped for, her face took on a pained look. "I need to talk to you about Rosston."

A vise gripped his heart. "What?"

"For better or worse, I am quite in love with you, Duncan. But my responsibilities—"

"I told you I'd help you."

She took his hand and squeezed. "I should like nothing more. But I must pay the estate taxes this week. 'Tis possible that with the canal loan from Sir Alan, I can negotiate a delay. You told me you need more time to figure out how to get back, and if you and Undine believe that that could happen soon, I would wait. Will it work? Oh, Duncan, I dinna like to put so much on ye, but will ye be able to help us?"

He hated to douse the hope in those eyes. He hated that he was powerless here, that neither his brains, nor his wealth, nor his determination brought him any closer to being able to help her. He was quite confident that with time and access, he could convince Sir Alan to make the loan. But was it fair to let her believe he might be able to help her with a gift of money when in fact the only help he could offer was by convincing Sir Alan to make a loan, an outcome he could not guarantee?

"Duncan?"

He gazed at the delicate bones of her hand. "I canna give you money. I talked to Undine. Nothing of concentrated wealth can travel through time."

Her eyes turned a forlorn blue. "Oh."

"But I can convince Sir Alan," he said hurriedly. "I *promise* you. It's what I do."

"Duncan, you know I canna risk the fate of my clan. If it were just me—"

"Only till Friday," he said urgently. "Believe in me. Please."

"You know there's another way, and you and I have to accept that if—"

"No! Dinna talk to me of Rosston and his gold. Will ye sell yourself for money?"

She looked at him as if he'd slapped her, and in his heart he knew slapping would have wounded her less.

"Yes," she said, eyes glistening, "I will. And you know it, ye two-faced rogue. Ye were happy enough to buy me when it was your turn. And I will sell myself again if I have to. Whatever it takes to save Clan Kerr."

"Every man between here and the gates of York?" The words were out of his mouth before he knew what he was saying.

The sting of her slap was not punishment enough. He wished she'd kill him.

"I'm here," a voice said. "I'm sorry."

Rosston. Standing twenty feet away, holding his horse's lead, and looking as if he, too, wished he were dead.

Rosston was wise. He stayed where he was, held

his tongue, made no move to punish Duncan for his unpardonable transgression. Why should he? Abby wouldn't have liked it, and in any case, Duncan had administered his own coup de grâce, saving Rosston the trouble of getting his hands dirty.

"I should go," Duncan said.

"Not till we're done," Abby said, as cool as steel. "We'll need three sets of hands for the body."

"I can do his part," Rosston said wryly, and blind with self-loathing, Duncan flew at him.

This time Rosston was better prepared. He twisted away at the last second and Duncan landed hard on a stretch of sunbaked earth.

No one said anything. Abby didn't even reach for an arrow. She turned, gestured to Rosston, and walked swiftly to the horse.

Rosston looked at Duncan, shook his head, and followed his fellow chief.

You idiot.

He was the most unworthy man in five hundred miles. But he wasn't a coward and he wasn't a quitter. He climbed to his feet, dusted off his plaid, and began toward the two people having a quiet discussion over a dead body.

Thirty-eight

ARCHIE WAS NOT NEARLY AS DASHING AS DUNCAN HAD imagined. His drawn face was gray and rubbery, and his mouth slack enough to show a mouthful of brown and missing teeth. He had died of pneumonia or something like it—Rosston referred to it as "the cough"—though one of Rosston's men had thoughtfully put a pistol ball through the man's heart and poured a jug of pig's blood over the clothes they'd dressed him in so it looked like he'd been crossed by a brigand on the road.

Duncan had already stuffed Archie's pockets and sporran with the bits of humanity he and Jock had gathered. Abby clutched the message about the attack and was debating with Rosston where on the body the paper should be hidden. That job was too important to be entrusted to Duncan, apparently, even though the plan had been his. Abby had not said a single word to him since his shameful remark. He felt about as worthy of her notice as Archie. Archie at least was beyond the reach of regret.

Rosston appeared beside him holding the plans. At

Duncan's instruction, the note had been written on silk. "Silk is silent," he'd explained, "and when it is hidden in clothing, it canna be heard the way parchment can." It was another lesson he'd learned from World War II novels.

Rosston held the note delicately between his thumb and forefinger, as if it were a lady's lace handkerchief, which gave him the look of a thuggish Cyrano. He waited expectantly. Duncan sighed and stepped aside, giving him access to the body. Rosston lifted one of Archie's unbooted feet and, with the precision of a surgeon, ran his hand carefully over the sock, stopping suddenly, triumphant.

"There's a secret pocket that runs the circumference of the sock," he said to Duncan. "If ye fold a piece of paper or banknote carefully when ye put it in, ye canna see anything. You're not the only one with ways to trick the enemy, ye ken."

Duncan resisted the urge to blacken Rosston's other eye and said with only slightly forced enthusiasm, "Well done."

The silk disappeared inside.

Rosston said, "I understand you will say you were hunting deer if you're found."

Duncan nodded. "It's the least I can do after getting her with child, don't you think?"

Rosston's dark eyes briefly registered the blow. "'Tis all the more remarkable, then, since she's the only one capable of using a bow."

"Well, it is a woman's sport, after all. Speaking of that, I hear you're quite the archer as well. Tell me, have you had a chance to shoot much lately?"

"Fouck you."

"We ought to wad up the silk," Duncan called to Abby, who had been adjusting the laces on her boot. "To make the hiding place more noticeable. I have my doubts about the general canniness of English soldiers."

She didn't register even the hint of a smile.

"I'm afraid your naïveté is showing," Rosston said. "There's not a man in the army who doesn't pick through every scrap on a dead man. They practically use a sieve. If he had a shard of copper under his fingernail, they'd find it and sell it."

The sound of someone singing in the distance ended the discussion.

"Rosston, take the body and get as far into the trees as you can," Abby said.

Duncan took a place behind a thick pine. Abby did the same. The singing drew nearer.

"Pastime with good company. I love and shall until I die…"

The man was definitely a soldier. The red coat was quite apparent, as were his pistol, sword, and musket. He was possessed of an exquisite tenor voice. The notes, pure and whole, filled the afternoon air.

"Grudge who lust but none deny…"

Abby met Duncan's eyes, but not long enough for him to communicate his regret. He wished he could beg her forgiveness. This might be the last time they were together for a very long time. But the soldier was nearly upon them.

"So God be pleased thus live will I…"

Up the slight rise of the clearing he went, scanning the edge of the woods as he walked.

The singing stopped, mid-line.

Electricity surged through Duncan's body. Abby withdrew an arrow and held it, nocked, at her side. From his vantage point Duncan could see the soldier look both ways then head into the woods a stone's throw beyond them. Had he heard a noise? Then, through the branches, Duncan saw the man loosen the tie on his breeks.

"He's taking a piss," Duncan whispered.

Abby nodded, still on high alert.

The woods were too thick to see him once he left the clearing. Duncan padded quietly from tree to tree, hoping for a glimpse.

"What do you see?" Abby whispered.

"Not a goddamned thing."

"I'm going closer."

"No."

"I am hunting a deer, Duncan. 'Twill be all right." She pelted east, hoping, he supposed, to maintain a safe radius from the soldier, who had been traveling northeast.

He wanted to throttle her. What had happened to the plan of staying together? He listened and looked, but without the knowledge that Abby was safe, he was too distracted to think.

The hell with standing. He'd rather die on the offense than the defense.

He ran in the direction she'd taken, listening for her footsteps, but she'd disappeared, like a doe in a thicket. The woods of Scotland were, after all, her element.

A shot rang out, and he burst into a dead run. Over fallen limbs, under drooping branches, he raked the tree-filled space around him for signs of movement.

He dared not yell, for fear he'd bring the soldier *to* them, not away. For all he knew, the man was shooting a grouse for his dinner. He had to find Abby. He had to know if she was—

He heard grunts and the hard thump of a body and headed straight for it.

The soldier had the barrel of his musket against Rosston's neck, pressing Rosston as hard as he could against a tree. Rosston had his hands on the barrel, pushing it away. His shirt was bathed in blood, and his eyes were practically bulging out of his head. Something flashed in a ray of sunlight. Duncan realized it was the blade of the soldier's bayonet lodged somewhere near Rosston's heart.

Where's Abby? Was she the one who'd been shot?

The horse and Archie were nowhere to be seen. Somewhere, Abby screamed. The soldier bellowed, "Enemy! Help!" Duncan's heart fired in his chest like a line of cannons. He had a short sword and no more. In a few seconds, Rosston's throat would be crushed. But he might be bleeding to death anyway.

Should he try to save the man? Or should he let him die?

Duncan drew his sword and charged. At the same instant, the soldier released his grip, and Rosston crumpled slowly to the ground. The soldier pulled the bayonet point out of Rosston, who let out a horrifying wheeze. The soldier turned, saw Duncan. He fumbled, trying to slip the bayonet back on the end of the musket. Duncan was ten strides away. He lifted the sword. The bayonet clicked into place. The soldier grabbed the barrel to raise it, but it was too late. Duncan closed his eyes and swung.

He connected with meat and bone, and his eyes flew open. The man's arm was half cut off at the shoulder, and blood was spraying everywhere. He would die from that wound. Duncan had killed a living man. The man took a step, and another, then dropped his musket.

"Fuck you," he growled, clutching the source of the spurting crimson. He screamed, "Clansmen!" Rosston made a faint, high-pitched moan.

"Clansmen!"

Die! Die! But the man kept screaming. Duncan's sword was covered in blood and gleaming bits of bone and tissue. He shook so hard, he couldn't focus. He held the point of the sword over the man's neck and drove it into the ground beneath him. For an instant, the man's mouth opened wide, as if one more scream would come out, then the light disappeared from his eyes.

"Duncan."

A full moment had passed, and Duncan realized someone had been saying his name over and over.

He dropped to his knees and crawled to Rosston.

"Duncan." The word was hoarse, remote. "Duncan, I'm nae dead."

"No."

"And nae are you."

Rosston's wound was deep, but it was not in his heart.

He heard voices in the distance. Many voices. "I have to find Abby. I'll come for ye."

Duncan sprinted deeper into the woods, trying to push the image of the soldier from his head. He rounded the bend at a thick stand of pines and ran right into Abby, standing by the horse.

"Oh, God, you're alive." He clutched her, and she him.

Then she saw the blood on him and wavered. "Rosston…?"

"No. The soldier who found him. Rosston's alive, but we need to get him to a surgeon. Abby, I was a fool when I said—"

"Aye, you were. We haven't time for that. There's a band of soldiers coming through. We are bound to be found. There will be a bloody war if they find a clansman and a dead soldier here." She tugged the horse's lead, and they hurried back to Rosston.

Rosston smiled when he saw her. Abby looked at the soldier and turned to Duncan. "Your work?"

He nodded. He didn't even want to look at what he'd done.

Getting Rosston onto the horse beside Archie was relatively easy—Rosston was still conscious and could help lift his weight—but getting the English soldier onto it was impossible.

Duncan said, "Perhaps with a rope—"

"No. We don't have time. He has to stay."

The sound of the soldiers was growing closer. There were a lot of them.

Abby said, "Give me your sword belt and plaid!"

"Why?" Duncan said but was already loosening the leather.

"Ye have to get Rosston to a surgeon and Archie to the agreed location." She stripped off her cloak and replaced it with his bloody plaid. "Their dead colleague and I will be a bonny distraction. He attacked me, ye know." She pulled the bloody sword out the soldier's neck and began to blubber theatrically. "I had no choice."

The full realization of what she was planning hit Duncan. "Oh, no. I am nae leaving you to explain yourself to a band of English soldiers."

"Ye took an oath."

"I don't bloody care."

"Ye took an oath," she said, "and I command it."

Damn her. Damn them all. "Bugger this bloody, foucking clan."

Rosston, who was barely holding himself on the horse, let out a labored chuckle.

"Go," she commanded. "Go!"

Duncan grabbed the horse's lead and ran. A mile later, with Abby and her dead attacker having long disappeared behind them, Duncan slowed to a walk, wondering what on earth he had left her to.

Rosston, as gray as the sky, said with a weak smile, "Ye look a wee bit like you've been attacked yourself, laddie, running through the woods in nae but your sark."

"Will she be all right?"

Rosston sighed. "She has been as long as I've known her. I expect today will be nae exception. Turn west here. Ye'll likely find my men just over the ridge. I think I am going to pass out."

Thirty-nine

Abby looked down the barrel of the musket, as grim and forbidding as the eyes of the soldier holding it. While she had very little feeling for the dead soldier at her feet, replacing the image of his body with the imagined picture of her mother, splayed awkwardly on the ground under her horse, had been enough to thoroughly wet her cheeks. The holes she'd torn in her gown and bleeding lines she'd scratched across her cheek completed the tableau.

"I told you I don't know why," she said, crying. "He asked me if I was alone…and then he…" She hung her head and made a low keen. Her experience of men was that crying unnerved them, and the more hopeless the tears, the more unnerved they found themselves.

A dozen more soldiers arrived and encircled the body.

"What *happened*?" one said.

"She says Dunworth attacked her," said the soldier with the musket. "When he turned his back, she grabbed her sword."

Abby cried harder.

"Why were you carrying a sword?" asked an older soldier, who surveyed her skeptically.

"My husband said I must. He said if I insisted on hunting badgers…I know I'm not supposed to hunt here, but the Elliotts are such a wealthy clan, and it has been so long since we had—"

"This ain't the Elliotts' land," the man with the musket said. "This land belongs to England."

Her eyes widened. "Oh dear."

The older soldier frowned. "So you say he attacked you, and you were able to reach for your blade?"

"I told *him*." She waved her shaking arm in the direction of the first soldier.

"Private Lynley. I'm Sergeant Rose," the older man said.

"I told Private Lynley that the man, Dunsmore, or whatever you said, couldn't…*do* what he intended. His cock wasn't ready. And he turned away from me so he could, well—"

"I think we have the picture." The older man flushed.

Undoing the dead soldier's breeks had been the final piece of prepping the scene. It was an act she did not wish to repeat—ever.

For a long moment the soldiers said nothing. Abby swallowed her anxiety. This was the moment her future would be decided.

Lynley gave Rose an interrogatory look.

"Private Bigham," Rose said, speaking to the man kneeling over his companion's body, "would you escort—I'm sorry, have we gotten your name?" He gave Abby a smile that came no higher than his mouth.

"Grant. Martha Grant."

"Would you escort Mrs. Grant back to the camp? I'd like to have someone write down her story.

Nothing to worry about, Mrs. Grant. You'll be free to go when we finish."

Abby rose unsteadily. "But my husband—"

"You'll be home before dark. We may even be able to throw in a badger." He gave her a courteous bow.

She bobbed a curtsy filled with regret and took Bingham's arm.

When the woman was out of earshot, Lynley said to Rose, "You couldn't take her statement here?"

"I could," Rose said, "but then the colonel wouldn't have a chance to talk to her. That's no crofter, my boy. That's the chief of Clan Kerr."

Forty

ROSSTON'S MEN DESCENDED ON THEM LIKE A SWARM OF bees, and Duncan accepted being shoved out of the way as they cut their chief free and dragged him from the saddle. Duncan had had to tie Rosston's hands around the horse's neck to keep him from falling off.

A minute later, Rosston's earsplitting cry cut through the hum. The whiskey they were pouring on his shoulder seemed to have jolted him out of whatever rest he'd been getting, and one of the men was threading a hideously long needle. Stomach rising, Duncan turned to get on with his duties. He needed to deliver Archie to the agreed spot, which as best as Duncan could calculate was still an hour away.

He tried to push the picture of Abby, abandoned and if not actually pregnant then as vulnerable as a woman who was, standing by a slaughtered English soldier out of his head. She had a given him an order. He would do it.

He adjusted Archie's plaid, which had become tangled in the process of transporting Rosston, and checked the hiding place in Archie's sock.

Duncan froze. His finger found nothing in the closely knit wool. He checked the other sock, in case he'd misremembered the side, but there was nothing in either of them. The silk and its message were gone.

The snugness of the hidden pocket and the light weight of the silk, made it impossible for him to believe the message had fallen out. He would have liked to believe Rosston had stolen it for a purpose Duncan could not imagine, but the truth was painfully obvious: Abby had taken it and intended to have the soldiers find it on her.

He pushed through the circle of clansmen.

"Watch yerself," one said. "We're working on him."

"I need to talk to him," Duncan said. "Alone."

Rosston, who was half-awake, waved his men off. The man with the needle gave Duncan a sour look, laid his work on Rosston's half-stitched shoulder, and rose. "'Twould be good to get him finished before he passes out again, ye ken?"

"I ken."

The moment the men were out of earshot, Duncan knelt down beside the makeshift surgery space, which evidently was the cleanest of the blankets the men had with them. Rosston had lost a lot of blood and his face showed it. The gaping hole in his shoulder had been replaced with a curved line of ragged, bloody Xs.

"The plans are gone."

Rosston groaned. "Christ, Abby."

"Why would she take it?" Duncan demanded, hoping Rosston had a different idea.

"Because she was sure to get searched."

"Dammit! She ordered me to deliver the dead

man—forced me to swear to it. Was that only to ensure I left her there on her own?"

"And to get me to a surgeon." Rosston turned his head in the direction they'd come. "Oh, Abby, ye headstrong girl."

"Where would they take her? I mean, if they searched her and found the note?"

Rosston licked his lips. "Outside a burned out castle just over the border. 'Tis the army's northern headquarters. Follow the vale till the firth. You'll see the wall."

"But I took an oath to her, as head of the clan. I am pledged to do as she says. Tell me, Rosston, must I heed her command to deliver the body? She may very well have a plan she has not shared with me that my arrival would destroy. Do I do as she says or as I think?"

Rosston closed his eyes, and for a moment Duncan thought he had slipped into unconsciousness again. Then the lips fluttered open. "In this case, as you might say, bugger the clan."

Duncan jumped to his feet.

"Wait."

Duncan stopped.

"I owe you my life," Rosston said.

"I was glad to help."

Rosston snorted but the motion made him wince. "You weren't. And I wouldna have been glad to help you." He shifted uncomfortably. His cheeks had already begun to shine with fever. "But as grateful as I am, I dinna intend to let you have her."

"Abby is not a woman one 'lets' do anything, ye ken, certainly not you or I."

"Ye saved my life, and I willna harm you. But I want your word ye will leave her alone."

"You're wasting your breath," Duncan said, impatient. "If she wants me, she'll have me." He stood.

"Damn you." Rosston grabbed his arm. "She's mine."

"Ye have no power to possess or bequeath," Duncan said, pulling himself free. "She is not a soup tureen or a crate of gold. If you would just realize that, you blistering fool, you might actually have a chance with her."

An unsettling confection of surprise and satisfaction appeared in Rosston's glazed eyes and he smiled. "Could it be ye dinna know what transpired between us last night?"

The words cut Duncan like a broadsword. Every particle of his being longed to know what Rosston dangled before him, but somewhere inside his chest a tiny ember of his trust in Abby flickered.

"Go to hell." Duncan turned for the horse.

"She negotiated the terms of our marriage," Rosston called and caused a number of men's heads to turn, and Duncan hesitated. "Do ye not want to hear the ones that apply to you?"

Forty-one

"MISSUS, ER, GRANT, IS IT? I AM EXCEEDINGLY SORRY for what happened."

Abby clutched the mug of warmed sherry that had been placed in her hand and nodded, taking care to keep her gaze downward. Soldiers, especially ones as vaunted as a colonel, did not care for women who showed neither deference nor fear.

The man's gleaming yellow hair was gathered in a resplendent queue, and a sizable gold ring sat on his right hand. His Lordship Colonel John Bridgewater of Her Majesty's Northern Regiments had inherited his title and fortune upon the death of his father a short time earlier. What he hadn't inherited was his father's wisdom or rank. Bridgewater's father had been commander of the Northern Regiments before him, but the late lord had been a general, and Abby knew from Undine, Colonel Bridgewater felt the slight keenly.

"Sergeant Rose, will you take the lady's plaid, please? We can provide you with a clean blanket, ma'am. I'm sure you have no desire to be wrapped in something soiled with the blood of your attacker."

"Actually, I—"

"Sergeant, find her something clean," Bridgewater said, slipping the sodden fabric from her shoulders. "'Tis the least we can do." He handed it to Rose and dismissed him.

She wondered for a moment if Duncan had been right, that she was being a fool to risk this. Of course, he didn't know the full extent of the risk. It would have been just one more thing for him to get hot-headed about. The gates of York, indeed. Why were men free to indulge themselves with as many women as they chose, but women were to limit themselves to one? On the whole, Abby thought one at a time was a more than sufficient nod to propriety.

"Please sit, Mrs. Grant."

An armchair upholstered in green damask stood near the colonel's desk. She gave him an uncertain look and he nodded encouragingly. She hadn't expected to be brought to Bridgewater, and would have strongly preferred for whatever story they needed to collect from her to be collected in the field. Murder in the defense of one's own person was rarely investigated, and even though Dunworth was an English soldier and she a Scot, there was little question a pregnant woman lucky enough to have gained the upper hand with a rapist would be considered innocent by authorities. And if her husband had been English, killing his wife's would-be rapist would have been his God-given right.

When she was seated Bridgewater said, "I am told by Sergeant Rose that you were not, how shall I say it, breached? I apologize for the indelicacy," he added hurriedly, "but it's important to get the details correct."

"No," she said, cheeks hot, "I was not."

"And the child…? It is unharmed, I trust?"

"It is, thank the Lord."

Bridgewater sank into his equally opulent chair. "Private Dunworth had shown himself to be a man of questionable morals before this, I'm sorry to say, and while he had never to my knowledge attempted a transgression of this nature, your report is regrettably not a surprise."

The statement did not require a response, and she offered none. It was just like the English army, she thought, to employ ne'er-do-wells and rapists.

"You say he came upon you in the woods?"

"I'd been hunting."

"Aye, the bow. We found it."

She'd been careful to choose the plainest unmarked bow she owned before setting off. Nonetheless, it was a wonderfully responsive tool, and it irked her to think she might not get it back. The sword, though far more costly, meant little to her. "I didn't realize I was on English land or I would not have trespassed." She nearly choked on the phrase "English land."

"Which is to say, you were happy to be stealing so long as it was from the Elliotts not England." He gave her a grim smile. "That is the truth, is it not?"

"I am not proud of what I did, sir. But my husband and I need to eat."

He pursed his lips sadly, as if he understood what people unlike himself could be driven to. "Well, let us not dwell on that. Dunworth had been assigned the patrol in that area. I presume he found you aiming at some sort of animal or another?"

"He did not. He came upon me in the woods. I had stopped to rest. I believe he intended to relieve himself. He was unbuttoning his breeks when he saw me." Best to keep the story as close to the truth as possible. She took a small sip of the sherry for realism, though she knew she needed to stay as focused as possible.

"And?"

"And he asked if I was alone. I didn't like the look in his eyes. I told him I didna want any trouble. I got up to leave. He grabbed me, and we struggled. He told me that he——" She took a deep breath, thinking of Duncan's story about spanking to heighten the color on her cheeks. "Do you really need to hear this?"

Bridgewater nodded apologetically.

She said with a shaking voice, "He told me he had no interest in long-plucked Scottish beaver, and that I could suck his cock or die where I stood."

Bridgewater gazed out the room's small window, the ugliness of the story reflected on his face. This was a hard thing to hear, she thought, even for a man like him.

"And you're certain of his intentions?" he said.

"Colonel, I am a six-year married woman. I am quite able to recognize a man in the mind of fornication."

For an instant she saw something rise at the corner of his mouth, something that suggested he was imagining the breadth and depth of her marital experience.

"I do not doubt you," he said gravely.

"If there is nothing more, can I assume you are done with me? You have been very kind, but 'tis a two-hour walk home."

"A few minutes more, madam. A few minutes more. Ah, here is Sergeant Rose with a cloak and a dish of quail. Would you care to join me? I'm starved."

Forty-two

DUNCAN HADN'T HAD TO GO ALL THE WAY TO Bridgewater's castle to find the colonel, nor even very far into the Debatable Lands. The tent in the distance topped by snapping red- and yellow-tailed pennants and surrounded by dozens of alert redcoats was the field headquarters of some army grandee. Even a number-crunching desk jockey could tell that.

Terms of a marriage contract.

He snorted. With effort, he banished the emotion simmering inside him, clouding his thinking. Cold-blooded calculation was what he needed. The time to talk would come later, if indeed he and Abby would ever talk again.

He looked through the spyglass he had stolen along with a fresh plaid and a sword from the saddlebag of one of Rosston's men. Oh, yes, Duncan could reive with the best of them—and she would soon know he could plunder and pillage too. Too bad her definition of a worthy man didn't include either of those qualities. Was she there? That was the question at present.

The tent flap opened, and he caught a glimpse of

her white bonnet. "Oh, aye, a bonny liar you are," he said, feeling spikes of anger-laced adrenaline. "Let's see if you do spurned lover equally as well."

The tent flap opened again, and this time a tall, broad-shouldered officer with blond hair and an air of elegance stepped from the tent. He closed the flap with deliberate care, stepped away from the opening, and gestured to one of his men.

The man stepped closer. Duncan couldn't quite figure out why the exchange seemed odd until he realized the men weren't talking. Everything being communicated was being done by hand gestures and head nods.

They know, he thought, as the spikes turn to fear. That had to be why they were avoiding talking. Despite Abby's confidence in her disguise, someone must have recognized her. And they didn't want her to know they knew.

He had to get to her.

Think, Duncan. Think before you hare off. Slowly, an idea took form. Jealousy has many uses. He reached for his sporran.

A moment later, he began toward the tent at a full run. Halfway there, he was met by a wall of redcoats.

"Put down your sword, Ginger," one called, advancing on him, musket drawn. The other men surrounded him slowly.

"Is she in there?" Duncan bellowed, thrusting the sword into the ground.

"Watch out, boys. We could light a fire with the flames in those eyes. Is he drunk too?"

"I've got no issue with you!"

"Good to know. I'll keep that in mind while I'm stuffing my boot up your arse."

Duncan had no escape. "I saw her there! Bring her to me!"

The first man exchanged glances with another. "Who, laddie? Did ye happen to lose yer wife?"

"My wife?" Duncan spat. "Not bloody likely. That's the chieftess of Clan Kerr, and I want her. Now."

Forty-three

A COMMOTION OUTSIDE THE TENT BROUGHT
Bridgewater's chewing to a stop. Abby had never been
so grateful for an interruption. The man had con-
sumed the quail followed by a joint of pork and four
chicken legs with a surgical precision that had turned
her skin to gooseflesh, stopping only a moment ago to
excuse himself to order more. She half expected him
to strop his knife between each course. And each bite
had been preceded by an offhanded question about
her husband, his farming, their neighbors, like the
king to Scheherazade, so that he might be entertained
as he ate.

At a loud *oof*, Bridgewater put down his knife. The
words, "Rose, what is going on?" had no more than
left his mouth when a man burst into the tent, nearly
knocking over the table.

The man was Duncan. Bridgewater stood.

Lip split and nose bleeding, Duncan snorted like a
bull who'd been separated from a cow in heat.

"Get up," Duncan growled at her. Two soldiers
flew in and caught him by the arms. Duncan flailed

impotently. "That's Lady Kerr," he cried, and Abby's heart dropped like a stone.

"I'm sorry, Colonel," one soldier said. "He got away from us."

Bridgewater sighed audibly. "Who is this?"

"Duncan MacHarg," Duncan said. "Where did ye find her? In the forest above the vale? Who was she with? Who was she with?"

"Shut your mouth," Bridgewater said calmly, "or I'll have one of my men shut it with the barrel of his musket." He turned to Abby. "Alas, Chieftess, I'm afraid our little tableau has come to an end. A shame, really. I was enjoying listening to you spin the tale of your simple farm life. You are, are you not, the Chieftess of Clan Kerr?"

Abby didn't know which man to look at—Duncan, spitting fury, or Bridgewater with his condescending smile. Of the two, Bridgewater seemed less a risk. "Aye."

"And you are not with child?"

"Not by me," Duncan said, grim faced. "I canna speak for any of the other men here."

She gasped.

"Oh dear, oh dear," Bridgewater said. "Do we have a lover's quarrel on our hands?"

Duncan glowered.

"Sergeant, what do we know about Lady Kerr's marital status?" Bridgewater asked.

Rose, who had slipped in after the soldiers, said, "She is thought to be engaged to a cousin of hers named Rosston Kerr, also a clan chief though of a less important clan."

The muscles in Duncan's jaw flexed.

"And is this man Rosston Kerr?" Bridgewater said.

"No, sir," Rose said. "He's about as tall, but Rosston Kerr has black hair."

"I see." Bridgewater returned to his chair and said to Abby, "You have nothing to add, I suppose?"

She shook her head, resolute.

"Mr. MacHarg, I take it you are bedding the lady?"

"Was." Duncan must have sensed a weakness in his captor's grip for he broke into another frenetic struggle.

"Oh, for God's sake, let the man go," Bridgewater said. "He's unarmed, and we all have swords. I, for one, would like to hear his story."

Abby would have been happy to put an arrow through the colonel's heart.

Duncan used his plaid to wipe the blood from his face. "She *told* me she would have no more of him. She *told* me that his money didn't matter."

Bridgewater shook his head. "Oh, Mr. MacHarg, you are very naive."

Duncan turned to the colonel. "You know her reputation, do ye not?"

Bridgewater looked to Rose, who made an embarrassed cough. "The lady has a propensity for incaution."

The colonel made an interested noise and looked at Abby. "I didn't know."

She colored.

"Oh, aye," Duncan said. "There was a tale, mind ye, that she took a grand coach with six footmen to York. You ken York, aye? 'Tis a journey of three days—three days there, three days back."

Abby shot to her feet. "*Shut up.*"

"Which meant by the time she returned—"

The look on their faces when Abby took her swing was the first thing that had given her pleasure all day.

Duncan's head lurched sideways.

Even Bridgewater was momentarily speechless. "Mr. MacHarg, I'm afraid you will not be receiving an invitation to the next Clan Kerr gathering."

The soldiers laughed.

But rather than show even the slightest regret, Duncan turned back to Abby with such a look of insult in his eyes, it seemed to her he was asking for another punch.

She obliged.

This time, however, he caught her hand and squeezed it painfully. "Touch me again, Chieftess, and you'll come to regret it." He flung her away.

She cupped her aching hand.

Bridgewater said, "Lady Kerr, please sit. I should very much like to hear why you were in the woods. I suspect badger is not what you were hunting."

"Aye, Abby," Duncan said darkly. "Tell him why you were there."

"Make him leave first," she said to Bridgewater.

"Oh, no, no. I think he has earned the right to hear."

She gave Duncan a smoldering look. "There is a man I meet there sometimes. A huntsman with a wife. Our assignations are infrequent. Only when I can no longer stand the awkward floundering of boys."

"*Whore*."

Bridgewater winced. "Mr. MacHarg, really. If your oath to the clan does not forbid such a remark, I would hope your manners might." He leaned back in his chair. "And what of the pillow under your dress, Chieftess? And Dunworth?"

She pulled off her bonnet, unapologetic. "The costume allows me to travel unnoticed. Dunworth, though, is a filthy predator who threatened to leave my body for the huntsman if I did not lay down for him, just as I said."

"Not *quite* as you said," Bridgewater replied, displeased. "Sergeant, is the washerwoman still here?"

"No, sir. She took the clothes back to her cottage. She'll return with them tomorrow."

The colonel sighed. "Lady Kerr, you are the chief of a clan and know the ways of war. You will understand I hope that by crossing into the Debatable Lands in a disguise you have left me no choice but to have you searched. 'Tis my duty as a representative of the crown."

She nodded.

"There are no women I can call on to do this, and I will not wait until the morrow. Rose, take her to my sleeping area, strip her to the skin, and go through her things. Make it as quick and painless as possible."

"Aye, sir."

Rose pointed to a small space cordoned off by a set of heavy, wooden folding dividers. Abby curtsied formally to Bridgewater, who returned a bow.

The soldiers holding Duncan looked as if they had missed buying the winning lottery ticket by a half a moment.

"Would you care to observe?" she asked one haughtily.

"Well, if you're offering—"

"*Collins,*" Bridgewater said sharply. "Mr. MacHarg, take a seat. I have a question or two for you, if you don't mind."

Duncan did not care to imagine the chill Rose would endure as he performed his assignment. Rose may have scored one of life's great unexpected treasures in being able to carry the image of a naked Abby to his grave, but he would likely never recover fully from the sense that a bit of shite scraped from her ladyship's heel would be of more consequence to her.

"May I assume Mr. MacHarg has been searched?"

"Aye," Collins said. "Thoroughly. He had a sword when he arrived. Nothing else."

"Nothing in his pockets?"

Collins blinked. "Oh, aye. A biscuit, some coins. Oh, and a button. The usual."

Bridgewater waved at Duncan to sit. He did reluctantly.

The colonel templed his fingers and gave Duncan a careful look. "You'll forgive me if I observe you look rather more like a strong arm than the lady's jilted lover."

Duncan nearly laughed. In the sleeping area, he could hear Rose's murmured, apologetic instructions to Abby. "Why can't I be both?"

"Why not, indeed? My concern is that your story is merely a construct."

"A what?"

"Made up."

"What she has done is no lie, I promise you."

"Then you wouldn't mind describing her to me, the parts, that is, that one cannot see."

Duncan filed away a plan to embed the man's teeth in the back of his head at some point in the future.

For now, he wanted nothing more than to get Abby and himself out of the Debatable Lands and back to Castle Kerr.

"She has a sizable scar on her chest," Duncan said. "From a musket ball."

"Oh, aye. I had forgotten the tale of her exile and return. Charming family." Bridgewater tapped his fingers on the desk. "Unfortunately, every soul from London to Glasgow also knows the story. I'm afraid I'll need something a little less well-known."

Duncan ground his teeth.

"Come, sir," Bridgewater said. "I am perfectly aware what a man keeps in his head. Is her mons dark or light? Are her nipples long or fat, pink or brown? Do her buttocks sit high? If you bedded her, surely you can give me a description that proves it."

The thought of murder simmered in Duncan's head. Perhaps once you'd killed one man, you grow more used to the idea. "Her nipples are small and pink," he said, seething, "as are her areolae. Her mons is dark—considerably darker than the hair on her head. And it is as thick as a pelt of fur."

"Thank you. I know this isn't easy. Rose," he called.

"Aye, sir."

"Is she undressed?"

"Aye."

"What is the color of the hair on her mons?"

For a long moment, Rose, who had, no doubt, been thrown into a shocked silence, said nothing, then, "Black as a raven's, sir."

"And her nipples? Cherries or currants?"

Duncan wondered for an instant what effect these

questions were having on the morale of the rest of the company.

"Currants, sir. Dewberries, even."

Bridgewater returned his attention to Duncan. "Jilted lover you are. I apologize for having to put her through this—though I suppose you don't much care at this point."

Duncan grunted.

Bridgewater leaned closer and met Duncan's eyes. "My thoughts, should you care for them: Forgive the trespass. She's a fine-looking woman. As canty as a horse in clover. And one never knows when one will need a similar sort of carte blanche oneself."

Abby, tightening the laces of her gown, reappeared in the main part of the tent, followed by Sergeant Rose, who seemed to be absorbed in the leatherwork of his boots. She stopped when she saw Duncan, and he, too, dropped his gaze. Duncan suspected Bridgewater was studying the texture of his blotting paper. Abby had that effect when she chose.

"Sergeant," Bridgewater said, "did we find anything?"

Rose deposited a handful of personal effects on the desk. To Duncan's immense relief, no silk square was among the items.

"And you checked her dress, pockets, shoes, stockings?"

"All of it, sir."

Bridgewater poked through the odds and ends, and picked up a small metal ball.

"Was this perchance the shot that pierced you, Chieftess?"

She nodded.

"Well done," he said. "I admire your spirit.

Sergeant, would you please review the supplies and make a report."

"I've already reviewed them, sir."

Bridgewater grimaced. "Then would you please review them again."

"Oh. Aye."

Rose tromped out.

Duncan's palms began to sweat. They had reached the end, though what the end entailed, he did not know.

"Chieftess," Bridgewater said, "I am not pleased to have found you, disguised, on land belonging to England."

Abby said, "The ownership of the land remains in dispute."

"Not to Her Majesty."

She straightened her sleeve. "I should think the death of your soldier might be of rather more concern to you."

"You were lucky, it seems. Dunworth was an idiot, and you have relieved me of the unwelcome task of removing him from my regiment."

"I was attacked and nearly raped, sir. 'Lucky' is most certainly not what I feel."

Bridgewater inclined his head toward Duncan. "Tell me the truth, Chieftess. Is this man your strong arm or your lover?"

Abby made a dismissive noise. "He is no strong arm, and he will never again be my lover."

True or not, the words were jarring to hear.

"He ran into a line of soldiers holding muskets without even his sword drawn," Bridgewater said.

"Then he is a fool."

"Perhaps. But I would think an experienced leader of men would see beyond the superficial interpretation and instead consider the depth of character such an act reveals."

My God! He's trying to reunite us!

Abby shifted.

Bridgewater looked at his desk clock. "I am required to sign off on our ordnance requirements before the messenger leaves. Would you excuse me for a moment?"

She dipped her chin, and he exited, apparently feeling no need to seek Duncan's permission.

Duncan breathed a deep sigh of relief. "You got my message then?"

"Aye." She opened her palm to reveal the tiny slip of paper with the words "He knows" Duncan had pressed into her hands after the failed second punch.

"Revealing you before he could was the only thing I could think of to disrupt his plan, whatever that might have been. And a forest dalliance explained your presence and lack of forthrightness."

"Not to mention fitting my reputation. Six footmen? Really?"

Duncan flushed. "Well, I—"

"Uh-huh. Can they hear us, do you think?"

Duncan considered the distance to the tent walls and the thickness of the canvas. "No. But I would certainly expect someone to be watching. So we must remain unhappy lovers until his return. You do realize he is attempting to reunite us?"

"Oh, aye." Abby lowered her head. "Is he dead?"

He knew she meant Rosston. Duncan took her

clenched hands in his. "He was alive and talking when I left him—with his men, who cleaned the wound and stitched him up."

He saw the wave of relief go through her.

"He's not a bad man," she said, eyes still downcast.

"He is not," Duncan said. "And though he is no great admirer of me, he was the one who encouraged me to come and offered the full help of his men, if I needed them. They are waiting in the woods for us. And while Rosston and I agree on little, we do agree on one thing: neither of us think you should have taken the message from Archie."

"Neither of you are responsible for the safety of my people."

She was right and he had no counterpoint. "Where is the note? Did you destroy it?"

She met his eyes, and a chill went through him. If that note was found on a clan chief, Bridgewater would have every right to put her to death.

"Oh, dear God, Abby. Where is it?"

"Very likely in his hands right now. Bridgewater is not quite the Cupid you imagine. He may be trying to reunite us, but his absence is also allowing him to search my cloak and plaid, which he took when I was first brought in. The note is in a false hem in the cloak."

"But once he's found the plan to attack…on *you*…?"

"I will face what needs to be faced. Duncan, you say you're from the future. It would give me peace to know…that is, if you dinna feel uncomfortable telling me…that Scotland survives this clash with England."

Her cheeks were as pink and full of hope as

the twinflowers at Candle Pool. He wished that Bridgewater would burst in here and drag him to a gallows. Anything rather than telling her what would happen.

"Abby, I don't think…" He blathered something about the risk of knowing one's future before one's time, terrified of what the truth would do to her. But she knew.

Her eyes filled and a single tear ran down her cheek and landed on her gown. "Is it awful?"

He owed her the truth. Even if it could not help her change it.

"Yes. The clans are routed. Those who do not bow to England are murdered. Everything we love here is taken from us. The Scotland we know ceases to exist. It takes no more than thirty years once it starts. And almost three hundred years later, it has not been undone. We are English, Abby."

She pulled her hands away from him, covered her eyes, and began to weep.

"Oh, my darling, my chieftess," he said, sweeping her into his arms, "I am so sorry." He felt the deep pain of their loss, and the shame of his twenty-first-century resignation to it.

Bridgewater swept back the tent flap, and Duncan clutched her tighter. He would die before he'd let anyone hurt her. Wordlessly, the colonel made his way to his chair.

"Chieftess, I see you have made your peace with the man." Bridgewater pulled his own pressed silk square from a pocket and handed it to her.

"Aye," she said, wiping her nose.

He sank into his chair, a different, uglier calculation weighing on him. Duncan scanned the room for something he could grab.

"It brings me less pleasure than you'd imagine to tell you your fate is in my hands. 'Tis my right to have you shot as a spy, you see, and 'twould do a great service to the people of England who've suffered the attacks and raids of your clan. Queen Anne would thank me for it."

The man lies with exquisite ease, Duncan thought.

"And yet," Bridgewater added, "I find I would prefer to offer you another choice."

Abby sat straighter, a Scottish queen unmoved by fear or threats. "What?"

"You are capable of being a voice of reason. I know your chiefs meet each fall. I want you to begin to spread the word of the benefits of cooperation. There is money to be made in a partnership with England. If we quell the violence in the borderlands, there is a great deal of money to be made, and the chiefs who ally themselves with us are the only ones who will benefit."

"I have always been a proponent of peace, sir."

"I have no interest in peace, Chieftess. I am interested in a swift resolution by Scotland to accept the Act of Union. I want your vote."

Her slim fingers worked the fabric of her skirt. Duncan could see the existential struggle in her eyes. What had he done by telling her the truth?

"Oh, Abby, don't listen to him—"

"I'll thank you for your silence, Mr. MacHarg," Bridgewater said. "With all due respect, this is an area in which you can have no understanding. Chieftess?"

"With all due respect," Duncan said, "go to hell. Abby, the things I told you? What if I'm part of the reason it happens? What if people like me tell people like you what we know and that dissuades people like you from doing what you know you should? Look at me, Abby. Nothing is ever certain. You know it and I know that. Let's change what we can, even if it's only a little."

He could see the struggle in her eyes as she weighed certain safety with the chance to protect the way of life her people loved.

"Chieftess," Bridgewater said, "I don't know what nonsense your acquaintance is spouting. But you are responsible for the lives of hundreds of men and women. You can protect them with a single hand-shake. Why would you not do it?"

She stood. Her hands were shaking. "I thank you for your offer, Colonel, but I should rather lick the boots of every man in the English army than vote for the act."

Bridgewater clapped his hands and laughed a single laugh. "That is exactly what I expected you to say. Still, 'twas worth a try. Then I believe our time here is at an end. Chieftess, I shall just need you to describe the nature of your meeting today on English soil and the happy resolution with Mr. MacHarg. Rose will set you up with paper and a pen. Then you'll be free to go."

"Why would that be necessary?" Duncan asked.

"Because Colonel Bridgewater wishes to hold a threat of exposure over my head, is that not true?"

"I'm afraid so. Ugly business, I know. One never

knows when one will need to diminish the reputation of an enemy among her peers or even destroy an advantageous alliance with a family sept. My apologies. By the way, I shall have to insist you include an account of the trip to York. I hope you understand."

Duncan began to rise, fists ready.

"Sit down," Abby said, tight-lipped. "We will accede to the colonel's request at once and consider ourselves lucky to have been offered such a choice."

"Mr. MacHarg, your chieftess is most wise." Bridgewater gave them an even smile and rose. "If that's all…"

Abby said, "May I have my things?"

"What…? Oh, the cloak and plaid? I had forgotten. Aye, of course."

Less certain, she added, "And my bow?"

He chuckled. "Yes, Chieftess, you may have your bow. You'll forgive me I hope if I keep the arrows. My men will not bother you as you make your way home, and I have heard the badger hunting has been very poor this season."

Forty-four

THEY WERE A MILE INTO KERR LAND BEFORE ABBY FELT
completely safe again. She stopped in the shade of a
beech near a crumbling stone wall at the bottom of a hill,
desperately glad the deed was done.

Duncan, who had been quieter than she'd expected,
leaned against the trunk. He'd changed so much since
she'd met him. Had it only been three days?

"You look like a Kerr," she said.

He gave her a wan smile. "Thank you."

"Well, except for the plaid. Does Rosston know
ye stole it?"

"I didna steal it from *him*. And I didna really steal
it. Just borrowed."

She threw the cloak and plaid she'd been carrying
on the ground, happy to free her aching, damp arms.
"If I never see those things again, 'twill be too soon."

She had checked for the plans with theatrical sur-
reptitiousness while still in sight of the army. "They
will expect us to check," she'd told him, fiddling with
the wool while they walked.

The silk had been where she'd put it, causing

Duncan a moment of anxiety, until she reminded him Bridgewater would want them to think they'd gotten away without it being found.

"But how will we know he's read it?" Duncan had asked.

"Because I put three strands of hair in the silk before I placed it in the hem."

"And are they there?"

"I dinna know. I didna dare have him or one of his men catch me pawing through the fabric. It would have planted a seed in his mind we would not be able to dislodge."

And now, under the beech's shade, Duncan bubbled with nervousness. "Will you not look now?"

She turned in a circle scanning the hills and fields. She was as familiar with these hills as she was the castle bailey, and if someone watched them, she would feel it. Satisfied they were alone, she adjusted the bow across her chest, sat down by the cloak, and carefully withdrew the nearly unnoticeable lump from its hiding place.

With a deep breath, she unfolded the silk. Had it only been three hours ago she'd written the words on it?

No hairs! Not a single one!

"They're gone!" she cried and jumped up. "He's read the note and thinks we plan to attack! We did it!"

She threw her arms around Duncan and he clasped her tight. The clasp transformed all too easily into a kiss and then the start of something more.

"Too soon," he said huskily.

"Is it?" she said, giddy. "Dinna forget I am your

chieftess. If I command you to possess me, you must. Dinna tell me you would prefer a bed. I have the grass stains on my arse to prove you're a liar. And tomorrow we shall prepare for Sir Alan's arrival, and you will convince him of the great opportunity he has to invest in our canal."

But her effervescence was not contagious. Duncan hardly met her eyes.

"What it is?" she said.

"Rosston told me you negotiated the terms of a marriage to him."

"Duncan—"

"Abby, you dinna owe me anything. And I don't care whether you're married or nae, or if ye take me to your bed or nae. I will stay at your side, as your strong arm, for as long as you'll have me there. And I willna make ye uncomfortable for it. If I am of use to you, that will be enough."

"You are willing to serve while I'm married to another? To wait for the infrequent note: 'Come to me, Duncan. My husband is away.' To take your ease while his bairn wriggles inside me, a big as a pumpkin?"

Duncan didn't blink. "I am."

"Why am I the only one of the three of us who isn't willing to do that? I didna negotiate the terms of our marriage, Duncan. He did—and I will thank him in person next time I see him for describing it that way to you," she added darkly. "I told him I couldna marry him, that while I am fond of him, I do not love him. And do you know what he proposed then? Did he tell you that as well?"

"He tried. I told him I didn't want to hear. I

decided that if I trust you, I must trust you in all things. And I walked away."

He cupped her hand between the two of his, just as he had done in Bridgewater's tent, only this time his touch was as gentle and warm as the other had been angry. He smelled of salt and wind and a touch of Bridgewater's sweet cologne.

"No more words, Abby. You carry the weight of a clan on your shoulders—and now you are tasked with changing history. I will abide by your decision."

She laughed. The sense that she had someone she could depend on completely was inebriating. For the first time since she was a girl, she didn't feel alone. "Thank you."

"However, if you care to give me leave, I'd be happy to kick Rosston's arse for being fast and loose with the truth."

"Oh, good. More fistfights. That will help us overcome England. Perhaps you two should just lift your plaids and we could get out the ruler instead?"

Duncan tapped his chin. "Might save some time."

"Gah!" She rolled her eyes. "What is it with men? You behave as if this inconsequential palmful of flesh—"

"Inconsequential!" He spun her around and pinned her, giggling, to the tree.

"—no bigger than a very average turnip—"

"When they're *soft*! But hard—"

"Oh, aye, hard they are invested with the pomp and splendor of a common least weasel. And yet somehow we are to believe they are the divine lightning rod of God's glory here on Earth."

She laughed so hard at the look of shock on his face, she could hardly breathe.

He lifted her to the tip of her toes and gazed down his aquiline nose. "You will take that back, Chieftess."

"Never."

"You will take that back *and* you will raise a hallelujah chorus before I am through with you tonight."

He kissed her hard enough to make her long for nightfall.

"And for the record," he said, his breath tickling her ear, "I would win."

Forty-five

THE SMALL NUMBER OF CLANSMEN WHO KNEW WHAT
had transpired—and what had been avoided—were
in a celebratory mood, and Abby had ordered a lavish
supper of roast beef, smoked ham, asparagus, and
toasted pears in her private dining room. Duncan,
who had damned it all and claimed the seat next
to Abby, was enjoying some very fine whiskey and
watching her eyes sparkle as she repeated the story
of her wayward farm wife, well, at least a heavily
edited one.

One of Rosston's men passed along Rosston's
greetings, saying he was awake and resting comfortably in his room. Jock reported that his crew had put
the finishing touches on the crumbling chapel on the
Esk that would convert it, at least for the time being,
into a rustic Kerr fishing lodge. Sir Alan would while
away a day or two knee-deep in Duncan's not incon-
siderate charm and some of the best fishing waters in
all of Britain.

All was well.

At evening's end, Abby excused herself to drop

in on Rosston and thank him for his help—though Duncan rather hoped there would be some arse kicking as well. And she had instructed Duncan to take the secret passage to her room once the halls emptied, which was why he was currently taking the steps on the main staircase two at a time, whistling.

"You seem rather happy," said Nab, whom he found bent over a pair of dice on his bed when he entered his room.

"I am."

"What was the private supper for?"

"What's the word on the street about it?"

"Huh?"

"What do the men think it was for?"

"Well, they know Rosston was stabbed. He says it was a soldier. But some of the men think it was you."

Duncan rather liked that. "If that were true, I doubt Lady Kerr would have been quite as willing to include me in the supper invitation."

"Unless it was a battle for her hand. Like Penelope and her suitors."

Duncan lifted a brow, not just at the reference, which surprised him in an unschooled boy in the eighteenth century, but the implications. All of Penelope's 108 suitors had been murdered by her returning husband. "I certainly hope you're assuming I'm the Odysseus in this contest."

"*I* might be, but the men are staking you at seven to one against."

"What?!"

Nab grinned. "I'd be betting myself, but you still havena paid me."

Duncan tousled the boy's hair. "I'll be paying you, ye wee thieving fox. Give me another week. Speaking of fox, what sort of information has Rosston been pumping you for on me?"

"The usual. Where you're from, for one thing." Nab crossed his arms around his knees. "I'd like to know that myself."

Duncan took a seat near the boy. "It's not far. My grand-da lived a couple of miles from here."

Nab looked away. "I know you're not from around here. Not really. It's all right if you don't want to tell me."

Duncan was speechless. His reticence had hurt more than just Abby. "It isn't that I don't want to tell you, Nab. It's just that there are things that even one's business partner…"

Nab scooped up his dice and hopped off the bed.

"Stop," said Duncan. "I'm from Scotland. I grew up in Edinburgh. I'm just not from…now."

Nab turned, eyes narrowed.

"I'm from a time ahead of this one," Duncan said. "I was called here by…well, that part's still a little unclear, but I suppose the answer is a combination of me, Lady Kerr, and Undine."

He was glad he'd thrown in Undine. It wasn't till he'd mentioned her name that Nab relaxed his scowl slightly. The boy's face was a mixture of desire to believe the fabulous tale and fear Duncan was mocking him.

"Prove it," Nab said tentatively.

"Oh, I see. First, you want the truth, then you dinna believe it. What do ye want to know?"

"When does that fat old queen die?"

"Tut, tut. Disrespectful, even in a Scotsman. And the answer is 1714." Duncan sifted through the faint remnants of his secondary school history lessons. "More or less. Followed by a long line of King Georges—Georges of every shape and size." He sized up Nab with a gimlet eye. "I should think you'd live to see the third one, who, by the way gives Anne a run for her money in the rotundity department. But he's actually best known for a war he wages on America."

"America?" Nab hooted. "Ruffian upstarts. They wouldna stand a chance."

Duncan chuckled. "Aye, well, it wouldn't matter if I told you they lost or won. You have no way of proving me wrong."

A look of concern came over the boy's face. "Oh God, you're not an American, are you? That's not why your accent's so odd?"

"Are you impugning my Scottishness, ye cad? I am not an American by birth, nae. A bit by sensibility, though, I fear. They have a hell of a fine idea about liberty. Keep your ears open when you're a grown-up. As a Scotsman, I think ye'll like what you hear. Now swear to me. Ye canna tell the men what I told you. Ye canna tell your friends. Ye canna tell your ma. Ye canna tell anyone."

"I never tell my ma anything." He held up his hand. "I swear."

"And with that"—Duncan glanced at the clock—"I believe I shall take my leave."

Nab rolled his eyes. "Another secret mission?"

"In a particularly rewarding engagement."

Forty-six

DUNCAN EMERGED FROM THE WARDROBE, CLOSED THE doors, and did a little tap dance.

A cascade of giggles brought him up cold. He turned around.

Three young women in robes and diaphanous chemises stood before Abby's fire. One was Nora, the maid who'd overheard him offering Abby his companionship his first night at Kerr Castle. The other two he did not recognize.

"Lady Kerr asked us to ensure you were comfortably settled," said one of the unknown ones, a blond with fine, wide cheekbones.

"Did she?" He took a step backward and tripped over Abby's bow, catching himself with the bedpost only by luck. A tidal wave of heat crashed over his cheeks. "I am actually as uncomfortable as a man could be," he said, prompting another dizzying peal of laughter from the two he didn't recognize.

Nora frowned at her companions. "There's brandy on the table, and Sionnach brought up a pitcher of hot water if you wish to wash before you begin. Would you like me to take your plaid?"

His hands shot up as if she were brandishing an ax. "I am quite attached to it at present," he said.

"As you wish. Lady Kerr is really the best at this, but she does not wish for you to have to wait. She told me to tell you that Sionnach has strong, steady hands, and that she can have it out of you in no time. Then you can relax."

"Um…"

"I brought a strip of leather, but I dinna think you'll need it. Forgive the girls for laughing. 'Tis perfectly reasonable for someone to be shy and perhaps even a wee bit scared about such a thing. It must hurt terribly to have a splinter in your…well, gentlemanly parts. And dinna worry, we won't say anything about this to anyone. You can return to your bedchamber the same way you arrived."

Duncan breathed an enormous sigh of relief. "I thank you for your kind offer. I should never submit proper young ladies to such a thing. Lady Kerr, though hardly less proper, is more used to the wounds of battle. So long as I move with care, I am in very little pain. I will wait for her attention."

Attention that will include a proper punishment for the mischief she has made.

Sionnach and the other girl curtsied and left. Nora drew closer, sympathy in her eyes. "The notion that you will be attended upon in this matter by the woman who spurned your advance must be doubly embarrassing to you," she said. "I am sorry." She lowered her voice. "I also wish to tell you that the same thing happened to my sister's husband after the Battle of Dunkeld, and for many weeks he was afraid he had lost the use of the thing entirely. But you may rejoice. With my sister's patient help, he was able to regain full claim on his male pride."

"Oh, I am verra glad to hear that."

"There is a girl here—Caileag—who works in the distillery." Her voice fell to a whisper. "She is...not verra particular about certain things. She may be able to help you should it come to that."

Oh, Abby, you will regret this... "Thank you. I'll remember that."

"You're welcome."

Nora scurried out and closed the door. The brandy looked too good to pass up. He headed straight for the bottle, only to jump when he found Undine leaning against the wall by the door.

"Jesus," he said, "do you ever knock or hum or *anything*?"

"Almost never. I hear you served your chieftess well today, sir."

"Nailed it. Which reminds me"—He pulled the bag of herbs from his sporran and tossed it on the table—"I think you gave me a defective pack. You said it would begin to warm when I'd fulfilled my role as a strong arm. Feel it. Colder than a witc—"

He stopped.

She cocked her head. "Pardon?"

"Colder than one would wish. Maybe it's the same problem you're having with Serafina."

"I doubt it."

"In any case, there's no rush." He filled two goblets with generous portions of brandy. "I think I'm going to stay for a while."

"I see."

He offered one of the goblets to her, and she shook her head.

He shrugged and took a long sip. "Between Sir Alan's visit and the canal and, well, Abby, I've pretty much decided that I want to—"

"Sir Alan isn't coming."

The words drained the happiness from him. "How do you know?"

"I received his messenger during your supper. It seems Sir Alan was made privy late this afternoon to a statement regarding various indiscretions on the part of our chieftess—a statement, it seems, that was signed by the voluptuary herself."

Bridgewater's messenger would have had to *run* to Carlisle to put it into Sir Alan's hands. That bloody bastard.

"According to the messenger," Undine said, "Sir Alan feels his original determination was the correct one. He has no reason to impugn Lady Kerr's name, and will certainly keep her indiscretions to himself, but the Kerrs under their current chief represent too great a risk for the Bank of Scotland. He will not be able to recommend an investment to his board of directors."

"Indiscretions? If indiscretion made a man a bad risk for investment, half the world's empires would have failed." He felt sick. "Does Abby know?"

"Not yet. But someone will have to tell her." The look on Undine's face made it clear who she thought that someone should be.

He gazed, unseeing, into the fire, his brain spinning through the options a mile a minute. "Well, this much is true," he said quickly, his mouth a half step behind his brain, "there are more banks here than just the Bank of Scotland. And more investors. The hell with Sir Alan! All we need to do is create an offering!"

"Duncan."

"It wouldn't be hard. The location is unbeatable. And the work has already begun. There are blueprints around here somewhere. There must be. If I could just get to Edinburgh. That's where the men with the money are. That's where I could—"

"*Duncan.*"

His planning dribbled to a stop.

"The time for schemes is over," she said flatly. "The estate taxes are due, and she doesn't have the gold to pay them. You must tell her to marry Rosston."

The traces of brandy on his tongue lost their sweetness. "I did tell her. I told her I would support whatever decision she made."

"With you standing in the wings, reminding her every day of what she's given up? You're her adviser, aye? What would be your advice if she were a man and Rosston an heiress?"

He didn't want to hear it. "No."

"Have you considered the possibility that the herbs aren't warming because you haven't actually fulfilled your duty?"

"Oh, I see. And if I tell her to marry Rosston, suddenly I'll be free to go?"

"Not free to go. Compelled. The herbs are not some bloody door you swing open and closed whenever it suits you, like the door on Abby's wardrobe. At the first ray of dawn, on the day after you have fulfilled your duty, the herbs will heat, spark, and burn out. And when they do, you will be sent back to your own time instantly, never to return."

He felt like he'd been sucker punched. "Then I will never tell her to marry Rosston. Not if that's to be my fate."

"And that is how you would serve the woman you love?"

Abby opened the door and slipped inside with Grendel behind her. "*Och,*" she said with a grin. "I've never been so happy to see a bottle of brandy—and my two favorite people, of course, though at this point the brandy comes first. Will you stay for a drink, Undine?"

"I won't." She gave Abby a long embrace and kissed both cheeks. "I shall find you in the morning. First thing, do you understand?" Then she met Duncan's eyes. "Do your job, eh?"

Forty-seven

"WHAT JOB?" ABBY SAID. "I CANNA THINK THERE ARE too many jobs left in this day. I feel like the day has already been long enough for ten. Did you enjoy my little joke? Though I suppose I wouldna be laughing if you had tried taking them up on anything."

"Aye, especially after they screamed for the footman."

"More likely slipped a knife in your heart. They are always armed."

He led her to the settee and put the second goblet in her hand.

"Are you sure this is where you want to start?" Her eyes twinkled wickedly as she sipped.

"I do not wish for it to start at all." He hung his head. "Sir Alan's messenger arrived during dinner. He willna be coming."

"Not tomorrow?"

"Not ever."

Her lip made the smallest quiver, but he knew she would not cry. Not yet.

He explained what Undine had told him regarding Bridgewater, Sir Alan, and the statement.

She put the brandy on the table. It seemed as if both of them had lost the taste for it.

"Bloody English prick."

He said, "You were right, you know. About how he would use the statement."

"I didna think it would be so soon."

He took her hands and caressed them with his thumbs. "We took a risk. It didn't work. That doesn't mean we shouldn't have done it."

"And what is our plan now?"

He thought about everything that had happened since his arrival and how nothing in his life before her could have prepared him for what he was about to say. "The plan is simple. You will marry Rosston."

"I don't want to marry Rosston," she said, surprised. "Why are you saying such a thing?"

"He has the funds to bail out your clan and build the canal. With a partner like Rosston, you will make your clan strong again. He'll do whatever you want. I have no doubt. And he'll do it well. The man is smart, Abby. And he cares about you."

"You said I wouldna have to marry him. You said—"

"I was wrong. I *wished* you wouldna have to marry him, but I do not possess the means to change what must be."

She shook her head. "Couldn't we go to Edinburgh or Glasgow? There are men my father knows—"

"No, Abby, the time has come to accept what's best for the clan. Think about it—you pay your taxes, your people eat, your clan grows, and the canal fills your coffers. With Rosston as your husband—"

She pulled her hands away. "You said you would fight for me."

His throat tightened and he struggled to stay on course. It would be so easy to carry her down that narrow staircase, climb onto the back of a horse, and marry her in the nearest church. He could support her as a bookkeeper. She'd never again have to worry about anything here.

Here. Bloody, bloody *here*.

"Abby," he said softly, "that was a dream. It was a dream I wanted to believe. But it canna be. I'm telling you as your friend: if ye do not accept Rosston's proposal and save your clan, ye will die an unhappy woman."

The balance in her eyes tilted unsteadily, back and forth, between the wild hope of a life with Duncan and the reality of what was before it. He watched as the balance settled slowly, slowly on the side of her clan.

Done.

The herbs on the table made an almost inaudible hiss, though it could have been the fire. Her acceptance was so complete, it had transformed their closeness into a breach of etiquette. Duncan slid away. "I believe I shall say good night."

He was almost to the wardrobe before she spoke.

"I shall always have ye as a friend, will I not?"

He stopped but did not turn. "I havena told you everything."

"Nae," she said, voice brimming. "Ye canna push me into Rosston's arms and leave me too."

"I shouldna stay. You and I both know that. Besides," he said, coming round to face her, "I should die if I had to be here."

Her face contracted and she clasped her hands, but only someone who didn't know her as well as he would assume she was stricken. Her silence was an act of girding. She'd lived through a mother's death and a brother's, through an exile and violent and unhappy return, and she'd looked into the face of death and the destruction of her people. She would survive his leaving. The question was would he?

He began to say good-bye but found himself too overcome to speak.

She ran toward him lightly and put her hands on his face.

Robbed of speech, he was now robbed of the power of movement as well.

"When will you leave?"

"Dawn. I—I—It's not me. It's Undine's herbs." He gestured weakly toward the packet. "I have done what I was called here to do, Abby. The spell will send me back to my time the moment the sun rises."

She picked up his hand and cradled it to her cheek. "You are a strong arm."

The softness of her skin physically hurt him.

"Come to my bed," she said.

"You canna ask me that," he croaked. "I dinna have the strength to say no. You must stop us. I cannot."

She pulled him to the bed. He lay on his side and she curled behind him, her arm clutching his. Grendel leaped up beside them and stretched out, staring sadly into Duncan's eyes.

"I didna mean to make love," Abby said. "I just want to hold you."

He pressed himself into her embrace, tantalized by the closeness, trying to collect and preserve every sensation.

"Will your family be glad for your return? You have a family, aye? I know of your grand-da, of course. And ye said ye had no siblings. Oh, dear, I never asked if you have a wife. Do you?"

He made a bittersweet chuckle. "No." Nor did he ever expect to. Not now. "My mother's gone. No siblings. My grand-da is all I have. I will be glad to see him."

"Will ye tell him about me?"

"He'll be glad to hear I was in love with a Scottish girl. I live in America now, you see, and he is desperate afraid I'll marry one of them."

"*Och*. An American? Ye would never find happiness with any but a Scottish lass. I knew that the moment I saw ye."

"Did ye now? Was that before or after you threatened to put an arrow between my eyes?"

"'Twas your shoulder—barely. And knowing ye need a Scottish lass is not the same as wishing to be the girl myself, ye ken? That came a bit later. Just around the time you stood before me naked."

"Oh, I see. I wanted to talk to you about that, actually."

"*Och*, I hope you're not expecting an apology for none will be offered. Your eyes feasted on my body. I intended to enjoy the same privilege." She sighed. "And enjoy it I did. Regarding your marriage, though—"

Duncan groaned.

"I do think a Scottish girl would be best. I thought that from the moment we first talked."

"Even when you threatened to have me locked in my room?"

"Oh, aye. Many's the knave who's been improved by a provident marriage."

"Knave, is it? I guess it's an improvement over simpleton."

"Oh, Duncan, how I will miss this."

For a long moment she was still, and only the slightest twitch betrayed her tears. He chose to give her privacy and to try to mortify his longing. The business of growing calluses must begin. In a few hours more, neither of them would have a choice.

"I will nae forget you, Duncan MacHarg."

"Nor I you."

Grendel put his head between his paws and let out a long, doleful whimper.

❧

Duncan emerged from a fright-filled dream in which he had been falling and falling. He reached for Abby. She was still there. As was he. The room was dark but not black. The coming sunrise lived like a rat-gray promise in the sky outside the window.

Why did I wake? Let her sleep through it at least. Oh God, let her sleep.

They had talked until they could talk no more. He had told her every shred of history he could remember regarding this dark time for Scotland. He didn't care if his telling changed history. He didn't care if his telling swept the future clean away. He hoped it would take him with it.

She had asked a hundred questions, making him

repeat the stories until she had memorized every detail. She was a canny lass, as canny as they come. He had also gotten her to promise to pay Nab for his work and to give him a position in the clan. Duncan had left Scotland's future in good hands.

He stretched his legs, wondering if he would feel the removal before it happened.

She caught his arm, as awake as he.

"Not yet," he said. "A few minutes, at least."

The grip relaxed. She uncurled herself and made a noise, as plain an invitation as he'd ever heard, and he kissed her. She tasted of brandy and sad longing, as he probably did. But however heavy his heart was, his mouth and loins stirred with desire. He wanted her.

"I will have ye," she said.

She climbed to her knees and lowered herself onto him. Wool and linen tangled between them as they ground their hips roughly. He could barely make out her face but her hungry breaths told him what he would see. He found her buttocks, bare and warm, and clasped them roughly. He wanted to blister her thighs, and she wanted it too.

He was lost in the feral taking. She stretched her arms, reaching, reaching for the peak that would bind them forever.

"Give me your child," she whispered, drunk with fire and desperation.

"Abby, no."

He was helpless to stop it. She began a long, slow arch, and he heard a sizzle. The room behind her lit up like a Guy Fawkes celebration.

"Duncan," she cried. "Oh, Duncan."

He landed on a damp, dark patch of grass, under the first bleak rays of a Scottish dawn, with the distant sounds of the A7 replacing the heartbreaking cry in his ears, his ejaculation two beats too late.

He put his hands over his eyes. "*Och*, Abby."

Forty-eight

DUNCAN GRABBED AN IRN-BRU FROM HIS GRAND-DA'S fridge and gulped down several swallows at the kitchen sink. He'd done five miles on the treadmill and was on his way upstairs for a little free-weight time. He watched his grand-da bag bulbs at the small patio table outside.

"You ken that stuff will kill you, aye?" the elder man called.

"Everyone has to die somehow."

"Come out here. It's a glorious day."

Duncan sighed and opened the screen door. His grand-da gestured to the only other chair, one of the folding variety with woven straps that he'd owned since long before Duncan's birth. One of the straps had disintegrated, leaving a fairly wide hole. Duncan opened the chair, purposefully turned it toward the house and sat down.

"Have ye ever thought of buying a couple new ones, Grand-da? I could loan you the money if you're tight, aye?"

"Fouck ye. I like the ones I have."

Duncan chuckled. His grand-da was eighty-one and still carried himself with the gravitas of the private who had crawled for a mile under North Korean artillery fire to save a company of twenty-one men who'd been cut off from their flanks. When Duncan was twelve, he'd watched a man on the streets of Edinburgh who had been in that battle come to a dead stop when he'd spotted Duncan's grand-da. He'd called his grand-da's name then saluted him. The man had been a colonel.

Tall enough to have to duck under door frames and with hair the color of an autumn bonfire, Duncan's grand-da provided his grandson with a somewhat unnerving look into what his own old age would be like. Duncan hoped he'd be able to do it with as much irascible grace.

"Why exactly are you here, laddie?"

"*Och*, and ye wonder why I don't visit often."

"You've never stayed for three weeks before. Hell, you've never stayed longer than three days."

Duncan fingered the fraying edge of his running shorts, feeling the slipperiness of the fabric. The shorts had been his at university, and he'd kept them, along with a small stash of other clothes, at his grand-da's. He'd worn the shorts hundreds of times, but now everything he put on here seemed odd and slightly foreign to him. "I told you. I have holiday time I need to use."

"Bullshite. And why the new treadmill? I've never known ye to run inside."

Duncan shrugged. "The outdoors is overrated. I want to be able to read when I run."

"Which explains why you haven't touched a

newspaper or book since ye got here." Duncan's grand-da began sorting the bags into baskets. "I have a theory. Would you like to hear it?"

"Not particularly."

"It's a woman."

"There's no woman in my life. I'm a free spirit." Duncan chugged more Irn-Bru. The sun on his face reminded him of the day at the crumbling chapel. He hated the sun.

"You've been running yourself raggit on that thing. Two, three times a day you're on it. I didna do that much running when I was in basic training. And when you're not running, you're sleeping."

It wasn't always sleep, Duncan thought. In fact it was hardly ever sleep. Lying in bed gave him an excuse to inhale the scant remains of her scent on his plaid.

"It's a holiday, Grand-da. Sleep's what you do."

"Have ye even looked at my garden since you came? Look how you're sitting. We've got the most beautiful view in Dumfriesshire here and you're facing the house."

Duncan hid a wince. "I did look at your garden, I swear. But I would certainly love to look at it again." He crossed the yard reluctantly. Beyond the fence, rising gently for a half a mile, was the hill where he and Abby had watched the singing soldier approach. Everything in this damned county reminded him of her. He hated being here, but he couldn't bring himself to leave.

He dropped his gaze to the exuberant beds of yellow and pink at his feet. Tall and short, of every shape and variety, the flowers in his grand-da's fervently culti-vated garden took his breath away. In the twenty-first

century, an amassment of blossoms like this had to
be engineered. Roads and suburbs crisscrossed the
land, and green space near even small towns had been
reduced to carefully carved-out parks, keeping flowers
from covering the hills with their glory naturally. He
thought of the path he and Abby had walked that day
to the chapel, and the cranesbill and twinflower that
had blanketed the hills. If he closed his eyes, he could
smell the lush scent on the wind and see the tiny pink
blooms beside which they had lain.

"Grand-da, do you have twinflower here?"

His grandfather stopped his sorting. "Now that's an
odd question."

"Is it?"

The man leaned back in his chair and gave his
grandson a curious look. "Aye, it is. Twinflower has
been extinct from Scotland for a hundred years."

"*Oh.*" Duncan turned back to the garden, hoping
he hadn't opened a can of worms. He heard the
squeak of the chair. *Shite.*

"To be fair, *extinct* is a bit of an exaggeration," his
grand-da said, coming up beside him. "But it grows in
so few places, it might as well be." He looked down
his long nose at his grandson. "Have ye seen it, then?"

Duncan shook his head. "How could I have?"

His grand-da made a thoughtful noise. "Aye, how
could ye have?"

"I must have heard someone say it."

"No doubt. It's a beautiful flower. Sad shame it's
not around. In fact, one of the few places it does exist
is not far from here. Would ye have any interest in
taking a walk?"

Duncan's chest tightened with the fear of what he might be forced to remember. "Actually, I should probably call New York before—"

"We'll be back soon enough. Grab a couple of waters, laddie. It's time to get a little sun on your face."

❧

Duncan made his way moodily up the rock-strewn path. They'd walked through the town, past the football pitches, and into the untamed Lowlands. On paper, he was the more agile hiker, being fifty years younger. But since his grand-da knew the paths and Duncan didn't, he looked like an amateur, stumbling on unseen rocks and slipping on waterweed as they splashed across a small stream.

"This is great," Duncan said, squeezing the water out of his muddied shorts.

"*Och*, what's a little dirt?"

The hill began to rise more steeply, and the muscles in Duncan's calves labored.

"Are you thinking about settling down at some point, lad? It's not good for a man to live alone."

Duncan considered pointing out that his grand-da had lived alone since his grandma's death a decade before Duncan was even born, but he held his tongue. "Haven't given it much thought, actually."

"Men like you and I need a strong lass. Brains, wit, independence—as interesting out of bed as she is in. We're bored otherwise."

Duncan wished he was dead. Or deaf. Or both. "I'll keep that in mind."

"Flitting from one bed to the next makes a man dull

and empty. A wine with no depth. You're starting to have that look to ye."

"Gosh, thank you."

They crested the long edge of the hill's peak, and Duncan's breath caught. There, below them, was the snaking curve of the Esk and the exact spot where he and Abby had first made love. The chapel was gone. Not a stone remained. It was as if someone had decided to remove every piece of evidence that their relationship had ever existed. For a moment he wondered if Abby had done it as a way to forget, but he suddenly had a heart-stopping vision of her sitting on the steps of the chapel, bow at her side, staring into the distance, with Grendel baying his sadness.

The vision was so wrenching, he wove a bit.

His grandfather, who'd been observing him, said, "Are you okay?"

"I think I'll sit." Duncan dropped onto the hillside and put his head between his knees. "I wonder if I'm getting a stomach bug."

"I wonder." His grandfather took a seat on a nearby boulder. "Duncan," he said gently, "is this where you saw the twinflowers?"

Duncan lifted his head a degree. His grandfather watched him with worried interest.

"I told you I haven't seen them."

"Did you meet a girl here?"

Dumbstruck, Duncan struggled to respond. "Why would you ask that?"

"Because I'm beginning to think you may have traveled to the past."

Duncan was so dazed by his grandfather's statement,

it was several moments into the older man's explanation of the power of this site in pagan times before he'd gathered his thoughts enough to reply.

"Hang on," Duncan said sharply. "You wouldn't ask me something like that based on a single mention of twinflowers. That's not enough."

"All right, how about the fact ye arrived on my doorstep at dawn three weeks ago in a handwoven plaid with blood on you?"

"I told you I went straight to the airport from a reenactment."

"Ye did tell me that. But the fact ye arrived from the 'airport'"—he drew quotation marks in the air to underscore the amount of credence he put in the idea—"without a bag and without a car or taxi, or even a goddamned pair of roller skates, led me to believe ye were lying."

Duncan sighed. Octogenarians were more sharp-eyed than he'd bargained for, at least this one.

"And the fact you've been moping about like a boy who lost his puppy made it obvious a woman was involved. At first I thought perhaps you'd stopped at Catriona's place before you came around mine and she threw ye out on your ear."

The fling with Catriona had not ended well, and Duncan had had the unfortunate luck to have her take a teaching position in the same town as his grand-da. "Oh, for Chrissake, I haven't talked to her in years."

"So, I understand. I stopped by her place last night with some cuttings."

"Oh, Jesus."

"The twinflower reference got me thinking, but it

was the look on your face when we crested the hill that told me what I needed to know."

"You know what? That's a load of shite. You can't take some obscure flower reference and add it to a look of surprise and come up with time travel. I don't care what your instincts tell you, Sherlock. There's something more going on here. What is it?"

His grand-da gave him a stony look. "I know ye were time traveling because I did it myself once. Now, tell me and dinna lie. Where were ye before ye arrived on my doorstep?"

There was no lying to his grand-da. There never had been. Less shocked than relieved, and feeling like an overfull water balloon that had finally been pricked, Duncan told the story in a rush—everything from the moment he'd run into the volley of rubber-tipped arrows in Pittsburgh until the moment he'd walked, bedraggled and despairing, to his grand-da's door. Everything, that is, except the part where he'd fallen in love with the chieftess of Clan Kerr.

"And that's all?" his grandfather said.

"Everything."

His grand-da made a doubtful noise. "Well, I suppose ye hardly need to tell me ye bedded the lass."

Duncan flushed. "It wasn't like that."

"Wasn't it?"

"No."

"A beautiful young chieftess who knows what she wants? Seems like your type."

"I said it wasn't like that."

"Did she throw you out? Or did ye sneak away when she wasn't looking?"

"*Neither!*" Duncan said. "I canna sleep! I canna eat! Jesus God, I can barely draw breath, and you're accusing me of abandoning her? I loved her as I will never love another." He dropped his head and bit back the tears.

His grand-da rubbed his back and pulled him close. "I'm sorry, laddie," he said softly. "I had to be sure. Call me a greedy old man, but if I'm sending you back to her, I had to know it was worth it."

Forty-nine

"I CANNA GO BACK. IT'S NOT POSSIBLE." DUNCAN WAS hurrying to keep pace with his grand-da, who was practically trotting down to the river.

"How do ye know?"

"She told me. The white witch told me. 'It's not a door,' she said, 'that one can swing through at will.'"

His grand-da stopped and looked at Duncan. "Your boss told you no one made partner before the age of thirty. Your first-form teacher told you boys who threw spitballs would never go to university. Your mum told you too much masturbating would make ye blind. I dinna recall you listening to any of *them*. Why would you listen to the witch?"

"Well…"

"As I thought." He returned to his descent.

"Wait. You haven't told me about *your* trip."

His grand-da didn't reply. He scurried to the bottom of the hill and turned to wait for Duncan. "Careful where you step. Now come over this way a bit. There." He point to a small, wet mound of rocks at the river's edge on which a few dozen narrow stalks topped by fairy caps of pink stood. "Twinflowers."

Duncan crouched to look. They were exactly as he remembered. The faint sweet scent filled his head, and he realized for the first time that was the scent Abby wore. "And this is the only place you find them in Scotland?"

"Oh, there are one or two others."

"They look so delicate."

"Aye, they do. Rip 'em out."

"What?"

"Grab 'em by the head and rip 'em out. We need their magic."

Their magic, it turned out was what had taken his grand-da on his journey. He'd been hiking in the Grampians twenty-some years ago when he'd first spotted a small patch of the flowers. Knowledgeable enough to know he shouldn't touch them, yet drawn by an irresistible desire, he'd torn the entire bunch free and immediately found himself in a public house outside the Inverness of yore. There he'd met a beautiful, golden-haired woman from Dingwall named Raineach. At thirty, Raineach was long past the age of marrying, but with the encouragement of her mother, she had decided to accept the proposal of an older merchant in Edinburgh she admired but did not love, and was waiting for the carriage that would take her to him. The carriage did not arrive, and her only other choice was a tinker's wagon. Having no other place to go and no way to return home, Duncan's grand-da decided to join her, though the banging of the pots kept them awake all night. By the end of the first day, they were in love, and on the final night, he bowed to her plaintive request to show her what she could never expect to have with her husband. He'd slept that night with her in his arms, and at dawn he'd been whisked back to his own time with no warning.

He'd fretted about her for many years, but it wasn't until he'd read about the discovery of the small patch of twinflowers so near his home that he'd even considered the possibility of returning. But by then he'd lost his courage. Too many years had passed.

"Are you sure you don't want to do this yourself?" Duncan said, still eyeing the flowers.

"Nae. I had my happy marriage. She deserves a chance at hers."

Duncan turned the idea over in his head, too afraid to believe it might work. "It's been three weeks, ye ken. Abby may have already married the man with the chest of gold."

"We don't even know if the flowers will work for ye or not. Let's cross that bridge first, aye?"

Duncan straightened and looked at his grand-da. "There's no guarantee I'll be able to come back."

"There's no guarantee I'll even be alive tomorrow. We can't base our decisions on something that might or might not happen."

"Grand-da…"

The man softened. "Aye. It will kill me to lose ye, Duncan. You're all I have left of your ma. But no grandparent in his right mind would deny his grandson a chance at happiness."

"She canna marry me, ye ken. If I return, it will be to be her strong arm. Nothing more."

"Duncan, if I could have stayed to be the man who shined Raineach's shoes, I would have done so without a single regret. You have a chance to do a lot more than that. You have a chance to change history." The older man's eyes shone. "To serve a woman as well as a country? Outstanding!"

Duncan laughed, but his heart was breaking. He threw his arms around his grand-da and squeezed tight. "Thank you for everything you've given me. I've never known a man I admired more than you."

"There, there, *a leannan*. You've made me verra proud."

They drew apart and Duncan wiped his eyes. "Are we ready?"

"You're sure now? Have ye thought about your work in New York?"

"Not once."

His grand-da laughed a booming laugh. "That's my lad."

Duncan took a deep breath, folded his hand around the stalks, and pulled.

Fifty

DUNCAN LANDED WITH A WHOOSH ON A COOL stretch of hillside surrounded by wildflowers. He was dressed, he realized belatedly, in his shorts, T-shirt, and runners, any of which would likely get him in big trouble here, assuming "here" happened to be the borderlands in 1706. But that worry was immediately displaced by dread when the quiet of the afternoon was broken by the peal of church bells and the sound of applause just over the hill. With his heart in his throat, he flipped to his stomach and began army-crawling toward a place he could see what he was hearing without being seen himself.

He'd gone no more than a dozen feet when he found himself staring into the disbelieving eyes of an overjoyed wolfhound.

Woof!

"*Shhh!*" warned Duncan.

The dog licked Duncan's face and shook with excitement.

"Grendel?"

Oh, Christ. Nab!

Duncan jumped to his feet and with equal amounts of speed and reluctance, stripped off what he was wearing and hid everything under a rock. He was completely naked when Nab appeared.

"What are ye—?"

"Dinna ask. Give me your plaid."

"It willna cover you. Where have ye been? Lady Kerr said you were called back to your home."

Grendel was probing Duncan's balls, and every press of the wet snout was making Duncan jump. "I was."

"Without saying good-bye?"

Duncan pushed the dog aside. "I foucked up, aye?"

"Foucked up?"

"Made a mess of things. And I owe you an apology—a big one. But right now, what I need more than anything is your plaid."

Nab sighed and untied the knot at his shoulders. Duncan took the piece and wrapped it around his waist like a bath towel, tucking the edge in at his waist. Then he padded quickly to a place from which he could see.

It was the chapel on the Esk. But Jock had done what he'd promised. The thing retained its stout bell tower, but almost everything else had been rebuilt to look like a lodge. The doors swung open and Duncan inhaled sharply. Knowing Abby had to marry was one thing. Seeing her on Rosston's arm would be another.

Jock stepped out, a hearty smile on his face, then turned and held the door for someone else. That someone else was Sir Alan. And he was followed by a handful of Rosston's men.

Duncan's knees nearly gave way.

"This wasna the wedding?" he demanded of Nab.

"Nae. Rosston has underwritten the canal. With his guarantee, that fop from the bank is willing to invest as well."

Abby's clan had been saved. Duncan was glad for that, at least.

"Then they are married?"

"Who? Rosston and Lady Kerr? Oh, no."

"*No?*"

"Not till two." He squinted into the sun. "Oh. Which looks to be now, doesn't it?"

The wedding, Nab reported, was to be in the Lady chapel, and Duncan flew up the path to the castle with Grendel galloping beside him and Nab, shirttails flying, just behind.

"I dinna understand your hurry," Nab called between gasps. "I'd have thought watching her wed was the last thing ye'd want."

Duncan faltered for an instant. Why was he running? He couldn't articulate the reason, but he knew he had to get to her.

"I'm leaving you behind, lad," Duncan said, bursting into a hard sprint. "I'll catch you in the chapel."

Up the rise he went, and under the portcullis. He scanned the ramparts, ignoring the stares his attire was drawing, and saw clumps of people milling about the chapel's entrance. Duncan had been to enough wedding ceremonies to know the crowd meant Abby's had either just ended or was just about to start. He grabbed the arm of a maid hurrying past.

"Is she married yet?" he said.

"No. Nor will she be if the gardener willna give us the right flowers for her hair. 'I canna wear gardenias,' she cries. 'The shoes aren't right. I want the emerald earrings, not the rubies. Where is my dog? You can hardly expect me to marry without my dog.' No, milady, I could never expect any bride to marry without her dog at her side. In fact, I believe there's a trencher of meat scraps on every altar for just that purpose. God, give me strength." The girl pelted away.

"Is she upstairs?" he called.

"Aye—though I canna recommend visiting."

Duncan raced into the castle and up the staircase. Grendel ran to his mistress's door and waited for Duncan. Duncan paused to evaluate the impression he'd make in his current gladiator garb versus a clean sark and plaid. He opted for the latter and sped into her brother's room, hoping no one else had moved in while he was away. No one had. He dropped Nab's plaid on the floor and threw open the wardrobe doors.

"I can see why Abby regrets your absence," said Undine, who had appeared behind him.

"I don't know about that," he said, too focused on Abby to be surprised or concerned, "but I can certainly see why she's had locks installed on the doors." He grabbed the nearest sark and slipped it over his head then reached for a plaid.

"I don't know what you're doing here, Duncan—"

"I convinced her to marry him," he said, arranging the wool in as close an imitation of correct usage as time would permit. "I did just as you told me."

"Then why would you take the risk of coming back here to undo your good work?"

"I just want to see her."

"To what end? Duncan, her happiness depends on a marriage to Rosston. You know that."

A winded Nab stumbled in. "Duncan, remember the whore I told you about? I just saw her walking right down——" He stopped when he saw Undine.

"I see your friendship with Duncan has expanded your vocabulary, if nothing else," she said coolly.

"I came for my plaid," Nab said, uncomfortable.

"What whore have you seen?" Undine said.

The boy looked to Duncan for a sign. Duncan shrugged. A whore on the grounds of Kerr Castle was hardly going to shock Undine, not unless the lass was scaling the ramparts like Spider-Man or something. Even then he wasn't so sure.

"The whore I told him about," Nab said, intentionally obscure, adding to Duncan, "behind the tavern in town? Giving dancing lessons?"

"Oh. *Oh.* Here?"

"Right in the hallway."

Duncan walked around a dubious Undine and peeked down the hall. The only person there was Molly, Lachlan's nurse. She was playing a game of tug of war with Grendel with a towel, ringlets of hair escaping from her bonnet. "Her?"

The look on Nab's face gave him the answer. Duncan frowned. Molly? Hopping with Jock behind a tavern in town? Molly, Lachlan's favorite? The lass Jock feared would carry the son who could displace Abby as chief?

He froze.

Undine, seeing the expression on his face, pushed him gently out of the way to have a look for herself.

She narrowed her eyes. "What is it, Duncan?"

"Who hired Molly?" he demanded.

"The same person who hires everyone around here: Jock."

Duncan closed the door and looked at Undine. "I think Molly's not the only one around here who's been had."

It didn't take Duncan long to find the second set of books. Not once he knew what he should be looking for. The book's spine read *England's Greatest War Heroes*. Jock hadn't even bothered to lock the thing up. No one in Castle Kerr would ever pull that book from the shelf. Duncan needed only scan the first pages to see the way the estate's profits had been systematically skimmed. He was in the middle of trying to figure out where the money might have gone when Jock opened the door.

He saw Duncan at his desk and reached for his knife.

"Easy, aye?" Duncan said. "Others know. Killing me willna do you any good."

"Might make me feel better."

"Where's the money?"

"Ha. Ye'll never see it again, lad."

"That, my friend, remains to be seen. Do you suppose Molly has any thoughts on the matter?"

Hatred flared in Jock's eyes.

"The only trouble with partnering with a prostitute," Duncan went on, "is that they're not too particular about whom they bed. You told me she was bedding Lord Kerr. But your plan was to get her pregnant yourself and say it was his, putting your own child in power, was it not? And when old Kerr insisted on Rosston as regent for the lad, you would have become Rosston's closest adviser. I wonder how long Rosston would have lived with an adviser as skilled as you?"

Jock didn't reply. He didn't need to.

Duncan said, "Well, you'll be surprised to discover, I think, that Molly is one step ahead of you. I'm fairly certain she's decided to cut out the middle man and just snag a child from his lordship directly. Why share the influence with you when she can give her child the blood of a true nobleman and save herself the trouble? But you'll have to take that up with her. Let us hope for her sake she's achieved her objective already, for her days at Castle Kerr are over." Duncan leaned back in the chair and sighed. "I wasn't sure who shot the arrow at me, but now that I see you have a lovely view of the bailey from here, I think I have my answer. I'd stay, but I must let Lady Kerr know she'll be in need of a new nurse and a new steward."

A sheen of perspiration appeared on Jock's forehead.

"There is one thing I want to know," Duncan said. "And I'm willing to consider advising Abby to let you go in exchange for the answer."

"I told you you'll never find the money."

"It's not about the money."

Jock's eyes narrowed for an instant then he laughed a booming laugh. "You *are* in love with her, aren't you? No, I dinna think I will tell ye if Rosston was a part of this. You'll have to take it up with him."

Duncan's heart fell, and he felt the guilt of his disappointment. If Jock had confirmed Rosston's involvement, it would have ended any chance the man had for a life with Abby.

Jock said, "I will tell you this, though. Rosston would have needed to partner with someone to pull off a plan like this. He's not canny enough to do it alone."

"Apparently, neither are you." Duncan stood. "Now I should very much like for you to make yourself comfortable while I lock you in here. I found these in your desk"—he jingled a small ring of keys—"and I'm assuming they'll do the trick." He rose from the desk and faced Jock.

The man swallowed. The blade in his hand caught the afternoon sun. "I can still get away. You're the only thing between me and an escape."

"Not the only thing."

The sound of a *click* made Jock turn. Nab stood in the hallway aiming a pistol.

"Hurry, Duncan," the boy said, arm quaking.

Jock scoffed. "Does he even know how to use the thing?"

"Well enough—at least I hope. In fact, if you wouldn't mind angling a bit to the left? The thing's cocked, and I'd prefer not finding out if the ball can travel through your heart to mine—*Oh God, Nab!*"

Jock leaped out of the way, which gave Duncan the opportunity he needed to grab the man's wrist and jerk the knife to the floor.

"Jesus," Duncan said gleefully, "you fell for that?" He kicked the knife toward a grinning Nab and kneed Jock in the stones for good measure. "Rule number one: never turn your back on a pissed off Scot."

Duncan locked the door and ran to the hallway

window. The chapel-goers were moving inside. He grabbed Nab. "Make sure Undine is able to stop the wedding. I'm going to Abby's room."

He raced down the hall, but his steps slowed before he reached her door. He knew Jock had drained the estate, but Duncan had no evidence Rosston was involved. Would Abby stop the wedding on a suspicion? And to what end? Rosston's gold would save her. And it wasn't as if Duncan had found the money Jock had hidden. Yes, he could stop the wedding, but if he did, he would destroy Clan Kerr in the process.

The disappointment was too much. To have come back and come so close to saving her, only to have her still joined forever to Rosston.

He stared at the door. Would seeing her change anything? Was there enough magic in the world to save two despairing lovers? Even if the answer was no, he knew he had to see her one last time.

He knocked. "Abby," he whispered.

Was she already lost to him?

The door opened, and Duncan's heart broke. Rosston, brushed and polished, gave Duncan a whiskey-fueled smile. "Not here, lad," he said, waving the goblet in his hand. "Not yet, at least." He opened the door and waved Duncan in. The room was filled with flowers, including several fat bowls of twinflowers. The bed—their bed—was dressed in gleaming white sheets covered in rose petals, and the airiest of chemises lay across the chaise before the hearth. The wardrobe was gone, replaced by a painting of Scots fighting the English.

"The Battle of Dunkeld," Rosston said.

The battle in which Rosston reigned victorious.

Darkness burned in Duncan's belly. "Ye canna marry her. And if ye played a part in the destruction of her estate, I'll kill ye."

Rosston put down his drink and balled his fists. "'Tis time for this to end."

Fifty-one

THE FOOTMEN FOUND HER ON THE ROOF, DESPERATE for someone to tell them what to do about the battle being waged in her locked room. Nothing calmed her like launching arrows as far into the empty hills as her strength would allow, but she flung the bow over her shoulder and stuffed her bleeding fingers into the pockets of her gown.

"Who is it?" she asked as they ran down the tower stairs, but her heart had already begun to cling to the possibility.

"We don't know. We assume one is Lord Kerr. No one inside would answer."

The door was still closed when they arrived though nothing raged beyond it. The room was deadly silent.

"'Twas ten minutes, easy, they were going at it," said one of the footman. "We looked for you everywhere."

"Open the door," she called.

She heard a groan inside and nothing more.

"Watch out." She took a step back and nocked an arrow. With a powerful *thwang*, the lock exploded in a hail of metal and wood. Abby turned the knob.

The room lay in shambles. The settee was in pieces, every table had been overturned, and Rosston's painting had been flung into a corner. Rosston lay on the bed, hand over his eyes, blood everywhere. Duncan's unmoving legs were visible on the floor beyond the bed.

"What have you done to him?" she shrieked.

Rosston groaned. "I'm bleeding too, ye ken."

"Sorry, mate." Duncan crawled into view, nostrils bleeding, two large gashes in his cheek. She'd never been so happy—and so irritated—to see anyone.

"That's all," she said pointedly to the footmen, who gazed at the scene openmouthed. They shuffled out, and she closed the door behind them.

"We were having a discussion," Duncan said, running a finger over his bloody teeth.

"I see that."

"About Jock." He climbed unsteadily to one knee. "Jock?"

"He's been robbing you." Rosston turned gingerly onto his side. "Duncan found a second set of accounts."

Abby's eyes stung. There were few lashes crueler than those of betrayal. "Oh."

"He's locked in the estate office," Duncan said, "awaiting your disposition."

Rosston said, "The whereabouts of the money, however, are not quite as clear." He offered a hand to Duncan, who took it and stood, wobbly legged, and immediately sunk onto the bed.

"You have not mismanaged the estate, Abby." Duncan rubbed his temples. "However, you are still bankrupt."

"And I could save you," Rosston said. "But I rather

think I won't. Duncan has informed me in some detail of the relationship you share—"

"Oh, Duncan."

"Dinna fear," Rosston said. "He paid dearly for the pleasure. I believe one of his teeth is on the floor near the hearth. Possibly two. But he also told me he loves you as he has loved no other. Abby, I am wise enough to see marrying me would bring you little pleasure and vain enough to wish to protect myself from such a blow. I hope you dinna mind, but when I inform the priest the marriage is off, the story will be you lied to me to save your clan, since that story is, in fact, the truth."

"I think that's your right, Rosston. I'm sorry for hurting you."

"I'm not a bad man," he said. "Just a man unloved by you. 'Tis possible that in a few weeks' time my heart will soften enough that I will see my way clear to giving you the money you need. But if I do, you will have to merge your clan with mine. On that point, I willna negotiate."

"I understand," Abby said, and she did. Fully. "I would do no less myself. I hope it does not come to that, but I will accept it if it does."

Rosston chuckled and stood, which immediately changed the chuckling to a hiss. "You are your father's daughter. That much is certain." He tried rearranging his sark to hide the bloodier parts but gave up the attempt. "I know you will marry him, Abby, but it would spare me some pain if you did not do it today. I have no right to ask for such a consideration, but—"

"We willna marry today," Duncan said. "I give you my word." He held out his hand.

Rosston wiped his palm on his shirt and took the extended hand. Abby decided she would never understand the ways of men.

A faint knock sounded, followed by a hesitant "Abby?"

It was Serafina, and Abby realized that it was well past the time for the ceremony. "Come in."

Serafina slipped in and was immediately dumbstruck by the chaos. "What *happened*?"

"A peace treaty," Abby said. "I lied to Rosston, and he has rightfully withdrawn his offer of marriage."

Serafina's eyes went straight to Duncan. He gave her an unsteady smile.

"And the canal?" Serafina asked.

"In limbo," Abby said. "My clan no longer has the financial backing of the Kerr sept, and Sir Alan has made it clear my reputation for indiscretion has made me an unreliable risk on my own."

"I wish I had the money to lend you," Serafina said sadly.

"Thank you. I wish you did too. And now, if you'll all excuse me, I believe I will pass the word to the priest and Sir Alan and his wife and the other guests that—"

Serafina's cheeks turned the color one only sees on redheads—nearly as bright and almost the same shade as Duncan's after his emotions had been stirred but before his voice rose to match them. "Sir Alan is married?"

Rosston frowned. "Aye."

The men as usual were miles behind, but Abby recognized in Serafina's question a nascent fury that could only come from one thing.

"He tried to bed me!"

"The upright Sir Alan?" Duncan blinked. "I remember him talking to you after the dinner."

"Oh, he found me entrancing. And I admit I rather enjoyed being seen that way, even if it was just for a time. But I had no intention of taking him to my bed. My God, the man is *fifty* if he's a day! He knocked on my door after everyone was asleep. I thought perhaps he lost his way to the privy. But when he made his intentions known, it took some verra stern words to force his retreat. '*Indiscretion*'? Ha! The man should be horsewhipped." She added sotto voce, "I sometimes wonder if all men shouldn't be. Present company excluded, of course."

Abby gave her battered companions a dry look. "I'm not so sure the exclusion is warranted. I'm sorry, Serafina. I have reasons to want to see Sir Alan horsewhipped myself. I wish someone had overheard him. How utterly delightful it would be to share such an account with his wife."

Something sparked in Serafina's eye. "And if the account included him referring to my breasts as 'the apples of Aphrodite,' my arse as 'the pillow of Apollo,' and, my, well—"

"Oh *dear*."

"—as 'a velvet sheath licked with crimson in which only the most noble blade should find purchase'?"

Rosston blinked. "Sir Alan of the Bank of Scotland said '*licked* with crimson'?"

"He should be horsewhipped for the bombast alone," Duncan said.

"He didn't say it," Serafina cried, exuberant. "He

wrote it! He sent me the most disgusting note the next morning. I hardly knew what to say. I ignored it *and* him."

Abby said a desperate prayer. "What did you do with the note?"

"Well, I would have tossed it, but I was afraid someone might see it. So I balled it up and stuck it in a shoe. It's still there!"

Abby cheered. So did Duncan. Even Rosston managed a smile.

"I'm sorry," Serafina said. "I should have thought to offer it to you before. I have no scruples about using the pressure of potential embarrassment to convince a man like Sir Alan to undo a terrible wrong. But in my experience, at least, there's very little that embarrasses an unmarried man, especially if he is rich and powerful."

Abby met her friend's eye and made a polite cough, the implications of which encompassed the scene before them. "I agree. A wife is just the lever we need to untighten this knot." She opened the door and called for a footman. "Tell Sir Alan I need to speak to him on an urgent private matter in my—well, not here, I suppose. And the estate office seems to be out as well. Make it the dining room. Tell him to wait there until I arrive." She nearly closed the door, then opened it again, "Oh, and do include my apologies: I am relegated to a velvet of verra ordinary black."

The footman nodded, uncomprehending, and made his exit.

Grinning, Abby said, "I will ask Sir Alan once more about making me a loan, and I canna say how, but I have the most inexplicable feeling he will have changed his mind." She did a little jig.

Rosston took her hand and kissed it. "Well played, cousin. You have overcome every obstacle thrown in your path and become a bloody fine clan chief in the process. You still need my men, though, and I will expect a visit before too much time has passed." He gave Duncan a resigned look. "If you insist, you may bring him too."

His compliment had been heartfelt, and Abby stood a little straighter. "Thank you, Rosston. Your words mean a lot to me."

"As for you," he said to Duncan, "I know you will take care of her."

Duncan bowed. "Thank you."

"You willna live long if you don't."

"And there's the thorn on that rose."

Rosston cleared his throat to catch Serafina's attention. "Shall we...?" He tilted his head toward the hall.

"Oh!" She realized she and Rosston were now intruding on an overdue reunion. "I will gather the letter and slip it under the door. Please give Sir Alan my regards."

Rosston took her elbow and guided her out.

At the click of the door, the shock Abby had managed to subdue for the past moments returned. Duncan sat before her, real and whole. The shaking rattled her knees, then rose to her chest in a wave that carried her across the room and into Duncan's waiting arms.

"God help me," she said. "I canna stand."

"God, you're quaking." He pulled her into a small, safe ball in his arms.

He smelled of flowers and sweat and blood, and she shook even harder.

"Stop, lass," he whispered. "You'll unman me."

"How did you…?"

"My grand-da showed me how. He's been here too. *Stop*," he said, as desperate as she. "I willna leave you. I promise. I love ye, Abby."

She clutched his damp shirt and calmed her breathing. "I spent every moment from the time my brother died building a wall around myself. And in four days you taught me I might as well have been building a fortress out of Lachlan's spun sugar. Ye made me ache for you—not just my body for your hands, but my ears for your words and my eyes for that crooked smile."

"*Crooked?*"

"I, who never wanted a man beside me, had fallen as hard as a starry-eyed milkmaid. And then ye left! Oh, Duncan, I hated you for coming, and I hated you for leaving, but I will nail your bloody feet to the Great Hall floor if ye try to abandon me again."

He laughed, and the rumble's vibrations erased her own.

"I've sworn an oath to ye, Chieftess. I will do as ye command."

She ran a hand across his rough cheek and straightened a little. "So you say. And yet you were verra quick to promise Rosston we wouldna marry."

"Today, milady. But I shall have ye as my wife, make no mistake."

"But do ye understand what that means?" she said in earnest. "I canna defer to you in any matter. My word is sovereign here. There will be times when

ye must be no more to me than a clansman who has
sworn his fealty. There will be times," she added sadly,
"when you must be no more to me than a footman."

Sunshine sparkled on the lochs in those eyes. "I
will be a footman, aye—when I must. But I will be
the footman who makes you cry his name in the dark,
who makes you claw the bedclothes, who gets you fat
with child."

Her breath caught. "I am nae ready for a child.
England's hot breath is on our collar. The Union must
be stopped. We cannot marry yet."

"We'll marry when ye command it. And I will fight
with ye, heart and soul. But the getting begins now."

"Now?"

He laid her on the pillows and drew a finger down
her Cupid's bow, stopping just inside her lower lip.
"Now."

Acknowledgments

Thank you to the wonderful team at Sourcebooks—Gene Mollica, Dawn Adams, Skye Agnew, Eliza Smith, Susie Benton, Amelia Narigon, Heather Moore, Todd Stocke, the entire sales team, and especially Deb Werksman, who knows a good Lowlander when she sees one. I'd like to thank Madhu Wangu and the dedicated writers at Mindful Writers, whose focus helps keep me on track. Claudia Cross, we did it again. As you say, more to come. Lester, Cameron, Wyatt, and my new daughter, Jean, I love you so much.

Legend of the Highland Dragon
by Isabel Cooper

---— ❧ ——---

He guards a ferocious secret

In Victorian England, gossip is as precious as gold. But if anyone found out what Highlander Stephen MacAlasdair really was, he'd be hunted down, murdered, his clan wiped out. As he's called to London for business, he'll have to be extra vigilant—especially between sunset and the appearance of the first evening star.

Mina wanted to find out more about the arrogant man who showed up in her employer's office, but she never thought he'd turn into a dragon right in front of her. Or that he'd then offer her an outrageous sum of money to serve as his personal secretary. Working together to track a dangerous enemy, Mina finds out that a man in love is more powerful and determined than any dragon.

---— ❧ ——---

"An outstanding read! A fast-paced, smartly written plot—fraught with danger and brimming with surprises—makes it impossible to put down."
—*RT Book Reviews* Top Pick, 4.5 Stars

"Mesmerizing, ingenious, slyly humorous, and wonderfully romantic."—*Library Journal*

For more Isabel Cooper, visit:

www.sourcebooks.com

The Highland Dragon's Lady
by Isabel Cooper

❧

He's out of the Highlands and on the prowl…

Regina Talbot-Jones has always known her family home was haunted. She also knows her brother has invited a friend for an ill-conceived séance. But she didn't count on that friend being so handsome…and she certainly didn't expect him to be a dragon.

Scottish Highlander Colin MacAlasdair has hidden his true nature for his entire life. But in his hundreds of years, he's never met a woman who could understand him so thoroughly…or touch him so deeply. Drawn by the fire awakening inside of them, Colin and Regina must work together to defeat a vengeful spirit—and discover whether their love is powerful enough to defy convention.

❧

Praise for Isabel Cooper:

"Cooper's world-building is solid and believable." —*RT Book Reviews*

"Isabel Cooper is an author to watch!" —*All About Romance*

For more Isabel Cooper, visit:

www.sourcebooks.com

Night of the Highland Dragon

by Isabel Cooper

---— ❧ ———

William Arundell is a detective working for a secret branch of the English government. When a young man is found dead, William's investigation leads him to a remote Highland village and the strangely youthful, intoxicatingly beautiful lady who rules MacAlasdair Castle. Nothing could have prepared him for the discovery that the charismatic Judith MacAlasdair is the only daughter in a long line of shape-changing dragons...or the fact that together they must put aside years of bad blood to save the British Islands from its deadliest foe...

---— ❧ ———

Praise for the Highland Dragons series:

"The mix of adventure and romance is just perfectly entertaining." —*Star-Crossed Romance*

"Magical, fantastic, and a great read for any dragon lover..." —*The Romance Reviews*

For more Isabel Cooper, visit:

www.sourcebooks.com

Lord of the Black Isle
by Elaine Coffman

— ❧ —

A Warrior's Life...

Laird David Murray would give his life to pull his clan through this time of strife and conflict. With enemies both inside and outside his keep, he has never felt so alone and desperate. Until he meets a beautiful healer with uncanny knowledge from another time...

Meets a Healer's Heart...

Elisabeth Douglas was a doctor in her own time. Now she's the only one with the knowledge and skill to help Laird David save the lives of his family...

— ❧ —

"Coffman's writing is deft, capable, and evocative." —*Publishers Weekly*

"Full of action, danger, passion, and drama...A must-read for medieval and time-travel fans alike" —*RT Book Reviews*, 4 stars

"Delightfully infused with suspense, humor, heartache, an entertaining plot, well-drawn characters, and a wily ghost, this story is a keeper." —*Romance Junkies*

For more Elaine Coffman, visit:

www.sourcebooks.com

The Return of Black Douglas

by Elaine Coffman

A *Booklist* Top 10 Romance Fiction of 2011

———————— ❧ ————————

He'll help a woman in need, no matter where she came from...

Alysandir Mackinnon rules his clan with a fair but iron fist. He has no time for softness or, as he sees it, weakness. But when he encounters a bewitching young beauty who may or may not be a dangerous spy, but is surely in mortal danger, he's compelled to help...

She's always wondered if she was born in the wrong time...

Thrown back in time to the tumultuous, dangerous Scottish Highlands of the sixteenth century, Isobella Douglas has a lot to learn about her ancestors, herself, and her place in the world. Especially when she encounters a Highland laird who puts modern men to shame...

Each one has secrets to keep, until they begin to strike a chord in each other's hearts that's never been touched before...

For more Elaine Coffman, visit:

www.sourcebooks.com

Kiss the Earl
by Gina Lamm

---— ❧ ———

A modern girl's guide to seducing Mr. Darcy

When Ella Briley asked her lucky-in-love friends to set her up for an office party, she was expecting a blind date. Instead, she's pulled through a magic mirror and into the past...straight into the arms of her very own Mr. Darcy.

Patrick Meadowfair, Earl of Fairhaven, is too noble for his own good. To save a female friend from what is sure to be a loveless marriage, he's agreed to whisk her off to wed the man she truly wants. But all goes awry when Patrick mistakes Ella for the would-be bride and kidnaps her instead.

Centuries away from everything she knows, Ella's finally found a man who heats her blood and leaves her breathless. Too bad he's such a perfect gentleman. Yet the reluctant rake may just find this modern girl far too tempting for even the noblest of men to resist...

--- — ❧ ———

Praise for Gina Lamm:

"Gina Lamm writes excellent [time-travel romance] with humor and great storytelling." —*Books Like Breathing*

"Snappy writing and characters who share a surprising, spicy chemistry." —*RT Book Reviews*

For more Gina Lamm, visit:

www.sourcebooks.com

How to Handle a Highlander
by Mary Wine

In a land of warriors playing a deadly game...

Moira Fraser has been given an ultimatum—marry the elderly Laird Achaius Morris, or risk another deadly clan war. She vows to do the right thing, as long as she can steer clear of the devilish charms of one stubborn Highlander...

How do you avoid becoming a pawn?

Gahan Sutherland knows there's a dangerous plot behind Moira Fraser's wedding, and will stop at nothing to foil it. But where a hot-headed, fiery Highland lass is involved, trust and honor clash with forbidden attraction, threatening to blow the Highlands sky-high.

"Well-written and filled with delightful repartee, this is a feast for medieval fans." —*RT Book Reviews*

"Mary Wine weaves a tapestry of a tale with adrenaline-pumping action, political manipulation, sweet and spicy love scenes, clan culture, and a touch of humor." —*Long and Short Reviews*

For more Mary Wine, visit:

www.sourcebooks.com

The Highlander's Bride Trouble

by Mary Wine

Her clan is in chaos

Nareen Grant is strong, confident, well-educated—and skilled with a bow and dagger. Betrayed by her family, she makes her way alone, until she lands in the lap of Saer MacLeod. But she wants no help from a savage man of the Isles.

And rivalries are deadlier than ever

Saer MacLeod is considered fierce even by Highlander standards, but he's enchanted by the headstrong Nareen. When an old feud endangers her life, Saer feels a ferocious desire to protect her...and claim her for himself.

"Wine's rip-roaring ambushes and beddings make for a wild ride through fifteenth-century Scottish eroticism." —*Publishers Weekly*

"The rapid pace, wonderful prose, and deeply emotional scenes make this book a marvelous read." —*RT Book Reviews* Top Pick, 4.5 Stars

For more Mary Wine, visit:

www.sourcebooks.com

My Highland Spy
by Victoria Roberts

This Highland laird won't bow to the crown

Laird Ruairi Sutherland refuses to send his only son away to be educated by the English. So he does what any laird would do—he lies to the king. The last thing Ruairi expects is a beautiful English governess to appear on his doorstep.

But this lady spy might make him...

Lady Ravenna Walsingham is a spy who is sent to the savage Highlands to uncover a plot against the Crown. Playing the part of an English governess, she infiltrates the home of Laird Sutherland, a suspected conspirator.

If she doesn't betray him first

Ravenna soon discovers that the only real threat Sutherland poses is to her heart. But will the proud Highland laird ever forgive her when he discovers the woman he loves is an English spy?

"Her lyrical prose grabs readers' attention, and the high level of emotional tension simply adds to the depth of the story. This book begs to be read and reread." —*RT Book Reviews,* 4.5 Stars

For more Victoria Roberts, visit:

www.sourcebooks.com

Kilts and Daggers

Highland Spies

by Victoria Roberts

———— ✦ ————

When Fagan Murray is charged with escorting Lady Grace Walsingham back to her home in England, he expected tension with the headstrong lass. But he didn't expect to be waylaid by Highland rebels. Fagan soon realizes he'll do anything to protect Grace, even if he has to protect her from himself.

Lady Grace Walsingham hated the Scottish Highlands—well, one Highlander in particular. Ever since she discovered her sister was a spy for the Crown, Grace has yearned for adventure. But the last thing she wanted was to encounter danger in the Highland wilderness, needing the one man she despises to protect her.

———— ✦ ————

Praise for *My Highland Spy*:

"An exciting Highland tale of intrigue, betrayal, and love." —Hannah Howell, *New York Times* bestselling author of *Highland Master*

For more Victoria Roberts, visit:

www.sourcebooks.com

The Highlander's Heart
by Amanda Forester

She's nobody's prisoner

Lady Isabelle Tynsdale's flight over the Scottish border would have been the perfect escape, if only she hadn't run straight into the arms of a gorgeous Highland laird. Whether his plan is ransom or seduction, her only hope is to outwit him, or she'll lose herself entirely…

And he's nobody's fool

Laird David Campbell thought Lady Isabelle was going to be easy to handle and profitable too. He never imagined he'd have such a hard time keeping one enticing English countess out of trouble. And out of his heart…

"An engrossing, enthralling, and totally riveting read. Outstanding!" —Jackie Ivie, national bestselling author of *A Knight and White Satin*

For more Amanda Forester books, visit:

www.sourcebooks.com

True Highland Spirit
by Amanda Forester

Seduction is a powerful weapon...

Morrigan McNab is a Highland lady, robbed of her birthright and with no choice but to fight alongside her brothers to protect their impoverished clan. When she encounters Sir Jacques Dragonet, she discovers her fiercest opponent...

Sir Jacques Dragonet is a Noble Knight of the Hospitaller Order, willing to give his life to defend Scotland from the English. He can't stop himself from admiring the beautiful Highland lass who wields her weapons as well as he can and endangers his heart even more than his life...

Now they're racing each other to find a priceless relic. No matter who wins this heated rivalry, both will lose unless they can find a way to share the spoils.

"A masterful storyteller, Amanda Forester brings new excitement to Scottish medieval romance!" —Gerri Russell, award-winning author of *To Tempt a Knight*

For more Amanda Forester books, visit:

www.sourcebooks.com

About the Author

Gwyn Cready has been called "the master of time travel romance." She is the winner of the RITA Award, the most prestigious award given in romance writing. You can visit her at cready.com.